"Known for her heartwarming stories."
Publishers Weekly

PAMELA MORSI
Nationally Bestselling Author of
No Ordinary Princess and
Courting Miss Hattie

"Morsi writes romances that read like fables or parables. Her books capture a certain sweetness grounded in human fallibility that is utterly charming . . . The most appealing aspects of NO ORDINARY PRINCESS lie in the author's ability to write about everyday people . . . and find what is right and good in those people and show them learning how love brings out grace and nobility in the most ordinary of souls."
Miami Herald

"Pamela Morsi has a knack for transforming everyday people into memorable giants."
Rendezvous

"Morsi is a pro . . . NO ORDINARY PRINCESS is no ordinary book, but a loving tale of life and self discovery."
CompuServe Romance Reviews

"Pamela Morsi writes with laughter, tenderness, and most of all joy."
Romantic Times

Other Avon Books by
Pamela Morsi

THE LOVE CHARM
NO ORDINARY PRINCESS

Pamela Morsi

Sealed With a Kiss

AVON BOOKS ◆ NEW YORK

AVON BOOKS, INC.
1350 Avenue of the Americas
New York, New York 10019

First Avon Books Printing: May 1998

AVON TRADEMARK REG. U.S. PAT. OFF. AND IN OTHER COUNTRIES, MARCA REGISTRADA, HECHO EN U.S.A.

Printed in the U.S.A.

WCD 10 9 8 7 6 5

To Carrie Feron
Executive Editor at Avon Books,
cheerleader and slavedriver
through eight of my eleven novels.
I pay the highest compliment
an author can give an editor:
You bring out the best in my work.
I also appreciate how you always correct
my use of there, they're, and their

And for Carrie's grandmother
Gladys Clover

Chapter 1

ALL WOMEN have moments of blissful success: the social triumph of being belle of the ball, the magic and majesty of a grand wedding ceremony, or the birth of a sturdy child. For Prudence Belmont, sitting serenely in the front parlor of the charmingly cluttered church parsonage, at age twenty-seven this was her moment of triumph. Her own splendid success. At long last, all her dreams and efforts and ambitions had been realized. For Prudence, the taste of victory was very sweet.

"Ladies," meeting hostess Mavis Hathaway boomed out in a voice that would have been an asset to her husband, the reverend. "The ballots in our special election have been tabulated. It is my duty to present to you the new president of the Chavistown Ladies' Rose and Garden Society, our dear Miss Belmont."

Two dozen pairs of white-gloved hands broke into muted applause.

Pru kept herself absolutely and purposely still as she allowed the announcement to wash over her like a warm, lavender scented bath. Not one eyebrow twitch or lip bite betrayed her pent-up anxiety or grateful relief, though her long, gangly legs trembled slightly beneath the frothy layers of her silk skirts. She had won. She had won.

Prudence had wanted this so badly, worked so hard for it, and now it was hers. Her achievement. Hers alone.

Allowing her gaze to wander the room, she smiled with what she hoped passed as serenity, gratified as the eager welcoming expressions of the finest ladies of local society beamed back at her. It had not always been so. These same admiring faces had gazed at her in the past, occasionally in censure and sometimes in pity.

But not today. Today she was their favorite daughter, the girl next door, the homegrown heroine who made good. Winnifred Beauchamp's unexpected demise had thrown open the most auspicious position of Rose and Garden Society president. And from the day of the funeral Prudence had prayed, hoped, finagled, prayed to have it. An interim president would serve out the rest of the year. But it was almost certain that without any unforeseen difficulties, that person would be selected in January to a full two-year term.

Prudence turned to her rival, Bertha Mae Corsen, and with a palms-open shrug, attempted to portray her win as unexpected and unsought. Bertha Mae Corsen was clapping politely along with the rest.

In truth, Bertha Mae had been the natural choice for the office. She was a founding member of the club. She had served as vice president under Mrs. Beauchamp for several years. And Bertha Mae, a kind, even-tempered woman in her early fifties, had a flower garden that was greatly admired. She was a longtime member of local society. But to be president, one's decorum must be perfect. And like most creatures on earth, Bertha Mae had her weaknesses. Unfortunately, her chief one being the telephone.

Her son, Elmer, had the newfangled machine in case of emergency. However, for Bertha Mae, it was love at first sight. The lonely widow discovered, in short order, that it could fill her long and empty days with friends and conversation.

And gossip.

Giggling behind her back the younger set began referring to her a Bertha Mae *Central*. There were only fifteen telephones in the whole community, it was joked, but at any given moment, night or day, Bertha Mae was talking on the other end of one of them.

The story always evoked a chuckle, even from Bertha Mae's closest friends. The telephone, it was generally agreed, was noisy and crass and should be avoided when at all possible. One might even consider it as a danger to propriety. With one ring of its loud bell a decent woman might shockingly find herself speaking to a man to whom she had never been introduced. And no ardent declaration of "Wrong number!" could heal such an etiquette breach.

There was no question about it, the telephone had cost Bertha Mae Corsen the presidency.

Prudence Belmont was kindhearted enough to feel a pang of sympathy. But the truth was Bertha Mae didn't *need* the Rose and Garden Society. Bertha Mae was a widow, a coveted position it seemed to Prudence. And she was the mother of two grown children. She owned her own house and land and was firmly ensconced within the hierarchy of the community. No, Bertha Mae didn't need the Rose and Garden Society, but, Prudence did.

Prudence had none of those things. Prudence Belmont was unwed. And since among the ladies of Chavistown, Texas, a woman's consequence was measured by how well she married, a spinster remained forever inconsequential.

Pru glanced over at Aunt Hen, who was looking pleased and proud in her fetching new strawbraid hat. Like herself, her aunt was long and rawboned with large, almost mannish, features. While such a plain appearance was unfortunate in the first bloom of youth, it aged well, and even now, well into her middle years, Aunt Hen might correctly be described as a handsome woman. Unmarried herself all her life, it was Aunt Hen who had taught Prudence that a woman can rise above her circumstances.

And now, at long last, she had. It was her moment of triumph. With her gloved hand upon her heart, Pru rose to her feet and took her place at the center of the group.

"I am overwhelmed," she said.

Her breathless appreciation so impressed those present that she was applauded once more. She allowed the praise to subside before she spoke again.

"And I am so flattered at your confidence in me," Prudence told them. "The Rose and Garden Society is by far the most prominent ladies' organization in town. To be chosen its president is the highest honor ever bestowed by the women of this community."

A murmur of approval rustled through the crowd. Among the ladies of Chavistown, it was *modesty* that was the best policy.

Prudence glanced down nervously and caught herself rubbing her palms and picking at the thumb seam of her cream silk gloves. Deliberately she hid her hands in the folds of her skirt.

"I want to take this opportunity to thank my aunt, Henrietta Pauling, a founding member of this club and a lady of gardening much to be admired."

Blushing uncharacteristically, the older woman attempted to wave away the kind words.

"Aunt Hen has taught me everything that I know about roses," Pru said. "I know that your faith in me is due in large measure to her own."

The ladies cooperated in a polite ovation. Prudence joined in. In truth, Pru was a voracious reader of gardening pamphlets and naturalists' texts, acquiring much of her knowledge of plants and soil from her own study. But it had been Aunt Hen who had first introduced her to the soul-pleasing pleasure of watching flowers grow.

Pru had been only a tall, gangly, thin, motherless girl of unfortunate circumstances and twelve years of bad luck when she came to Chavistown and her Aunt Hen.

Pru had always been grateful to her. Aunt Hen had seen to her schooling, her deportment, her launch into small-town society. Aunt Hen taught her to be self-reliant and to hold her head up high. And Aunt Hen had dried her tears when she had fallen hopelessly in love with the wrong man.

That was all behind her now. Today, this very day, September 11, 1895, with the ballots cast and counted, it was Prudence Belmont who was chosen as best able to lead the Rose and Garden Society into the twentieth century.

Clearing her throat, Pru steeled herself for the acceptance speech that she had practiced a dozen times in the barren privacy of her bedchamber.

"My dear ladies," she began, "the leadership of the Chavistown Ladie's Rose and Garden Society is an honor and a challenge that I take up gladly. I will strive to prove myself worthy of your trust. And to truly *serve* the membership from this office. I will endeavor to do my part to make the Rose and Garden Club the . . ."

A loud clattering in the hallway erupted.

"Ah . . . to make the Rose and Garden Society . . ." Pru tried to continue.

The voice of a housemaid could be heard calling out.

"You can't go in there!"

The parlor door came flying open and slammed back against its hinges. A dirty, disheveled boy, missing his jacket, as usual, stood in the doorway.

"Sharpy Kilroy!" Mavis Hathaway scolded loudly and crossly. "What are you thinking of, busting in here like that?"

"His name is Milton." Prudence corrected her automatically, but her attention was fixed upon the small boy with the wild look in his eye. "Milton? Milton, what is it?"

"Old Man Chavis done collapsed on the ginning floor. They're carrying him home now."

"Oh my heavens, no!"

There were startled cries all around the room.

Prudence, too, felt her heart fly to her throat. Peer Chavis was more than the landlord of nearly every foot of Main Avenue real estate, the owner of the cotton gin, and the city's most prominent citizen. Peer Chavis was the bulwark of the community.

Pru's gaze flew to Aunt Hen. The older woman was as pale as death itself, her eyes wide, her lips colorless.

"They done sent for Doc Phillips," Sharpy announced. "But Ollie Larson said it weren't no use.

SEALED WITH A KISS

Chavis looks nearly good as dead now and weren't long for this world nohow. Mr. Larson said they'd save time and money to skip the doctor and just send for the next of kin."

A gasp escaped Pru's own throat.

In her moment of triumph, disaster.

The cowboy was long and lean, sun-browned and slit-eyed as he stepped off the train. He carried no gripsack or portmanteau, just a pair of worn saddle-bags thrown over his shoulder and a well-oiled Winchester in his hand. From the weather-beaten platform he surveyed the bustle of the busy little town for a long moment before easing his hat brim a bit lower over his eyes.

The train gave a long mournful whistle as it steamed heavily, indicating its readiness to leave.

For a moment he was tempted to leave with it. He could just get on the train and keep on going. There was nothing to stop him. Nothing to keep him here. Nothing . . . nothing except old mistakes and some cold anger. His fingers went to the crisply folded Western Union missive in his pocket.

"All aboard!" the conductor called from behind him.

He didn't dare look back. He had come this far, he at least had to proceed one step farther.

Determinedly he headed down from the platform and along Main Avenue, the pegged heels of his trail boots making a distinctive sound against the planking. He was dressed in Western style. The sturdy weight denim trousers he wore were held up, not with suspenders or galluses, but with the cinched belt that allowed the easy movements necessary for a man who threw a rope for a living. His twilled cheviot overshirt was indigo blue and unadorned by even so much as collar button. At his throat was no tech scarf or Windsor tie, but a paisley neckerchief, handy for covering the mouth and nose on a dusty trail. His appearance was incongruous in this place, but he was familiar.

Familiar but changed, he was changed. The town was changed. Eight years could do that. As he walked he noted both what was new and what remained as it had always.

The streets were still unpaved, but residents were now protected from the omnipresent mud or dust by raised platforms on either side of the street. Fenton's Dry Goods had a new front facade, but the front windows still hung, awkwardly mismatched. The shoemaker still had his little shop above the barber. And old Mr. Crane was still selling cigars where he always had, if the brightly painted wooden Indian in front of his doorway was any indication.

His eyes had grown accustomed to the long beige-and-gold horizons of the arid Pecos. Now he gazed almost lovingly upon the civilized green of Texas's Black Waxy Prairie in the distance. There was a feel of nostalgia to his stroll and a hint of dread in his step.

It was the same. Chavistown was the same as he recalled. But it was different, too.

When he'd left, the new courthouse in the square was still under construction and rimmed with scaffolding. Today it stood stately and majestic, the center of town both literally and figuratively.

Overhead wires crisscrossed in amazing patterns. Telegraph warred with telephone and electric lines in a weave as intricate as any spider's web.

There was a nickelodeon where the Straight Shot

Saloon used to be. And next door to it was a soda fountain. He kept his face averted from the patrons of the latter as he passed. But the ne'er-do-wells spending their hard-earned nickels on peep shows were too occupied to notice him.

One youthful loafer did catch his eye. He seemed far too young to be hanging out in such a place, and yet he stood, legs spread, hands folded across his chest as if he owned the joint. When the little fellow, clad in ragged knee pants looked up, his shrewd expression immediately turned to youthful awe. Nothing was more certain to impress children than a real genuine cowboy.

He nodded to the child as he passed.

On the north corner of town square, the intersection of Main and Market, he spied Ollie Larson. He couldn't quite repress a grin. As always, a small crowd was gathered around the man as he stood on the raised platform created from a box of Pure Dreft Soapflakes. As in times past the unflagging pessimist spouted his latest dire predictions. The cowboy recalled diatribes against the gold standard and agrarian socialism. Today, however, the old man's theme was law and order.

"It is an onslaught of crime like none seen in Texas before," Ollie declared to the crowd. "No household in Chavistown is safe as long as this phantomlike burglar remains in our midst."

The cowboy kept his eyes down avoiding the chance for Larson to get a good look at him. He headed up the street without pausing.

A half block farther he chanced upon a shiny new saloon, the only one he'd seen on the street. Carefully lowering the brim of his hat once more, he stepped a

little reluctantly through the brightly painted green
shutter doors.

The interior was exactly as he expected. He'd been
inside hundreds of joints just like this one. All a little
dark and a little dusty, with the distinct smell of drink
hovering over the place.

He glanced around at the customers. There was a
table full of poker players intent upon the game. One
tired, sort of half-pretty woman looked up hopefully
and pulled her feet out of the wooden chair next to
her. He didn't even bother to meet her gaze. A couple
of rowdy farmhands looked to be starting early on a
weekend drunken spree. A few other men were
drinking calmly as if it were their business. No one
that he recognized.

At the near end of the bar a dandied-up gentlemen
in a plaid coat and summer derby sat alone, his well-
worn traveling bag at his feet.

The cowboy almost smiled. If there was anyone unlikely to be a local, it was a tired drummer in a plaid
coat. With no appearance of haste or purposeful intent, he took the seat right next to the traveling bag.

The barkeep sauntered up and wiped clean the area
directly in front of him.

"What'll ya have?"

"Beer," the cowboy answered.

With a nod he turned to the keg behind him, and
drew a glassful of the dark golden liquid and set it in
front of the cowboy.

"Five cents a glass," the barkeep told him, walking
away.

The cowboy nodded and began rifling through the
change in his pocket as the man left to wait upon the
farm boys. He placed a nickel on the bar and began
to move it around with one finger in a smooth tight

circle, never moving too fast, never quite letting it go.

He glanced over at the drummer beside him.

"Afternoon."

The little man looked up eagerly.

"Good afternoon to you, sir," he answered, and in true salesman fashion, offered his hand across the bar. "Arthur D. Sattlemore, Big Texas Electric Company."

The cowboy's only answer was an indecipherable grunt as he imbibed a great gulp of beer.

The drummer continued to look at him expectantly, as if he would surely introduce himself. When he didn't the silence dragged out uncomfortably.

The cowboy waited.

The drummer cleared his throat. "I'm new in town," he said. "Been here a week now. I'm staying at Johnson's Boardinghouse."

The cowboy nodded.

"It's a real clean place if you're looking for somewhere to stay," the drummer said expectantly.

"I'm not looking for a place to stay."

"You're a resident here?"

He shrugged. "Just passing through."

"Oh."

Once more the conversation waned. The salesmen went for the tried-and-true topic.

"Hot weather we've been having."

The cowboy nodded. "A miserable summer," he agreed. "But good for cotton."

"You are a farmer, sir?"

Clearly the drummer was surprised.

"No," the cowboy answered. "But when you're in Chavistown, it's hard to talk about anything else."

The drummer chuckled and nodded understanding. He leaned closer. "You have the right of it there, sir," he admitted. "I was asked to come present my company to the Commercial Club. I've been here a week and haven't been able to get a word in edgewise. The whole town is talking cotton and what will happen without old man Chavis."

The cowboy blanched. "He's dead?"

The drummer shook his head. "Not as of this morning, but without him to run the gin and the cooperative, the farmers are worried that their cotton will sit in wagonloads by the side of the road."

"The picking is surely not even finished," the cowboy said. "The old man will be up and around before it's over."

The drummer shook his head. "Not the way they're telling it. Seems Chavis is bad off. Weak as a kitten, they say, and the quacks warn that he won't live to see winter."

"Doctors have been wrong before," the cowboy said.

The drummer nodded. "The whole town hopes you're right. The old man ain't got no one to take over for him. The gin is closed down, and the cotton just waiting."

The cowboy nodded.

"The Commercial Club had a meeting early in the week and voted to send for young Chavis, the old man's son."

"They voted on it?" the cowboy asked curiously.

The drummer nodded. "And it was a darned close vote, too. Doc Phillips said to send, but don't nobody know if he'll show up. And a lot of folks just as soon he didn't."

"Is that so?"

"Young Chavis created some bit of a scandal in this town eight years ago," the drummer explained. "Nobody's seen so much as his shadow since. They say his daddy disowned him and that it would be against the old man's wishes to bring him back to town now."

"They didn't ask Chavis to send for his son?"

"Oh the poor old fellow can't talk a lick anymore," he answered. "He tries, but nobody can understand so much as a word."

The cowboy listened quietly, intently.

"So they sent for the son, and they're hoping that he'll come and save their biscuits," the man said. "But for myself, I just wouldn't trust him."

"No?"

The traveling man tutted and shook his head. "They say he jilted a local gal, just left her high and dry."

"Is that what they say?"

The drummer nodded. "And I ask you, what kind of man blessed with plenty of money, an influential name, a fine place in the community and an innocent young sweetheart who expects to marry him, runs off with some round-heeled, painted-up, saloon gal?"

The cowboy took his finger off the nickel. Slowly he picked up the beer and drank it down in one long swallow. He banged the glass on the bar with enough force to catch the attention of every man in the room.

"What kind of man, indeed," he said to the drummer.

Without another word, the cowboy walked out the door. He stood for a long moment on the wooden sidewalk. First he gazed west, up Main Avenue, where the chimneys of the city's finest houses peeked out over the treetops. Then he glanced in the direction of the railroad station once more. He hadn't been recognized. No one knew that he was here. He'd found out what he wanted to know. So why was he as unsure now as he'd been when he'd stepped off the train?

Gidry Chavis, former resident of Chavistown, Texas, now an itinerant cowboy and drover, had not been sent for by his father. The old man didn't even know that he'd been asked to come home. What if he was unwanted? What if after all this time he was unforgiven?

Still he turned his boots westward. In the years he'd been gone he'd become a decisive man, quick to action, fast on his feet. But this place, these people, brought back memories of uncertainty, bad decisions, misplaced loyalties, and past mistakes.

Was he going there? Was he to see the house he'd grown up in? Was he to visit his father? To visit the man who had been both his hero and the standard to which he had failed to measure up. Was he to admit how wrong and foolish he was? To make peace with him at long last.

What about her? Would he have to see her? The image of a blushing young girl gazing up at him adoringly flashed before his eyes. Was he returning to . . . no, no. It was impossible. He had made it impossible, irrevocable.

He touched the telegram still in his coat pocket. His father was ill. It was not at all certain that he would live. His father who had struck him in anger, who had declared him a shame, who said that he never wished to see his son again, might soon have that wish come true. He perhaps would soon lie in cemetery shade, only a stone to differentiate his resting place from pasture grass. Maybe he was ready for that. Maybe he could be content with it. His son could not.

Gidry made his way up Main Avenue toward the grand home of his boyhood. His father might have no wish to see him again. But Gidry wanted very much to see Peer Chavis. Though clearly he remembered his words when he didn't.

"I don't want you or her or any of this!"

He had screamed at the old man that long-ago night just before he left. At twenty-one, Gidry had had a mind of his own, and it did not in any portion resemble his father's.

"I am not you. I never have been," he spit out. "And you wouldn't let me even if I wanted to be!"

Peer Chavis was quaking with anger, red-faced, furious.

"You . . . you *are* like me," he bellowed. "You are exactly like me, that's the dadgum problem, and I'm determined that you won't make the same foolish choices that I did."

"Choices? When did I ever get choices?" Gidry hollered right back. "It's always what *you* want. What *you* think is best. Well I'm done with that. Now I am my own man."

"You're not a man at all," his father answered. "You're just a boy and an untried, ignorant boy at that, all lust and no learning."

"That's what really galls you, isn't it?" Gidry challenged. "That I'm spending my nights with the finest-looking female in town while you're living like a monk."

"Don't talk more stupid than you are."

"You want me to get married," Gidry said to him. "You say it's time for me to think about responsibility and companionship. I'll marry all right. But I'll marry the gal that *I want*, not the one you think I should settle for."

"Gidry, you cannot seriously think to marry that floozy," his father said with certainty.

"Of course I can," he insisted. "You can't stop me. I can do whatever I want."

The old man's eyes were as hard as glass.

"And what you *want* is to embarrass me, humiliate your sweet young betrothed, and scandalize this town."

Gidry had no answer for that and held his silence, anger cloaked around him like medieval armor.

"You've had it too easy, too soft," his father said. "You've been given every thing that you ever wanted. You're no man at all, just a boy. A boy that's had it too soft."

"Soft? When have I had it soft?" he shot back "When have *you* ever been soft on me? You've cuffed me, cursed me, berated and blasted me. Did you ever wonder that I didn't ask why my mama left you? It's because I know exactly. You probably didn't treat her a bit better than you've treated me."

His father's face had been florid with fury.

"You know nothing about your mother and me," he bellowed at his son. "And you could never understand it if you did."

"I know she doesn't want to live here in *your* house, in *your* town, and neither do I," Gidry answered.

"My house and my town have given you every thing that you've ever needed, everything that you've required!"

"Well, these days I require a lot more. I require the freedom to do what I want, choose my own friends, marry who I please."

"Are you willing to give up your family for that?"

"I won't have to," Gidry answered, challenge in his youthful tone. "After we're wed we'll go to Alabama and stay with Mama."

"You wouldn't know your mother if she came

walking up Main Avenue," Peer told him.

"And whose fault is that?" Gidry's words were an accusation. "I've lived here in your boring town with your boring people all my life. I never once received a kind word or even a nod of approval from you, just blaspheming and the back of your hand."

Gidry raised his chin and through clenched teeth voiced his defiance. "I've had my fill of it, old man. And as for you and this town and all the people in it, well as far as I care you can all go straight to hell."

His father slapped him. He could still hear the sound of it reverberating in his mind eight years later. He could almost feel the burning sting of it against his cheek and taste his own blood as the corner of his lip gave way.

"I will not be cursed at in my own home!" Peer had shouted. "Not even by my own son."

Gidry's eyes were slits of anger. "It won't happen again, old man," he'd said. "It won't happen again 'cause I'm leaving."

He'd picked up his bag, but his father was not yet finished.

"You walk out that door, Gidry Chavis," he said, "and I'll never let you walk back through it again."

"As if I would ever want to," he shot back before slamming the door behind him.

Eight years later, Gidry stood out in the street a hundred yards from that front door wanting to walk back through it very much. And wondering if he should take his father at his word.

He stopped in the middle of the tree-lined streets to gaze upward at the grandest house in all Chavis County. The *manse* his father had called it. He had it built in plantation style in honor of his wife and to remind her of her family home in Alabama. There was not one iota of his stern, practical father in the fashionable design. He had fashioned it deliberately for her. It had not even been completed before she'd deserted her husband and returned to the bosom of her fine Southern family.

When Gidry had left home, Alabama had been his destination. The round-heeled saloon gal had been only an excuse. He'd never asked her to marry him. Truly, he'd never even considered it. His father was right about that. There were gals a man married and ones just for practice. The red-spangled gal wasn't even interested enough in him to practice. She'd let him pay her way to San Antone, but he'd headed eastward.

He'd soon realized his mistake.

His strangely childlike and selfish mother and her aggrandizing, narrow-minded relatives had been as cloying and repellent as the Alabama summer. He was too much like his father, she'd told him. Too common to appreciate the finer points of Southern gentility.

Of course she could never have been happy in Texas, not even as mistress of this fine reproduction of an antebellum house. Gidry had always admired his home with its wide verandas curved around the east corner, both stories adorned with spindlework friezes and balustrades. On the lower one a white plankboard swing hung in the corner. The place was in some need of a fresh coat of paint, but its intricate woodwork and the majestic cross-braced gable were scuffed but still welcoming.

Gidry was not certain that it was meant to welcome him.

His eyes were drawn to the second-story window of his father's room. The old man would be lying in there. Perhaps he was dying. If he was, there were things he wished to say to him. He wanted the chance.

Gidry had learned a lot in the years he'd been gone. He'd learned to fend for himself, to face his fears, to stand up as a man. He'd driven cattle, tended horses, and hung fences. He could cook a rattlesnake over a campfire and scrub his clothes clean with lye. He'd discovered that a man is only as good as his word. And that a vow unkept was more loathsome than vermin. In his years away from home Gidry Chavis had learned to respect his father. He knew now that his father had been right. He *had* been too soft, too safe, too selfish.

He wanted another chance. He ached for another chance. But he knew he didn't deserve one.

His father was only a short distance away. Up in the room beyond the window. What would his father want? That was the question that plagued him. His father needed him now.

The town needed him now. Peer Chavis had controlled cotton in this community as if it were he himself who created it. The market was low and uncertain. A firm hand and an iron will was necessary to secure a good price for the crop. The people of Chavis County had depended on Chavis Cotton Company to provide that for the last fifty years. Gidry Chavis could continue that for the old man, for the community.

Gidry was uncertain. He'd made a life for himself out in the cattle country of west Texas. It was a plain life full of hard work and hard-won respect. But he was proud to call it his own. Out there, alone, he was nobody's son, only a man with a job to do. And Gidry had learned to do it well. He wanted to hurry back to it. The hard, hot sameness of it suddenly held bright appeal.

But he wanted to stay here also. He wanted to help out. To somehow atone for his past. To say with his deeds what perhaps he could never say with his words. He knew now what he'd thrown away. And he was not without regrets about it. He wanted to show that.

There was something more that he wanted. He wanted, at long last, to admit that he was wrong, to say that he was sorry. He wanted his father's forgiveness.

But he was unable to confront his father, to ask him what *he* wanted. And he would not force his presence upon the sick old man against his will.

As he hesitated, deep in his thoughts, a movement at the corner of his eye caught his attention.

He glanced over at the garden of the house next door and a grin spread across his face. With her back to him, on her hands and knees, Henrietta Pauling was working in the rich black soil of her flower garden. Her faded, shapeless gown hung upon her shoulders like an oversize cotton sack, and a huge unfashionable sunbonnet hid every wisp of her scraggly hair and protected her face from the harsh rays of a Texas afternoon.

"Aunt Hen," he said quietly to himself.

She'd been their neighbor and his family's closest friend all of Gidry's life. When his stubborn father would listen to no one else, he continued to accept counsel from the outspoken, rawboned spinster next door. She had helped shape Gidry's life. She had treated him fine and fairly, even when he was in the finest devil of trouble. Which had been most of the time.

Of course, since his departure, the older woman

would have good cause to dislike him. But in all honesty, Gidry knew that she wouldn't hold a grudge. It just wasn't in her nature. A man could confess to Aunt Hen that he had been in prison and know, somehow, she'd manage not to think any less of him.

Aunt Hen would be happy to see him, no matter what. And she would know how his father was doing. She would know whether he wanted Gidry to come home and do his duty or stay in exile forevermore.

Hopeful, Gidry made his way to the front of the Pauling house and through the narrow, blooming, trellis gateway. The garden was much improved since last he'd walked here. Aunt Hen loved growing things, but he had not recalled such glorius roses. The thorny bushes grew in great variety with large blooms all along the narrow garden paths. He made his way with some stealth remembering how he used to sneak up on her and startle her as a child.

He was already grinning broadly as he slipped up behind her.

"Well if it isn't the crankiest old maid in Chavis County," he said.

She turned in a flash to stare up at him in surprise.

Gidry's smile froze as the face of the wide-eyed woman who gazed up at him from the depths of a gingham slat bonnet was not familiarly lined with ancient mirth and motherly goodwill, but one many years younger and equally familiar. A face he had hoped to avoid entirely for the next thousand years.

"Prudence?"

"Gid! . . . ah . . . ah . . . Mr. Chavis."

He was stunned into clumsy speechlessness.

Hastily she rose to her feet. The threadbare Mother Hubbard gown she wore looked at least twice her own age and bore two dirty prints at the level of her knees. A pair of seemingly giant men's plow boots peeked out from beneath her skirts. Altogether it was an incongruous and unattractive costume.

"Prudence, what are you doing here?" he asked stupidly.

Her expression was momentarily puzzled. "I live here," she answered.

"Here with Aunt Hen? You mean you never married."

Her cheeks blazed vivid red. "I certainly had offers!" Her tone was strident, defensive.

"Of course, of course," Gidry insisted quickly, wishing both to bite his own tongue and to have lightning strike him dead on the spot. There was a smudge of dirt upon her nose and one tendril of sweat-dampened brown hair stuck to the side of her cheek.

Gidry turned slightly sideways, making it less necessary to meet her eyes. Good Lord! What a disaster! Of all the people in Chavistown, Prudence Belmont was the one particular woman he decidedly wished to avoid.

They had once been close, perhaps too close. For years they were devoted playmates, partners in mischief, and complete confidants. Pru was his friend, the favorite part of his day, his perfect pal. For that crime he had rather publicly jilted her.

"I . . . I was looking for Aunt Hen," he said. "That's why I'm here. That's why I said . . . well, where is Aunt Hen anyway?"

"She's with your father," Pru answered, brushing ineffectively at her mud-stained dress.

"Has he worsened?" Gidry asked, glancing toward the big house.

"No, no," she assured him. "Aunt Hen likes to spell

the nurse. I think she doesn't quite trust her with his care."

Gidry nodded.

"Yes, she has always been so good to him."

"She still is."

The silence between them lingered. Gidry wanted to take his leave. He didn't want to have to look at her. Like most men, he would have preferred facing a whole pack of rabid coyotes than the one true friend whom he had wronged.

"We did not know you were returning home."

Gidry patted the pocket of his coat. "I received a telegram from the Commercial Club. I . . . thought perhaps that I was needed. I hoped Aunt Hen would be able to tell me if my father might want me to step in."

"Well she is there, with your father," Pru said, indicating the house. "You can talk to both of them at once."

Gidry hesitated, glancing toward his home briefly before turning once again to Prudence.

"Could you simply tell her when you see her that I am in town," he said. "I will go get myself a room and try to catch up with her later."

"You are not staying at your house?" Pru sounded completely dumbfounded.

"Probably not," he admitted evenly. "I . . . I'm not sure that I am welcome."

Her cheeks visibly reddened.

"It was all such a long time ago," she said a little breathlessly. "Surely, all is forgiven."

"Is it?" he asked, looking her straight in the eye for the first time.

His direct look apparently caught her off guard. But

she raised her chin higher, as if refusing to see more in his words than what was on the surface.

"I'll go get her for you."

"Thank you. Thank you, Pru. I . . ."

"Don't mention it," she said quickly as she hurried away.

He was quite certain that she was not referring to this moment, this small favor. *Don't mention it*, she had said. His father had wanted him to marry Prudence Belmont. Prudence had wanted it also. He had formally asked her. He had given her a ring. And he had run off and left her. It was a long time ago. And yes, it was by far best not to mention it.

Chapter 2

SHE HAD heard people relate moments in which they wished that the earth would open up and swallow them. For Prudence, seeing Gidry Chavis in her garden this afternoon fit that bill entirely.

She made her way as quickly as possible to the back door of the Chavis house.

I certainly had offers! She heard her own words again and wanted to scream in frustration. Why had she said that? What malicious unkind devil had put those words in her mouth? How bitter and disappointed she sounded. He would be all built-up and full of himself that she had pined away for him for eight long years. *Poor jilted spinster, he would say to himself, she never married, you know.*

It had not been a lie, of course. She had had offers. Shortly after Gidry had left, old Henry Tatum had diligently attempted to court her. When she resisted his more amorous attentions, he'd come straight to the point stating clearly that he needed a wife and he thought she'd do.

Still aching from rejection, she had not believed *he* would *do* at all.

Not more than a year later, Stanley Honnebuzz began walking her to church. He was a stern, sober young man who'd just hung up his law shingle. Pru had seriously considered marrying him, but when he finally did ask her, she couldn't go through with it.

And not three years ago, when Amos Wilburn's wife passed on, Pru had been the first woman he'd approached with the opportunity to take on the rearing of his rowdy brood. By then Prudence was so involved with her roses, she was completely uninterested in the rather stern older man and his seven half-grown children.

She'd had offers. She wanted Gidry Chavis to know that. She would be horrified if she thought he felt sorry for her.

She glanced down at her dirty gown and nearly moaned aloud. What unkind fate should bring Gidry Chavis back into her life on the same morning she intended to replant the rugosas that were getting too much sun along the fence row. She was dirty, perspiring, and wearing a dress more suited to liming an outhouse than meeting her former betrothed. One look at her in this morning's outfit and how could any man not feel sorry for her. She looked absolutely wretched.

In all her imaginings of seeing him again, and she had imagined it more times than she cared to admit, she had always been poised, dignified, well-spoken, even witty. She would be standing tall in her gray worsted jacket with the wide pompadour sleeves adding to her presence, her best mignon hat perched upon her perfectly dressed hair. She would titter ever so drolly about their past relationship, denigrating with fine humor the quickly passing passion she had conceived for a gentleman so clearly unsuited to her self-assured and independent nature.

It was to be a sharp contrast to the calf-eyed young girl who had worn her heart on her sleeve from the moment she met him. Who had so openly declared her undying love for him.

Pru stepped in through the side-entrance door to find Mrs. Butts, the hired nurse for Mr. Chavis, sitting comfortably at the kitchen table enjoying a cup of tea.

The huge, overbearing woman glanced up, perusing Pru's costume with distaste.

"Don't bring the whole garden in with you," the nurse scolded.

Prudence gave the woman a frosty glance. She never allowed herself to be talked down to by anyone. Experience had taught her that position, once forfeited, was hard to regain.

"Is my Aunt Hen upstairs?" she asked loftily.

The nurse's tone changed to deference immediately.

"Oh yes, yes, ma'am. She's just giving me a little break from time to time. Your aunt is such a good woman to help."

Pru nodded, although in truth she knew that it was the nurse who occasionally helped Aunt Hen and not at all the other way around. Since the day Peer Chavis fell ill, Henrietta Pauling had been by his side nearly night and day. It was only her aunt's long-standing reputation that kept the situation from being a scandal. Unmarried women, even ones nearing fifty, did not take on the care of men other than a father or a brother. No neighbor did such a thing, no matter how many years one had lived next door. And certainly a maiden lady would never care for a married man. It simply was not done.

That unalterable fact was seemingly lost upon Aunt Hen however.

"I will speak to her a moment, if you please," Prudence told the nurse in a tone that precluded the suggestion of a request.

"Take your time, ma'am, all the time you want," the nurse assured her.

Without further reply, Prudence hurried through the doorway to the main hall and up the wide stairway. Her thoughts were not upon the nurse, Aunt Hen, or Peer Chavis. As ever when he was within a reasonable distance, Pru thought about Gidry. It had always been that way, and she berated herself with every step that it still was.

She should have spoken up more cleverly. She should have been less flustered at seeing him. She could have uttered a glibly pointed witticism. Or offered only a stern and disapproving gaze.

Glancing down at her dress once more, she shook her head. She should have said anything or been anything other than a dirty ragamuffin in sad gown who'd *had offers*.

At the landing she paused at the carved mahogany seat that perched beneath the grand stained-glass window. The bright green vines and purple grapes obscured her view, but from the beveled edges of the window she could see him still standing in her garden. Her breath caught in her throat. She would never have believed that he could be more attractive than he had been eight years ago. Then his flirty manners, jet-black hair, and dark, flashing eyes had set every young female heart aflutter, including her own. Today he was larger, more muscular, sun-browned and serious. The cowboy garb suited him. It made the beauty of his features more rugged and masculine.

Deliberately Prudence breathed again; her heart was hammering.

"No, not again," she vowed to herself quietly.

It had been pitiful how she'd loved him, yearned for him, longed for him, so hopelessly at nineteen. Allowing herself those feeling again now at twenty-seven would be pathetic and hideous. She would not, could not let that happen. Hadn't she humiliated herself enough?

I certainly had offers!

She nearly groaned aloud. Why had she allowed such words to come out of her mouth?

Shaking her head, Pru turned and hurried up the stairs and along the hallway to the front bedroom. With a little tap of announcement she caught her aunt's attention and brought her into the smaller bedroom.

Her Aunt looked at her curiously.

"Gidry is down in the garden," she whispered.

Aunt Hen nodded. "I saw him a few minutes ago standing in the street just looking at the house. Just looking at it as if it were the most beautiful sight he'd ever beheld." The older woman tutted unhappily. "It has been a long exile for him."

Prudence didn't comment. To her thinking, Gidry could have come home years ago if he'd been willing to swallow his pride. And he *should* have come home to take up his responsibilities. Once he'd run off with that saloon gal, no one would have ever expected him to marry Pru. But at least he should have . . . he should have returned to Chavistown when *she* had.

"So he spoke to you," Aunt Hen said. "Well, it's good to get that over with, I suppose."

"He thought I was you when he approached me in the garden," she said. "In my work clothes and this big old sunbonnet he couldn't tell us apart."

Aunt Hen laughed lightly. "That must have been quite a moment for the both of you then."

Pru didn't find it all that humorous.

"So what did he say?" Aunt Hen asked. "I'm sure you expected an apology."

"An apology?" Prudence was genuinely surprised. She had not expected any such thing. Although it was very much like her to insist on the obligations of refined manners. But an apology for not loving her? Somehow that could never be enough.

"You mean he didn't say anything about you both being too young to know what you wanted?" Aunt Hen suggested. "Or how often he'd regretted his hasty departure, not even taking proper leave of you."

"No, no we didn't talk about it at all," she said.

"Just both pretending that nothing happened," Aunt Hen said, shaking her head in disapproval.

"Nothing did happen," Pru insisted. "We were once engaged, and he broke it off. That was the sum of the incident entirely."

"Yes," her aunt said nodding. "So I have heard you say. It's not all that strange that I remember it a bit differently, I suppose."

Pru felt it necessary to defend herself, defend her actions when seeing him again.

"That's all water under the bridge," she insisted. "My youthful infatuation for Gidry Chavis has long since joined paper dolls and ball-and-jacks as remnants of my childhood."

"Hmmm," was Aunt Hen's only reply. She nodded but somehow still looked skeptical.

"Gidry is here because he thinks his father needs him," Pru said. "But he won't stay under this roof unless you think that's what his father wishes."

"Is that why he didn't come straight up to the front door?" Aunt Hen asked.

"He is apparently unsure of his welcome."

The older woman nodded and headed toward the larger bedroom and the man lying in the bed. She walked to his side and began gently to stroke the creases upon his forehead.

"Your son is home, Peer," she said. "You told the boy not to come into the house, and he hasn't."

The man's dark eyes, sunk deep in his head, looked up at her expressively. He appeared momentarily stunned and then irritated. He raised his right arm slightly as if grasping for something. Aunt Hen took his hand.

"He's downstairs in my garden, but he won't come up unless you invite him back into your house." A strange guttural noise came out of the old man's throat. It could not be called language or even gibberish. It was sound merely. Peer Chavis retained the ability to make sound, but the effort required to do so exhausted him completely.

Aunt Hen patted his hand and urged him to quiet. She looked at him a long moment before she spoke again.

"It's been a long parting," she told the old man. "Harsh words on both sides no doubt. But that doesn't matter anymore, does it? One thing about losing your health, you find out what really matters."

The old man swallowed visibly, a trail of tears beginning to seep out of both eyes, clouding his vision as he tried to form the words.

"Tell Gidry to come on up," Aunt Hen told Pru, swiping the wetness from his cheeks with her thumb. "Tell him that his father wants to see him."

* * *

Home was a paltry and inadequate word Gidry decided, as he silently walked through the rooms of his childhood. It was all so familiar, and yet he felt so removed from it. These walls, the stairs, the banister, the doorway, were as known to him as the back of his own hand. And yet they were not as he had remembered them. Because he was not as he remembered himself.

But if he were changed, his father was much more so. The afternoon sun slanted in from the south windows, illuminating the massive canopy shrouded sickbed of Peer Chavis. The strong, determined, opinionated man who for twenty-one years had ruled his life and to whom Gidry had railed against lay thin and gaunt and pale upon the bedsheets.

"Papa, I'm home," he said quietly.

The old man gazed up at him in silence.

Gidry turned to Aunt Hen, standing on the far side of the bed.

"Can he hear me?" he asked her.

She nodded. "Long as you don't whisper," she answered.

"It's Gidry, Papa," he repeated. "I'm home."

The old man's dark eyes were neither cloudy or vacant. He was there. Gidry saw at once that his father's mind was still sharp. Peer recognized his son. Whether he was pleased about it was not readily discernible.

He swallowed determinedly. He'd been given this opportunity, and he was not going to let it pass by.

"I'm home, Papa," Gidry said. "I'm home to say I'm sorry. I'm sorry about everything."

There was a long silence as he stared at the broken old man on the bed before him, waiting.

"He can't answer you," Aunt Hen said quietly. "He hasn't been able to make a word understood since the day he collapsed at the gin."

"Does the doctor say if he'll be able to speak again?"

"Doc says with apoplexy if they are not talking by the third day, they never will."

Gidry was startled. Surely it could not be true. He needed to talk with this man who shared his heritage as well as his temper. There was so much he needed to say, so much that he needed to ask. He looked back at the pale version of the vital father he had known once more. The old man's countenance was grim and accepting.

"He can't move anything on his left side," Aunt Hen explained. "He can't count on words or gestures to express his feelings anymore, so he has to rely upon his eyes."

Gidry felt the sting of tears in his own, but he blinked them back.

"There was so much that I wanted to say," he told her.

"You can say whatever you want," she replied. "He understands every word. I talk to him all day. Just because he can't reply doesn't mean he's not enjoying the conversation."

She smiled down at the old man and gently stroked his forehead. "When he gets tired of listening, he'll just doze on off. I swear, it's about the rudest thing I ever saw."

Her teasing eased the tension of the moment, and Gidry was actually able to smile.

"I'll leave you two to make your peace and catch up on the latest news," she said. "I'll be down in the kitchen sorting through the dirty linens if you need me. The laundress comes tomorrow."

Gidry nodded.

"What if he . . . ?"

"I'll be right downstairs," Aunt Hen said. "If you need me, just give a holler."

"Thank you, Aunt Hen," he said.

The old woman smiled at him.

"Welcome home, Gidry," she said as she closed the door soundlessly behind her.

Gidry followed his father's eyes as he watched her go. The old man obviously needed Aunt Hen as a buffer as much as he did himself.

"Aunt Hen's a fine old gal," Gidry said. "When I was a boy I used to wish that you'd married her."

The expression on his father's face was a strangely curious one.

Gidry shrugged.

"I was a kid. I pretended that she was my real mother and that the woman from Alabama in the photograph was just a made-up story."

Gidry chuckled lightly. "I suppose I was thinking more of what I'd want in a mother than what you'd want in a wife," he explained. "After meeting Mama, it seems pretty clear that Aunt Hen just would not have been your type. And she's always been perfectly content with her spinster status. A man can't really change a thing like that."

The silence seemed to speak for itself.

"There are a lot of things that just can't be changed," Gidry admitted quietly. "I wish I could have been a better son to you. I wish we had not parted with such rancor. But I learned a lot, Papa. I learned a lot on my own. I also discovered the truth in so much that you taught me."

The words were out, and Gidry didn't regret them. He was alone with his father. Alone, in the silence of the dimly lit sickroom. There was so much that he wanted to say. So much that he wanted to account for. But he had no idea where to begin.

He'd said he was sorry, but it seemed so paltry against what he'd done. At that moment he realized with perfect clarity the enormity of his crime. He had scandalized a town. He had hurt Prudence Belmont. But even more than those things, he had stolen the years of his father and himself together. The years when they might have been men of mutual respect. The years when he might have acquired the wisdom that the old man had learned alone. As cruelly and as thoughtlessly as any robber he had stolen those things. Both from his father and from himself.

"I'm sorry," Gidry said again. "I've wasted so much time."

He stood unsure and uncomfortable. "I suppose Aunt Hen would say, 'No use fretting about the past. Best to make the best of what you have.' Aunt Hen always knows what to say to us. Even when neither of us knew what to say to each other."

Gidry pulled a chair up next to the bed.

"I want to sit here with you, Papa," he said. "I'm sorry you can't talk to me, but I'd be pleased just to look at you again."

Gidry did not immediately avail himself of the chair. It seemed almost disrespectful to sit in his father's presence without the old man's leave to do so. Silently he marveled at his own thoughts. His father had never been such a stickler for form. And Gidry had never been the type of son who adhered to such deference.

"I . . . I believe I'll stand," he said simply. He

couldn't truly offer an explanation, so he didn't bother to do so.

He had no idea what he would say to his father. A one-sided conversation with a man he hadn't seen in eight years would be difficult for anyone. But when the man was a father he now respected but had long ago reviled, it was an even more complicated task.

Gidry looked down into the face of the broken man in the bed.

"I should never have stayed away so long," he said.

His father's fine blue eyes gazed at him for long moments as if studying the familiarity of his son and assessing the changes in him. He knew he looked different. Hard times and heartache don't just age a person, they alter him, too. Gidry was much altered. But a quick glance in a mirror revealed him more like his father with each passing day.

Could his father see that? Did he recognize himself in his son? Gidry felt uncomfortable within the scrutiny, but he steeled himself against stepping away. He owed his father so much, surely he could stand for inspection. He did avert his eyes, which had become inexplicably moist.

Peer reached forward and took the arm of Gidry's coat. He was almost smiling as he fingered the long leather fringes along the seam.

"They wave with every move and the slightest breeze," he explained to his father. "It keeps the flies off me."

The old man continued to look at him.

"Flies are hell on earth among a cattle herd," Gidry said, and then added quietly, "I'm a cowboy, Papa. I've been making my living as a cowboy."

That seemed to amuse his father. Gidry shouldn't have been surprised, he realized. Cowboys, lonely and lonesome on the range, had made a tradition of telling stories around the campfire to amuse themselves. Many stories were based on actual events and true happenings on the range. But as often as not they were wild-eyed lies told straight-faced to the deception of none and the amusement of all.

The cowboys had gotten so good at tall tales, that Eastern dandies had taken up the idea and had begun to write stories of their own based on tales told around the campfire. The dime novels of his grandfather's day were long past, still the cowboy stories were told in pulp magazines and comic strips. People found them endlessly entertaining. And Gidry knew himself to be better at storytelling than most.

"Yes, I'm a cowboy," Gidry said. "I can throw a rope on a steer at full gallop and turn a herd into the wind in the middle of a snowstorm." He chuckled lightly and spoke more softly, as if betraying a confidence. "And I've had days to sit so long in the saddle that a chair could not be found to conform to my backside."

There was telling laughter in his father's eyes.

Moving closer to the old man's side, Gidry gave a wide grin. "Did you ever hear how the bald-face maverick saved the Republic of Texas?"

The old man's eyes gleamed with delight and interest as Gidry launched into his story.

It was a pleasant diversion, entertaining his father with trail talk and cowboy lore. It had lightened those first moments between them and made their reunion easier to bear.

Gidry had come back to see his father, to help out until the old man was back on his feet, and to get the cotton ginned. He saw now, as he gazed down into his father's now-sleeping countenance that he would not be returning to ranch life. Not soon. Perhaps not ever.

Walking to the window, Gidry stared out into the darkness. How many nights from how many lonely distant places had he imagined this view? Perhaps a thousand would not be an overstatement. Chavistown was his home, his heritage, his people. How easily he had cast it away. How difficult it was to recapture.

Peer Chavis needed him. So Gidry was back. He was back, and would run the business and more than likely the town as well as his father always had. From the moment he'd been mustered out of the Army of the Confederacy, when Peer had been younger than Gidry was now, his father had managed to run everything. He managed to build a community from the ashes of war. With such an example, how could a man fail?

Gidry might well fail without help from the townsfolk, he mused. They had no reason to want him or trust him. He wasn't sure even if they would be willing to accept him back. He'd left in a high-blown hubbub. And his shabby treatment of his bride-to-be was blatantly unforgivable.

Gidry's brow furrowed as that moment, he saw his former fiancée at the back of the house next door. She was somewhat obscured within the glow of the lantern she carried as she left the back of Aunt Hen's home and hurried with almost furtive haste to the illkept and ramshackle milking shed on the back edge of the property.

Her destination sparked Gidry's curiosity. From the look of the shed, Aunt Hen had not kept a cow in at least twenty years.

To his complete surprise the shed door was opened from the inside as she arrived.

His jaw dropped open immediately, but it took a couple of seconds for his mind completely to form the conclusion that his thoughts were drawing. Prudence Belmont was making a secret assignation.

Gidry was momentarily shocked almost beyond belief. Chavistown was a very upright and moral community. In that he was certain the place had not changed overmuch. Even the mildest peccadillo was not easily overlooked. His own youthful rowdiness was cause for much disapproval, and his jilting of a perfectly acceptable young woman had put him almost completely beyond the pale.

But a single female meeting a man in secret was far more scandalous than any circumstance that he could conjure up. If found out, she could likely find herself tarred and feathered. It would take a hasty marriage and lifetime of virtuous living even to begin to overcome it. Why would Prudence Belmont risk such a thing?

Why indeed. Gidry shook his head in wry acceptance. He'd learned a few things about the ways of the world in the last eight years. People would cheerfully destroy their own lives and the lives of those around them as well. They did it for *love*. Love.

He knew from personal experience that Prudence was a woman capable of deep and healing love. She had loved Gidry with all her heart and soul and mind. It had been an all-encompassing and all-consuming love. And he had neither understood nor appreciated it.

She had offered her whole being, her life, her future to him as a precious gift. He had accepted it with about the same amount of awe and pride as the scrap of ribbon given him for winning the sack race at the Fourth of July picnic.

He had been her closest confidant and best friend, but the mystery of her deeper nature had never sparked his interest.

It had, apparently, sparked the interest of others. Pru was not an unattractive woman, although she'd looked less than her best this afternoon. It would be no great surprise that men in Chavistown would find her of interest. Hadn't she just told him this afternoon that she'd *had offers.*

Apparently not all of them included marriage.

Chapter 3

THE EARLY-MORNING sun slanted through the kitchen windows, affording enough light for Prudence to read the latest bulletins from the American Rose Society. Although the group was mainly for commercial growers, Pru prided herself upon being as knowledgeable on the subject as any professional.

She tutted with concern over an article comparing blossom production in urban areas with rural sites. In the past it was thought that soil content and overuse might be the cause of this disparity. This author, however, postulated that it was the noise of trains and trolleys and the herds of humans moving along on sidewalks that was jarring plant root systems and inhibiting growth.

The changes in modern life, being untrue to nature, are a threat to plant and flower production.

Pru shook her head. It was all true, of course. She had seen the smoky, smelly cities. It took no convincing for her to agree that nothing was a bigger danger to her roses than the hubbub of industrialized society. She was so fortunate to live in a quiet place like Chav-

41

istown, where her plants could grow and prosper as God intended that they should.

She had a difficult time concentrating upon her reading this morning since Gidry had been summoned home. Having come face-to-face with him yesterday was as close to a waking nightmare as she ever wanted to imagine.

It had been eight years. Eight long years, yet in some part of her heart it was as close as yesterday. His walk, his voice, the expressions on his face, the slightly crooked grin and the straight-shouldered stance were as familiar to her now as if they had been imprinted upon her soul.

She could not remember when she did not love him. He had always been a part of her from the first day she had arrived in Chavistown following her mother's death. After years of rootlessness and travel, she had fallen in love with her solid new home and everything about it. The causal friendliness Gidry had bestowed on her younger self had seemed the most perfect part after the drama of her first twelve years.

Her father, Harvey Belmont, had been a handsome gambling man, forever pursuing that lucky streak that would put him in clover. And where he went, her mother followed, despite that all Evelyn Pauling had ever wanted was her own little house and a gaggle of children. Pru never doubted her parents loved each other from the day they'd met till the day her mother died, but the jealous arguments, money problems, her father's fondness for bourbon, her mother's declining health from consumption, and the constant moves from flophouse to grand hotel had been draining.

They buried her mother in Dubuque, Iowa, and Pru

had boarded a train to Texas to live for good. She had been blessed enough to find the home her young heart had yearned for, and Gidry became an inextricable part of that dream. In the gangly years that followed, she had been his shadow. At first he had treated her with the benign tolerance of an older brother. But as she matured, and as she pored out her love and admiration for him as generously as springwater in a flood, he beamed with pride at her and claimed her as his own.

They had been inseparable. And they had done everything right. He had escorted her to church every Sunday morning. Promenaded with her in the park in the afternoon. She attended every social function and Chautauqua lecture upon his arm. And chatted endlessly together in the relative privacy of the garden bench. They played endless games of Parcheesi and Twenty Questions under the watchful eye of his father. And tried their hands at pyrography with the help of Aunt Hen. Together they decided what furnishings to have in their house. What wonders they would visit on their honeymoon trip. And what names they would give to the nine sons they would have. Nine boys. Gidry had insisted. Enough to field a Chavis family baseball team.

It was a warm and beautiful fantasy. Burst as easily and irrevocably as a soap bubble in the Wednesday wash. He was still the youthful desire of her heart. But her heart no longer desired youth.

She had become a woman. On one long-remembered night of sleeplessness followed by a simple terse letter.

My dearest Prudence,

I have determined that it is best that we do not wed.

You are my truest friend, so I know that you will understand.

I am off to find new people and places and to do at last, the things that I want to do.

I am not the man who can make you happy. Please forgive me and recall me with fondness.

Good-bye,
Gidry Chavis

She had not wanted to believe that it was true. He'd only gotten cold feet, she'd assured herself. The things that he wanted to do, included marrying her, having a family. She did know him. She did know what he wanted. It was all some terrible misunderstanding. She would joke with him about it. Tease him out of it. They were meant to be together and would be for all time. Theirs was a perfect romance and nothing could tarnish it. She was certain of that.

It was only after receiving the pitying glances of the town gossips and hearing the whispered speculation of his affair with Mabel Merriman that she begun to understand that it was really so. That after gladly giving everything of her heart, her self, she had been cast aside almost carelessly. She had loved him utterly. And apparently he had loved her not at all.

The hurt had been sharp, paralyzing, agonizing. More than her foolish young heart was able to bear. To survive the pain of it, Pru had taught herself not to feel—and not to love. Pride was her comfort now. And what a dependable, faithful comfort it was.

"Good morning."

Pru glanced up from her reading as Aunt Hen entered the kitchen. The old woman's housedress was scrupulously clean and pressed, and every hair upon her head was neatly in place. But she looked older than her fifty years, tired and thin, with dark circles under her eyes.

"Oh, I was hoping that you would sleep late," she said.

The old woman shook her head, as if the idea itself was preposterous. "Who can sleep when the sun has come up?" she asked rhetorically.

"You're putting in so many hours at the Chavis house, you really need to rest," Pru told her.

"I'll rest when I'm dead," she answered. "Until then I'd best stay busy. The day is plenty short enough as it is without wasting any of it."

"Well, at least sit and allow me to fix you a good breakfast," Pru said. "All you ever eat anymore is cold biscuit and jam."

"I *like* cold biscuit and jam," Aunt Hen insisted as she stepped over to the larder to retrieve exactly that. "And I haven't time for anything else. I need to get over to the house."

Pru closed her pamphlet and looked up at her aunt, her brow furrowing with worry.

"Surely you don't need to rush over there now that Gidry is home," she said.

"As much as ever," her aunt replied as she seated herself at the table. Her plate held two cold biscuits, yesterday's fare. Next to them she spooned out a generous portion of plum jelly from a blue mason jar. "Gidry will be needing to go down to the gin. With the place closed down, there'll be work and trouble piling up all over the place and every businessman in town will be itching to talk to him and the rest of us will be wanting to hear what he has to say."

"I can't imagine what people think that Gidry

might have to tell them," Pru related tersely. "He's been away from the cotton business for eight years. And it seems to me that even when he lived here, he was not a common sight down at the gin."

Aunt Hen settled a big dollop of jam upon her biscuit.

"He was just a boy back then," she pointed out.

"He was twenty-one," Pru reminded her. "Twenty-one years old, lazy, self-indulgent, and spoiled."

Aunt Hen chewed her biscuit thoughtfully. "Is that why you fell in love with him?"

Prudence had the good grace to blush. "I was a child myself," she admitted painfully. "And it certainly wasn't *love*."

The older woman raised her eyebrow and gave her niece a long look. "That's sure what it seemed like at the time."

Pru met her aunt's speculative gaze with one as equally stubborn. "It's so long ago, I don't know how you can even recall it. I barely remember it myself."

Her aunt laughed aloud at that.

"Well anyway," Pru continued, "I am quite pleased to see Gidry back in town. It is his responsibility to take care of his father, and that certainly frees you from any obligation you might have."

"It is good that the boy's back," Aunt Hen agreed. "I think having him home may be good for his father. But a sick man needs a feminine touch. I'd best be there to watch over Peer in Gidry's absence."

Pru looked at her aunt's haggard features. The lingering illness of Peer Chavis was as visible on the lines of her face as the old man's own. Prudence loved her aunt and could not imagine why she should risk her own health. She steeled herself to voice disapproval.

"Now Aunt Hen," she chided. "I know that Mr. Chavis has been a good neighbor to us always. But he has a nurse employed for his care."

Her aunt sniffed derisively as she jellied another biscuit. "The woman's only half-lazy," she replied. "And even if she weren't, folks in their last days shouldn't be left to strangers."

"I'm sure that after these weeks, Mrs. Butts's face is no longer strange to Mr. Chavis," Pru replied. "And he's a married man, Aunt Hen. It is Mrs. Chavis who ought to be here taking care of him."

"As if that woman even cares if he lives or dies," Aunt Hen pointed out. "She walked out on a faithful husband and an infant child because she was just too hot in Texas."

Prudence knew well her aunt's opinion of the absent Mrs. Chavis.

Her aunt huffed angrily. "I hope Alabama has been hotter than hell itself for the last twenty-five years."

Pru tutted reproachfully. "Now Aunt Hen, we don't know all of the circumstances behind their marital troubles. It's not for us to judge."

"I'm not judging, I'm stating the facts," Aunt Hen insisted. "And the fact is, his wife will not be coming back here to take care of him. In the absence of family it is friends who ought to be by his side."

Pru wasn't willing to let it rest. "I don't see any of the other women in town wearing themselves to a frazzle to take care of him," she said.

"Other women have their own families to attend to," her aunt countered.

Prudence didn't agree. "Other women also have more experience tending the sick."

Her aunt bristled at the criticism.

"I tended my own father until his passing," she

said, rather affronted. "I do what I can, and I believe my help is appreciated."

Pru regretted her words. "I did not mean that you aren't a blessing to the old man. You're far too good to him."

"Peer Chavis has been very *good* to me, Prudence," she said. "And he's been good to you as well. When I couldn't pay the taxes on this place five years ago, he quietly bought it up himself so no one would know, and the two of us have lived here without paying so much as a penny of rent."

"He doesn't need our money," Pru pointed out. "He owns half the county; one tiny little cottage and a rose garden wouldn't count for much."

"Still he's never said so much as a word," Aunt Hen reiterated.

"Yes, yes, he's been a wonderful neighbor. And I know . . . well, I know that he always felt bad about the . . . the problem between me and Gidry and perhaps . . ."

"He didn't do any of it because of you and Gidry," Aunt Hen said with certainty. "I don't want you believing that. It had nothing to do with his generosity at all."

"Well, no matter what his reasoning," Pru replied. "I am grateful that he helped us out. But maiden ladies do not care for the personal needs of ailing older men."

Her aunt actually chuckled at that.

"A man is a man is a man," she said. "I've seen nothing yet to scandalize me."

"But still, people talk," her niece insisted.

Aunt Hen shook her head.

"Pru, you give the weight of other people's opinions far more concern than is healthy," she said.

The younger woman was stung by the truth of her aunt's words. For eight long years Prudence Belmont had been the epitome of moral behavior and social decorum. At first she had done it to quiet any scandal that Gidry's behavior might have caused. And then she had done it because . . . because it just seemed the easiest way to live, taking no chances, running no risks.

Lately, of course, she had begun to risk more than she'd ever imagined herself willing to do. She gave a quick glance out the back window toward the little milk shed at the back edge of the property. She had not meant for it to happen, but it had. She had begun by risking the pity and scorn of the community and had now, it seemed, begun to risk her heart.

"Following the rules of society is not something for which I should apologize," she answered defensively.

"I wouldn't have you facing the world in any other way," the older woman said. "But if you look to other people for approval, you may often find yourself being disappointed."

"I enjoy the approval, but I do not seek it," Pru said. "I live up to the highest standards of my community because I choose to do so for myself. I take some pride in my impeccable behavior."

Aunt Hen raised an assessing eyebrow. "They do say pride goeth before a fall."

Pru glanced guiltily out the back window once more. God only knew what the people of Chavistown would think of that aspect of her impeccable behavior.

Gidry stood out in the room full of gentleman like a wild animal among a complacent flock of neatly sheared sheep. His cowboy clothes were casual and plain in the formal setting of the Commercial Club.

He had not intended to appear so out of place, but there was no help for it. He'd found his dress suits still hanging in the wardrobe of his old room. But his shoulders had grown much too broad for the fancy-cut coats. Though he could have worn one of his old dress shirts, they were all designed for button-on linen collars and not one of those, starched and ready in his chest of drawers, would fit comfortably around his thickened neck.

So he'd come downtown looking like a stranger, but the men around him knew him very well. Or at least they knew the young man that he used to be.

Conrad Peterson was a well-to-do farmer whose land holdings rivaled Chavis's own. Albert Fenton had run the dry goods store since Gidry was a boy. Oscar Tatum owned the livery stable and Silas Crane the cigar store. Of course Reverend Hathaway was there, along with old fellows like Amos Wilburn, Plug Whitstone, and Judge Ramey.

There were also men closer to his own age. He and the young banker, Elmer Corsen, had attended primary school together. Oscar Tatum's son Henry was only a few years ahead of him. And the young lawyer, Stanley Honnebuzz, to whom he'd taken an immediate dislike, was in his late twenties or early thirties, too, he supposed.

He needn't have worried about his mode of dress. The men were so busy firing questions at him, he doubted they had time to criticize his inappropriate garb.

"With the price of fiber as low as it is, I don't see how any of us are going to make enough to get us through next winter, let alone show a profit," Albert Fenton complained.

"Farming has never been a sure living," Plug Whitstone declared philosophically. "We've been riding high for a lot of years now. I suspect it's time for a downturn."

Stanley Honnebuzz huffed angrily. "I, for one, sir, have invested too much in this year's crop to be satisfied with last year's success."

The old man stopped jawing his tobacco long enough to give the young lawyer a disdainful frown.

"Don't you be talking down to me, young feller," Plug said. "I done forgot more about cotton than a knothead like you'll ever know."

With a smoothness acquired from working with hair-triggered cowboys, Gidry effectively separated the two with soft-spoken words.

"I'm sure everyone wants a successful year," he said. "But farming has always been a risky pursuit."

His memories of dealing with the men of Chavistown had not been good ones. At twenty-one Gidry had been routinely treated with dismissive and even casual derision. He was a spoiled rich boy for whom no one had any real respect. He had anticipated this morning to have to win them over. But clearly today it was not needed. The gentlemen of Chavistown were far too concerned with local problems to see the arrival of the heir to the community's wealthiest citizen as anything but welcome.

"How has Chavistown managed to prosper continually while other cotton towns suffer good years and bad?" he asked.

" 'Cause we had your father," Conrad Peterson explained. "The old man never let us down, not once. Not even when your mama left him or when you . . . well, he always kept his eye on the good of the community."

The words were spoken almost as a challenge. As

if the men expected him to disagree with their interpretation of his father's life. Perhaps at twenty-one he might have, but not now.

"I am certain that my father still wants what is best for Chavistown. Unfortunately, he can no longer tell us what he thinks that is," Gidry replied.

The long moment of quiet thoughtfulness in the well-appointed meeting room above Champion's Tin & Hardware was almost a silent prayer.

"Peer Chavis can't tell us what to do," Gidry said evenly. "So we must figure it out for ourselves."

The men around him raised their eyes to look at Gidry, hopefully. They wanted the answer simply to be given to them. And they wanted him to be the one to hand it out. In a way, it was almost too easy. Gidry should not, to his own mind, have been allowed to come home with no questions asked, no reprimand given. He had walked away almost carelessly, without looking back to see what trouble he left in his wake. Now he was being allowed to return not as the errant troublemaker he had been, but as the prodigal son, for whom they were dutifully killing the fatted calf.

"Tell me how you operate," Gidry said. "What exactly does the Commercial Club do for Chavistown."

"We *are* Chavistown," Stanley Honnebuzz declared with some self-importance.

"Mayor Paxton is our only elected official," old Mr. Crane explained. "And he's a mere figurehead."

"Judge Ramey oversees our dealings with the big boys in Austin. It's the Commercial Club that has the constable on its payroll," Albert Fenton said.

The judge spoke for himself. "I preside over our County Council, but all the councilmen are current or former members of the Commercial Club. We pretty much do what we like here in Chavistown. Your father liked it that way, and the folks that live here do also."

"Them council fellers take care of the official business," Plug told him. "But we, the Commercial Club, we're the ones what always takes care of Chavistown."

"Good business makes for good towns," Elmer Corsen piped up.

There were murmurs of agreement and approval all around. Gidry nodded and managed to look noncommittal. In his travels, he'd seen dozens of Texas towns like this one. Run exclusively by a small group of men as if it were a medieval fiefdom. It was not a very representative form of government, but it was a very efficient one.

"How have you and my father managed to keep business so good?" Gidry asked.

"We've always managed to top the commodity price for cotton by selling the whole county cooperatively," Corsen said.

"Your father would deal directly with the mills," Fenton went on. "By selling every bale in a hundred-mile radius at one time, he could command a higher price."

"And when the production of the whole county is headed for one destination," Conrad Peterson added, "Peer could negotiate for a sweet shipping price by rail."

"And your old papa weren't against slipping the railroad men a dollar or two under the table now and then," Plug pointed out.

That declaration produced a room full of knowing chuckles.

"The railroad men get twice the joy out of a dollar

under the table than they do a tenspot above board," Albert Fenton joked.

Reverend Hathaway cleared his throat meaningfully, and the jocularity subsided.

"Well," Gidry said, "I don't see any reason why we can't continue in just the way my father would."

The men looked around sheepishly at each other, each one seemingly hesitant to speak.

"Is there something else I don't know?" Gidry asked.

Judge Ramey spoke up.

"There are upfront costs in this cooperative," he said. "The fuel for operation of the gin, the shares paid to farmers, the baling costs, all of that was regularly taken care of by your father."

"He always took the risks," Peterson explained. "That's why he took the largest share."

Gidry was silent and thoughtful for a long moment. They needed money. Of course that was why he was so easily taken into the fold; finances, not friendship, forged this renewed respect.

"I haven't even been to the bank," Gidry told them. "Elmer, I assume my father had money set aside for this."

"He did indeed," Corsen assured him. "And as you're the next of kin, I'm sure the judge can set up the paperwork for you to have access to it."

Slowly Gidry nodded. They needed him. But, strangely, he needed them as well. This community was his father's greatest achievement. He had let the old man down eight years ago and lived to regret it. It was not a mistake that he would make again.

"If I'm risking my father's money, I would prefer handling the business arrangements myself," he told them. "But I could certainly use some help. Perhaps you already have among you someone who is adept at driving a hard bargain."

"Albert Fenton has the first nickel he ever saw," Elmer Corsen said.

Fenton looked momentarily taken aback, and sat up in a more defensive posture as if the words were a criticism. Before he could reply, Gidry smiled at him.

"Then perhaps you are our man, Mr. Fenton," he said. "Driving a hard bargain is a skill as worthy and in need of constant practice as throwing a lariat."

"Well I don't know I . . ."

"What was it you said, Mr. Corsen?" Gidry asked rhetorically. "Good business makes for good towns. Your own business, Mr. Fenton, has been extremely successful. If you are willing to use some of what you've learned to help the community, I'm sure we'd all be appreciative."

"I . . . well of course I'd be willing to help," Fenton conceded. "But I know absolutely nothing about cotton mills or shipping. Your father always did that."

"And I'm sure he kept good records," Gidry replied. "I'll go over the books at the gin. I'm sure all of the places we've sold to and the prices we've paid will be noted right there in my father's hand."

"But that won't tell us where to sell to this year," Honnebuzz said.

"No," Gidry agreed, "but it will give us an idea of where to start."

Men nodded to each other; murmurs of approval could be heard among those gathered.

"Mr. Wilburn," Gidry suggested, "if you could get the word out to the farmers, we can start ginning day after tomorrow. Have them bring their crops to town as soon as they are ready."

"I'll let them all know," he said.

Gidry turned to Main Avenue's most prosperous merchant. "Mr. Fenton, why don't you begin tentative talks with the railroad men about shipping costs and destinations."

The man nodded agreeably.

"Elmer, if you and Mr. Peterson would keep an eye on the current commodity prices and report regularly to us, that would be helpful," Gidry said.

"Yes, sir," Elmer replied.

The respectful form of address hung in the room for a long moment. Gidry felt himself go cold and still inside. He was a young, rootless cowboy who'd thrown away his life here for wild ways and fast women. The men in this room were mostly older and surely wiser than he himself. He was undeserving of their trust or their deference. Calling Goodtime Gidry Chavis *sir* was certainly only a slip of the tongue. Yet no one remarked upon it, and no attempt was made to retract it.

Plug Whitstone chuckled. "It appears you've turned out to be more like your daddy than we thought."

Gidry was genuinely humbled by the old man's words.

"I intend to try to live up to my father's example," he said.

"I suspect that's all we can ask," Plug replied.

Gidry nodded acceptance.

"Then is that all the business we need to take care of?" he asked the group.

"That ain't even the half of it." Henry Tatum spoke up with a troubled sigh.

"The town's major concern right now is the crime troubles," Reverend Hathaway explained.

"Crime troubles?" Gidry's brow furrowed in curiosity.

The reverend nodded. "We have a thieving sinner in our midst."

Hathaway's dramatic biblical reference was very much to the point and earned nods of approval all around the room.

"I heard Ollie Larson on his soapbox yesterday," Gidry said. "But I thought he was exaggerating."

"I wish he was," Stanley Honnebuzz complained. "My house has been broken into a half dozen times. We've got a burglar or a gang of burglars in this town. And the sooner we figure out a way to stop them, the better."

"What were they after?" Gidry asked.

Honnebuzz looked momentarily uncomfortable.

"I done been burgled twice," Oscar Tatum said. "And somebody's got to do something about it."

"Twice?" Gidry was astounded. "Who would rob a livery stable?"

"These thieves'll rob near anybody for nearly anything," Plug told him.

"They stole Gimp Watkin's wooden leg," Silas Crane added. "I told his widow she should have buried him with it."

"It's almost as if they know us," Reverend Hathaway said. "As if they are familiar with when we are at home and when we are not."

"You've been robbed, Pastor?" Gidry questioned.

He nodded. "On a sunny sabbath afternoon," he answered. "Mrs. Hathaway and I always take a Sunday stroll, weather permitting. They took a lovely inlaid mother-of-pearl hairbrush and a photogram of my wife's uncle Lucius in his Confederate uniform." The reverend sighed sadly. "He was killed at Manassas in '61. It was the only image ever taken of him."

Gidry was very puzzled. "They didn't take your silverware?"

The reverend shook his head. "No, nor any of my wife's jewelry either. It is a modest collection, but certainly worth more than the hairbrush or poor, dear Uncle Lucius."

"Why would a thief steal a photogram and leave jewels?" Gidry asked, almost to himself.

"It doesn't matter *what* they steal," Stanley Honnebuzz said. "What matters is *that* they steal, and it must stop."

Plug Whitstone looked at Gidry assessingly. "I heard you come into town carrying a Winchester. Did your life out in the Pecos teach you how to use it?"

Gidry stared back at the old man evenly. "I can protect myself and what's mine. I wouldn't willingly take on the task of protecting a whole town."

"Well, somebody's got to do it," Oscar Tatum said. "If not you, then one of them Rangers or peacemakers."

Amos Wilburn shook his head stubbornly. "I'm not voting to bring in no stranger. Especially one with a gunman's reputation. I got daughters to think of."

"Don't be a knothead, Wilburn," Plug ordered.

The meeting erupted in pandemonium as simultaneously every member of the Commercial Club decided to voice his opinion.

Gidry allowed the shouting match to proceed unchecked. He was thinking about his father. He was thinking about his duty to the town. He was thinking about a thief who passed over the valuables to take souvenirs.

He was thinking about the woman who lived next door to him who used to love him and now carried on discreet liaisons in her aunt's milking shed.

Chapter 4

HENRIETTA PAULING raised the window shades in the sickroom to let the morning sunlight shine in. It was still hot as summer outside, but the beginnings of the fall season could already be seen. The twittering birds were mostly sparrows and barn swallows. The plants still blooming, were latecomers and hangers-on, periwinkle and lantanas. The last of the crepe myrtle blossoms lay like bits of confetti beneath the bushes. Though the trees still had full foliage, here and there they had begun to turn the bright colors of autumn.

Across the wide lawn she could see her own neat little house and the garden that she had spent so many long years tending. It was Pru's garden now, of course. Henrietta worked in the soil there from time to time, but she was glad to give up the responsibility of it to her niece. She had other concerns now. Other troubles to fill her days and disturb her nights.

"It's a beautiful day, Peer," she announced to the man who lay still and silent in his sickbed. "A beautiful, fine day. It always puzzled me why folks make so much of spring, when the fall can be just as lovely.

It doesn't rain nearly as much. And the first cool breeze after a grueling summer can be more invigorating to a tired heart than the warmth of April."

She turned to face Chavis. His eyes followed her, but the frozen side of his face made his expression unreadable.

"I know what you're thinking," she said. "You're thinking how can a woman who's spent the better part of her life tending to flowers not prefer blossoming time over the browning of autumn."

The old man remained silent.

"Well, I didn't say I *preferred* the autumn," she told him. "Only that it has a beauty of its own that I'm clear-thinking enough to appreciate."

She stepped closer to the bed and his right hand, trembling, reached out for her own.

They entwined their fingers as Henrietta seated herself on the edge of the bed. The contact eased him somehow as if the very touch of her skin had the power to heal. It tugged upon Henrietta's heart.

"When we have a beautiful fall day like this," she told him softly, "I often think about the sweet old days when I was a girl."

He looked up at her. His smiling eyes could not quite be matched by the crooked, half-downturned curve of his lips.

"Yes sir, I *do* know what a long time ago that was," she said, feigning offense. "But it's easy to forget. Except for these tired old bones and this face in the mirror, I'm still that same young gal. Willing and able to pick cotton all day on my hands and knees and then dance all night like I hadn't a care in the world."

She laughed softly and shook her head.

"I guess back then I really *didn't* have a care in the

world," she said. "I just thought things would always be as they were."

Her expression sobered.

"Change," she said. "That's a thing that's hard to get your mind around. We rail against it and try to hold it back, but it's inevitable. And it's as natural to life as breathing."

She was staring down at the flowered pattern in the chenille rug at her feet.

"Change was something I'd never expected," she said. "And even after all these years I still find myself fighting against it."

She felt the pressure of his grasp tighten and turned her attention to Peer's face. His gaze was solemn now, solemn but full of strength. They stared at each other for a long moment. Henrietta finally smiled.

"Here I am supposedly nursing you to health and you have to waste your energy keeping me from drifting off into old maid's melancholy," she said. "Peer Chavis, how did a smart fellow like you get your life in such a tangle with mine?"

He didn't answer, but a gleam of fine humor could be detected in his eyes.

"I'll bet it was those pigtails of mine," she postulated. "I remember how you couldn't keep your hands off of them. Sticking the ends in your inkwell and jerking on them pretending they were bell ropes. I must have complained to my mama a million times, 'Peer Chavis is pulling on my pigtails.' I can't even guess how many switchings you took for torturing me."

She smiled and shook her head.

"And all that complaining didn't do a lick of good," she admitted. "You just kept on teasing me until I finally got mad enough to tease back. Now that was a fortunate turn of events. It was fine enough that I could call you names and giggle at you behind your back. But once I started getting my girlish curves, you were one dumbstruck fool."

She put her hands on her hips and glared at him, pretending superiority.

"I know you'd deny it if you could," she said. "Fortunately for me we've finally reached a place in life when you, Mr. Chavis, do not always get the last word."

Slowly she allowed her mouth to widen into a teasing grin.

"We were quite a team, two peas in a pod," she told him. "You could begin a sentence, and I'd be able to finish it off. Both of us always knew what the other was thinking. Now I have to do the whole sentence by myself with you just lying there being waited on hand and foot."

She looked down at him, laughing, but her heart in her eyes.

"I know what you are thinking now," she whispered.

A melancholy silence lingered between them. Henrietta deliberately threw if off.

"Do you recall that dance at Krueger's barn?" she asked him.

His mood seemed to lighten with her words.

"We must have paired up for every tune that night," she said. "I'll bet the whole town was talking about it. That was some of the finest fiddle playing that I can ever recall. And in my new party dress, I thought I was about the prettiest thing that ever waltzed in Texas."

The expression in his eyes seemed to admit agreement.

"You were liquored up tighter than a clock spring," she said, tutting at him disapprovingly. "And sneaking me away into the darkness like that. You should have been ashamed!"

Her disapproval was mostly feigned.

"If my mama had found out about that," she told him, "there wouldn't have been a switch left on a tree in this town."

She shook her head.

"And all that drama, telling me that you were running away to join up the regiment. Asking me how I could send you off to fight to the death without allowing you a kiss from my lips. Do you remember that?"

Her laughter was warm and heartfelt.

"You *do* remember how I slapped your roguish face good and proper," she said. "Your ears are probably still ringing."

He pulled the back of her hand to his face and closed his eyes as he rubbed the smoothness of it against his cheek. A tear escaped from the corner of his eye and dampened her own flesh.

Henrietta closed her own eyes to the sight for a long moment, savoring the tenderness of the gesture. Then she guarded her heart against the longing that swelled up in her. And she grinned at him.

"That's a rough old jawline, you've got there, Peer Chavis," she said. "I guess you're trying to tell me how much you need a shave."

She hurried to her feet, attempting to pull away from him.

"It's washday, and I'm going to get you all cleaned up and these linens changed," she told him.

His weak, trembling hand held hers firmly.

"You'd best let me go. I've got a world of work waiting."

Their eyes met, and his gaze restrained her even more securely than his grasp.

The look that passed between them didn't require words, but Henrietta spoke them anyway.

"I know that you love me, Peer Chavis," she said to him quietly. "I know you would have married me years ago if you could have. Change may be inevitable, but the things we want changed often remain the same."

It was true. So very true.

"I love you, now more than ever," she admitted. "And I have loved you ever."

He relaxed his grip as if breathing a sigh of relief.

She touched his wrinkled brow as if to erase the lines of worry and pain. It was almost more than she could bear, seeing him this way. But bear it she must because she would not be any other place than at his side.

"You're in danger of having to make an honest woman of me," she said, putting her hand on her hip and shaking a threatening finger at him.

"Just a few years away from a brand-new century. It's not like divorce is completely unheard of. I know I've always said that it would create too big of a scandal," she said. "But it seems my reputation is already in shreds."

His eyes widened slightly in surprise.

"It's true," Henrietta assured him. "My own niece told me so."

Peer's expression turned curious.

"Imagine that," she told him. "A right-living maiden lady of my advanced years creating a scandal in Chavistown."

Henrietta chuckled and shook her head.

"I wonder what wicked deeds the gossipmongers have conjured up for me to be doing in this room all day?" she asked. "Maybe they think I'm having my way with you, taking advantage of your weakened condition."

That statement brought a lopsided grin to the old man's face.

"Or more likely they just think I'm making a fool of myself," Henrietta said.

She hesitated at the foot of his bed for a long moment. The tone of her words became soft and sweet with memory. "I suppose it's not the first time I've made a fool of myself over you."

Gidry's return from downtown led him unerringly not to the doorstep of his father's manse, but to the tiny vine-covered gate of Aunt Hen's garden. He entered with some hesitation. In the Chavistown he had always known, any victory, no matter how big or small, would have to be immediately shared with Pru. His acceptance today by the men of the Commercial Club was nothing short of a spectacular victory.

Certainly they needed his money. They would have done a requisite amount of bowing and begging to get it. But they were proud, practical men. They would never have recognized him as their leader had they not thought him up to the task.

Gidry wanted to talk about it, revel in it, relive it in the eyes of someone who had not been there. He wanted to confide it to Pru.

She was on her hands and knees in the far northwest corner of the garden within the shade of a huge old elm.

"Hello!" he called out a bit tentatively, unsure of his welcome.

She looked up. Once more she was clad in work clothes, but these at least were neither threadbare or overlarge.

"Hello . . . ah, hello, Mr. Chavis," she answered.

He was a little put off by her choice of address. *Mr. Chavis* had always been his father. Somehow it seemed very wrong for this woman, the person who had perhaps known him better than any other in the world, not to refer to him as Gidry. Had she called him that yesterday? He had been so surprised to see her, he couldn't remember. But he knew he didn't like it. It made him uncomfortable, as if he were some stranger. Perhaps they were strangers to each other after all these years.

"My aunt isn't here," Pru volunteered. "Are you home for luncheon?"

Gidry shrugged.

"Yes, it's about that time," he explained. "But I came to see you, actually."

Pru looked straight at him, but her expression was one with which he was completely unfamiliar. It was masked and guarded.

"I don't mean to disturb you if you're busy," he said.

"I'm planting purlane," she told him. "Nothing else will grow very well in the shade of these old trees."

Gidry looked up at the grand stately tree that had probably been here before his grandfather was.

"I'm surprised that anything will grow beneath it at all," he admitted.

"Purlane will," she assured him. "And it will come back every year and be the prettiest pink you've ever seen in your life."

Momentarily Gidry thought to compare it to the blush in her cheeks.

"Of course, this year it won't come up at all," she said. "I should have planted it in the spring. But somehow I just didn't get around to it back then."

"Sometimes that happens," Gidry said.

"Gardening involves lots of planning for the future," she said. "But sometimes it's hard to realize how much you are going to miss something in bloom until you see it's not there."

Gidry nodded slowly, not sure what to say in response. Her words had been spoken casually, but he heard them with meaning of his own.

The silence between them lingered overlong.

"You surely must be getting hungry," Pru said.

"I don't want to trouble anyone at the house," Gidry replied without thinking.

Pru seemed momentarily taken aback. "Oh . . . well, I'm sure I can scare up something in the kitchen."

"I didn't mean that I expected you to feed me," he assured her, mentally calling himself a thousand kinds of fool for his inadvertent intrusion.

She carefully set down her gardening tools and slapped the dirt from her hands.

"Do you still like turnips?" she asked.

Gidry's mouth began to water at the thought.

"I haven't had a good plate of turnips since I left town," he admitted.

"I boiled a potful this morning," she told him. "It's funny I can't get Milt—ah . . . a lot of people don't like turnips."

"That leaves more of them in the world for me," he answered.

It was a reply he'd given often before. It seemed to transport them back in an instant to the laughing young couple that they had once been. Their eyes met. And just as quickly they were returned to the uncomfortable pair of near strangers they now were.

Gidry followed her to the house. She slipped off her muddy gardening boots at the kitchen door, and motioned for him to enter. He shook his head.

"It's a beautiful day," he said. "I'll just eat here on the back step."

She nodded and left him there. Gidry sat down, eyeing for the first time with any real interest the changes around him. September wasn't the best month for flowers, yet the garden was still perfectly kept, with bright-colored blossoms of varied appearance. He didn't know very much about blooming plants, but he recognized marigolds and petunias. And there were roses, of course. There seemed to be dozens of varieties. Clearly they must be her favorite. That was something he had not known. He thought back over time, eight years past. Had the rose been her favorite flower then? Why had he not known what she liked best? She knew that he liked turnips.

Pru came out the kitchen door with a plate in each hand.

Gidry stood immediately to help her.

"It's not Sunday dinner fare," she told him. "But it will keep you from fainting during the afternoon."

Their hands touched beneath the warmth of the plate.

"Not that there was much danger in that," he said.

She seated herself beside him on the step, their shoulders almost touching. Carefully, she tucked her dress around her, perhaps a little more modestly than necessary. Her long, narrow feet, covered in black cotton stockings peeked out below the hem of her skirt. The sight caught in his chest somehow. It made her seem more a woman. She had always been just Pru to him. Warm, easygoing Pru, who induced none of the edgy, tingling emotions he associated with the female gender.

Inexplicably, Gidry's gaze was drawn to the milk shed on the northeast corner of the property. In the full light of day it looked even less a site for illicit romance than he'd imagined last night. He must have been mistaken. Pru would not be involved in such a thing. Not his Pru.

His Pru.

The thought lingered

His dinner dish was heavily laden with soft, saucy turnips, a pile of bread-and-butter pickles, and a huge hunk of corn bread.

Gidry inhaled the aroma and sighed with pleasure.

"There is nothing in the world better than Aunt Hen's turnips," he said.

"Well, these are *my* turnips," she corrected.

He savored the first bite.

"And they are just as good," he told her.

She waved away the compliment. "There is nothing magical about boiling turnips."

Gidry grinned at her. "Ma'am, believe me," he said. "I've eaten my share of turnips cooked in restaurants, boardinghouses, and on the cattle trail. And never do they taste this good."

He finally managed to draw a pleased smile from her.

"It's sugar," Pru explained. "Just a smidge of sugar while they're cooking, it makes all the difference."

He nodded gravely at her, savoring another bite.

"Thank you for revealing your secret, ma'am," he said teasingly.

She blushed brightly as if she had in fact disclosed something personal.

It was a strange and somehow wonderful familiarity sitting next to her like this. There had been so many similar moments in the distant past. They had talked and teased and laughed together so easily back then. He'd have told her all his fun and foibles. She'd have listened with rapt attention and given advice if she'd thought he needed it. Then he'd have placed a chaste kiss upon her pretty lips as he took his leave.

He watched her stocking-covered toes curl along the edge of the back step.

There would no longer be any kisses between them, chaste or otherwise.

"I talked to the gentlemen of the Commercial Club this morning," he told her. "The ginning should start day after tomorrow."

"That soon?"

"Yes, it seems that the farmers up on the ridge rise were able to pick a bit early this year," he said.

Pru didn't appear surprised.

"That soil up there is downright sticky with nitrogen," she said. "And the balance of sun and rain has been nearly perfect this year."

Gidry raised an eyebrow.

"I never imagined that you knew so much about farming," he said.

She shrugged carelessly, as if to suggest that it would be no surprise to anyone else.

"Farming is just gardening on a larger, more serious scale," she explained.

"Do you know anything about cotton?" Gidry asked.

She made a face that was comic with question.

"You mean that scraggly white stuff that grows in

every field and unclaimed dirt plot within a hundred miles of here?" she asked him facetiously.

"Yes, that's the one," Gidry told her. "The cruelest crop they call it."

"And rightly so," she pointed out. "What do you want to know about it?"

"Basically how we are supposed to make a living growing it," he said. "When the crop is ruined and there is nothing to sell, the price is high. But when you've had a good year and everybody's got cotton, it's not worth anything."

"Gidry Chavis," Pru said, shaking her head and tutting fatalistically. "Just back in town one day and already you're quoting the farmer's eternal lament."

He nodded and scooped up another big bite of turnips before he continued.

"Even if we manage to get a really fine price above the commodity index," he said, "with the market for cotton this low, we'll still lose money."

"Then the gentlemen of the Commercial Club had best figure out another way to make what we have pay," Pru said.

"I think they are counting on me to do that," he said. "I wish you could have been at the meeting this morning. They treated me with a lot more respect than I ever deserved."

Her expression softened, as if she were proud of him. "Then you'll have to make certain that you don't let them down," she said.

He considered her words for a long moment.

"We could modernize the town," Gidry suggested. "Try to bring in more industry, so we aren't always at the mercy of the cotton markets."

Pru nodded thoughtfully.

"But that will take years, I suppose," Gidry pointed

out. "And what kind of industry would like to settle down in the middle of cotton country?"

Pru shrugged.

"With the recent panic in the currency," Gidry continued, "not a whole lot of companies are expanding or—"

"What do you do with the seed?" she asked him, interrupting.

"Huh?"

"The cottonseed?" Pru leaned an elbow on her knee and gazed at him speculatively. "What do you do with the cottonseed."

The ginning process separated the fiber from the hull, the seed was left behind as a waste product.

"The cottonseed belongs to the farmers," Gidry said. "Chavis Cotton has never kept the seed. My father always gave it back."

"And what do the farmers do with it?"

"They use it for next year's planting, I suppose," Gidry said.

"Not all of it," Pru pointed out. "The cotton on just one small farm makes enough seed to plant the entire state of Texas."

"That's true," Gidry said, surprising himself at what he remembered. "It only takes about a half bushel of seed per acre. And there is nearly a half ton of seed for every bale."

"So what do they do with the rest?" she asked.

"I think they use most of it in feed," he said. "And the rest of it is just compost for fertilizer."

"Why don't you sell it to one of the oil mills?" Pru suggested. "I read a pamphlet just recently about all the new uses they are finding for cottonseed oil."

"I think because it was never worth the trouble," Gidry said. "It costs nearly as much to transport as it pays. It was always just easier to plow it back into the ground."

Pru was thoughtful once more.

"What if you didn't have to transport it? What if Chavis Cotton started its own cottonseed-oil production right here in Chavistown."

Gidry's eyes widened with excitement and appreciation as he considered her idea.

"There isn't a cottonseed plant in the entire Black Waxy," he said, almost breathlessly. "We could buy cottonseed from the whole region for practically nothing. And these days they are making everything but mother's milk from it."

The two of them stared at each other with pent-up excitement for a long moment, then burst out with delighted laughter.

"How much would a processing plant like that cost?" Pru asked.

Gidry shrugged. "Maybe a lot more than we're willing to invest. But we don't know until we check into it."

"I think it would be foolish if you didn't check into it," she declared.

"Yes, of course we should check into it," he agreed enthusiastically.

He just gazed at her in wonder and shook his head.

"I knew that I should come talk to you," he told her. "You're smart and capable. And you've always been the one to help me sort things through. I'm always at my best when I'm with you."

His words of compliment had completely the opposite effect of what he had intended. She looked as if he had dashed cold water upon her sunny heart.

She grabbed up his plate and rose to her feet.

"I have things to do this afternoon, Mr. Chavis,"

she said. "I'm sure you have your own work to attend to."

Gidry wanted to kick himself. He wasn't sure exactly what he had said, but it had clearly been the wrong thing. He was determined to make amends.

"Pru," he began lamely, "I think we need to talk about the past, to talk about what happened between us."

"Not today," she told him firmly.

"There are things that need to be said," he insisted.

"Perhaps so, but they have waited eight years, I don't think it's essential that we delve into them immediately, just because it is suddenly convenient for you."

"Pru, I—"

"I hope you enjoyed your meal, Mr. Chavis," she said. "Remember in the future, just a smidge of sugar and you can cook your own turnips for yourself."

It was unfair to wish that Gidry Chavis had never returned. His father needed him, the town needed him. Prudence Belmont, however, was determined *not* to need him. And she certainly didn't want him to need her.

She knelt in the hot afternoon sun and furiously attacked the crabgrass that grew unwanted along her back fence row.

I'm always at my best when I'm with you.

There was a time, long ago when she would have taken that as a compliment. But no longer.

The slats of Aunt Hen's old bonnet shaded her face, but not enough to keep the perspiration from her brow. She was damp and miserable from the heat and work, but she continued angrily to push herself.

You've always been the one to help me sort things through.

She wasn't certain at what she was most angry, the crabgrass that dared to encroach upon her carefully cultivated gardens, Gidry Chavis, who seemed completely content to pick up their friendship right where he dropped it eight years ago, or herself.

Herself.

She jerked at the long weeds with such force she could almost feel the cut of the blades through her heavy gloves.

She was very angry at herself. Eight years had gone by, eight years to become stronger, smarter, wiser. Eight years and yet, when she'd heard him call out to her, her heart had begun pounding.

Do you still like turnips?

Why had she remembered? Why had she asked him to stay? Why, feeling the tingle of his nearness in her veins, had she not sat in the kitchen and allowed him to eat alone.

Pru knew the answer full well, and she didn't like it one bit. She had wanted to be near him. She had wanted to talk to him. She had wanted, just like Gidry, to forget everything that had gone before.

She groaned in frustration as she wiped the sweat from her brow.

Eight years ago she had loved him to distraction, trusted him totally, and handed him her heart freely. He had broken it carelessly, callously, completely.

Then she had the excuse of being young and foolish. She would not allow herself such foolishness again.

She would not.

Her reaction to the nearness of Gidry Chavis had been immediate. And it had been extreme. His dark good looks and handsome smile were certainly capable of turning the head of most women in the state of Texas. But there was something more that thrilled her down to her very soul. It was the way he gazed at her as if she mattered, as if her opinions were important to him, as if they were two sides of the same coin.

They were not, she reminded herself.

No doubt during the past eight years Gidry Chavis had gazed at women all over Texas. He had set other feminine hearts to pounding and engaged with them in thrills with which prudent Prudence, the Chavistown spinster, was still unfamiliar. She had living evidence of that fact.

Pru ripped at the crabgrass blinking back angry tears.

She had loved him. He had loved elsewhere. It should be over, finished, forgotten.

She had eyed him glancing at her stocking feet; her breath had caught in her throat. It was not an indiscretion, and yet she had felt as if she were exposed. She had tucked her skirts more securely about her to counter the sudden inexplicable desire to jerk them up, to let him see the curve of her knee, the line of her calf, the trimness of her ankles.

Pru was embarrassed by her own inclinations and angered by the direction of her thoughts. What would people think if they knew? It was pitiful, wretchedly pitiful. If someone were to detect such longings in her, what would they say?

Gidry Chavis did not want her in the fresh bloom of her youth, the gossips would whisper. *Does she expect that he would desire her now?*

The sting to her pride was as painful to her as if the words had actually been spoken. Never. *Never* would she allow herself such feelings. Her heart had pounded only because she had loved him once, because she had been alone so long, because in her whole life no man had ever looked at her the way he had.

"I sure wouldn't want to be a weed with you around."

Pru gave a startled gasp of surprise.

"Aunt Hen, I didn't hear you approach."

The older woman nodded. "I suspect your own thoughts were a bit too loud," she replied.

Pru rose to her feet guiltily.

"I was just trying to get this crabgrass out of the fence row," Pru answered.

Aunt Hen eyed her niece curiously and shook her head.

"Maybe this is something you've read in one of those naturalist pamphlets," she said, "but it's my experience that crabgrass pulls easier in the early morning after a good rain."

Pru blushed with embarrassment, but had the comfort of knowing that her complexion was already so flushed with effort, her discomposure could surely not be detected.

"You are undoubtedly right," she assured her aunt. "I'll leave the rest of it for an earlier, damper day."

The two women stepped into the relative coolness of the shaded garden as Pru peeled off her work gloves and discarded her bonnet.

"Have you had anything to eat since breakfast?" she asked. "I have turnips on the stove."

Her aunt shook her head. "I'm not hungry," she replied.

"You really should eat," Pru insisted. "You are losing weight."

Aunt Hen chuckled, unconcerned. "Oh, I always seem to manage to keep enough meat on these old bones to scare the buzzards away," she said.

Pru didn't join in her laughter.

"Turnips?" she said. "That must have been nice for Gidry. That's his favorite still, I suppose."

Pru glanced at her aunt startled.

"Oh, I saw you two eating out on the back step," Aunt Hen said. "That was probably smart. It wouldn't do your reputation a lot of good to invite him into the house when you are alone."

"I would never dream of doing such a thing," Pru answered quickly.

Her aunt raised an eyebrow and gave her a long look. "I don't believe that a woman can be condemned for her dreams," Aunt Hen said.

"I am not *dreaming* about Gidry Chavis," Pru assured her.

"Well, maybe you should be," the older woman suggested. "I don't believe I ever saw such a likely couple as the two of you."

"That was a very long time ago."

Aunt Hen was thoughtful. "Eight years is not all that long," she said. "Just about the time required to turn a rebellious boy into a reasonable man or a fanciful girl into a philosophical woman."

Pru slapped her canvas work gloves against the garden bench with a loud thud, ostensibly to flail the dust out of them.

"I think you are mistaken," she said. "Eight years has been just enough to solidify my position in this community and convince me that I shall never marry. And I don't believe that you know Gidry as well as you think you do. There are things ... things that have never come to public light."

Aunt Hen eyed her curiously.

"Whatever do you mean?"

Pru just shook her head.

"I don't think it proper to give details to anyone," she said. "But you must believe me when I tell you that there is more in Gidry's past than people know."

Aunt Hen seated herself upon the bench.

"Prudence, there is no such thing as a man without a past," she said. "They live in a world quite different from our own. A world with influences and temptations that clearly make no sense to a thinking woman. But once a good man, a fine, ordinary man, settles down to marriage and family, he can be counted upon to give up his errant ways."

"Perhaps Gidry Chavis will *settle down to marriage and family*," Pru told her. "But it will not be with me."

Aunt Hen was momentarily silent.

"That's disappointing to hear, Prudence," she said. "Marriage is a wonderful thing."

Pru looked at her incredulously. "You have never been interested in wedding bells," she pointed out. "You've always valued your independence. And you've always told me that being a happy, fulfilled woman is not synonymous with being some man's wife."

"That's absolutely true," Aunt Hen agreed. "But neither does being a man's wife, a man that you love, necessarily rule out independence. Being a helpmate, being a mother, those are very independent vocations."

"Now you sound like Reverend Hathaway," Pru complained, joining her aunt upon the wooden garden bench. "The next thing I know you'll be saying that it is a woman's duty to marry."

"It is a woman's *duty* to make of her life the best

that she can," Aunt Hen said. "It is her duty to herself. God gives each of us a share of talents and opportunities. When we find a balance between those two, happiness can no longer elude us."

"Happiness has not eluded me," Pru insisted. "I am very *very* happy."

"Well, you needn't shout so about it," Aunt Hen told her. "You'll frighten the neighbors."

Pru's words *had* become overly adamant; she moderated her tone.

"Have you ever had regrets about not marrying?" Pru asked her.

The older woman was thoughtful.

"No, I don't believe I have."

"Me neither. We are very much alike," Pru pointed out. "Everybody says so."

"In some things we are," she agreed. "But to me you are always more like your mother, sweet and gentle, good and forgiving."

Pru's brow furrowed slightly and then with a shake of her head she dismissed the statement entirely.

"No, I'm not at all like Mama," she assured her aunt. "Mama was fragile, in body and spirit. I'm strong, like you. We look a lot alike, we care for the same things."

Aunt Hen shrugged.

"Yes, in ways you are like I was at your age," she said. "But you have to remember that I come from a different time, and I had different choices."

"You chose not to marry," Pru said.

"I came of age during the war," Aunt Hen said. "My parents didn't want me to risk widowhood by marrying before the men left to fight. By the time they came back . . . well not that many of them did come back."

Aunt Hen hesitated.

"And those who did come back were changed," she said. "We were changed. The world had changed."

Pru listened to the strange hollowness in her aunt's voice and reached out to take her hand.

"Oh, Aunt Hen, did you love someone who died in the war?"

The older woman looked at her strangely for a moment and then shook her head.

"No, no," she assured her niece. "Nothing like that. I just wanted you to understand that my choice not to marry was made in a different time from now, under different circumstances. After the war there were so few men available to wed, and I didn't love any of them."

Aunt Hen squeezed her niece's hand and looked her straight in the eye.

"But it seems to me," she said to Pru, "that a certain young man is very much available, and that you may still love him very much."

Pru shook her head adamantly.

"Oh no," she said. "I've made my choice already, I'll not waste so much as one more thought on marrying that man or anybody."

Aunt Hen held her silence for a long moment before she spoke.

"Being a spinster has allowed me to do many things that a wife could not," she told Pru. "I was able to devote myself to my parents every day that they lived. I've been unhindered in my community work and faithful in support of my church. I've had the opportunity to raise my sister's child as if she were my own. And to influence the life of the motherless boy next door. I have lived a lifetime worth of seasons in the most beautiful part of Texas God ever created.

And I've had the freedom to cultivate my garden as I saw fit. It may not have been the grandest life in the eyes of others. I have some regrets. But mostly, I would not have wanted it any other way."

Pru smiled at her, comforted somehow to hear the words.

Aunt Hen raised an eyebrow and regarded her skeptically. "But then, I never had the good fortune to fall in love with Gidry Chavis."

Chapter 5

THE GIN was located on Sante Fe Boulevard, next to the railroad tracks. It was a rambling set of buildings, sided and roofed in corrugated tin that gleamed brightly in the midday sun. Gidry carried the key in his pocket, but it wasn't necessary. The door was only latched closed. He let himself inside, somewhat uneasily. He had never really liked the place. Outside it appeared large and spacious, but inside it was crammed full of machinery. Wheels, pulleys, and belts of enormous size made the interior crowded and close. It was a dangerous place. As a boy he had, at his father's bidding, spent hundreds of hours running errands up and down the narrow stairs between the machine level and the ginning floor. Because of his small size he was often sent scampering around the low-hanging lint flues and beneath the churning mechanism for misplaced tools or broken lengths of rawhide.

Gidry hated that. It made him feel like a mouse amid clockworks. Small and insignificant in comparison to the grand and glorious production of the cotton engine. And the noise, the sheer screaming noise that shook the ground as far away as Main Avenue, kept ringing in his ears for a week after the place shut down for the season.

Today he walked through the strangely silent building feeling only an odd nostalgia for the boy he had been. He had the sensation of being closed in on all sides. He had agreed to gin the cotton, to take the financial risk, to stand in his father's place. For so long he had grown accustomed to doing as he wished, working where he wanted and leaving when he set his mind to do so.

There would be no such freedom for him now. He was a Chavis. And in his town his name had meaning that went beyond something merely to answer to.

Gidry tried on the feeling. It was narrow, restrictive, but in some way it was comforting as well. This was where people knew him, the worst as well as the best. If a man could earn respect among those who knew his failings, he had acquired something precious indeed.

He was, from that moment, determined. He would do for this town, his town, as his father would do. As Pru had suggested, he would not let them down. He would prove himself to those who doubted. Gidry owed the old man that at the very least.

The small office above the engine room was little bigger than a kitchen cupboard and had a ceiling so low Gidry had to remove his hat to stand straight without brushing against the ceiling. The place was so cramped with cabinets and furniture that sitting in the high-backed desk chair seemed not just the best, but the only course.

He found the ledger inside the top drawer and opened it to the most recent year's production. Gidry inspected the crisp, neat entries in his father's handwriting. The date was inked in at the top of the page. Each farmer's name was carefully printed at the left. Beside it was listed the grade of their cotton, the number of bales ginned, and the price paid.

As Gidry leafed through the pages, he did so almost reverently. The plain, functional accounting was as much a history of cotton farming in Chavis County as any that would ever be written. Touching it was akin to touching his father's life, to knowing him as he never had.

He thought of his father as the man had been the night before. Silent, suffering, and very old. He'd never imagined his father becoming old. He'd always been vital, vigorous. Peer Chavis had been his son's definition of strength. But the reality of life was that the sturdiest rope would eventually wear and fray, the sharpest blade became dull with use. It was a lesson taught daily, because it was so hard to learn.

"Howdy, mister." The little voice startled Gidry to attention.

He glanced up to see a barefoot boy standing in the doorway of the office. The child, still sporting a baby-toothed grin, looked strangely familiar. Dark hair and eyes, a long-limbed arrogant stance reminiscent of portraits Gidry had seen of his father's young cousins. Of course the boy's clothes precluded his being any much distant kin. All his relatives had been prosperous farmers. This ragamuffin was obviously not from such a substantial background. At that juncture Gidry recalled seeing the fellow in the nickelodeon when he'd passed by the previous afternoon. So of course the boy would look familiar.

"Howdy yourself," he replied to the youngster.

He pointed down to the boy's bare feet.

"You should wear shoes inside the gin," Gidry told

him. "The spines on the cotton bolls are as sharp as needles."

The little fellow shrugged. "My feet is tough as hell," he said. "Ain't nothing bothers them."

Gidry didn't argue the point.

"What are you doing in here?" he asked. "This is no place for a child to play."

The child straightened his narrow little shoulders. "I ain't playing," he declared adamantly. "I work here."

Gidry propped his elbow on the chair arm and gazed at the boy skeptically.

"You work here?" he asked.

The child nodded. "I'm the what-cha-man," he said. "Old Mr. Chavis pays me two bits a week to keep an eye on the place. With all the thieving going on in town, it was damned well worth it to him."

Gidry felt like laughing out loud. The little devil couldn't be much over six years old. Only his empathy for the young fellow kept him from smiling. He deliberately cleared his throat.

"So, Watchman, what would you do if you caught a thief on the property?" Gidry asked. "Truthfully, son, you don't look big enough to bring down a burglar."

"I ain't your son," the boy told him with a proud tone that belied his youth. "And it don't take no big sheep-bugger to ring the yard bell for help. I do my job around here. Ain't a soul touched this gin nor any property belonging to the Chavis family since I been on the job."

Gidry found himself admiring the foul-mouthed whippersnapper's insolence. He was absolutely right. Night watchmen were more typically older men, no longer strong enough for a full day's work. They wouldn't be expected to overpower an intruder, but rather to deter him by their presence, or call for help if he was not.

"I done my job," the boy continued. "Ain't nobody so much as touched a damned thing. But I ain't been paid now since the old man popped his cork. Three weeks' wages, I'm owed. Seems to my thinking the Chavises don't need to be running no credit line with me."

"No, I would think not," Gidry agreed.

"So if you ain't going to keep me on," he said, "at least you'd better pay what you owe me."

"Have a seat," Gidry told him.

The youngster hopped up on a ledger bench. His feet dangled several inches from the dusty floor.

Gidry tried to imagine who the little fellow might be. With the community prospering so well the last few years, the boy was obviously not a farmer's son. In fact, his family had to be almost certainly landless for the youngster to be free enough of farm chores to hire himself out to work. Even if his father were a sharecropper, there would be more than enough to do at home.

"What's your name?" Gidry asked. "I never hire employees whose names I don't know."

"Kilroy," the boy answered. "Milton Kilroy's my name, but folks mostly call me Sharpy."

Gidry raised his eyebrows in good humor.

"I bet they do," he agreed.

Milton Kilroy. There were a goodly number of Kilroys in town. Gidry couldn't recall one, however, who would be of an age to be this child's father. That is except for the old crazy drunk. His brow furrowed as he tried to remember the man's name. Befuddle. That was what they called him. Befuddle Kilroy. The old ne'er-do-well had burned out his brain with wood alcohol when Gidry was a boy.

"Are you kin to Befuddle Kilroy?" he asked.

The boy's answer was guarded. "He was my pa, I guess," the little boy replied with studied casualness. "I don't know nothing about him. He's been dead since I was a baby."

Gidry's throat narrowed in sympathy for the fatherless boy. Of course he was out in the world trying to make a living. Befuddle didn't have a pot to piss in or a window to throw it out. Nor any way to acquire either. The fellow scarcely knew day from night, and what little he did know he kept fogged up with corn liquor. He would have left his widow with even less. Sharpy was probably trying to support her and maybe a couple of little siblings, too.

"How old are you?" Gidry asked him.

"Seven," the boy lied with a straight face. "Almost seven and a half."

"That old?" Gidry replied with sufficient gravity. The way he calculated it, young Sharpy might then be even less than six and merely tall for his age.

"Do you live around here?"

"Here?"

"I mean down here near the railroad."

"No sirree," Sharpy stated flatly. "I ain't never living near the tracks. Too many damned kids."

"You don't like kids?"

"Not all them squalling babies I don't," he declared. "If you're living near the tracks, they's always more and more damned squalling babies, if you know what I mean."

"What do you mean?"

"Aw them trains come by twice a night," he explained gravely. "Wakes all the menfolk, and they

want to do something to help 'em get back to sleep.
Next thing ya know their woman's got another squalling baby pissing diapers and sucking at tit."

Gidry was struck speechless. Even granting poor
luck in paternity and a widowed mother, who was no
doubt scrounging for every scrap, there was something very, very wrong in a six-year-old having such
knowledge of the world.

Sharpy didn't appear to notice anything amiss.

"Are you a real cowboy?" he asked Gidry.

It took him a moment for Gidry to adjust to the
abrupt change of subject. "Sometimes," he said finally. "Sometimes I'm a cowboy."

"I'm going to be a cowboy when I grow up," he
said. "It'd be mighty nice to be out away from folks,
where nobody knows you. And sitting atop a fine
horse. I'm going to buy me one damn good horse
someday. I'll take it out West cowboying with me."

"That's a fine ambition," Gidry agreed. He'd seen
more than one landless nobody with a will to work
earn enough riding herd to get a start in the world.

"I got lots of am-bitchen," he assured Gidry. "I'll
be a cowboy, or maybe I'll run my own peep shows.
There's a world of money in peep shows, you know."

"I had no idea," Gidry admitted. "But don't you
think you're a little young to be looking at peep
shows?"

"I don't look at peep shows," Sharpy said loftily.

"Well, that's good."

"I got my own dirty postcards. You wanna see."

"Dirty postcards?"

"Yep, I got postcards with pitchers of ladies in their
underwear."

Gidry stared at the little boy in disbelief as he dug
his personal peep show out of his bib pocket.

The boy jumped down from his perch and walked over to prop himself against the edge of the desk. He started to hand them over to Gidry and then hesitated.

"I don't usually show 'em for free," he said.

Gidry jerked the postcards out of the boy's grubby hand.

The heavy three-inch-by-five-inch cards were slightly grayed from age and dog-eared from over-handling. Gidry's eyes widened as he stared at the photograph of a petite but well-rounded young female wearing only a pair of frilly drawers and black lace stockings. She held in her hands what appeared to be a live snake, its body spoiling the view of her naked breasts.

"Good Lord!" Gidry exclaimed aloud.

The next one was even more shocking. The female was naked in her bath. Though her limbs were hanging over opposite sides of the bathtub, obscuring her most intimate parts with sudsy water, her breasts were totally bare and with her hands upon her head they were raised to the viewer's eyes.

"Where in the devil did you get these?" Gidry asked shocked and angry.

Sharpy demurred.

"I charge two fer a penny to look at 'em," he said. "If you want to buy one to keep, it costs a nickel."

Gidry had no intention of handing back such vulgar material to such a young child. He was far too young even to be seeing such a thing, let alone *selling* it.

A brunette with her bloomerless backside to the camera was bent to the waist adjusting the buttons on her shoes.

"I'll take all of them," Gidry said, sliding the post-cards into the top drawer of the desk. "And I'll pay you your back wages. But if you're going to work for me, young man, I have some rules that must be followed."

The little fellow crossed his arms stubbornly.

"I'm listening," he said.

"No more cussing," Gidry said firmly. "I've always believed that a man who can't corral cattle without cussing them, ain't much of a cowboy."

"Hell's fire and damnation!" the child complained. "What difference does it make how I talk?"

"It makes a difference to me," Gidry insisted.

Sharpy shrugged. "The woman won't let me cuss from supper to bedtime nohow. Guess quitting the rest of day won't matter much."

"Good," Gidry answered, grateful that the boy's mother apparently still had some control over his behavior. "And no more postcards. I don't want anybody in my employ peddling pornography."

"What's po-knock-rafee?"

Gidry jerked open the desk drawer with the postcards inside. He tapped one finger upon the curved belly of a portly female, wearing only a salacious grin, draped across a chaise lounge.

"This is pornography," he said.

The boy's brow furrowed unhappily. "Hell . . . I mean heck, I make a bit of money on that po-knock-rafee."

Gidry nodded, not at all surprised to hear it. As a youngster, he would have gladly coughed up his last penny to view pictures of naked ladies. It seemed clear that boys were still boys.

"We're starting the ginning day after tomorrow," Gidry told him. "They'll be more work for a young fellow than just watching out for the place."

Sharpy still didn't look pleased. "I got more postcards where these came from. Can't I jest sell what I already done got?"

"Bring your inventory to me," Gidry answered. "I'll buy up all the pornography you have in stock. Then don't get any more. That's a condition of your employment here."

The little boy weighed his choices carefully. Finally he sighed in resignation.

"All right," he agreed.

He jumped to his feet and headed for the doorway. "I'll work for you, do without cussing, and quit selling the postcards. But I sure hate to give up my best business."

"Don't worry," Gidry told him. "I'll try to keep you on steady work. Neither your mother nor any of your family will go hungry, I promise."

Sharpy turned from the doorway to eye him curiously.

"I ain't got no family," he said. "Never had nobody but Mama, and she up and died over a year ago."

Pru had spent the coolness of the morning fighting black spot powder that had inexplicably appeared upon her newly planted Eglantiers. She had plucked the infected leaves before the dew had dried. And then ripped apart a cigar and spread the tobacco around to smoke the base of the plants. She didn't want to lose them, and, even more important, she didn't want the mildew to spread to other bushes. Although that seemed unlikely given the continuing good weather.

Having done all she could do, Pru left her flowers to the will of God and embarked upon an even more daunting task.

She was determined to clean the milking shed. She

had been biding her time, not only because the small building was thick with dust and overrun with vermin, but because the sometimes inhabitant of the place assured her repeatedly that he was not at all bothered by the presence of cobwebs in the dark corners or the long-term accumulation of grime.

"Just let it be my place," he'd pleaded with her. "I ain't never had a place that was truly mine."

Pru had assured him that he was welcome to the shed and that she would respect his privacy. To her mind, however, that was quite separate from her insistence on certain hygienic standards. He had not been at all pleased with her edict that he would wash up nightly and bathe completely once a week. But he had reluctantly agreed, and Pru was certain that he was pleased with the results. Making the milk shed clean and neat would also be accepted once he had experienced it. Like roses that grow more hardly in tilled soil free of weeds, people more harmoniously thrived in healthy surroundings.

And she wanted him to thrive. She wanted all the best for him always. He deserved it and had been denied it. She deserved it also. He could have been her very own.

She was only a half dozen yards from her objective when a movement at the corner of her eye caught her attention. Immediately she changed her direction. Nobody must suspect that she had someone living in the milk shed. She turned to walk toward the tall profusion of four-o'clocks that grew upon the trellis in front of the outhouse, then realized that it would look as if the outhouse was her destination, an impression she didn't want to encourage.

Pru swerved her path and made a beeline for the small plank bench supported by an old tree stump on one end and solid log on the other. Shaded by a stately pecan tree and set amid the oldest and most beautiful of the roses, it was the lovliest place in the garden.

It was only after she had taken her seat that Pru realized what a bad choice the site was. It was here, upon this very bench, that Gidry Chavis had last kissed her. And it was toward this bench, with her seated now as she had been then, that Gidry Chavis now walked.

She'd thought a lot about what Aunt Hen had said the day before. Her choices *were* different from her aunt's, certainly. But some things happened irrespective of one's choice. Gidry Chavis had jilted her. She'd had no say in it. But she did have a say in their future dealings. And her choice, she reminded herself firmly, was to have only the most casual of acquaintance with him. The best way to ensure that happened was not to encourage his visits. If Aunt Hen was thinking about the two of them together, could the scrutiny of the rest of Chavistown be far behind? She would never allow herself to become the object of their gossip or pity. Deliberately, she made her expression cool and distant.

"Good afternoon, Pru," he said.

She realized that she was nervously straightening her dress. Deliberately she clasped her hands together and held them still in her lap.

"Good afternoon to you, Mr. Chavis," she answered.

He stood in front of her for a long moment just looking at her.

"May I sit with you for a moment?"

Of course that had been what he was waiting for. A mundane, polite offer to be seated.

"As you will, sir," she answered, far too formally.

She couldn't stop herself as she unthinkingly drew her freshly washed skirts aside as if she dreaded any inadvertent contact.

Pru wanted to be distant and nonchalant. That was how she should be. But there had never been any distance between the two of them. Their shared past was very long ago. They were both changed and grown now. It made perfect sense that she would regard him only as a neighbor she vaguely knew.

So why did her heart beat so rapidly when he was near? She answered the thought in her own mind. Because he reminded her of the young woman that she used to be. She could not, would not be that young woman again.

"You used to call me Gid," he told her, that too-handsome grin lighting up his face. "When you say, 'Mr. Chavis' it sounds like you're talking to my father."

"I used to call you Gid when we were children," she answered. "We are no longer that."

"No, Pr . . . Miss Belmont, we are not," he agreed.

A silence ensued. It was difficult for Pru to refrain from making conversation with him. At one time she would have chatted away like a magpie. For so many years nothing, virtually nothing, in her life was worth experiencing without being allowed to share it with Gidry Chavis. They were the cutest young couple in Chavistown. And she had been the envy of all her girlfriends.

With perfect clarity she could recall discussions about secret spooning and the sweet mysteries of boyfriends.

"You can never let a boy think you like him," Leda

Peterson had declared. "The more you care about him, the less you can show it."

Pru had giggled with disagreement.

"I love Gidry," she stated baldly. "He knows it and you know it and I don't care if the world knows it."

"You and Gidry don't count," Leda insisted. "You two aren't like ordinary courting couples."

And they hadn't been. Their romance had been perfect. They had shared everything, said everything, lived in each other's pockets.

Gidry cleared his throat as if determined to put forth the effort to talk with her.

"I went down to the gin today," he said. "We are set to open tomorrow, and we should be filling trains with bales of cotton for the next few weeks."

"That's good," she said lamely.

"I thought myself to be almost completely ignorant about cotton markets," he admitted. "But my father's records are very good, and I have surprised myself with what I actually know."

"How nice," Pru responded.

"Of course, I do, in fact, know nothing about stopping the recent thefts," he said.

"Naturally not."

The one-sided conversation lagged once more. Pru knew she wasn't doing her part. Sitting beside him once more, here of all places. It was simply too much. She was through *bringing out the best* in Gidry Chavis.

It was here, upon this bench, where he had formally proposed marriage to her. Here, where he had kissed her lips so sweetly. It was here that she had declared her undying love for him.

Desperately she hoped that he didn't remember. Even more desperately she wished that she could forget.

A long uncomfortable silence lingered. At one time she would have cheerfully entertained him with a thousand stories of her days. Now she was determined to speak civilly, but only when spoken to.

"Pru . . . I mean Miss Belmont. We can't be enemies," he said. "I know somehow yesterday I managed to say the wrong thing. I'm not sure what it was, but I plead stupidity. I want us to talk together, to be friends as we once were."

"We are both grown and changed, Mr. Chavis," Pru replied. "I don't think reviving our former friendship is possible."

"While I was away, I would think of Chavistown and I would always think of you. You are as much this place to me as is the courthouse or the gin."

She was not warmed by the words.

Oh, now I am just another landmark, she thought unhappily.

Pru straightened her shoulders and raised her chin pridefully. "Mr. Chavis, I have no enemies," she assured him loftily.

"Perhaps not," he said. "But there was a time when I would have casually presumed you to be my friend."

It was true, she supposed. They had been friends, but for her part it had been so much more. Eight years was a long time. But she'd been hurt, very hurt. Sitting here now, she found that her heart ached still.

"I suppose an apology would help," Gidry said.

An apology for not loving her? It was ludicrous. Pru knew from her own experience that one could not choose where and whom to love. If such were possible, she would have married another man years ago. Gidry Chavis did not love her. It was a fact as unchangeable as the color of his eyes or the good fortune of his antecedents.

"An apology is not necessary," she assured him.

"I think more than likely it is," Gidry answered. "An apology as well as an explanation is more than overdue."

"Please, no." Her voice was a mere whisper.

Somehow she could not bear the words if she heard them aloud. Her heart was steeled so tightly against them, that surely it would shatter once more. She no longer cared for him, she assured herself. The crumbs of his affection were no longer precious treasures to her.

Yet her heart still ached. And she despised her enduring devotion to him. It was hopeless and pathetic. But as certainly as he couldn't love her, she couldn't stop loving him.

She was eight years older now, eight years wiser. She had been publicly humiliated eight years ago. She'd worn her love for him like a prized possession. When it was ripped from her, she was forever changed. She would not allow herself to go back to the naive foolishness that had brought her so low before.

"Please do not apologize for anything," she said firmly. "The past is forgotten. It was a part of my childhood. Let us never speak of it again. I am not the only woman you ever walked out on."

She gave a light humorless laugh and looked him straight in the eye.

Gidry's brow furrowed in question, but he didn't pursue the comment.

She knew about him. She knew things about him that he, perhaps, did not know himself. He was a faithless man, one who could not be counted upon.

Some men were just that way and nothing could change them.

Pru focused her attention upon his scuffed, square-toed leather trail boots. Why was the man still dressing in such an informal manner? Chavistown might not be a cosmopolitan city, but for a gentleman of means a jacket and tie were required for afternoon attire.

"Lightning bugs are out," he said.

She looked up and smiled. The flickering little insects were the first portents of evening. As childhood friends Pru and Gidry had spent many hot summer nights capturing the small creatures to make light in a jar.

Absently she caught sight of the house next door.

"Aunt Hen is on her way home," she said.

Gidry looked at her curiously. "How do you know that?" he asked.

"On her way out she always switches on the landing light behind the stained-glass window," Pru answered.

"That window was made for Aunt Hen." Gidry told her.

"What?" Pru glanced first at him and then at the window. "For Aunt Hen?"

Gidry chuckled lightly. "At least that's what Papa told me when he had it put in. I must have been five or six at the time."

"It was done by the same workmen who did the window at church, wasn't it?"

Gidry nodded. "Papa contracted the glaziers and had liked their work on the Good Shepherd so well, he asked them to come to our house to do a flower garden in spring bloom."

"Where does Aunt Hen fit in?" Pru asked.

He gazed at the window, smiling as if recalling the memory. "Papa told me that Aunt Hen shared her garden with us. We could view it all day. But at night her garden was as dark as the rest of the world. So we were putting a garden in a window and that with the light shining behind it, we could share it with Aunt Hen all the night long."

Pru felt a wave of tenderness for Gidry as he told the story. She mentally resisted the emotion, determined to keep her feelings neutral. Not an easy task seated beside his handsome, smiling visage, within sight of his long legs, muscled and male, stretched out before him beneath tight-fitting denim trousers. Could any woman remain indifferent to that?

"I hadn't thought about that in years," he said, shaking his head. "I think I'd forgotten it completely until just now."

"It seems a rather strange gift for a neighbor," Pru said. "The sight from a window."

Gidry shrugged in agreement. "Maybe Papa just made the story up. Parents have been known to do that from time to time," he said. "They make up a simple story when the true one is too hard to explain."

"It's hard to imagine your father, serious and venerable Peer Chavis, making up silly stories for his son," she said.

"Then you don't know Papa all that well," he told her. "He loves tall tales. I sit at night and entertain him with the most outrageous cowboy lies you've ever heard. He just loves it."

Pru nodded slowly, thoughtfully. "It is strange that I've known him so long and yet I don't really know him that much at all. I feel the same way about Aunt Hen sometimes."

"Really?" Gidry shook his head. "Maybe it's because they lived so much of their lives without us. So much happened to them before we were ever born, so much we will never know."

"Perhaps you are right," Pru agreed. "The other day Aunt Hen was talking about the war and the choices she made in her life. I'd never thought of the war as having affected her at all."

"I know it affected my father," Gidry said. "He was just past twenty when he'd run off to join the Confederacy. Papa always felt that the war stole away his youth, his family, and his fortune. It must have been a terrible time."

"We have been so lucky to grow up in peaceful times," Pru said.

He nodded. "As long as those nasty, scrapping Europeans are confined to their own shores, it appears that for the western hemisphere, at least, permanent peace is almost guaranteed."

"But for Aunt Hen and your father," Pru said, "it was very different. Apparently the entire country was being torn apart, brothers fighting brothers, and young men left their homes and families to defend the causes they'd hardly heard of and could only begin to understand."

"The Chavis family supported the South in principle," Gidry told her. "But at rather a bit of distance, I think. Since the Republic of Texas had joined the Union voluntarily and as an autonomous government, Texas retained the right to leave that union at will. So the fight for Southern secession was really not our fight."

"What about slavery?" she asked.

Gidry shook his head sorrowfully. "What a thing for a man to give his life defending."

Pru agreed.

"Papa could have, probably should have, stayed home and attended to his family's business," Gidry said. "Sometimes I wonder why he didn't. Do you think he was a hot-tempered, hardheaded young adventurer like me?" His grin was mesmerizing.

"I suppose it's possible," she said. "They do say the apple doesn't fall far from the tree."

"I suspect it would have been hard for me to be content to grow cotton when there were battles to be won and glory to be achieved," he said more seriously.

"He certainly looked glorious," Pru said. "I've seen the photograph downstairs, with him in his dress uniform of gray, a cockade in his hat and a saber at his side."

Gidry laughed. "He certainly did look rakish and devil-may-care," he agreed. "The war must have changed him. Or maybe it was his marriage. He arrived back in Chavistown with his new bride and a new baby on the way, and there was no one at the station to meet him. Cholera had killed his whole family. He said once that vagrants had taken his house and weeds had taken his cotton."

"It must have been awful for him," Pru said.

"He just began again, clawing a life for himself and his own from the dirt that had been his family's for years. He succeeded, but I guess it wasn't soon enough. Mama was unused to hardship, I suppose, or simply lonesome for things familiar. She went home for a visit and never came back."

It was not easy to lose the woman who gave birth to you. Pru knew that from her own experience. No amount of caring people around you could ever truly make up for it. Their shared motherlessness had been one of the first ties to bind their friendship.

"I know you missed her," Pru said finally in a whisper.

Gidry thought about it a moment before he answered. "I missed not having a mother," he said. "That couldn't be helped. But Papa tried his best, and I had Aunt Hen and I had you."

"Me?"

Pru was startled to be included as if *she* were one of his parents.

"Well . . . yes, of course . . . you were there and you loved me. I . . . I needed someone to love me."

Pru felt her face flush with color and her anger rise to the surface just as rapidly. "I had a girlish infatuation for you," she told him firmly.

"I meant that you loved me as a friend," Gidry assured her quickly. "You loved me as a friend. And I loved you. I loved you the same way."

Abruptly she rose to her feet.

"Is that why you asked me to marry you? Because you loved me as a friend?" she asked. Her voice had risen perceptibly.

"I . . . I knew it was what you wanted," he answered. "It was what you wanted. It was what my father wanted. It . . . it just wasn't what I wanted."

"And as we all know," Pru snapped furiously. "Gidry Chavis always gets what he wants."

"Pru . . ."

"We were friends, you say," she countered. "Yes, we were friends. As much friends as two people could be when one of them wore her heart on her sleeve for all the world to see."

"You were my good friend," Gidry told her. "My childhood sweetheart. And you would have made a good wife to me. I know that, Pru. I'm willing to admit that. But I had grandiose visions and I was grown-up. Twenty-one years old, and you seemed merely a girl."

"I was the girl that you had promised to marry," she pointed out.

"Pru, I have nothing to say for my behavior except that I am sorry," he told her. "I have tried to apologize . . ."

"I don't want your apologies!" she shouted.

"Then what *do* you want?" he asked her.

She wasn't given a chance to reply as Aunt Hen called out to them from the gate.

"What on earth is all the shouting about?"

Without another word, Pru fled to the house, through the back door, and into the kitchen.

"The truth is I think I can remember enough about cotton ginning to keep the town on the right track," Gidry told Peer Chavis as he paced the narrow floorboards at the foot of his father's bed. "But I don't know one thing about crime or thieves or how to make a town safe from burglary."

Gidry was still disconcerted from his visit with Prudence. He knew that he'd not done as well as he'd hoped. He knew their relationship could never be what it once was. Eight years ago she had been in love with him. Of course, she no longer felt that. But she had been a dear friend and happy confidante as well as his sweetheart. As a young man he had shared every thought and dream with her. He wanted it to be that way once more. To be able to talk to her about what he was thinking, what he was planning.

Clearly, Miss Belmont was not interested in anything that he had to say. She wanted to have a merely casual acquaintance. As casual as could be had in a town of five thousand.

Unable to share his thoughts with her, he had chosen to share them with his father.

"I don't think hiring a lawman with a fancy reputation would quite suit Chavistown," he continued. "Yet I can't imagine what more we can do on our own."

He stopped pacing long enough to put his hands in his pockets and stare out the window. There had to be an answer somewhere. He tried to think about what he knew.

"On the trail drive we would take watches at night," he said. "While some slept, others would ride the perimeter and keep an eye on the herd. There was always danger of wolves or coyotes getting a calf, rustlers stealing from us, or bad weather spooking the cattle. But a couple of men could alert us all."

His brow furrowed thoughtfully as he turned to his father.

"We could put volunteers on the watch," he said. "Have someone on every street to do citizens' patrol."

Gidry shrugged. "Of course a smart criminal would just wait until the watchman had passed and then do his thieving."

He shook his head. "I don't know how smart these fellows are. Why in the blazing devil would somebody rob a livery stable and not take horses? Who would steal a dead man's wooden leg or an old photogram of somebody's relative?"

Gidry stood thoughtful, curious, lost in speculation for a long moment. Then as if recalling where he was, he glanced at his father once more. The old man lay, as he always did, thin and pale, his sharp eyes watching his son.

"I don't know why I'm boring you with this," Gidry told him. "If you ever knew anything about fighting crime, you undoubtedly forgot about it during the last forty crime-free years in Chavistown."

He dragged a chair up next to his father's bed and seated himself, crossing one booted foot over his knee. His father's hand moved forward on the bedcovers and Gidry spontaneously clasped it in his own. It was an old hand, withered by age and use. It was the hand that had cuddled him close as a baby. It was also the hand that had struck him on the night he'd left home. Gidry grasped it tightly as if willing his own strength to flow into his father.

He looked up into the old man's eyes, so much like his own.

You're going to get better. He told the old man silently. *You are going to walk again and talk again and be my father as you once were again.*

More time. I wish we had more time.

The words were a prayer on Gidry's heart. When he actually spoke his tone was lighter, deliberately causal.

"No, Papa, I bet you can't tell me a thing about fighting crime in Chavistown. If you want to learn about the ways of lawless badmen," he said in the understated dramatic tone that he used for storytelling, "you need to take a tour of the Pecos."

His father's eyes brightened immediately, recognizing the tone as the one Gidry used for his tall tales.

"An old cowboy I met, who swears he was there at the time, related to me a story of the James boys. You've heard of the James boys of Missouri? As wild and wicked a gang of thieves as ever existed. This is a true accounting of a robbery they made, the full story of which is rarely heard. Rarely heard because

it was not a tale that Jesse and Frank would want
placed in their legend. And rarely heard 'cause the
railroad men are not shown in the light of great in-
telligence themselves. You see on this night, this rainy
moonless, west Texas night, the James boys made the
mistake of robbing the same train twice.''

As Gidry repeated the timeworn piece of Wild West
fiction, he watched his father's face. In the very short
time since his son had been back in town it was clear
that Peer had grown attentive and anxious for the stories that Gidry would tell. It was almost as if the old
man wanted to experience what his son had experienced, to know for himself the unrelenting boredom
of the cattle trail. To escape from the confines of his
sickbed and live the wild and colorful cowboy lies
related around the campfire.

Gidry wanted to escape as well. He wanted to escape the truth about himself and about what he had
done to Prudence Belmont.

He had tried to apologize, to explain, to make her
understand. But he truly didn't know how and was
not even certain that he should.

He had promised to make Pru his wife. He had
wanted to make her his wife. Of all the upright, decent women in the world, there was none other that
he'd rather have to share his life. But then he had
discovered that not all women were upright and decent. And not all of them expected an offer of marriage.

It was natural that a young fellow, soon to marry,
should sow his share of wild oats. If he was to settle
upon one woman for life, at least he should have in
mind what some other women were like. And how
could a man teach his wife the facts of life when he
himself had little knowledge of them? The nature of

these discussions with other men his own age had led him to seek out sexual experiences with women whose reputations were no better than they should be.

His father had discovered his unsavory liaisons and had ordered that they cease. Prudence was a clean, decent girl. Gidry's behavior, unchecked, would likely bring her heartbreak, if not disease.

But it was not so easy. Once having tasted forbidden fruit, visiting with sweet, innocent Pru had become increasingly tedious. She had been his best friend and his betrothed. But he certainly could not share with her his new knowledge. It had been unthinkable back then. It was unmentionable even now.

He'd gone to her that night, that last night of their engagement, in the privacy of the flower garden. She had accepted his advances with stoic assent. She sighed beneath his callous caress as if his touch was true tenderness. And she had sparked to a sensuous passion as surprisingly powerful as his own. She'd made no protest when he dared beyond decency to hold her ample young breasts in his hands. When he'd flicked his tongue across one thickened raised nipple, she'd gasped in shock, but she hadn't jerked away from him.

Gidry had kissed her and caressed her and wanted her that night. But he hadn't wanted the commitment that taking her innocence would have meant. He had wanted to be young and careless and foolish. He had wanted to keep company with flashy females dressed in bright red spangles.

So he had spurned the only woman who'd ever loved him. Then he'd left a note. He couldn't recall what he had said, but it spoke nothing of the guilt he felt or the injustice of what he'd done. He'd dismissed her feelings as if they had no value. And he had walked away.

There is no one quite as difficult to deal with as the person whom one has genuinely wronged. And he had genuinely wronged Prudence Belmont.

Gidry ended the Wild West story he was telling his father with the chagrin of the James boys and a fine joke on the railroad conductor. Peer Chavis settled more contently into his pillow and lowered his eyelids, allowing sleep to overtake him.

Gidry put out the lamp at his father's bedside and sat in the darkness, gazing at the man's face in the moonlight. He was thinking, wondering, regretting.

He stared down into the dark, silent garden where he had thrown away her love as worthless. He hated the young man who had done that to his Pru. He hated the man that he once had been. He could not even console himself that he had honorably spared her deflowering. It he had taken her virginity, then he would have married her. He was not, nor ever had been, as much a cad as that.

He'd run straight from her arms to the noise and smoke of the Red Slipper. There he had drunk a jug of corn liquor before facing his father. The girl in the red-spangled dress was heading south on the night train to San Antone.

"Save me a seat," he'd said, slapping her playfully on the backside. "My very favorite seat."

After eight years Gidry still felt shame at his behavior. Much shame and stupidity as well. His interest in the red-spangled dress had faded by the weekend. And he'd learned all too quickly that there were a dozen women just like her in every Texas town.

In eight long years he had yet to meet another woman like Prudence Belmont.

His attention was captured by a trickle of light seeping out around the old warped doorway to Aunt Hen's milk shed.

Gidry raised an eyebrow. Was she out there again tonight?

Who was the man? And why did he meet her in secret?

Because he was a married man, seemed the most likely answer. It would only be a married man who would sneak to her place at night and wait in a milk shed. An old milk shed would not be Gidry's idea of a romantic hideaway.

A single man would have courted her openly. He would have walked her to church, sat upon her porch, taken her for a discreet promenade in the park on Saturday. A single man would have most likely married her before expecting to sample her favors.

No, most likely it was a married man. A married man bored with his middle-aged wife and sick of the sound of his squabbling youngsters. He might find Pru's more mature years a great preference over the simpering expectations of a young miss. And Gidry could well imagine that the fellow had been pleasantly surprised at the sober spinster's very passionate nature. A married man could not be held to soft words or promises. A woman went into such a liaison knowing full well that the alliance had no future. Divorce might be legal in Texas, but upstanding people did not engage in it. Even his own parents, separated for twenty-five years, had to his knowledge never given a serious thought to severing their vows permanently.

It was a married man who was secretly meeting Prudence. And if the two were caught, the man's wife might never quite forgive him, but the community

would. It was always the woman who was held completely to blame. Prudence had no male relatives. She
had no father or brothers to protect her from worthless adulterers who would prey upon her lovestruck
nature. She had no one to exact revenge if the illicit
romance became the whisper of scandalmongers.

Gidry watched and watched. He watched for what
seemed a lifetime. He squared his jaw and slapped a
clenched fist into his palm. If he heard one bragging
whisper from her no-account lover, he'd personally
break the man's neck.

The door to the milk shed opened. Prudence held
the lantern in her grasp and he could see her clearly
in the doorway. Even at this distance, he could see
that she was neatly dressed with every hair in place.

Gidry snorted to himself in derision. The fellow
must not be much of a lover. If Pru had just spent half
an hour in Gidry's arms, she'd be tousled and jelly-
legged from the experience.

What the devil was he thinking about? Prudence
Belmont was never going to spend even one minute
in *his* arms. What a ridiculous idea! It was as if he
thought he could turn back time, as if he believed that
people got second chances.

He watched her walk through the night gloom of
her back garden, the lantern in her hand to help her
see the way. Of course it worked otherwise as well.
He could clearly follow her path even in the thickest
of shadows. That was worrisome. If he could see what
she was up to, others in the neighborhood might as
well.

Gidry shook his head. When one was up to dis-
graceful deeds, darkness was definitely preferable.

His brow furrowed thoughtfully. Then a smile
curved upon his face.

That was it!

He put his hands upon his hips and reared back almost laughing out loud he was so delighted with himself. That was the best answer to crime in Chavistown.

Chapter 6

THE GINNING had begun at dawn. There was no question about that. The machinery was loud enough to be heard in every corner of town. And for those fortunate enough to be deaf as a stone, the ground vibrated underfoot like an ongoing earthquake.

Prudence walked through her garden anxious about the root systems of her plants. If the trains, trolleys, and heavy footsteps of city dwellers could harm roses, heaven only knew what the tremendous shaking of a steam-driven cotton gin might do. It was only for a few weeks, she assured herself. Though her plants lived through the quaking every year, it worried her. Modern life seemed so incompatible with the laws of nature.

Pru had little time to dwell on the fact, however. A town meeting was called for twelve noon at the courthouse square.

The news spread through town from one citizen to the next with a speed and efficiency that Western Union could only envy. Especially considering that a person must scream to one's neighbor simply to be heard.

Ethel Peterson had informed Pru. Ethel's husband was influential in the Commercial Club, so it would make sense that she would get the news early. In fact, she got it quite early. Her husband didn't have a chance to tell her. The Petersons had a telephone, and Bertha Mae Corsen rang up every number in town.

The ladies in the community, noting the time of day, took part by organizing an impromptu picnic. As president of the most prominent ladies' organization in Chavistown, Prudence was immediately drawn into the center of the enterprise.

It was not a position that she relished. Some women could take a scrap of fatback and a peck sack of butter beans and competently manage to feed five thousand, while receiving lavish compliments from every satisfied stomach. Pru could certainly cook well enough to keep herself and her aunt from starving. But huge, public meals that fed hundreds of people were clearly not her forte. She had never had a large family, never lived in one.

Resolutely, and grumbling only beneath her breath, Prudence took up the mantle of picnic production. With the tremendous rattle and shake of the cotton gin numbing her brain, Pru made out lists upon lists upon lists notifying the ladies of their respective assignments. Even Aunt Hen was appropriated from the sickroom and set to frying chicken in the kitchen of the Chavis house.

The town was overflowing with people. Farm families, their wagons loaded high with cotton, took their places in line around the gin. The queue spanned the length of Austin Street from Sante Fe to the courthouse, then circled around and went another block

and a half down Main Avenue. The combination of
the first day of ginning and a town meeting had the
city crowded and bustling as a grand metropolis. The
carnival atmosphere was so seductive that classes
were let out at the public school. And once those children were running loose and cavorting in fun, Erma
Beth Whitstone's Normal School for Young Ladies
dismissed students as well.

By eleven-thirty makeshift plank tables were
draped in bunting and set up on the north side of the
courthouse. By a quarter to twelve they were sagging
under the cumulative weight of five dozen covered
dishes. Corn pudding, string beans with snaps, beet
pickles, and squash fritters sat among mountains of
mashed potatoes and cooked cabbage.

At exactly twelve o'clock the horrendous noise and
endless shaking of the cotton gin abruptly stopped.
The resulting silence was so startling and welcome
that the women looked at each other and spontaneously laughed out loud.

Pru spotted Sharpy Kilroy racing toward the
square. His ragged clothes were sweat-soaked and his
face was dirty, but there was a big smile on his face
and he sported a shiny new pair of shoes.

He stopped abruptly in front of the first table and
held out his dinner plate.

Cloris Tatum shooed the boy away angrily. "Get
away from here, you dirty little beggar," she said to
him. "These vittles are for decent folks."

Pru watched the little boy's smile disappear and his
cheeks pale in humiliation. Her own emotion was immediate boiling rage. Cloris was a Kilroy by birth. Her
family's neglect of the orphaned child set the tone of
treatment to him by the whole town.

"Milton," she called to the child softly. She motioned for him to come to her.

He did as he was bidden, his visage frozen in a cold, beaten expression that would have sat more reasonably on a man of forty than a child of seven and a half.

She looked down into that little face, her heart aching. *He could have been mine*, she told herself not for the first time. *He could have been my very own child*. But he wasn't. He was a pitiful orphan, unclaimed and all alone. Reviled by the community that had produced him.

Prudence took his dinner plate from his little grubby hands.

"Milton, sweetie," she said. "Why don't you go wash up at the trough, and I'll fix your plate." She learned forward and added a conspiratorial whisper. "I know where the best food has been put back."

The suggestion of getting something to which only the favored were entitled appealed to the touch of larceny in the boy's little soul as Pru knew it would. His beautifully gleaming baby-toothed smile reappeared, and he rushed off to do as she'd suggested.

Pru began piling up the child's plate with enough food for three boys his size.

"It's doesn't do to coddle little beggars like that," Cloris warned Pru snidely. "They begin to think the world owes them something."

To Pru's mind, the world clearly owed this child a full belly and this community owed him a lot more, but she deliberately maintained her silence. Never would she reveal what she suspected, what she thought she knew.

"That child ought not to be running wild in the

streets," Cloris continued. "He should be in an orphanage somewhere."

Mrs. Hathaway was nodding agreement. "I have said that very thing to the reverend a dozen times at least."

"He's doing very well by himself," Pru insisted. "A lot of men have gone out to make their way in the world when they were mere boys."

"Not that young," Mavis told her.

"He's almost eight," Pru said.

Mrs. Hathaway looked genuinely surprised. "Has it been that long?" she asked skeptically.

Cloris waved away her words. "Nonsense, he still has his baby teeth."

Pru couldn't imagine what teeth could have to do with it. She piled his plate high with the foods she already knew to be his favorites, fried chicken, creamed peas, snap beans in fatback, and plenty of beet pickles. As he hurried to her she found him a shady spot under one of the native pecan trees that had been planted along the edges of the square.

The little boy seated himself cross-legged on the ground and dug bare-handed into his food.

"Don't you have a spoon, Milton?" she asked him.

He shook his head with unconcern.

"I don't need one, Miss Pru," he said. "I can always manage to get the da . . . the danged food to my mouth."

Prudence squatted beside him and tenderly brushed his thick dark hair away from his brow.

"You've been working hard this morning?"

His mouth was full, but he nodded eagerly.

"I want you to be very careful around that dreadful machinery," she said. "More than one man has been maimed at such a job, and you are very small to be doing it."

"For the work I do, you got to be small," Sharpy answered. "Mr. Gidry, he done told me that he did the same scooting and fetching when he was a boy."

"Well, I still want you to be very careful," she said. "Even scooters and fetchers have been known to be injured."

He nodded once more, intent upon his food.

"I see you have some new shoes," Pru said.

"I didn't steal 'em," the little boy declared.

"I never thought for a moment that you did," she assured him.

It was terrible the way people always thought the worst of someone like Sharpy. The poor boy was undoubtedly the frequent target of accusation and censure.

"I assumed that you had already made enough in wages to purchase the new shoes yourself," she told him.

Sharpy's mouth was mostly full once more, but he nevertheless managed a reply.

"Mr. Gidry done traded 'em to me," he said. "And they's just exactly my size."

"Gidry Chavis bought you these shoes?" Just the sound of his name on her lips had her heart beating a little faster. "That was very good of him," she said.

"I *traded* him," Sharpy insisted defiantly. "I don't take a God—a gosh darn thing from nobody never."

"Oh yes, of course," Pru agreed solemnly. She knew perfectly well the young boy's fears of being indebted to someone.

"What did you have to trade?" she asked.

The youngster looked momentarily evasive.

"I traded him some *valuables* I got."

"Valuables?" She smiled warmly at him. "What kind of valuables would that be?"

"Men kind of valuables, Miss Pru, nothin' you'd be interested in," he said gravely.

Pru ruffled his hair lovingly. He never pulled away from her like most children his age would have done. It was almost as if he needed her mothering touch almost as much as she needed to bestow it.

But she could not linger long at his side. She didn't want to draw attention to her obvious preference for the boy. Part of having taught herself not to feel had made Prudence one of those women who simply did not dote upon children. She had never allowed herself to hold them, kiss them, talk baby talk, or even squeeze a fat pink cheek. It had been a safeguard for her own heart. She never talked with the young mothers about their children. She had never joined in a game of ring-around-the-rosy, never so much as showed a vague interest in anything said or done by anyone less than legal age. Those very facts now made her feelings for young Sharpy more inexplicable.

She could not allow her tenderness for the boy to bring him to public notice. People might start asking questions, thinking things through, coming to conclusions. Very likely the same ones that she had come to herself. She must protect the young fellow as she protected herself. It was not such a hard deception to endure. Especially when he obviously knew that she cared for him.

And she had plenty to do. Deliberately she left him alone with his vittles. She made her way back toward the table, purposely stopping to make a fuss over Leda Peterson's twin boys and homely Constance Redfern's surprisingly pretty daughter, Sassy. Let folks imagine that she was growing a soft spot in her heart for children. That was mostly what they expected of a spinster anyway. An *unfulfilled* female like herself would cherish the attention of even the most unruly and unattractive youngster. To have it thought that her barren womb led her to be unnecessarily attached to Sharpy Kilroy was humiliating. The true reason was even more so.

Within minutes a parade of laughing, joking men was spilling into the square from the gin.

Against her will Pru's gaze was drawn to Gidry Chavis. It was not Gidry himself that she was looking at, she assured herself. It was that he was still dressed in his body-hugging, inappropriate cowboy garb. Among the crowd of workingmen in overalls and the few upstanding citizens in sack suits, he appeared tall and broad-shouldered and far too good-looking for any useful purpose.

Defensively she raised her chin. After the previous afternoon's fiasco, Pru was more determined than ever not to allow any foolish notions concerning Gidry Chavis to be unloosed. But it was difficult to ignore him when he so clearly stood out in a crowd.

The men began lining up for food, and Pru was quickly caught up in the hubbub of getting everybody fed.

By some kind of unwritten protocol, the gin workers ate first, followed by the farmers, townsmen, and laborers. Once the men had filled their plates, women lined up as well. But not on behalf of themselves. They procured food for their children, their mothers, their ancient old-maid aunts. It would have been considered an egregious breach of etiquette for a woman in fine health and the prime of life to so much as taste a bite before the food was cold and the rest of the community overfed and drowsy.

Because Pru was neither too old nor still growing, and a spinster, no child at her breast or growing in her womb, she was one of the last to eat. In fact the meeting had already begun.

Stanley Honnebuzz was already arguing with old Ollie Larson. Judge Ramey had to get between the two to shut them up.

"If I could just have your attention for a few moments here," the judge called out.

The crowd began to hush and settle.

Pru found a solitary spot in the shade and seated herself. Although she was naturally interested in the affairs of the town, those concerns were almost exclusively centered around cotton. And as she had no such crop to tend to and worry about, her concentration was more upon her meal than the business at hand.

"I want to thank you all for coming out today," Judge Ramey said. "I know that it probably had more to do with the gin being in operation and the ladies fixing this fine meal than anything you thought you might hear from an old politician like me."

There were light chuckles heard throughout the square.

"In fact a fellow on this very spot once told me, 'Ramey, I wouldn't vote for you if you was Saint Peter!' "

The judge reared back slightly and locked his thumbs at the clips of his suspenders.

"I told him, 'Sir, if I was Saint Peter, you *couldn't* vote for me. 'Cause you wouldn't ever be living in my district!' "

The menfolk guffawed at the great joke. The ladies tittered a bit uneasily.

Pru managed with difficulty to keep a smile from turning the corners of her mouth. A spinster lady probably should pretend that she didn't even comprehend the meaning. Feigning ignorance had never been something at which she was particularly adept.

Judge Ramey continued.

"As most of you know, Gidry Chavis is back among us," he said. "He's got some new ideas for us. I'm going to let him tell you about them himself."

Gidry stepped up to take the judge's place. There was a spattering of applause, mostly from the men of the Commercial Club and the gin workers. The rest of the community had not yet decided what they thought of the prodigal's return.

He smiled warmly at the crowd. He was not as easy with speaking as the judge had been, but he had a natural bent for leadership.

"I don't suppose I need to tell any of you that the gin is in operation as of today," he began.

There was notable laughter in the crowd. Certainly anyone who was not dead and in the grave would be aware of the morning's noisy clatter.

"As I told the farmers first in line," he continued, "what seed you don't need back for your farm we're going to try to process ourselves. Elmer Corsen and Conrad Peterson are checking into building a cotton-seed-oil plant right here in Chavistown."

There was a collective intake of breath from the crowd, followed immediately by excited chatter as each and every person on the square felt the need to share his or her opinion with whoever might listen.

Pru was as pleased as most everyone else, perhaps more so as it was her own idea.

"As we all know, there is not a cottonseed-oil plant in the entire Black Waxy Prairie. If we can get one started, donate our own seed for free processing, then we can use the income generated to pay off the construction."

There were murmurs of agreement everywhere.

"Mr. Shipley has assured us that Farmers and Merchants Bank would be willing to lend the Commercial Club the start-up money for construction," Gidry continued. "Within three to five years, whether cotton prices are high or low, we should be out of the red and beginning to pay off dividends to members and shareholders."

The applause for that announcement was hearty and genuine.

"That's a fine idea the boy has," one old farmer was heard to say.

There were nods all around him.

"Everybody knows the price of cottonseed oil is more stable than the fiber," Amos Wilburn answered.

"Those industry folks is coming up with more things to do with that dang oil ever' day," Plug Whitstone added, punctuating his words with a spit of tobacco. "If we got a processing plant, it'll bring new business to town faster than buzzards to a dead skunk."

"He's right about that." Pru heard someone agree.

"Now wait just a minute!" Ollie Larson hollered out. "Wait just a dad-blamed minute."

The talked stopped as people craned forward to see what Know-It-All Larson, the soapbox orator, had to say.

"You don't like the idea of us producing our own cottonseed oil?" The question came from Gidry Chavis.

The wiry old man shook his head. "I ain't opposed to making some money from that worthless cottonseed," he assured the crowd. "But that ain't my main concern here. It don't matter how much new business comes to town nor how much money we make if they is thieving no-accounts among us going to rob us blind."

An immediate clamor arose at his words. It was true. For the people of Chavistown, times were already good. Crime was a bigger issue than prosperity.

"I've got some ideas for that, too," Gidry announced.

"He's going to bring in one of those west Texas lawmen," one man suggested.

"He'll do better to run all the vagrants and lowlifes out of town," another declared.

"I'll not have some outsider telling me where I can go and when I can be there," a third man vowed.

Gidry raised his hands to quiet the crowd.

"The gentlemen of the Commercial Club have already discussed this at length this morning," he said. "We think we have come up with what is a very practical plan."

"You all talk and we pay!" Larson declared with challenge. "It'll ruin our way of life and cost us a pretty penny, I'll bet ya."

"No, Mr. Larson," Gidry said calmly. "It won't bring any unwelcome change to the way that we live. And will also not involve assessing any tax burden upon the good people of the community."

There were sighs of relief in the crowd. Solutions without a price to the populace were always welcome.

"So what is it?" Ollie asked. "What's the big answer the Commercial Club has come up with?"

Gidry turned to a small, unfamiliar man in a plaid coat.

"Ladies and gentlemen of Chavis County," Gidry said, "please allow me to introduce to you Mr. Arthur D. Sattlemore, a representative of the Big Texas Electric Company."

The stranger held his bowler hat in his hand and seemed a bit nervous at the prospect of addressing a crowd.

"Mr. Sattlemore is going to talk about the latest innovation in combating burglary and pilferage, residential electric street lighting."

There was a startled gasp from the crowd. Pru sat up straighter.

Gidry was still speaking.

"Within the next four years, these last before the new century, the darkest, dimmest corners of our fair Chavistown will be glowing with the brightness of modern electricity even on the cloudiest moonless night."

The gentlemen of the Commercial Club clearly expected an enthusiastic round of applause. They were doomed to disappointment. Most of those in the crowd were stunned to speechlessness. The streetlights on the four corners of town square were a necessary evil, but to light the entire town day and night. Was such a thing even possible? And, if possible, was it in any way desirable?

"It's unnatural!" Pru whispered worriedly to herself.

She glanced around to see if anyone had heard her exclamation, or if anyone shared her concern. The Commercial Club was going to light up the whole town. All that electricity in the air couldn't possibly

be good for people. However would they sleep at
night if there was no darkness.

"What will such a thing do to our gardens?"

Prudence Belmont asked herself the question and
from that moment was determined to get an answer.

Gidry lingered on the courthouse steps as the
crowd dispersed. He felt strangely deflated. The meeting had not gone as well as he had hoped. Installing
residential street lighting appeared to him as such a
fine, unintrusive answer to the problem, he'd assumed that everyone in town would be as enthusiastic
about it as he was.

Judge Ramey simply waved away his concerns.
"Oh, that's just what you get in politics."

"I'm not interested in politics," Gidry told him.

The old judge laughed. "Not that many folks are,"
he assured him. "But it's like professing a disinterest
in your elbows. If you're just sitting around doing
nothing, it's easy not to care about them. But as soon
as you see something that needs doing or fixing, you
find that a lack of elbows can be a genuine detriment."

"I just want to do something to help the town,"
Gidry said.

"If *the town* was just streets and buildings you could
do that," Ramey said. "But the town is people. And
people and politics are two sides of the same coin.
There is no nation, congregation, or quilting circle
small enough not to be affected by it."

"Lighting just seems so obviously better than polic-
ing," Gidry pointed out. "Is it because it is me? Because it is my idea that people are opposed to it?"

The old man shook his head. "When it comes to

politics," Ramey told him, "there is always going to be a certain number of againers."

"Againers?"

The judge nodded.

"No matter what you come up with—they're going to be against it," he explained. "If you wanted to hand out twenty-dollar gold pieces on Main Avenue, there'd be some folks opposed to the idea."

Gidry was thoughtful.

"Can those people, the againers, can they cause enough dissension to derail a project?" he asked.

"Not by themselves," the judge assured him. "Ollie Larson on his soapbox may get a lot of attention from people, but folks don't necessarily agree with him."

"So we needn't be concerned?"

Judge Ramey was not so certain.

"By themselves the againers are not much of an impediment," he said. "The real danger comes from people with convictions."

"Convictions?"

"Those folks who look quite honestly and openly at the same things that you do and interpret what they see entirely different."

"What do you mean?" Gidry asked.

"I mean that people can disagree about things for perfectly valid reasons," he said. "And determining who is truly right or truly wrong on the subject may very well only be decided with certainty when we get the chance to ask God face-to-face."

"What possible exception could anyone find to merely lighting up the streets to keep criminals from stalking in the dark?" Gidry asked. "It's a very good idea."

The old judge chuckled.

"I agree with you," he said. "But believe me, we

will soon find out that a lot of folks don't, and we'd better be ready to defend our *very good idea* with every possible scrap of knowledge and clear thinking we can come up with."

Gidry prepared himself to do that through the rest of the afternoon. With the cotton gin in full noisy operation once more it was impossible for a man to do much more than make explanatory gestures to his fellow workers and keep his thoughts to himself.

The ginning was kept up at a frantic pace. Farmers would drive their wagons up underneath the scales in the overhang area between the gin and the seed house. The wagon would be weighed with its full load. Then a large tubular pipe attached to a reverse fan inside the gin sucked the cotton from the wagon into the maze of troughs in the rafters above the gin stands. The empty wagon was then weighed and the difference noted in that farmer's tonnage of gross weight cotton.

The ginning process separated the cotton lint from the seed, the latter representing about two-thirds of the gross weight. The method, called by some cat-clawing, was to have the multitoothed gin stand gently pull at the cotton tufts to separate them as if the claws of a mischievous kitten had hooked them out. The lint was then compacted and baled into five-hundred-pound blocks that could be more easily sent by rail to the mills that spun and wove it into sturdy, marketable fabric.

To be ginned, the cotton needed to be dry. So as wagons waited their turn, farmers cast a nervous eye toward the sky, fearful of rain. The necessity of avoiding wet weather pushed the entire ginning processes into a perpetually anxious hurry.

Among the noise, the heat, the hard labor, and the

people, Gidry's thoughts were a worrisome jumble. He kept his eyes upon everything and helped out where he could. He supervised the weighing, and watched for bog-downs on the gin floor. When a belt wore through on the machine level, he hurried down there to be an extra pair of hands in replacing it. And once a bale was compressed and wrapped, he was another strong back to get it down the platform and loaded for the rail cars.

The only other person involved in so many different phases of the process was young Sharpy. Gidry watched the little boy scurrying here and there running errands and saw himself as a youngster. Acquiring the knowledge that he had today by being involved in the work when he was still just a child. Sharpy worked with a happy heart, unlike Gidry as a child. He had not truly minded being with the other men, but he had resented his father for insisting he help. And the older he got, the less obliging he had become.

How grateful Gidry was now that he had been forced to learn so much. He would never have been able to run the gin without his father if he had not spent every summer of his youth learning about its operation.

As the light waned it became necessary to quit for the day. The workers, quiet both with weariness and the pleasant cessation of the gin's infernal noise, lined up at the office door to collect the day's wages. Outside the farmers held their wagons in line as they unhitched the teams. The more affluent would find a night's lodging at the hotel or one of the local boardinghouses. Those who were poorer would camp with their wives and children in the vacant area on the far side of the railroad tracks.

After everyone had left, Gidry totaled up the day's work and noted it all with date and observations, his own handwriting so distinctive from the previous entries written by his father. As he replaced the ledger in the top drawer, he could not fail to notice the stack of dirty postcards. He had acquired more of the tawdry things that morning.

He had intended to stop by the tailor's to get measured for some more suitable town clothes, but as he'd passed by Tavers Shoemaking he recalled how the foul-mouthed little boy scampered barefoot across the hulls and bolls that were strewn throughout the gin.

With the sun almost up and the owner just arriving at the shop, Gidry had quickly purchased what Mr. Tavers assured him would fit a good-sized youngster of about six years of age. Initially he hadn't known how he would get the proud child to accept the gift. But it had fortunately not been much of a problem. The rascal had shown up with a half dozen postcards, more vulgar than the last Gidry had seen, and had gladly *traded* them for the handsome new shoes.

It was not a particularly good idea simply to leave them in the desk. He gazed for a moment at the one on top of the stack. A short-limbed rather plump young woman sat bare-breasted upon a fainting couch. She stared straight into the eye of the camera, the smile on her lips suggesting lascivious satisfaction.

Did Prudence Belmont look at her lover that way?

The thought, coming from out of nowhere, startled Gidry. What on earth was he thinking about? He didn't bother to answer his own question. He needed to get rid of the blasted postcards. They were definitely not something he could keep in his office.

But neither could he take them home with the two women spending so much time there. What if Aunt Hen or Mrs. Butts happened upon them!

He needed to burn them with the rubbish. Out of sight, out of mind. Wasn't that what people said? He would burn the bawdy things and be done with them. But he had no time to watch a fire tonight. Dry weather was good for ginning cotton, but it was dangerous for prairie grass. Not even the tiniest blaze could be taken for granted.

He set the dirty postcards back in the drawer, careful to turn them picture side down, and rose to his feet. It was late and he was tired. He would think of what to do with them tomorrow.

Gidry secured the door, replacing the peg formerly in use with a new spring-shackle padlock of solid bronze. Young Sharpy might well be in charge of guarding the place, but he hoped to keep it shut tight enough that the little fellow's brave heart would not be needed.

He walked up Third Street to the courthouse, where the four gas streetlamps glowed hazy and yellow in the night. He crossed the square to Main Avenue and headed toward his home. Once away from the center of town, the street was so dark that the overhang of trees barely cast a shadow from a sliver of moon. He tried to imagine this street, his street, lighted and safe. Free of places for evil to stalk and hide. In truth, he couldn't quite picture it, the electricity turning night into day.

But as he neared his home, he got a small example. Aunt Hen's house was as brightly lit as a beacon upon the street. The tiny cottage did not boast the wonders of Mr. Edison's lightbulbs, but from the look of the place, every coal oil lamp and candelabra was burning. And the distinctive chatter of a gaggle of ladies could be heard all the way to the corner.

Gidry shrugged. It must be some sort of sewing bee or quilting party, he surmised. But at this time of night?

Chapter 7

A N EMERGENCY meeting of the Ladies' Rose and Garden Society was called at the home of Henrietta Pauling. Aunt Hen was not at home, occupied as usual with the tending of her sick neighbor, a fact that caused no small amount of tittering behind her niece's back. Pru, however, had no time to be overly concerned with her aunt's unconventional behavior. She had felt so strongly about the threat to the town's gardens and gardeners presented by the Commercial Club that she had rashly insisted that waiting until the next day was simply not possible. That, she decided very soon, was likely a mistake. The group virtually never met at night, as that would have been an inconvenience to the husbands of the membership. Pru's unconcern for spouses highlighted her concern.

Having served a huge community meal at midday, Pru made no attempt to provide refreshments beyond tea and coffee. She considered even those bows to convention completely unnecessary. This was no social occasion. This meeting was earnestly serious.

Mavis Hathaway, as parliamentarian, tapped decisively upon her saucer with a demitasse spoon.

"This meeting will please come to order," she said firmly. As the room quieted, she turned to Prudence. "Madam president."

The two women nodded formally to each other as Mavis returned to her seat and Prudence gathered her notes and placed them upon the foldout parlor desk that served as makeshift podium.

"My dear ladies," she addressed the membership, "I do hope that most of you have had opportunity to look over the tracts and leaflets that I have made available to you. I am convinced from our discussions this afternoon and prior to this meeting that we are of one mind on this subject. And the literature agrees with us. We cannot under any circumstances allow the residential lighting project proposed by the gentlemen's Commercial Club to come to pass."

Prudence paused waiting for any words of dissension. There were none. Even Bertha Mae's group of followers could not find anything in the proposal to dislike.

"But how are we to stop it?" Edith Champion asked. "When it was presented on the courthouse square, it was already worked out, the entire negotiation complete."

"Perhaps we can come up with a petition," Miss Ramey suggested.

"A petition!"

Clearly the word scandalized more than one of the ladies.

"Don't be ridiculous, Alice," Mrs. Hathaway scolded. "We are not suffragists. We will not degrade ourselves in that manner."

"We are women," Ethel Peterson agreed. "And as such we have no vote, no voice, no say in how the gentlemen manage the community."

"But we have our opinions," Pru said. "And I believe that ours are equally valid."

"The opinions of females," Bertha Mae pointed out, "are almost as welcome to men as scabies in summer!"

Her words brought a scattering of laughter through the group as well as murmurs of resigned acceptance.

Cloris Tatum nodded solemnly. "As long as the only opposition is ladies, nothing will be done."

"But however will we get the men on our side?" young Mrs. Peterson asked.

"We could refuse to cook so much as a bean or bake as little as a biscuit until they take notice," Mrs. Johnson suggested, with a degree of seriousness.

"Quicker yet would be send them all to bed down on the back porch until they change their way of thinking," Eula Whitstone said, chuckling. "The whole matter would be set to right in less than a week!"

Her words were met with screeches of scandalized humor.

Mavis Hathaway, however, gave her a censuring glance.

"Eula! There are maiden ladies among us."

The older woman refused to accept the scolding.

"Then I suspect they must allow us to take care of it for them," she said.

Pru's cheeks were a vivid scarlet, but she did not allow embarrassment to intimidate her. "I believe that we could lure men to our cause," Pru told them. "Not by shirking our . . . our natural places, but by simply winning them over by reasonable discussion."

The women ceased their giggling to listen.

"Today we were not ready for an intelligent interchange of ideas," Pru told them. "Today we were caught off guard. But I believe that I can formulate our feelings into an interesting presentation. We can ask for another meeting where we can present our side of the story."

"Do you really think that they will listen?"

"I think they will listen," Pru said with certainty. "And I think that some of them will agree."

"And once some of them agree," Cloris finished for her, "we will no longer be merely ladies in opposition to the plan. We will be a group of citizens."

"So we need to have another meeting," Mavis said.

Pru nodded. "Yes, we need to have another meeting as soon as possible. Are we agreed?"

There were nods all around.

"He won't allow us to speak."

The words captured the attention of everyone in the room.

"What on earth do you mean, 'He won't allow us to speak'?" Pru asked, her expression incredulous.

"Mr. Chavis won't allow us to speak," Alice Ramey confided. "Mr. Honnebuzz asked him about it, and he indicated that he was not interested in our opinion."

It was well known that Stanley Honnebuzz was keeping company with Miss Alice. A gentleman of the law, like her father, he seemed the perfect suitor for the young woman. For some reason, and to her father's obvious dismay, Alice continued to hesitate.

"With the gin in operation and the cotton being shipped, Mr. Honnebuzz says that everyone is far too busy to care about having another meeting."

"But this is our community, too," Pru said. "We may not vote, but we have a right to a say."

"Mr. Honnebuzz says that we have no rights at all," Alice told her. "The lighting project is a gift of the

Commercial Club, no taxpayer money is to be spent. When someone gives a gift, you can't put specifications on it, you just have to accept it."

Tiny mouselike Mary Dixon sighed thoughtfully. "And I suppose he is correct in that. It certainly would be rude."

"Rude?" Pru was incredulous. "What is rude is saying that we must take this without even voicing dissent. If someone gave you a rattlesnake for Christmas, would you say 'Thank you very much' and build the reptile a cage next to the chicken coop? I don't think so."

"So what can we do?" Alice asked.

"What we truly need," Bertha Mae announced, "is to speak to Gidry Chavis personally. This is his idea; all the other men in town are going to follow him."

There were murmurs of agreement all around.

Bertha Mae directed her attention to Pru, her expression challenging.

"We all realize, dear Prudence, considering your past heartbreak, that you would undoubtedly prefer to keep your distance from Mr. Chavis," she said.

Pru felt the woman's words as keenly as if she had been kicked in the stomach.

"Although it is the president's obligation to do this," Bertha Mae continued, "allowing the unfortunately personal circumstances, I would be willing to contact Mr. Chavis myself on behalf of the club."

There was a spattering of muted applause.

"It is absolutely unnecessary for you to trouble yourself, Mrs. Corsen," Pru assured her firmly. "I have already reacquainted myself with Mr. Chavis upon two occasions. We were childhood friends."

"Yes." Bertha Mae nodded sagely. "We all remember how you doted upon him."

Pru purposely ignored her.

"We are merely asking Mr. Chavis for a fair hearing and a public meeting. I am perfectly capable of requesting both."

Bertha Mae looked doubtful and deliberately pitying.

"Mr. Chavis has always been a fair and reasonable man," Pru stated with a calmness and strength of purpose she did not feel. "Surely his experience in the West has not changed him overmuch."

Mrs. Corsen and her followers still looked skeptical but adopted an attitude of acceptance.

"We'll try this," Mrs. Whitstone said jokingly. "If it don't work, then we'll send them out to the porch."

The second day of ginning did not go as well as the first. A loose belt flew off the platens, barely missing Edmund Krueger, who could have easily been decapitated as was clearly evidenced by the huge chunk of the building's south wall that was broken open. The near brush with eternity so disconcerted the man that he began to shake so badly that he could not work. Running a man short put extra pressure upon Gidry who now, more than the day before, needed to be everywhere at all times.

Stanley Honnebuzz stopped by to see him twice to warn him that a group of ladies was all het up over the lighting project, but he put the man off both times because he was too busy.

They still managed to gin twenty-seven bales. But at the end of the day, when Gidry sat once more at his ledger, he was bone-tired, drenched with sweat, and not a little bit cranky.

An hour later, cleaned up, well fed, and relaxed, he

wondered aloud at his decision as he sat in the chair at his father's bedside.

"Honnebuzz said that it's best not to give the opposition an even chance," Gidry explained. "He said that allowing the ladies a forum to air their objections is the same as legitimizing their concerns."

Gidry, his brow furrowed, looked longingly into the expressive face of his father, wishing the old man could advise him.

"I'm sure he probably knows what he's talking about," Gidry said. "Still it seems very high-handed to me not to allow the ladies to speak their piece."

There was a light knock at the door, and Aunt Hen entered without preamble carrying an armful of linens and a pitcher of hot water.

Politely, Gidry rose to his feet.

"I thought you had surely gone on home," Gidry said to her.

The older woman shook her head. "I haven't changed the bedsheets," she said. "I can't do it by myself, and today Mrs. Butts was simply not at her best and couldn't help me."

"I'm not too adept at bed making, ma'am," Gidry admitted. "I will do what I can."

"Actually, if you could just lift him off the bed and into that chair," she said. "Mrs. Butts and I usually roll him from side to side, but I believe that you could probably move him. And he might enjoy sitting up for a few minutes."

Gidry was momentarily taken aback. He could not imagine that he would be strong enough to lift his large, powerful father. But Aunt Hen's rather generous faith in him kept him from saying so.

As she pulled down the covers, Gidry saw that his father's striped flannel nightshirt hung upon him as if a half dozen sizes too large. Determinedly, he put one arm around the lower part of his father's shoulders and the other beneath his knees. Taking a deep breath, he hefted his father into his arms. To his complete astonishment, Gidry was able to lift him easily.

"My God! He doesn't weigh anything!" he exclaimed.

"No," Aunt Hen said quietly. "No he does not."

Gidry held his father in his arms for a long moment. It was hard for him to get his mind around it. It was hard for him to comprehend. His father, who had so many years ago held him and carried him and had been his strength, now lay in his arms, no more weighty than a child himself. The silence in the room lingered.

Gidry sat his father in the chair at the side of the bed. He looked better sitting somehow. He was gaunt and pale, but if Gidry ignored that, it was as if the man was his strong, powerful father once more.

"Get the basin and a rag," Aunt Hen directed. "Mrs. Butts usually washes and shaves him, to spare my modesty, of course. Perhaps you will do a better job than she does."

Gidry had never washed another human being in his life. But gamely he set himself to the task. Beneath the nightshirt, the evidence of his father's decline was even more pronounced. His ribs showed as distinctly as the pickets of a fence. His arms and legs lay like wasted sticks at his sides. Gidry felt the sting of tears come to his eyes and gritted his teeth against them.

"Were you telling your father more stories of the Wild West?" Aunt Hen asked.

Gidry was grateful for the distraction.

"Not yet," he answered. "I was telling him about the day's work at the gin and relaying a discussion I had with Stanley Honnebuzz about the electric-lighting project."

Aunt Hen had stripped the bed and shook the tick thoroughly before turning it over and replacing it on the spring mattress.

"Electric lighting all over town," she shook her head. "It's hard even to imagine."

"Yes, it is," Gidry agreed.

The woman was thoughtful for a long moment and then a soft, sweet smile brightened her face as if a pleasant thought had pulled at her heart.

"Peer, do you remember that perfect pumpkin year?" she asked with a faraway chuckle.

The question was not directed at Gidry, so he made no comment. Aunt Hen apparently required no answer.

"There were flowered vines in every corn row in the county. The weather was good. Not too rainy, not too warm and plenty of sunshine. By the fall, we had so many of those great big pumpkins we couldn't have stored them all for winter if we'd emptied out every barn."

She laughed lightly as she snapped the bedsheet open with a firm jerk and spread it upon the mattress.

"That was something, wasn't it, Peer? We ate pumpkin cookies, pumpkin bread, pumpkin cakes, pumpkin pudding. There was roast pumpkin, pumpkin fritters, pumpkin soup, even pumpkin butter. But we still couldn't eat them all up," she said.

Gidry ran the damp soapy cloth along his father's emaciated chest and looked up into the old man eyes. His father was looking at Henrietta.

"Finally toward the end of the season when not a soul in town could bear the taste of pumpkin for one more meal we began feeding the seedcores to the hogs and making jack-o'-lanterns."

Aunt Hen was smiling to herself, evidently lost in thought for long moments before she continued. "Those jack-o'-lanterns really lit up the town," she said. "Every post and porch and pillar sported some garish-looking face and a bright orange glow."

She carefully tucked the corners of the sheet under the mattress.

"And it was just the kind of excuse that young people needed to roam around at nightfall."

She shook her head. "You were tall as a tree in long pants and I already with my hair up, but we ran up and down the streets like two children let loose at the fair," she said.

"We met friends and made up stories and laughed and giggled our fool heads off. And you held my hand all night long," she said with a soft, sweet sigh. "You held my hand all night long."

Gidry cleared his throat.

"It must have been beautiful," he said.

Aunt Hen glanced over at him, as if just remembering that he was there.

"Yes, it was pretty," she agreed. "The town all lit up like that, it was really pretty. And I suppose you could say it was romantic, too. More than one young couple made a hasty trip to the altar that winter."

Gidry felt uncomfortable and in the way. He turned his attention to his father's bath and hurried to finish. He got him into a clean nightshirt.

"Would you like to stay in the chair for a while, Papa?" he asked.

His father's neck and jaw were trembling as if the weight of his head was almost more than he could manage to support.

"You'd best put him back to bed," Aunt Hen said quietly. "It saps all of his strength to sit up."

Gidry nodded and tenderly laid his father back in the fresh, sweet-smelling bed.

Aunt Hen pulled the coverlet up over him and tucked it carefully around his shoulders. Gidry noticed, perhaps for the first time, how the old woman's care of him was as tender as it was efficient.

She looked up into Gidry's eyes. He saw no embarrassment there, but there was wariness. There were a million questions he wanted to ask. There were a thousand things that he wanted to know. And clearly the jut of her chin spoke silently that none of them were any of his concern.

"Is that what your electric lighting is going to be like?" she asked.

"What?"

"The electric lighting," Aunt Hen repeated. "Is it going to be as pretty as having a town full of jack-o'-lanterns?"

Chapter 8

SHE SHOULD speak to Gidry immediately, Pru decided bright and early the next morning. She had lain awake most of the night, anxious about seeing him again. Her fine, brave words in front of the club ladies were all good and well, but in all honesty she would as cheerfully walk over cactus barefoot as face Gidry Chavis.

She dressed in her Sunday best, determined to make a good impression. The silver-gray silk suit was stern and serious enough for a discussion of business. The trim-cut jacket and wide sleeves made her appear formidably buxom and tiny-waisted. This morning, however, she regretted the ruffled shrimp pink blouse. She had thought it sheer beauty when she'd sewn it. Now, however, it appeared much too pretty for her severe state of mind.

Gidry had not seen her except in her gardening clothes. At the town meeting, when she was finally dressed fit for company, he hadn't noticed her. It was important for him to see her well dressed. But she didn't want him to think that she was dressing up for him. Her heart was no longer on her sleeve. She wouldn't give the man the satisfaction of believing that she still had feelings for him.

She was ready to go just after breakfast, but decided that it was best to wait and catch him during the mid-day luncheon pause. The gin was already bellowing out its noisy business. Pru had no desire to carry on a discussion within the deafening noise of it in oper-ation. It would be difficult enough to talk with him at all. It would be impossible to scream at him over the roar of machinery.

Determined to wait, Pru seated herself primly in Aunt Hen's front parlor. It was something she'd grown accustomed to doing back in her girlhood days of loving him. She had waited for him to come sit on her porch. She had waited for him to walk her to church. She had waited for him to notice that she was now quite grown-up and desperately in love with him. Deeply enough in love to want more than hand-holding and sweet words: she had wanted his kisses, his touch. He had not noticed. At least not until that night, that last incredible, unfath-omable night when he had held her in his arms, whispered words of desire, and made her feel for once truly like his woman.

Pru closed her eyes, savoring the memory for a long moment. It was all she would ever have of him. That one wicked, star-crossed night was all she would ever have. It simply could not be enough.

Her eyes flew open at the direction of her thoughts. No. Absolutely not. She would not allow herself to start thinking that way, wishing for those things. She was no longer in love with Gidry Chavis and she re-fused to allow herself ever to be so again. Theirs had been a perfect, tender love. And he had torn it to shreds, ruined it for all time. She would never, could never care that much for anyone again.

She rose to her feet. She could wait no longer. Noise or no noise, she would see him now and get it done. Like ripping a bandage from a wound, the pain would be momentarily searing but quickly over.

Pru gave herself one last examination of her appearance in front of the looking glass. She was handsome, she assured herself, and businesslike. The ruffled bodice was a bit frilly, but it rounded her silhouette nicely and she couldn't quite regret it. She was heavily corseted, an unusual circumstance for her. Being a lady of the outdoors generally, and one who was past the first blush specifically, she saved extravagant underpinnings for Sunday only. But facing Gidry Chavis again required the most forbidding corset a woman could muster. Like a soldier fitting himself for battle, she donned her flat straw bonnet with the braid trim, satin roses, and the matching shrimp pink ribbon.

"You'll do," she assured her reflection in the mirror.

She gathered up her papers and her parasol and hurried purposefully through town. She was certain that the Rose and Garden Society would be allowed to present their case once she had voiced their concerns to Gidry. He had always been a fair and reasonable man. And he had, by his own admission, always listened to her advice.

He had not loved her and had ruined their romance. In all conscience, a man could not be blamed for that. When a woman took so little care of her heart she must expect that it would get broken.

She walked with deliberate sedateness down the tree-lined boulevard that was upper Main Avenue into the business district. Except for the noise and a slightly increased pace of business, things appeared very normal. People hurried to and fro. Farmers were buying, merchants were selling. Old men sat on benches and watched the world go by them. Chavistown was exactly what it should be, safe and familiar.

As she neared the area of the railroad tracks, the roar of the machinery was made more untenable by the flurry of activity and hordes of people, all forced to yell to make themselves heard. Farmers' wagons loaded with raw cotton were queued up in lines that snaked this way and that along the streets and across the open ground around the gin.

She smiled and waved at people as she passed. Having lived in Chavistown all her life, she had at least a nodding acquaintance with practically every man, woman, and child in the county.

One face that caught her attention was very familiar. Sharpy Kilroy came running out the door to give the *next haul* signal to the weigh master. The scales dropped beneath an overhang between the gin itself and the seed house. The tonnage of the heavily loaded wagon had already been noted. When it was empty, it would be weighed again and the difference noted as the amount of cotton. Pru watched as the man lowered the flue into the back of the wagon. A huge fan inside began sucking up the light, white cotton bolls.

Pru watched the procedure for several minutes with as much curiosity as the little boy.

He turned finally and caught sight of her. He waved joyously and headed in her direction at a boyish lope. He was so proud of his new job. Last evening he'd talked incessantly about it, hardly even pausing to give himself a chance to draw breath. He'd also talked about his new hero, Mr. Gidry Chavis. There was justice there, she thought. Some sort of sweet justice. She wondered briefly once again if she should say something. But no, it was none of her concern. Gidry Chavis and his life were none of her concern.

But somehow the little boy who was now running toward her grinning ear to ear, delighted to see her, had wormed his dark-haired, wide-eyed, devilish little self into her heart.

"Milton, I hope you are not working too hard," she called out to him.

"What?" he hollered back at her.

They were standing only paces apart, but the noise level was excruciating.

"I hope you are not working too hard," she tried again a little more loudly.

"What are you doing here?" he asked.

"I need to speak with Mr. Chavis," she answered.

"What?"

"*I need to speak with Mr. Chavis.*"

Pru pointed meaningfully at the gin.

The little boy nodded eagerly and motioned for her to follow him.

Although the gin was only two stories high, it was the largest building in town, bigger in area than the new courthouse that had four stories as well as a basement.

He led her through the small doorway near the end of the building. Coming from the bright morning sunshine outside, she was momentarily blinded within the dim interior. The noise was almost unbearable, and the lint-filled air burned her eyes and tickled her nose.

Young Sharpy tugged on her hand and as her eyes adjusted to the darkness, she allowed him to direct her to a very narrow set of stairs, nearly hidden within the churning, cranking, screaming machinery. The steps were barely twelve inches in width and there was no handrail, giving Pru the sensation of ascending a ladder.

She made her way tentatively as the little boy scrambled up with childish self-assurance. At the top of the stairs was a low-framed door which Sharpy opened for her with such good manners, that she nodded at him approvingly.

The gin office was empty. Somehow she had expected Gidry to be sitting here waiting, but apparently there were many things for him to do that required more than sitting alone in a tiny and sparsely furnished room. The high stool at the ledger desk was awkward for a lady in skirts, so Pru was forced to remain standing. She hoped that she would not have to do so for very long.

She surveyed the room curiously and then turned to see Sharpy still behind her. He had closed the door, but stood waiting for her directions.

"Go get Mr. Chavis," she told him.

"What?"

"Go get Mr. Chavis."

"What did you say?"

"Go . . ."

She should have waited. The noise was too intense for her even to give orders. It would be absolutely impossible to have any kind of meaningful discussion with Gidry.

She should just turn around and go home. But, of course, he would hear that she had come to see him.

She had already worked up the courage and did not want to lose the initiative.

She would write him a note, she decided. She would simply request an opportunity to speak to him away from heat and noise of the gin. Sharpy could deliver it right into his hand. Yes, that was the perfect solution, she would write him a note.

The pen and ink were atop the ledger desk in plain sight. A piece of paper was not so easily obtainable, however. She did momentarily consider tearing out a corner of a blank accounting page, but thought the better of what might be construed as damaging the business records.

She opened the top drawer of the desk, hoping to locate just a small piece of scratch paper, but no luck. There were, however, a number of stacked postcards tucked into the corner. Grain and seed companies often advertised their products on cards such as these, which was undoubtedly why they were there. One of them would work perfectly well as a note card, Pru decided. And selected the one on top.

She didn't bother to glance at the opposite side, her concern was only on what she should write. It was important that her words be chosen with care. Even the salutation was difficult. To address him as Gidry was entirely too familiar. Writing *Mr. Chavis* was perfectly correct, but seemed so awkward. They had known each other since childhood. It felt almost insincere to put such a formal distance between them.

Finally she settled upon *Sir* as most appropriate and dipped the pen in ink and began to write with her best penmanship.

There was no need to discuss specifics in such a small missive. She would merely indicate an urgency to speak with him away from the noise and heat and bad air of the gin.

She glanced down at what she had written, satisfied. It said exactly and directly what she wanted and there were no misspellings or grammatical errors. It would do very well, she was certain. Neatly she signed herself as Miss Prudence Belmont. And carefully blotted it with the green felt-covered block.

She turned to give the note to Sharpy for delivery. The little boy stood still as a stone, staring in horrified fascination.

"Milton?" she asked curiously

He made no reply but continued to eye the note in her hand ominously. His strange behavior prompted her to glance down at what she held. It was only a postcard, a small three-by-five postcard. What on earth could cause the young boy to be so mesmerized.

It was at that moment, for some unknown reason, Pru turned it finally in her hand to see what was upon the back of it. A buxom female stood stark naked in her boudoir, facing a large, curved mirror. She had one hand upraised and buried in her upswept hair. Grinning coyly, her only concession to modesty was the one dainty palm that covered the apex of her thighs.

Prudence gave a startled cry of alarm. Never in her life had she seen such a thing, never had she imagined that a woman would pose for such a photograph.

She glanced down at the little boy beside her. Clearly he had known what the postcards were. And he had known that they were lewd and vulgar, else he would not have looked so guilty.

Unexpectedly Sharpy grabbed the postcard out of her hand and looked to be making a run for it. Prudence had other ideas. She caught him easily as he made it to the doorway. The postcard slipped out of his grasp, but she didn't give it a thought. All of her concerns was for the sweet, young, impressionable child.

"Come with me, young man," Pru said decisively, grabbing the child's arm and half-leading, half-dragging him out the door and down the stairs. "You will not work one more moment in a place such as this."

"What?" he called out to her unable to hear her words above the noise surrounding them.

She didn't bother to answer. Milton Kilroy was leaving this male den of iniquity, and she vowed fervently that he would never return here again.

The third day had gone better than the first two, Gidry decided. There were no major breakdowns and, thankfully, no injuries, not even so much as a cut or bruise. All the men reported to work, however young Sharpy Kilroy had inexplicably disappeared. No one noticed his leaving, but he was nowhere to be found by midmorning, and all of them had to make up the difference very inefficiently by running to and fro themselves. Gidry was genuinely surprised at the boy's absence. He considered himself good judge of character, and had anyone asked he would have bet money that the young ne'er-do-well was as dependable as sunrise.

Gidry walked through the gin, the evening quiet unappreciated as the echo of the stilled machinery continued to ring loudly in his ears. Stanley Honnebuzz had stopped by to see him. The ladies of the Rose and Garden Society had apparently held a special meeting last night about the lighting project and wanted to present their case in opposition at a public meeting.

The man had assured him that he had nothing with which to concern himself.

"I nipped that in the bud," he'd told Gidry proudly.

Gidry couldn't imagine what the ladies had to protest about. Certainly deterring crime in town would be a benefit to persons of both genders. It was probably some silliness, Honnebuzz told him. The ladies probably feared that artificial light could allow men to see through their window shades or some other such nonsense.

He wished he could discuss it with Pru. Being such an avid gardener, she was undoubtedly involved with the group. But Pru appeared determined now to keep him at a distance. Perhaps Aunt Hen was a better choice. She was an eminently sensible woman, much like her niece. Thoughtful and contemplative. Not at all the type of woman Stanley Honnebuzz would have described as prone to hysterics.

His thoughts lingered back to his father's sickroom. Aunt Hen's tender care and her quiet devotion to his father were both very precious and very confusing to him.

Had his father and Aunt Hen . . . no, it was foolishness even to think such a thing. They were friends, longtime friends. His father had never . . . had his father ever?

It was difficult to imagine that a man as robust and healthy as his father had remained faithful to an absent wife for thirty years. Of course, a son could never truly know a father's life, but there had never been any evidence of any female consort. There was never any indication of any illicit liaison.

Why had his father been so faithful in his vows?

Surely it must only have been honor. There were no residual feelings between Peer and Gidry's mother. Clearly, there was nothing at all. In truth the only thing his parents seem to have in common, besides himself, was their complete disinterest in each other. As a child Gidry had often asked questions about his mother. Peer had not seemed to care. As an angry young man, he attempted to taunt his father by writing frequent letters to the woman who had given him birth. He had hoped to stir Peer's wrath, but the older man would not be baited. The level of contact his son wished to have with his mother was completely up to Gidry, his father had declared. It was clear that Peer was not only unconcerned but uninterested.

Other men with unhappy marriages were frequently rumored to seek out the company of women with questionable reputations living on the edges of the respectable community or even those wilder females plying their trade in the saloons and dance halls along the railroad tracks.

Not one whisper of suspicion had ever been leveled at Peer Chavis. And Gidry had had his ear to the ground, listening. His father's seeming near perfection in morals had in many ways been the catalyst for Gidry's youthful wickedness. If his father was above base scandal, Gidry had been determined to revel in it.

But perhaps his father had not been as perfect as Gidry had believed. Perhaps he had been involved with a woman no one would have thought to suspect.

Aunt Hen?

Gidry gave the idea long, thoughtful consideration, then discarded it. His father might have been susceptible to a fall from grace, but Henrietta Pauling was incapable of the duplicity necessary to carry on a long-term affair in secret.

No, Gidry was certain that when they reminisced together it was as old friends recalling things long past. If they had ever loved, it was long ago in their youth, a love without doubt uncomplicated and unconsummated.

He reached the narrow stairway to his office, tired and ready to shore up the books for the night and head for home. It was strange how the work physically drained him, yet invigorated his soul. His life as a cowboy had been outside in the elements unencumbered by sturdy walls and enclosed rooms. He had thought he loved that about it, but realized now that he loved this feeling of accomplishment even more.

He was smiling to himself when in the dim light, he caught sight of something that was not supposed to be there. What appeared to be a small card lay on the lint-dusted floor beneath his feet. One of the men must have dropped it, he decided as he leaned over to pick it up. They all passed this direction on the way to the door. It undoubtedly slipped out of a bib pocket or a hatband.

It was one of those dirty picture postcards, Gidry realized immediately. He hoped young Sharpy had kept his word and wasn't selling them anymore. Of course, there was no telling how many the little smut peddler had sold in the past.

Gidry started up the stairs, thinking that he would put this one with the rest of the tawdry collection and get rid of the whole stash. He had taken one step up the stairs when he noticed the writing on the back. He stopped still, staring at it in disbelief as he read the words

> *Sir,*
>
> *I am in urgent need of a moment alone with you. As soon as is convenient, please come to me in the quiet privacy of my home.*
>
> *Miss Prudence Belmont*

Gidry's mouth dropped open. He turned the postcard over once more and glimpsed again the naked female smiling so seductively. What man receiving such an invitation could doubt its meaning? Gidry certainly didn't. Some man, some man in his employ, had received this. He had dropped it accidentally as he was leaving. Most likely he was in such a hurry to claim his prize that he was incautious. Even now he might be sated and satisfied, lying spent between her soft white thighs.

Gidry set his jaw tightly, a surge of jealous anger sweeping through him.

"Damnation!" he cursed aloud.

Knowing she was seeing a man on the sly was one thing. Holding in his own hand the suggestive evidence of their illicit affair was quite another. Gidry sat down on the narrow stairs, reading again the words that were intended only for the lecherous eye of her lover.

Urgent need. Quiet privacy.

She was so bold. It was difficult to imagine. Of course she was very bold and well-spoken in general. But a woman like Prudence, he had always been sure, would be submissive and quiet beneath the bedsheets. She had been so shy and sweet. On that long-ago night when they had spooned in the garden, she had been virginal and modest. But she had allowed his touch and had been aroused by it. He'd always felt so guilty about the liberties that he'd taken with her. Obviously she was no longer so affronted by the baser needs of humankind.

He shook his head incredulously.

It was one of the men who worked with him. Somehow that made it worse. A faceless lover whom she met in secret was troublesome. But a man that he knew personally. Gidry could hardly fathom it.

One by one he mentally went down the list of the men working at the gin.

Too old, he thought of one.

Too young, another.

Devoted to his wife.

Ruled by his mother.

Too ugly.

Too clumsy.

Too mean.

There was not a man among them, Gidry decided, who was in the farthest stretch of the imagination worthy of Prudence Belmont.

He glanced down at the postcard again. The naughty Nellie smiled up at him. What was he thinking, the men were not good enough for her? What kind of woman purposefully chooses to involve herself in secret love affairs when she should rightly be raising children and tending a husband?

She should have married years ago.

She should have fallen in love and wed when she was young.

She had fallen in love. She'd fallen in love with him.

Then she should have married him!

Gidry's brow furrowed. No that was not it. He hadn't wanted her to marry him.

But she should have anyway!

He was so angry. His thoughts so confused.

He slammed his fist against the wall in frustration. "Ow!" he bellowed. He shook his hand, wincing. He examined the injured knuckles and shook his head.

He didn't understand his feelings. He didn't understand any of it. But he didn't like it. He didn't like it one bit.

Chapter 9

"I¹T'S MY job, ma'am," Sharpy Kilroy explained for at least the dozenth time. "It's my job. I told him I do it, and I got to keep my word."

"Absolutely not," Pru replied. "I told you *no*, young man, and that is the end of it."

The two were standing in the milk shed, the last rays of the afternoon sun slanting through the doorway. She had half led, half dragged the resisting child from the gin back to her home. Though much sheltered in her lifetime, Prudence was not unaware of the baseness and crudity that existed in the world. She understood that no one could be protected from these evils indefinitely, but believed that children should remain children as long as possible. The little boy beside her had perhaps never truly been a child.

"Where on earth do you get all of these things?" she asked, attempting to make order out of the chaos of the room. "And why do you keep them."

She held up a well-worn beaded cinch strap. It was far too old and flimsy to gird adequately any saddle horse.

Sharpy jerked it out of her hand.

"It's pretty, ma'am," he said defensively. "And it's mine."

Prudence shook her head without understanding. How could one little boy with nothing and no one of his own manage to accumulate so much in such a short time? Sharpy had been living in Aunt Hen's milk shed for only a few months, but he had dragged in a wagonload of worthless possessions in that time.

"I'm not about to take them away from you, Milton," she assured him. "I just don't know how you'll manage to have room for everything."

The tiny shed would have been adequately roomy for the narrow cot, small table, and two chairs that Pru had provided. It was extremely overcrowded, with the piles upon piles of whatnots, whatsits, and whatfors that the little boy had acquired wherever. In his own way, he had made the lonely, miserable milk shed his home, and Prudence couldn't fault him for it. Young Sharpy needed a home.

One frosty morning last winter she'd found the little boy sleeping upon her garden bench wrapped only in a worn saddle blanket. Up until that moment she'd never given one thought to the orphaned child of Mabel Merriman and Befuddle Kilroy. She'd assumed, as she supposed the rest of the town did also, that somebody was taking care of him. Milton Kilroy was taking care of himself.

"Whose portrait is this?" she asked, holding up a framed photogram.

"It's my father," the little boy answered, snatching it away from her.

Pru looked at the child, her brow furrowing in worry.

"Milton, that is not your father," she told him firmly.

Sharpy shrugged. "It might be," he answered. "I told you that my mama said Befuddle Kilroy wasn't my real papa. Old Mr. Chavis just arranged for him to marry Mama so I'd have a name."

"Yes."

"So this fellow might be my real father," Sharpy said. "I think he kind of looks like me, don't you think?"

Pru's heart was breaking.

"Not at all," she told him. "You are much more handsome than this fellow. You have a very strong jaw and a noble brow."

Her words of praise straightened his young shoulders proudly.

"Of course some boys are better-looking than their papas," he pointed out.

"Does it mean so much to you, Milton?" she asked. "Does it mean so much to know who your father might have been?"

"Naw, I don't give a da—I mean I don't care for nothing," the boy insisted with plucky self-assurance that wasn't totally genuine. "I just pretend sometimes. I know *pretend* is a baby game, but I play it once in a while, for fun."

Pru nodded quietly.

"Miss Prudence," the boy interjected quietly, "I don't want to give up my job at the gin."

"Milton, it is not a nice place for a young boy to work," she said.

"But it's the place where I got work," he answered.

"You can find some other job," she told him. "I'll speak to Reverend Hathaway. Perhaps he knows of some other employment."

"I don't wanna work for Reverend Hathaway," Sharpy insisted. "I like Mr. Chavis."

Prudence wasn't surprised. Gidry was the kind of man other men looked up to. It was perfectly natural for him to be the object of a little boy's hero worship, especially so for this little boy.

"Milton, I cannot allow it," she said.

Sharpy's mouth firmed into one stubborn line.

"Miss Prudence, I thank you for all that you've done for me," he told her. "You give me my own place to sleep and food to eat. And I ain't complained much about having to wash nearly every day, or saying prayers or sitting through the reading and writing lessons."

His tone expressed a gravity far beyond his years.

"But Miss Pru, I ain't giving up my job. It's a da—a darn good job and I like doing it. If that means I got to clear out of here, well then, I'd best be about it."

"Milton, where on earth would you go?" she asked.

He didn't have an answer, but it didn't seem to worry him much.

"A steady job is harder to get than a place to sleep," he told her. "Especially when a fellow ain't as big as the rest of the men looking for work."

Pru chose her words carefully, not wanting to hurt his pride, but certain that she was right. "Milton, you are not a man yet, you're still a little boy, and the gin is not a fit environment for you."

"What do you mean by that?" he asked. "What's fifth-a-fire-ment?"

Pru brushed a loving hand across his brow.

"A fit environment is a good place for a boy to spend his time. Working alongside grown men in the gin, there is just no telling the kind of unwelcome influence to which you might be exposed," she explained.

Sharpy was momentarily thoughtful.

"You're talking about the po-knock-rafee, aren't you?" he said.

Pru's eyes widened. "Where on earth did you ever hear such a word."

"From Mr. Chavis," he answered. "That's what he calls them dirty postcards."

"My God, he'd showed them to you?" She was incredulous.

"Well, not exactly," he replied.

"You knew they were there, didn't you?" she said. "You'd seen them before."

"Well, yes ma'am," he answered. "Truth is, I . . ."

"I can't . . . I can't believe my ears."

"I ain't lying, ma'am," Sharpy assured her. "It was really all my fault, ma'am."

"Oh my heavens, this is far worse than I had imagined," she said. "How could he do such a thing? How could he pollute the innocent young mind of a child, any child, especially . . ."

Her voice trailed off, her expression both angry and concerned.

Sharpy's brow furrowed, and his chest puffed out defensively.

"He didn't pole-luke my mind, ma'am," Sharpy declared. "My mind works just as good as it ever did."

"I know that, Milton," she assured him gently. "But Mr. Chavis should have never let you . . . well you simply should have been protected from his tawdry vices."

"There ain't no tar devices in the gin, Miss Prudence," Sharpy assured her. "Everything works with belts and pulleys."

Pru opened her mouth to explain, then decided not to bother.

"I just think, Milton, for your own good, I should try to find you some work elsewhere."

"I don't want other work," the boy stated firmly. "I'm thinking that I should find some other place to stay."

"What?"

"I know that you said I could stay here in your aunt's milk shed, that you would sleep better knowing there was a man about the place," he continued. "But now you are butting into my business, ma'am. You're saying I can't keep my job. Well, I'm going to keep it, ma'am. And if that means I can't stay here, then . . . then let me clear my things out."

"Milton! Don't be silly," she said. "I don't want you to leave. I've . . . well, I've grown very fond of you. More than fond of you. I care about you very much. You are to me like, well, like a little brother."

Her words seemed to please him, but he was adamant. "I've lived under a tree before," he told her. "I can do it again if I have to."

"I can't let you do that," she said.

"I don't think you can stop me, ma'am."

"But don't you see, the gin is no place for impressionable little boys," she said.

"I ain't so end-pressed no-bull," he answered. "And I like Mr. Chavis. I liked the old man, too. He treated me good. He helped me out. He talked to me about my mama. It was like he cared what happened to me. But the new Mr. Chavis, he likes me. I mean . . . well, he talks to me like I was a friend or a relative or something. Me, Sharpy Kilroy, I'm his friend. I ain't about to let him down."

Pru stood gazing down at the defiant little face before her. Sharpy liked Gidry. He wanted to be around him. He wanted to be like him. He wanted to be a friend or relative to him. She glanced at the framed photogram she still held in her hand. The vague shadowy image caught on light-sensitive paper stared back at her. He was a stranger. A stranger that the child pretended was his father. Gidry Chavis was no stranger. Didn't this innocent child deserve his chance to be close him, despite all?

"Sharpy," she said, "I will find a way for you to be close to Mr. Chavis. I will find a way for you to see him and talk to him. But I care too much about you to allow you to continue to work at the gin."

The child's brow furrowed. Pru felt his confusion. He didn't want to lose the safety and security of the simple place he called home. But he was unused to living within the restrictions of people who knew what was best for him.

"I won't work at the gin," he said finally, "if you promise that I can still see and talk to Mr. Chavis."

"I promise that you can," Pru said. "But stay away from . . . from sordid talk and from . . . from all forms of pornography."

"Yes, ma'am," he agreed eagerly. "I don't care much for it nohow."

"That's good," she said.

"And Mr. Chavis," Sharpy added. "He don't look at them much neither."

"Milton, I don't think . . ."

"I heard folks saying that he used to be your beau," Sharpy informed her.

Pru froze at his words. She hated being the object of gossip. And being part of six-year-old gossip was the worst.

"That was a long time ago," she said simply.

"Maybe he can be your beau again," Sharpy suggested. "He ain't married at all, and I like him a lot better than that old mealy-mouthed Honnebuzz."

"Milton, you shouldn't talk that way about people," she said. "And Mr. Chavis will not ever be my . . . my beau again."

"But there ain't no reason why," the child pointed out.

"There are plenty of reasons that you are far too young to understand," Pru said.

"I know you're kind of old, ma'am, but you don't need to worry," Sharpy assured her. "I think you're prettier than all them gals in the po-knock-rafee."

Prudence gasped.

"It's true, ma'am, I ain't just saying that cause you've been nice to me neither."

Pru held on to her composure.

"Milton, you must never, never compare ladies with the . . . females portrayed in those postcards," she explained patiently. "Ladies would never do that sort of thing."

His brow furrowed curiously.

"They was just getting dressed and taking a bath and stuff," Sharpy pointed out. "Maybe you didn't see them up close, ma'am. Those weren't paintings, those were picture postcards of real ladies. They just didn't have no clothes on."

"Milton!" Her cheeks were flaming with embarrassment. "There are certain things that are simply not spoken of," she told him sternly. "You must promise me that you will never, ever speak of those postcards again."

"All right, ma'am," he said.

"I have your promise?"

"I promise," he said.

"Very well," she said. "Now we won't mention it ever again."

He seemed to be agreeable.

"Since you no longer work at the gin," Pru said, "I will just simply have to employ you myself. I have an infinite number of jobs that you can do."

"That's my favorite kind, ma'am," Sharpy assured her. "The in-fun-et jobs."

Pru smiled warmly at him and ran a loving hand through his tousled hair.

"Let's begin by getting this place cleaned and straightened. If you are going to keep all these things, you at the very least must establish some sort of order about it."

Gidry awakened at dawn, tired and cranky. He'd spent most of the long night watching Aunt Hen's garden from the darkened window of his father's room. He had listened to the measured even breathing of the older man behind him and thought about the woman in the small house across the lawn.

They had been in there much of the early evening. She and her secret lover had been alone together in the tiny milk shed. The flickering light visible only faintly through the doorframe and boarded window indicated they were moving around a good deal. Perhaps they were pacing, worrying. Maybe he realized that he'd dropped her wicked invitation; maybe they were anxious about who might see it and if they were to be found out.

He hoped they were pacing. Other activities that might have caused the light to flicker did not bear contemplation. Perhaps the secret lover was having his way with Pru upon the table. Or against the wall. Or both. Fornication could cause a light to flicker. He hoped they were pacing.

Gidry had come home to supper determined to put

the thoughts that plagued him completely out of his mind. He'd taken his dinner with Peer, speaking about the workday past and the one to come, as if Peer Chavis were still his boss, as if the gin were still his operation. Afterward he'd told his father more wild rollicking cowboy tales, one after another until at last, exhausted, the old man had slept. He'd wanted to entertain and cheer Peer Chavis, but more than that, he'd wanted to conceal his own uneasy thoughts.

This morning, they were not much better. But at least it was daylight. There was work to be done and a purpose to be fulfilled. It was foolish for Gidry to allow such matters as the love affair of the woman next door to concern him. What was he? Some old gossip?

If Prudence Belmont wanted to engage in some sordid, morally imprudent romance with what was undoubtedly another woman's husband, it was no concern of his own. He certainly didn't want her.

Well, perhaps he did *want* her, but only in the very general, very physical way that any man wants a woman when he's not had one in a while. She was not special to him in any way. No, that wasn't true, she certainly was special. But not in that way. Or maybe it was in that way. Gidry could no longer figure it out. In fact, he'd decided, during his long sleepless night, that he didn't understand any of it.

She was a hypocrite, presenting herself to the people of Chavistown, even to him, as a dull, unattractive spinster. When in fact she was a sinful seductress luring weak men into her moonlit milk shed to break their marriage vows. That couldn't be Pru! But it was; he was certain that it was. Oh, how a person could change in a few years. And she had obviously changed for the worse.

It was these angry thoughts that were fresh upon his mind as he left his house in the morning and unexpectedly met up with her as she stood apparently waiting for him to pass her front gate.

"Mr. Chavis, could I please have a word with you?" she asked politely.

Morning glories bloomed up the arched gate and all along the fence, framing her in a vision of fresh-scrubbed tidiness and homey warmth. It was infuriating. The woman had spent an entire evening in heaven-knows-what lascivious sexual pleasures and stood before him now just after dawn, prim, proper and apparently rested.

It infuriated him.

"I'm in a hurry," Gidry answered coolly.

"It will only take a moment," she insisted. "And it is of the utmost urgency."

He did stop, however reluctantly, but made no attempt to hide his annoyance.

"Make it quick," he insisted. "I've got cotton waiting."

It was evident from the stern way she drew up her mouth that she did not appreciate his brusque manner. She raised her chin slightly in challenge.

"The Ladies' Rose and Garden Society met on Thursday and . . ."

"Yes, I know all about your little meeting," he interrupted. "In fact, I passed by on my way home from work. The house was lit up like Christmastime, and you could hear the chatter all the way to the street."

"I'm sure the discussions of the gentlemen of the Commercial Club can get a little loud as well," she said.

"Yes, of course," he agreed. "But men are brash and

noisy by nature. It's my understanding that ladies are to be quiet and demure."

"You obviously don't have a close enough association with *ladies*!" she told him sharply.

He raised an eyebrow and gave her a long glance from the tip of her toes to the top of her head.

"I'm very surprised that you would say that, Miss Belmont," he answered snidely. "My association with you was almost close enough to be scandalous."

That statement took the color out of her cheeks. He watched her flounder momentarily for some sort of appropriate reply.

Gidry was surprised at himself and sorry for his words. He should never have brought up the past. There was too much there and in it, he was all in the wrong. He regretted his harsh words and knew he should apologize, but he still felt such anger. He felt such inexplicable, irrational anger.

"I . . . I do not believe, Mr. Chavis," she retorted bravely, "that any long-ago history between the two of us can have any bearing whatsoever on the issue in question today."

"And what possible issue is that?" he asked. "The community is up against a band of thieves and a bunch of silly, bored females worry that electric lighting will keep them awake all night. Or maybe they are afraid that without total darkness a poor old henpecked husband might actually get a glimpse of the human body without the benefits of corset stays and horsehair bustles."

"Oh yes, Mr. Chavis, I am aware of your preferences in female attire," she snapped. "Simplicity is too grand a name for its description."

"I have no idea what you are talking about," he replied.

Her complexion was florid with embarrassment or anger or perhaps both.

"What I am talking about is the very essential need for another meeting on the subject of the residential street lighting," she said, appearing to draw her composure by taking a breath.

"I see no need for any further meeting on the subject," Gidry said.

"The entire populace is to be affected by this change, Mr. Chavis," she told him. "Surely all the citizens should have an opportunity to speak up about the issues involved."

He shook his head.

"A further meeting is totally unnecessary," he told her.

"It is very necessary," she insisted. "No other view was given a hearing."

"I don't believe that any other legitimate views exist."

"You don't believe it without even hearing what we have to say?" She appeared incredulous. "Another meeting is essential, or everyone will be as ignorant on the issue as you seem to be yourself."

"You might as well get that idea completely out of your mind," he told her. "There will not be another meeting. I will not let it happen."

"What on earth do you mean?"

"I mean, Miss Belmont, that I have no intention of allowing you and your female fellow naysayers to stir up some purposeless controversy."

"Then those in opposition to your judgment are to have no voice in this at all, sir? We are to be offered no public forum?"

"You want a *public forum*, Miss Belmont? Ollie Larson has a soapbox," he said. "I suggest you get one for yourself."

"Aren't you making this a bit personal, Mr. Chavis?" Pru pointed out. "You speak as if I am the only person in opposition."

"Aren't you?"

"No indeed, Mr. Chavis," she said. "I formally represent the entire membership of the Ladies' Rose and Garden Society, who voted unanimously to present our perspective to the community."

"Please reassure the ladies of your little club that they have no cause for concern. They should just leave these things to those who know best."

Her eyes widened, and her jaw opened in shock at his curt dismissal.

"Perhaps we would do that, sir, if we had any confidence that the gentlemen of the Commercial Club actually *knew* best," she retorted.

"You think that we do not?"

"I think that due consideration has not been given to all sides."

"In that you are wrong, Miss Belmont," he answered. "We have thoroughly and thoughtfully considered. And we have come to the conclusion that the only people who will find the illumination of our residential streets unwelcome are those who are engaged in nefarious activities that they would not wish to be brought to light."

"What on earth do you mean by that?"

"Exactly what you suspect that I mean, Miss Belmont," he answered. "Good day."

Chapter 10

"CAN YOU believe that he talked to me in such a manner?" Pru asked her aunt not two hours later as the two aired out the sickroom at the Chavis house.

That morning Mrs. Butts was claiming that an infirmity of the back prevented her from doing any heavy work, so Prudence had been recruited. For the moment, she regretted the decision. The young people had had some sort of tiff, and her niece could not rest until every word, gesture, and expression had been relived, analyzed, and conveyed.

Henrietta glanced toward Peer who was half-sitting, half-reclining on the mauve damask fainting couch that she had brought up from the front parlor. Peer seemed increasingly unable to catch his breath while sitting upright. The fainting couch was a vast improvement over being always in bed, but without many of the tiring effects of being up in a chair.

She tucked the coverlet around his shoulders. Although the day was quite warm, she did not want any casual cool breeze to chill him inadvertently. There seemed to be little chance of that, since only insects and the incessant pounding noise of the cotton gin moved the air.

"I can't imagine that Gidry would insult you without provocation," she answered her niece with only the vaguest concern.

Peer was groggy and sleepy today, not completely himself. It made her uneasy. Rest was a necessary part of the healing process, she hastily assured herself. The listlessness she detected in his eyes was undoubtedly caused by the effort of his body to move toward recovery.

"You believe I provoked him?" Pru asked her, sounding affronted.

"I didn't say that," Henrietta replied with a long-suffering sigh. "But I believe that the two of you have more unfinished business than either of you cares to admit."

"Our personal history has nothing to do with it," her niece insisted. "Surely, as a gardener, you see our point."

"Don't try to get me into the middle of it, Pru. Yes, perhaps there are things yet unconsidered and questions to be asked," she said. "But apparently you have not broached them correctly with Gidry."

"I was hardly allowed to broach them at all," Pru told her. "He was insufferable, intolerable, and inconsiderate."

"You will not convince me that Gidry Chavis is being deliberately difficult. He is not an unreasonable fellow," Aunt Hen declared. "I have known him too long and too well to believe that."

"We know how he used to be, but I can assure you that this morning he was as unpleasant as any person I have ever encountered."

"Perhaps you caught him at an inopportune time.

You did say that he indicated he was in a hurry."

"When would have been a good time?" Pru asked. "With the gin pounding every day, it is nearly impossible to hear oneself think, let alone have a discussion."

Henrietta couldn't argue that.

"I am determined," Pru confided, "that we shall have our meeting. Somehow we will get the entire town to attend, and I will not allow Gidry Chavis or anyone else from the Commercial Club to as much as say howdy-do. If they think they can silence us just because we do not agree with them, they are in for a big surprise."

Henrietta tutted ominously.

"I don't think that you should plan such things as if expecting a confrontation," she said. "Remember the adage that you catch more flies with honey than vinegar."

"Oh, I intend to be sweet, Aunt Hen," Pru assured her. "I intend to be so sweet I'll make Gidry Chavis's teeth fall out."

"Ah, so it's Gidry you are fighting here, not the Commercial Club," she said.

"Gidry represents the Commercial Club, just as I represent the Rose and Garden Society," she said. "If he can make it personal, then so can I."

"I'm not sure that is wise."

"Maybe not," Pru agreed. "But it is necessary. Gidry Chavis is rude and ungallant and . . . and . . ."

"And I would appreciate it if you would not speak that way in front of the young man's father," Henrietta scolded.

Pru was immediately contrite, glancing at Peer apologetically.

"I don't think he can hear us, Aunt Hen," she said quietly.

"Of course he can hear us," she said. "There is nothing at all wrong with his hearing."

"Except he does not appear to be listening. I'm not even sure if he is awake."

Her niece was quite correct. Peer Chavis reclined upon the fainting couch looking very pale, almost ashen in color and not at all asleep. His eyes were open and he was staring trancelike into nothingness.

Prudence had gathered all the soiled linens into a wicker basket. "Let me take these things out to the washhouse," she said.

Henrietta nodded an absent assent.

As her niece left the room, Henrietta regarded her patient with concern.

"Peer?" He made no reaction.

"Peer!" she said more sharply.

He glanced up at her then. He looked more like himself, and she released her breath slowly with relief.

"Where did you go?" she asked him

He didn't answer, but reached out with his one good arm to try to take her hand.

Henrietta grasped his palm in her own and knelt beside him. His thin, bony fingers trembled in hers, and she willed the health and vitality of her own body to flow into his.

"Where on earth did you go?" she asked again, this time her voice more teasing. "You must have been a million miles away."

She moved closer to him and laid her cheek against his shoulder.

"I always resented it when you went off places and left me here alone," she said. "Whether it was a business trip for the cotton cooperative or a three-day diversion to visit old friends. I've always hated being here without you."

She glanced up at him. His expression was dark with intensity.

"The first time was the worst, of course," she told him. "Being left in Chavistown while you went off to fight for honor and glory. I was furious when you left. You were so cocky and sure of yourself. I knew that you would be foolhardy and risk great danger. I worried about it every day."

Henrietta shook her head.

"And every day I also imagined your homecoming," she said. "Sometimes you rode up on your horse. Sometimes you alighted from the train. At times you were a hero carried upon the shoulders of other men. Occasionally you were wounded and lying upon a stretcher."

She chuckled lightly without much humor.

"But never, Peer Chavis, never in all my daydreams, did I imagine your homecoming with a new bride at your side and a child in her womb."

She moved away from the comfort of his shoulder to look into his eyes. They were bright with tears, and she felt the sting in her own.

"I forgave you for that long ago," she told him, tenderly caressing the gauntness of his cheek. "And I don't even wish that it had never happened. Your chosen wife never impressed me much, I admit. But she gave you as fine a son as a man can wish for."

Henrietta smiled with reflection, as if her own thoughts were suddenly far away.

"You know another daydream I lived with for years on end was about that boy," she said. "I used to pretend that he was my son, my very own."

Her heart lightened at the thought.

"And I know that you wished for the same thing," she said. "That's exactly how you got it into your head that he should marry up with my little Pru."

Henrietta tutted in disapproval.

"They were such a happy pair. The very best of childhood friends. Everyone knew that she loved him. And any fool could see that her tenderness would be the making of him."

She shook her head.

"But it was a big mistake to get into the thick of it like you did," he told him. "People find it difficult enough to live in paradise when God gives it to them. They are certainly not going to enjoy Eden if they get shanghaied into it, however well-meant."

He could make no comment, but she knew he agreed with her.

"That's why I'm not going to say one word about this lighting up the town business. I don't care if they go fifteen rounds on the courthouse square with a fury that John L. Sullivan would envy. If those two are fated be together, I would sure like to see it come to pass," she said.

When a day started off as badly as this one had for Gidry, it only made sense that it would get worse. After losing his temper with Prudence in the morning, he remained unable to find it all day long. Young Sharpy showed up saying that he'd quit and wanted the pay that was due him. He refused to say why he had left so abruptly or where he had been all the previous afternoon.

"Walking off the job is a termination offense!" he bellowed at the boy over the roar of the machinery.

"I didn't even take a turn at the fence," the little

fellow assured him soberly. "I went straight across town."

The weather was threatening rain, and a disagreement broke out in the line of farmers that nearly resulted in blows between two young hotheads.

At midday Albert Fenton came to tell him that the ladies were up to something. Another emergency meeting had been called for the evening and it looked as if they were not taking *no* for an answer.

"What on earth do you think they could do about it?" Gidry asked incredulously.

Fenton rolled his eyes.

"You ask that 'cause you're not a married man," he answered. "They don't have to do anything. Believe me, more men can stand up to savage torture than can live with a woman who assures him that 'nothing is wrong.' "

As they headed for their own impromptu meeting of the Commercial Club, Gidry mentally berated himself for mishandling the situation. Honnebuzz was probably right about not allowing the opposition to have a voice, but he should have heard Pru out this morning. At the very least he should have treated her with courtesy.

He had been unreasonable, and he'd been angry. Imagining her and her lover whiling away the hours together had simply soured his stomach. From the way he'd acted, one would have thought that he was jealous!

He needed a clear head and a respectful attitude. Perhaps she was behaving immorally, but she was not his wife, his daughter, his sister. Pru was nothing to him. And he was certainly not saint enough to be able to cast the first stone.

In his future dealings with Miss Belmont, he determined to be perfectly civil and unfailingly polite. The next time he bumped into her, he was going to be genteel and amicable. . . .

He bumped into her, literally, as she was coming out of the dry goods store. He and Albert Fenton were still discussing their options, and Gidry was not looking where he was going. She was apparently perusing the contents of her market basket and ran straight on into his chest at full gait.

She gave a little startled cry.

"Pru!" he answered with surprise, and reached out with complete altruism to steady her.

When his hands clasped around her waist she slapped at them and jerked away from him.

Her reaction was so extreme that Gidry was stung with humiliation. She made him feel as if he were a common masher attempting to accost her on a public street. Some worthless no-account cheating husband could make love to her all night long, but Gidry Chavis was not supposed to touch her, even to keep her from falling flat on her bustle.

"Pardon me, Miss Belmont," he said formally. "I did not mean to run you down."

The color in her cheeks was high as she straightened her hat and attempted to recover her dignity. There was something about upsetting her prim neatness that appealed to him in a primal earthy way. He resisted the inexplicable urge to pull her into his arms and kiss her.

"Perhaps out in the Pecos men just barge through doors as they please," she informed him coldly. "But in our town, Mr. Chavis, the rule is ladies first."

Her setdown was so superior, Gidry's brow drew down in anger. He would never have allowed another man to speak to him in that fashion. And he wasn't willing to let a woman do so either. Especially not this woman.

"I did not see you, ma'am," he said with deliberate quiet. "For that I do apologize; however, I would have assumed that a spinster would grow accustomed to gentlemen failing to notice her."

He regretted it the minute it came out of his mouth. It was unkind and untrue. Deliberate in its attempt to injure.

Prudence blanched, clearly wounded. She glanced over at Fenton and nodded to the man with embarrassment.

"Good day, sir," she said icily, and stepped past Gidry on to the sidewalk.

He followed her retreat, shaking his head with self-castigation. The very last thing that he wanted to do was to make this fight personal, but it already was.

"You know, Chavis," Fenton said, "Miss Prudence is not the best woman in town to make an enemy. Then again, I guess you two got off on the wrong foot a long time ago."

Gidry couldn't argue that. She had once loved him, and he had jilted her. That should have all been in the past. But somehow it was not. It was as recent as the morning's sunrise. And knowing that she was carrying on some illicit affair just sat completely wrong with him. So much for polite and amicable. It was open hostility between them, and nothing to be done for it.

He followed Fenton into the building and within a few minutes the other members of the Commercial Club began arriving. They stood together in the organized clutter of the back room, everyone talking at once.

Cotton and the rail shipment now being readied

should have been their main subjects of discussion. But they were not.

"Alice says that Pru Belmont is mad as a wet hen about not being given another meeting on the lighting project," Judge Ramey said.

"Those women are up to something," Elmer Corsen agreed. "They think they've been affronted, and women don't forget that easily."

"Yes, my wife has already started the silent treatment," Henry Tatum piped in. "You'd think I'd be grateful not to hear her chatter, but the silence is far worse."

"For heaven's sake, Chavis," Peterson complained. "Did you have to be so snippy with them?"

"We don't owe the opposition a platform," Honnebuzz insisted.

"When the opposition is from our wives, mothers, and daughters, we'd do better to give them the platform and get it over with."

"Then you men are just going to cave in?" Gidry asked.

"You've lived out on those lonely ranges too long, Chavis," Tatum said.

"He sure has," Plug Whitstone agreed. "A woman can't be fenced, led, or herded. A man just got to gentle up to her as best he can and pray she don't get a bee in her bonnet."

The other men chuckled in agreement.

"So you think we should give up the lighting project?" Gidry asked.

"Of course not," Honnebuzz answered. "What we need to do is hold our ground, but make it look like it's not our fault."

"How do we do that?"

"Actually, it pretty near done," Plug Whitstone said

with a chuckle. "Young Chavis done started things here. He ain't married nor got female relation of no kind. We let the ladies think that it's all his danged idea, and we just can't do a thing to stop him."

There was a whistle of appreciation from one man. A diabolical chuckle from another.

"It's perfect."

"The question is can you put up with it, Chavis?" Fenton asked. "There won't be nothing easy about having every woman in town ready to spit nails at you."

"Surely it's not *every* woman in town," Gidry said.

"Very nearly all of them are in the Rose and Garden Society," Honnebuzz pointed out. "And those that are not, want to be."

"Well, it won't be forever," Gidry pointed out. "Eventually they will get over it."

Plug spit a jaw of tobacco into the tin can he carried. "Yep, they say that eventually women forget. My Eulie caught me making eyes at one of them city gals when we was in New Orleans on our honeymoon. It's been thirty years ago, I'm expecting her to quit harping on it any day now."

Hoots of laughter filled the room.

"Maybe we should hear them out," Fenton suggested. "From what I've gleaned so far, perhaps they do have some legitimate concerns."

"Nonsense, Albert," Stanley Honnebuzz chastised. "How could they possibly understand anything about it? They are women after all."

"But Miss Prudence is very well read," Fenton defended. "I never talked to anyone who knew more about plants and gardening."

"Gardening she may know, but electricity she does not," Honnebuzz insisted.

"Fenton's got a point," Elmer said. "Miss Belmont is a very levelheaded woman. If she is mightily opposed to the lighting project, she must have a reason."

"That's so," someone in the back agreed.

"The year my sweet corn got tall as the house but didn't ear, it was Prudence Belmont that suggested I lime the field," Amos Wilburn told them. "I've had good crops ever since."

"Well, yes, I suppose she's smarter than your average woman," Honnebuzz conceded.

"You've talked to her, Chavis," Fenton said. "What do you think?"

Gidry hesitated, choosing his words carefully. He believed he knew full well what despicable *reasons* Prudence had for her opposition. But he would not, could not, by gesture or careless word, convey any hint of the sordid truth to these gentlemen.

"The woman has not conveyed to me any practical consideration that I would deem in any way worthy of discussion by this group," he replied.

Stanley Honnebuzz nodded with great self-importance.

"Just as I said," he concluded. "It's all featherheaded nonsense. If they were to be taken seriously at this juncture, it would simply give them encouragement for future interference."

There were nods of agreement on that score.

"What do you say, Chavis?" Oscar Tatum asked. "Are you ready to bring the wrath of the female population of Chavistown down upon your head?"

"I suppose, if it seems best," Gidry answered. "But Honnebuzz is a single man also; maybe he would prefer to do it."

The lawyer opened his mouth to reply, but the judge did it for him.

"Stanley is courting my girl, Alice," Ramey said. "And she is a great admirer of Miss Belmont. In fact, I'm worried that she might follow that woman's example and take up spinsterhood."

"Besides," Albert Fenton pointed out, "Prudence is already mad at you."

Gidry couldn't argue with that.

"If you're willing to take this on, Gidry," Judge Ramey said, "then we can hold fast and push our way through. But it's not going to be easy."

"Nothing involving women ever is," Plug pointed out.

Chapter 11

"AND MR. Honnebuzz said that all the gentlemen of the Commercial Club were agreeable to letting us speak our piece," Alice Ramey announced. "But Gidry Chavis wouldn't even hear of it. He just flatly refused."

"That's what my husband said, too," Ethel Peterson chimed in. "The men were all for hearing us out, but Chavis was dead set against it, and they couldn't go against him."

"Inexplicable!" Mrs. Johnson exclaimed. "Totally inexplicable."

"I can't think what his reasoning might be," Alice Ramey agreed.

"He certainly doesn't know the people of Chavistown very well if he thinks that he can just bully us into doing what he wants."

"He's spent far too long away," Cloris Tatum pointed out. "Why he doesn't even look like one of us anymore."

"Those clothes," Eula Whitstone tutted. "Completely inappropriate."

"I should think he'd had enough of cattle that he'd

186

not want to bring the smell of them into town."

That comment provoked a bevy of unkind giggles.

"Well I personally intend to give that young man the cut direct the very next time I see him," Bertha Mae announced.

"It will be no hardship for me to draw my skirts aside either," Edith Champion agreed. "Imagine the audacity of trying to bend the entire town to his will."

"Maybe his father is the richest man in Chavis County, but he hasn't even lived in this town for eight years."

"And as I recall," Bertha Mae said pointedly, "he did not leave under the best of circumstances.

Surreptitious glances were shot in Pru's direction, but she was determined to ignore them.

"You should have heard the way he talked to *her* at the dry goods store," Mrs. Fenton whispered. "He nearly ran her down with his rambunctious cowboy ways. And then talked to her as if *she* were in *his* way."

"Some men are just like that," Alice Ramey commented. "I personally don't have a civil word to say to that type."

Prudence ignored the conversation as best she could and surveyed the room critically. It was even more crowded tonight than the last time they met in emergency session. And unlike the previous meeting, tonight not one word had been uttered in complaint about taking them away from their families. The level of concern about the residential lighting project varied greatly among the membership. But being told that they could not have a voice in the decision making caught the ladies unawares. And the distinct possibility of a confrontation between Gidry Chavis and

Prudence Belmont was apparently something that few would risk missing.

Prudence brought the meeting to order. A hush fell upon the crowd, every eye looking up to her anxiously, questioningly.

"Ladies of the Chavistown Rose and Garden Society," she began. "Our function as an organization, our reason for existence, is clearly laid out in our Official Charter and Bylaws."

She held up the small worn set of papers bound together by a pink ribbon sewn into the left margin.

"If I may quote from Section One, Paragraph One, our stated purpose is 'to promote the civilization and beautification of our community through the care and attention of ornamental gardens.'

"Anything, I suggest to you ladies, anything that stands in the way of fulfilling our purpose must be somehow overcome," Pru told them. "Anything or anyone."

An anxious murmur filtered through the crowd.

"As most of you know, the Commercial Club is planning a major renovation of the residential areas of our town," she continued. "They are doing this for a cause quite altruistic and bearing the total expense of the project themselves. I believe that we can all appreciate their efforts, however wrongheaded we know them to be."

There was a titter of amusement at the expense of the absent gentlemen.

"Ladies, the Commercial Club has refused to call another meeting so that we might present our opposition to their proposed project. Fortunately, we are Americans and live in the great state of Texas, where the right of free assembly is guaranteed by the constitution. We do not need *the permission* of the Chavistown Commercial Club to speak," Prudence announced grandly.

There was a spattering of applause among the ladies gathered, impressed with Pru's glorious oration, but still many questions were on their minds and in their eyes.

Good order was momentarily lost as each one turned to confide her thoughts to the woman next to her.

Pru rapped her spoon against her teacup three more times, bringing about a reluctant silence to the meeting.

Bertha Mae Corsen raised her neatly gloved hand.

"The floor recognizes Mrs. Corsen," Pru said, nodding to her.

"We can gather all we like," Bertha Mae complained. "But until we get the menfolk to attend, it's a lost cause."

Once more pandemonium threatened to break loose. Pru controlled it with some difficulty.

"I have a plan," she told them. "It was Aunt Hen, actually, who set me in the right direction."

"It's good to hear that she's with us on this," Bertha Mae said snidely. "One wonders that she has any life at all. Mrs. Butts says she never leaves old Chavis's side."

The subdued hiss of gossip buzzed through the crowd.

It was on the tip of Pru's tongue to fly to her aunt's defense and point out that Mrs. Butts, although paid for her time, was quite willing to leave the patient's side at the drop of a hat. But that was what Bertha Mae wanted, she decided. She wanted to cause trouble. Dissension among them would result in failure. And failure was not to be tolerated.

"Actually Aunt Hen's advice is well-known to the ladies of this group and has been proven wise on many occasions."

She had recaptured their attention.

"She reminded me that one catches more flies with honey than vinegar," Pru told them.

Old Eula Whitstone shook her head. "If you're thinking to sweet these fellows up into letting you have your way, I think you've picked a tough row to hoe."

"No," Pru answered. "I'm still counting on logic to persuade them. But I am planning an irresistible temptation to get them to listen."

"So you've taken up my idea of making them sleep in the washhouse," Eula said.

Alice Ramey giggled.

Prudence blushed.

"Not exactly," she replied.

The rest of the ladies were agog with curiosity.

"I think we should have a Harvest Moon Dance."

For one long moment the room was completely quiet. No said a word. The silence was abruptly broken by squeals of delight, excited laughter, and a general hubbub of discussion.

"It's a perfect solution. The men have to come."

"To get them to listen and have fun as well."

"Ladies have never sponsored their own dance."

"Maybe it is high time we did."

"Oh pooh!" Mrs. Fenton whined unhappily. "It is times like this I hate being married to Albert. He is such a terrible dancer!"

Her words provoked laughter.

"For those who can't be lured in by dancing," Pru continued, "we will have plenty to eat, horseshoe pitching, the most talented songstresses in town and a historical tableau," Pru announced.

Her eyes twinkled with delight.

"How much time do we have?"

"When is the harvest moon?"

Prudence referred to an advertising calendar that touted a three-times-a-day regimen—ten, two, and four—for a popular new patent medicine.

"The fall equinox is the twenty-second," Pru told them. "And the nearest full moon will be the thirtieth."

"That gives us barely ten days," Alice Mae pointed out.

"It will be perfect timing. All the ginning should be done by then and the cotton on its way to market. The men will be ready to celebrate."

"But it doesn't give us much time."

"If we all work together, we can get it done in ten days," Bertha Mae replied.

"I'm willing," Mrs. Johnson declared.

"Count me in as well," Mavis Hathaway said.

"Wonderful! Wonderful!"

Pru was thrilled at their enthusiasm.

"Mrs. Johnson, if you would be in charge of the menu," she said.

"Consider it done," the elderly woman answered.

"Mrs. Champion, can you make arrangements for the music?" Pru asked. "Perhaps Mrs. Hathaway can help you. One of you can schedule the ladies' vocal presentations and the other see about the dancing."

The two ladies nodded agreement.

"Did you have someone in mind to supervise the historical tableau?" Alice Ramey asked very timidly.

"Why yes, I did have someone in mind," Pru answered.

"Oh." The young woman blushed with embarrassment.

"You are the exact person that I thought would be best able to think of an appropriate piece and present it in the most worthy fashion," Pru told her.

The young woman fairly gushed with pleasure.

"Oh, may I help with the costumes?" Leda Peterson asked.

Pru watched, proud and pleased as the ladies divided up into committees and immediately commenced with enthusiastic planning. She moved from group to group and listened to their plans. She offered an idea or two herself, but mostly she was impressed by the cleverness of the ladies themselves.

Even Bertha Mae and her close associates, having been volunteered for decorations, came up with a concept both pretty and practical.

Pru heard noise at the back door and slipped out of the parlor. Her Aunt Hen was home and looking as tired and worn-out as Pru had ever seen her.

"Aunt Hen, you look exhausted," Pru told the older woman.

"I can't imagine why," her aunt replied. "Peer has been sleeping most of the day. Except for that little time we spent airing his room this morning, I've been sitting doing nothing."

"Well *doing nothing* certainly has taken the color out of your complexion," Pru pointed out. "I think you'd better stay home tomorrow; you might well be coming down with something yourself."

Aunt Hen shrugged and shook her head.

"I feel better being there," she insisted. "Even if my whole day is doing nothing."

Pru tutted at her in disapproval.

"You are having another meeting." Aunt Hen's

words were more a statement than a question.

Pru nodded.

"We've decided to have a Harvest Moon Dance."

Aunt Hen raised her eyebrows, clearly impressed.

"I don't imagine the menfolk will be able to resist that," she said.

"I don't believe they will either," Pru said. "Isn't it just the best idea possible?"

Aunt Hen nodded. "Very good, very good indeed," she said. "I knew that you'd make a fine president."

"Mrs. Johnson is planning the food. Alice is organizing a tableau. Edith and Mavis are setting up the music. Even Bertha Mae is involved. She's doing the decorations."

"It all sounds promising," Aunt Hen told her.

"I'm counting on your help," she said.

Aunt Hen shook her head. "Don't," she answered simply. "I'll tend Peer, and you tend to the Rose and Garden Club."

"But he doesn't really need you all the time," Pru assured her. "And he certainly won't that day. Gidry will not come, I'm certain. So while he stays home with his father, you can help me."

"You haven't needed my help, Prudence, in a very long time," she said.

"You will come?"

Aunt Hen shook her head.

Pru sighed but reluctantly accepted her answer.

"I think nearly everybody will be there," Pru told her aunt excitedly. "None of the young people will be able to stay away, and I expect even the gentlemen of the Commercial Club will show up, too. Except for Gidry, of course. He seems to be the only one really opposed to us."

"Is that so?" Aunt Hen commented. "Doesn't really seem like him."

"It is very much like him, Aunt Hen, I assure you," she said. "He was absolutely rude to me at the Dry Goods store today."

Her aunt deftly changed the subject.

"What are you going to do at the dance, Prudence?" she asked. "If other women are taking care of the food, dancing, and entertainment, what is left for you?"

"I'm going to make our presentation on the dangers of residential street lighting," she said proudly. "For all the fun and excitement, we mustn't lose sight of our purpose here. We will have our forum."

Agatha Crane stepped into the room just as Pru's last words were spoken. She raised her hand in a defiant salute.

"And let Gidry Chavis just try to stop us!"

Gidry had taken the job of Commercial Club scapegoat with the disregard of a man who had never borne the brunt of a community's anger.

The women of Chavistown would cross the street in order not to pass him. And if perchance an encounter was unavoidable, it was as if they turned deaf and blind. Or rather as if he had become completely invisible.

And Stanley Honnebuzz had been right. Even the women who never darkened the door of the Rose and Garden Society, the ones who wouldn't know a gardenia from a billy goat, even those women were hopping mad. And they were mad at Gidry Chavis.

With the men it was little better. Having insisted that the refusal was not their own, but Gidry's, they could not appear openly friendly for fear that word would get back to their wives. It seemed like every human in Chavistown had neither a kind word nor welcome smile for him. The only opportunity he had for talk was at work. And the incessant roar of machinery didn't make discourse a pleasant prospect.

Being cut was his worst nightmare of returning to his hometown. And it had come true at last. If not for Arthur Sattlemore, the salesman from Big Texas Electric and young Sharpy Kilroy who, now unemployed, seemed to have a good deal of time just to sit around the gin loafing, Gidry would have forgotten what it was like to have conversation.

Maybe he could have felt good about it, thinking that being shunned was going to ensure the success of the lighting project. But it was clear that the ladies were going to have broad attendance at their Harvest Moon Dance. And they would present some fearful hysteria and make a few converts among the audience. The more people on their side, the weaker the commitment to change. And without change, the community could not prosper.

In truth, he'd thought that Pru was the only real opposition to the project. Her disfavor with it, Gidry was sure, was partly an attempt to conceal her current unsavory relationship and also because it was his idea. He was certain of that. He had treated her badly, and after all these years she still held a grudge. It had been made plain that day in the garden—she had not forgiven him for breaking her heart so long ago.

Although it was a puzzle why she should still be upset with him when she was apparently happily involved in an illicit romance with one of his employees.

Perhaps it was the same sort of jumbled confusion that he felt about her. It was like jealousy. But of course, it could not be jealousy. A man could only be jealous if he were in love. And he did not love Prudence Belmont. Of that he was certain, or relatively certain, or at least he didn't think so.

Gidry sat in his father's darkened room staring sightlessly out the window into the night. He was reluctant to admit it to himself, but he was watching for her. Waiting for her to meet her lover. Hating for her to meet her lover.

He no longer made mental lists of the principal suspects. The identity of her lover, Gidry had finally decided, was something he did not want to know. The anger when he thought about that man, that worthless cheating man, touching Prudence Belmont, his Prudence Belmont, was beyond reason. If he found the man out, he would, at the very least, create a scene. What he'd like to do is pick a fight. Or pound the man senseless.

He wondered if she loved him. Pru was capable of powerful love. He knew that from experience. Had she turned all her affections to her lover? Had he taught her to love physically as well as emotionally?

Gidry gritted his teeth miserably as he thought of the postcard. She shouldn't be doing that! She was a fully passionate woman. Awakened gently, she would be a worthy partner in sensual delights. It galled him unreasonably that some other man had done the awakening.

"I probably should have married her," he said.

His voice was startlingly loud in the still silence of the night. He glanced toward the bed. He couldn't see a thing in the dimness of the room, but detected no stirring or changes in breathing.

His father was hardly listening, he was sure. The old man had been so tired this evening, drifting in and out of wakefulness, that he hadn't even been able to listen to a tall tale. But Gidry had become so accustomed to talking to his father about his day, his worries, his concerns, everything that came on his mind, that it hardly mattered that he confess his deepest thoughts. After eight long years fending for himself, making decisions on his own it was a great luxury to be able to *discuss* things with his father. Even if the old man could not respond.

"You saw it way back then," he said, "but I could not. She is a bright, hardworking, dependable woman who would have made a devoted wife and loving mother."

He chuckled humorlessly.

"Of course a man of twenty-one has scarcely any use for hardworking, dependable, and devoted women," he pointed out. "A man of twenty-one wants only a nicely rounded female stuffed precariously into a bright red dress with spangles."

Gidry continued to stare out the window and rubbed his chin thoughtfully.

"What was her name?" he asked himself. "Mary? Or was it May?"

He shook his head. It was so long ago and of so little consequence that he could no longer recall.

He could remember how much he'd wanted her. He had not been wholly unfamiliar with women, but he never wanted one as he'd wanted her. He'd seen her dozens of times. She'd shake her sultry backside at him, and his body would go weak as jelly. Well, perhaps not all of his body.

He had been thinking of her one pretty spring day before he'd left town. At his father's behest he'd taken Pru on a picnic. Pretty little Pru, all fresh-scrubbed and wholesome. There was nothing about her that in any way resembled the hot, forbidden charms of a spangle-dressed female.

The day at the picnic she'd been all sweetness and sincerity. He could picture her in his mind as clearly as if it were yesterday and not eight years ago.

The two of them had found a shady spot along Hollering Creek just a short walk from the road. She'd been dressed in dark pansy blue. It was a color that rather suited her. Her broad-brimmed straw bonnet boasted a ribbon of the same color, which she tied neatly just below her left ear.

They had finished a very tasty meal provided by Aunt Hen. Gidry lay back with his hand behind his head, lazy and content. His pleasant hazy thoughts of the red-spangled female were abruptly interrupted.

Pru's familiar voice was unusually quiet and betrayed a slight tremble.

"I know a woman is not supposed to speak first," she said.

Gidry opened his eyes and looked up at her. Her cheeks were prettily pink, her eyes adoring.

"I know a woman is not supposed to speak first, but I cannot hold my feelings inside any longer."

He held his breath, willing her not to say it, willing her not to say it. To leave it alone for another day. She did not.

"I . . . l love you, Gid. I always have," she whispered. "You are the first thing that comes to my mind when I awaken in the morning and the last thought I have at the end of the day."

"Oh Pru."

"When I'm not with you I'm dreaming about you. I imagine conversations I want to have and remember the ones that we have had," she told him.

Her heart was in her eyes. He looked away, not wanting to see it.

"I love you, Gid Chavis, totally and utterly," she continued. "I want to be with you always. I want to share your name. I want to give you children."

"For mercy's sake, Pru," he had pleaded with her, almost angrily. "Don't just smother me with it. Don't you have any pride?"

"Pride?" she answered. "Pride is such a meager emotion when compared to love."

Gidry sat staring out the darkened window.

"Pride is such a meager emotion when compared to love," he repeated aloud.

He heard a sharp intake of breath behind him and realized that his father had awakened.

Gidry turned toward the bed and stared into the darkness.

"I'm still here, Papa," he said. "Still just thinking out loud."

He moved closer and clasped his father's hand in his own. His father's grip seemed to be growing weaker, but there was still much warmth in it.

"I was thinking about Pru," he told his father with deliberate good humor. "The ladies in town are all mad at me. And Pru is the maddest of all."

He was thoughtful for a long moment.

"But I wasn't thinking about how she feels now," he admitted. "I was thinking about when she used to love me." His voice quieted almost reverently. "That woman had a powerful love for me. No other woman has ever thought that much of me since."

Gidry shook his head ruefully.

"What was that you said to me that night I left?" he wondered aloud. "You said that foolish men have been throwing away paradise ever since the garden of Eden.''

He sighed heavily and gazed out the window once more.

"You were right," Gidry told him. "That night I threw away paradise."

Chapter 12

I T WAS going to be the most glorious community event ever held in Chavistown. That was a certainty to anyone even remotely involved in the planning of the Harvest Moon Dance. But it was not without its setbacks and problems. Those fell heavily at the feet of Prudence Belmont.

The dance was originally planned for the courthouse square, but Alice got word to Prudence that Judge Ramey said it was impossible to hold it there without permission. And that a permit would take as least six weeks to acquire.

Considering the impromptu meeting held at the same location by the Commercial Club, Pru was extremely doubtful of the judge's words. So much so that she donned her gray silk suit and went to accost the man in his courthouse chambers.

If she caught him by surprise, he didn't show it. And he readily admitted that the permit requirement was a sneaky, underhanded trick.

"But there is nothing I can do," the judge insisted in an opened-palm entreaty. "Gidry Chavis insisted upon it, and I can't go against him. He is a very powerful man, Pru. I'm a humble public servant."

She was skeptical. Humbleness was not a quality that Pru associated with the judge. And as for being a public servant, well, Ramey was a fair and honorable man. He was especially so when it best suited his personal interests.

"You will not stop us," Pru assured him firmly. "Not being allowed to utilize our own public property will only make us more determined."

The judge's expression was all feigned sympathy.

"Perhaps some farmer at the edge of town will allow you to utilize a field near town."

Having the dance out of the city would definitely lower attendance, if an appropriate place could even be found. With the cotton just in, hay meadows had yet to be mowed. Waist-high prairie grass was not conducive to dancing. And no farmer in his right mind would allow his field to be trampled even for a good cause.

"You will not stop us!" Pru vowed once more as she angrily took her leave.

"I am so sorry," the judge claimed. "It's all Gidry Chavis, you know. I would be on your side."

Pru had her doubts. There was something just too pat about it.

Her suspicions were further heightened when she approached Reverend Hathaway. The church grounds were not as large as the courthouse square, but they were in the middle of town.

"I couldn't go against Gidry Chavis," the reverend told her nervously. "He is completely in opposition to it, and I can't go against him."

"Sir, you are not dependent upon Mr. Chavis for the security of your position," she told him. "And do not try to tell me that Gidry now has the ear of the bishop."

"Well no, of course not, but . . ."

"Mr. Chavis can in no way endanger you or your livelihood," she said. "If you choose to do his bidding, it must be from personal preference."

"Oh no indeed, ma'am," he said hurriedly. "I assure you that *I* am in your support. But Gidry Chavis is . . . well he is a member of my congregation and . . ."

Pru's eyes narrowed as she leveled the minister a long look.

"Correct me if I am wrong, Reverend Hathaway," she said. "But Gidry Chavis has not darkened the door to this church since the day he set foot back in town."

The man was clearly flustered.

"Well no, he has not."

"The ladies of the Rose and Garden Society rarely miss your sermons."

"Yes, that's certainly true," he admitted. "But Mr. Chavis's father is ill, Miss Belmont," he answered. "Perhaps he does not attend church because he cannot leave the old man's bedside."

"He leaves it every day to work at the gin," she pointed out. "And if what I saw of the old man this week is any indication, prayer is probably the most that he can do for him."

"Miss Belmont . . ."

Pru interrupted him firmly.

"Reverend Hathaway, would you like to see the women of your congregation turn away from you in droves?" she said. "Then refuse to allow us to hold our event on these grounds."

The Reverend sputtered uncertainly.

"But a dance, surely a dance should not be held here."

"We are not Baptists, sir," she reminded him. "We can dance the night away with no fear of our salvation."

"Well, I . . . ah . . ."

"Perhaps I could speak to Mrs. Hathaway about it."

For Prudence that was her hole card. Her guaranteed win. Reverend Hathaway might not fear death, hell, or the wrath of God, but he was very much afraid of his wife.

Unfortunately, Albert Fenton was not afraid of his.

"Sir, everyone in town is aware that you have in storage decorations left over from the Fourth of July picnic," Pru told him. "We are offering to take them off your hands."

"It's like I told Mrs. Corsen," he said to Pru calmly. "I just can't sell you any decorations for your little sociable."

"It is not a *little sociable*, Mr. Fenton," Pru told him. "It's a Harvest Moon Dance. It is going to be the community event of the year."

"Then these decorations are entirely unsuitable," he said. "They are patriotic—red, white, and blue. Not at all the thing for a Harvest Moon Dance."

"Your wife and children will be there, Mr. Fenton," she told him. "In fact I believe that the whole town will be there."

He shrugged. "I have no objection to my family enjoying whatever harmless pursuits might be available."

"But you won't sell me the leftover decorations from the Fourth of July?"

"I cannot," he insisted.

"You don't have to tell me why," Pru answered.

"The answer would simply be Gidry Chavis. Gidry Chavis is your biggest account. You won't risk your business with Gidry Chavis."

Fenton looked at her blank-faced, revealing nothing.

"I ask you, Mr. Fenton, how on earth can selling a few frothy decorations to the Ladies' Rose and Garden Society be a risk to your business?"

He didn't bother to answer.

"The Chavis account may be your biggest, Mr. Fenton," she admitted, "but the purse strings of most of the households in this town are held by women. Women who want this dance. Women who want their say."

Fenton's words were calm as he spoke. "And those women will understand perfectly that I can't sell stock that I do not own," he replied.

Pru was momentarily struck speechless.

"What do you mean?" she asked finally.

"I sold all of those decorations this afternoon," he said.

"This afternoon? You sold everything?"

"Everything."

"To whom, may I ask, did you sell them?"

"Why to Mr. Gidry Chavis," Fenton answered.

Pru's jaw tightened. She was mad enough to spit.

"How much did he pay you?"

"That is none of your business, Miss Prudence," Fenton replied. "Business transactions in this store always remain confidential."

"All we really need are the Japanese lanterns," Pru told him. "I will give you twice whatever he paid just for the Japanese lanterns."

"I *am* sorry," he said. "I don't own them."

"Mr. Fenton, we have got to have them," she said.

"Even with a perfectly clear night and a bright harvest moon, a dance requires light."

"Light? It requires light?" The man chuckled and shook his head. "If you would just leave well enough alone, Miss Prudence, this time next year this town will have all the light that it needs."

Prudence repeated those words verbatim to the small group of committee leaders meeting in her kitchen that evening.

"I declare I could strangle the man," Pru said.

"I hope you are speaking of Mr. Chavis," Mrs. Fenton said defensively. "My husband clearly could not sell what he did not own."

"Mr. Chavis would not have owned the decorations if your husband had not told him we wanted them," Bertha Mae said pointedly.

"Well, we simply can't let this stop us," Pru said.

"We can make the decorations," Leda Peterson said.

"Make them out of what?" Cloris Tatum asked. "With no bunting or crepe paper, how do we even begin?"

"I say that we should begin in our gardens," Bertha Mae said. "If every woman in the club donated the last blooms of the year and the first leaves of fall, we will have enough color to decorate for a hundred dances."

"Of course you are right," Pru agreed. "And using our community's own natural beauty will make our point much better than any store-bought decorations."

"We've almost got our costumes complete for the tableau," Alice reported. "So we can certainly lend a hand in putting things together. Why Leda's fingers are so nimble she could stitch up dirt till you'd think it was a pie."

There was a flutter of congratulatory giggles. Leda blushed prettily.

"Of course, it doesn't matter how well everything looks," Bertha Mae pointed out. "If we can't figure out a way to light the place appropriately, nobody will even be able to see how it's decorated."

The truth of her words put a temporary damper on enthusiasm.

"Maybe it will be very clear and the moon very bright," Alice suggested optimistically.

"Still, we must plan some sort of lighting," Mavis Hathaway said. "A dance in the darkness would be scandalous."

"Maybe we could all bring our lamps from home," Alice said.

Edith Champion shook her head.

"No, that would never work."

The back door burst open banging loudly against the wall.

"Good heavens!" Mrs. Hathaway exclaimed.

"It's that Sharpy Kilroy," Mrs. Johnson said. "What is he doing here?"

The little boy stood frozen in place in the doorway, clearly unsure of what to do in such a roomful of ladies.

"You need to knock before you enter, Milton," Pru said quietly. "Do come on in, now that you're here."

" 'Cuse me, ma'ams," the little boy said. "I done got us a stage for Miss Alice's ta-blow."

"You did what?" Cloris Tatum looked at the boy askance.

Sharpy nodded enthusiastically.

"I heard Miss Alice saying to you yesterday, Miss

Pru, that folks wouldn't be able to see it all too well without a stage," he explained. "And you said that it would make your speech better, too, but there was just no help for it."

"And there doesn't seem to be," Pru said. "There is not a carpenter, woodworker, or even a man with a hammer in this town that would take on the job."

Sharpy nodded.

"But I done it," he said. "I got it for you, Miss Pru. Come and see."

The little fellow flew back out the door. Pru followed him and, rife with curiosity, the rest of the ladies did as well. In the yard sat a worn wooden platform about eight feet wide and four feet long. Clearly it had once been a part of something else, but what Pru had no idea. The worn wooden planks were nailed together and braced with sturdy timbers and showed evidence of having once been painted slate gray.

"Milton what is this?" Pru asked. "Where on earth did you get it?"

"It's a stage for your speech and Miss Alice's tablow," he said. "And it's mine, Miss Pru. I didn't steal it."

"Of course you didn't," she said. "I would never have thought such a thing."

"Where on earth did it come from?" Mavis asked.

"My house," Sharpy answered. "Or what was my mama's house. That old shack down near the creek off Sante Fe."

"Befuddle's old place?"

Sharpy nodded. "It's mine I'm thinking," he told the ladies. "But it ain't much. The roof's done caved in and can't nothing live there but old cats and spiders. But the porch here is in good shape. A couple of boards here to brace it in the back and a little paint, it'll make a dandy stage for us.''

The women stood staring at the unattached porch in silent disbelief. The little boy's eyes were so excited, so thrilled with his achievement, Pru couldn't help but laugh out loud.

"You are wonderful!" she told him, leaning down to plant a kiss solidly upon his grimy little cheek.

He drew back from her in obvious embarrassment and wiped the kiss away thoroughly. But Pru could tell that he was totally pleased.

The women inspected their stage with good humor and enthusiasm. The talk recommenced upon the decorations, and by dusk all were on their way, determined to see this course to the end.

Bertha Mae was the last to leave.

"It's too bad your young friend doesn't have some Japanese lanterns stashed away somewhere," she said, laughing.

Pru chuckled as well as she bade her farewell. She stood at the front gate for a long moment. Turning she stared at the house next door. The brightly lit garden of stained glass shone as beautifully tonight as ever. A light was burning in Mr. Chavis's room. The noise from the cotton gin had stopped a half hour earlier. Gidry was probably taking his dinner with his father. Aunt Hen said that he often did that.

Her anger at him was fading. It was clear to Pru, if to no one else, that one man, especially one just back in town after eight long years, couldn't possibly cause the Rose and Garden Society as much trouble as had been caused. All the men were in on it, every last one of them, she was sure. Gidry was just taking the blame. He was good at that.

He'd taken the blame eight years ago for the failure

of their romance. And in her heart of hearts, Pru realized that she was just as much to blame. Yes, he had rejected her. Yes, he had been the one to leave town. But she had been the one to push him in that direction. She had believed that everything was perfect, when it obviously was not. If she had not been so naive, she would never have risked so much. And without risking, nothing was ever lost.

She had wanted him so much, dreamed of him so much, that her whole life revolved around him. Nothing, no one else mattered to her. Not her aunt, not her friends, not her community, not her church. She was so wholly enraptured by him that she had ceased to exist as anyone except the person who loved Gidry Chavis.

That kind of love was not love at all. It was an abdication of her own self, her own life. Rather than be a person on her own she attempted to fill the world only with him. She couldn't have expected him to love her. There was no person inside her to love.

She sighed heavily.

His faithless jilting had hurt her deeply, it was true. But at least it had forced her at last to look around her and see, for the first time as an adult person, what life was and where its meaning lay.

Pru reached up to caress one tightly closed blossom on her morning glory vine. The flower was still as beautiful tonight as it had been at daybreak. She couldn't see it to know that, but she knew it just the same.

"Miss Pru."

A little voice interrupted her revery.

"Oh, hello, Milton," she said. "It's getting dark; you should probably draw some water and wash up a bit before bedtime."

"What did she mean about the Jack-a-knees lanterns?" he asked.

"What?" Pru looked at him momentarily puzzled, then chuckled lightly. "Oh, the Japanese lanterns. Mrs. Corsen was only making a joke."

"I don't get it," he said.

"We were all just so pleased that you got us the stage," she told him. "But we still need to find some lighting. We had hoped to purchase some Japanese lanterns from Mr. Fenton. But Mr. Chavis heard that we were planning to buy them and he bought them himself."

"What's Mr. Chavis going to use them for?" he asked.

"Why nothing," she replied. "He just bought them so we couldn't."

Sharpy listened thoughtfully and nodded.

"What do these Jack-a-knees lanterns look like?" he asked. "Are they some kind of paper?"

"Yes, they are made of paper," Pru told him. "They are made to hold a candle inside."

"I know where they are." he said.

"You know where what are?"

"The Jack-a-knees lanterns," he said. "I saw Mr. Chavis bring them to the gin this afternoon. He put them in the little wooden cabinet in the office."

"At least he did actually go buy them," Pru said. "I'm glad to hear that."

"I could get them, Miss Pru."

"What?"

"I don't work for Mr. Chavis no more," he said. "He ain't got nobody watching the place at all. I could get into the gin and get them for you,"

"Don't be silly, Milton," she said. "I'm sure the gin is locked up very securely."

"Oh locks don't bother me much, Miss Pru," he said. "I can pretty much get in wherever I like. Besides, there is still that hole in the wall where the belt flew off the platens and I tacked the tin back over it myself."

"You think you could get into the gin and get the Japanese lanterns," she said.

The little boy snapped his fingers confidently. "It'd be easy."

Pru considered it for a long moment.

"But it would be stealing," she said finally.

"No, ma'am," Sharpy insisted. "We wouldn't steal nothing. Mr. Chavis ain't using the Jack-a-knees lanterns, so we could just borrow them. When we're finished with them, we put 'em right back where we got them."

Pru looked into the mischievous eyes of the little boy. A grin tugged at the corner of her own mouth, getting broader and broader until she laughed out loud.

"It would be a very good joke on Mr. Chavis," she said.

He nodded.

"And he was very underhanded about buying them out from under us."

The little boy nodded again.

"But I absolutely can't let you go alone," she said. "If someone were to catch you, you'd be in terrible trouble. We'll go together."

"Tonight?" he asked.

Pru glanced up at the lighted window of the house next door.

"Yes, I think tonight will be perfect," she said.

Pru changed into a drab old work dress whose once rich color had faded to a dull, nondescript brown. She covered her hair with a dark scarf and hurried to the back door.

She looked toward the Chavis house once more. The light in the old man's bedroom had been extinguished. She grinned devilishly to herself. Gidry Chavis had already gone to bed, and she was setting out to make a fool of him.

"Let's get going," Sharpy called out to her in a whisper. "If we wait until most everybody has gone to bed, every dog in Chavistown will take up howling at us as we pass."

She nodded and grabbed up the lantern she kept by the doorway as she stepped outside.

"No, don't bring any light," Sharpy insisted.

"Why not?"

"People can see a lantern a mile away," he said. "And when they do, they get real curious."

"But how will we see our way?" Pru asked.

The little boy shrugged. "It ain't so dark that you don't get used to it."

Pru was uncertain but followed his advice. Certainly they could find their way across town in the darkness, but how on earth would they manage to get into the gin or find that cabinet in the office without seeing their way?

She almost backed out of the scheme. It was foolhardy and devious. It was not the kind of example to be setting for a young child like Sharpy. And if they were caught, it would be extremely embarrassing. But the thought of seeing Gidry Chavis's face when he found out, as he undoubtedly would, that the Harvest Moon Dance had been gaily lit by his own Japanese lanterns was worth the chance.

With a shrug of acceptance she extinguished the lantern.

*   *   *

Gidry stood at his father's window, quiet and watchful. Pru came out of her house, carrying her lantern as she always did. He expected her to make her way immediately to the milk shed. That's where she met her lover, that's where she engaged in her illicit affair. That's where . . .

The image of the pornographic postcard filled his brain, but the beautiful nude temptress in his imagination was no stranger. Her face was that of Prudence Belmont. Sweet, shy Prudence Belmont.

It infuriated him. It aroused him as well.

His brow furrowed as he watched the yard next door. Pru did not hurry to the milk shed. She seemed to be standing, talking to someone right there in her yard.

Was it her lover?

Gidry's heart pounded as if he had just run uphill a half mile.

When the light abruptly went out, he knew something was going on. In the vague shadows of moonlight, they appeared to be leaving together by the front gate. He glanced at his father, asleep in the bed, and then, slamming his Stetson upon his head, he was out the door.

He encountered Aunt Hen at the foot of the stairs.

"Good heavens, Gidry, where are you off to?"

"Can you stay with Papa a while longer tonight, Aunt Hen?" he asked. "There's a man I've got to meet."

He barely waited for the old woman's nod before he was out the door. He couldn't let them get too far ahead of him.

Gidry ran as far as the street and easily spotted them. They were clinging to the shadows, especially her companion, but he could follow their movement.

He made his way along the tree-lined side of the street himself, deliberately keeping his steps quiet and at a half a block distance. He didn't want to be detected. He didn't want them to know that he was following them.

The two made their way down the streets. In the dim moonlight he tried to make the two of them out more clearly. In one break in the trees, he glimpsed Pru clearly. Her lover less so. He seemed a good deal shorter than she. Pru was a tall woman, of course. Probably taller than a lot of men in town. Gidry stood several inches higher than most men and was proud of the fact.

The short fellow certainly seemed to know his way around town in the darkness. He unerringly led Pru around every pothole and stumble stone in their path as they skirted the edges of the business district.

At one point they slipped through a back gate. Gidry hurried to follow them without hesitation. They went through the garden and across the yard of Judge Ramey's house. It was as if the short fellow did this all the time. He skirted the ornamental fishpond and knew exactly which picket was loose in the far fence. He held it aside, and Pru slipped through. Gidry did so himself only a minute later to find himself within inches of Whitstone's carriage house.

Walking sideways, he eased himself around the building and into a deserted back alley, where he spotted them once more. They had picked up the pace considerably, and Gidry had to step lively to keep up with them.

He was completely lost. He had lived in Chavistown all his life. He roamed the area in daylight as a child and stumbled through in the night as a disagreeable youth, but these dark passageways were as familiar to him as the surface of the moon.

It was at the next cross street that he realized they were between Second and Third Avenues near Santa Fe. The gin was in sight. Gidry was astounded. They had avoided the light and activity of the courthouse square completely. And he had left her house only minutes before. If he'd known this shortcut, he'd have made it to and from work a good deal faster than typically.

The galvanized metal of the cotton gin shone brightly in the light sliver of moon in the sky. They were on the back side of the building, the side that was most overgrown in tall grass and sage bushes.

Gidry expected them to circle around the entire block toward their ultimate destination. He could not have been more surprised when the two of them stepped up to the side of the building. The little short fellow deftly peeled back one sheet of tin that appeared to the naked eye to be nailed down exactly like every other sheet.

Gidry watched in astonishment at the two scrambled their way inside his building. He stood staring in disbelief for a long moment. Had her lover wanted to show her where he worked? What was there to see in the darkness? Were they there to pour soap in the gin stands or to commit some other type of vandalism? Not likely. Did they have some sort of fetish and wish to perform an illicit act on the gin floor?

Gidry's eyes narrowed with displeasure. They had better not. Gidry was not the kind of man who was quick to fight, and the fellow seemed about half his size, but he thought he could cheerfully pound the man into a greasy spot upon the floor.

He did not follow the two through the loose sheet-

ing on the back wall but rather walked around the
gin to the front door. He quietly fitted the key into
the new padlock and opened the place up. He stepped
inside into total darkness. How could anybody see
anything, he wondered. He would never be able to
find them unless he tripped over them, he thought.

It was at that moment when he heard them tread
above him. They were in his office. He was incredulous. They were in *his* office! He decided to tear up
the stairs and confront them. Unfortunately, he had
no idea where the stairs might be.

He picked up the lantern hung by the doorway and
lit it. The matches were in a small box on the ledge
next to it. With one flick of the match against his
thumbnail he lit the wick. A bright yellow glow en-
circled him as he adjusted the burner and lit the wick.

He heard the steps above him in the office go still.
He glanced toward the stairway. The lanternlight
must have shone in the doorway. There were some
excited muffled whispers and then a scrambling.

"Run!" he heard a young voice call out clearly.
They were going to try to get away.

Gidry raced toward the stairs, only to be nearly
knocked aside by Sharpy Kilroy hurling himself down
the stairs. The boy landed upon the floor, rolled to his
feet, and stared at Gidry like an animal, caught in the
light. The two stood frozen for a long moment and
then, like a frightened deer, the boy startled away
through the darkness of the gin.

"Sharpy!" he called after the child sternly.

His word didn't even create a hesitation. He could
hear the rustle as the boy made his way back across
the deserted gin floor and the ring of metal as he ex-
ited through the loosened piece of tin in the back wall.

Gidry turned to glance up the stairway. At the top, in the doorway to his office stood Prudence Belmont looking white as a sheet.

"What in the devil is going on here?" he asked.

Her expression turned momentarily sheepish and then defensive. Without answering, she gave her back to him and reentered his office.

Exasperated, Gidry went after her, taking the stairs two steps at a time.

He entered the doorway to find her standing in the middle of the room. The cabinet was open and much of its contents were in a hastily discarded pile upon the floor.

"What is going on here?" he asked in a tone he knew from experience was cold enough to make hardened cowboys quiver.

She turned to face him, her chin held high. Her gaze defiant.

"I came for the Japanese lanterns," she answered simply.

Gidry's brow furrowed momentarily puzzled. A further glance at the littered contents upon the floor revealed brightly colored paper with long diaphanous strands.

Gidry hung the lantern on the hook next to the door and folded his arms across his chest obstinately. He gave the woman before him a long, thoughtful look. The yellow glow of light did not reach all the way into the corners of the room, but illuminated the two people who stared at each other. Beyond them there was nothing, no one else.

"You came here to rob me?"

It was a statement more than a question.

She did not reply.

"I heard there was a problem with thievery in this

town," he said. "But I never thought that group included small children and the president of the Ladies' Rose and Garden Society."

"I do not consider it thievery," she answered tartly.

"Oh? Then what do you consider it?"

"I was . . . I was merely borrowing the Japanese lanterns," she said rushing through her words. "We need them for our Harvest Moon Dance. I knew that you would not be using them for any purpose in the near future. As we have been neighbors for years, I simply assumed I would be allowed to borrow them."

Gidry used one finger to kick the Stetson a bit higher on his forehead.

"You are here to borrow them," he repeated.

"Yes."

"In the middle of the night, with no permission and no lantern, sneaking into the back of the gin through a loose metal sheet, you came to *borrow* them."

"Yes."

"Did you intend to return them the same way?"

"I . . . ah . . ."

She hesitated.

"Probably not," she finally admitted.

Gidry shook his head and tutted at her as if she was an errant child.

"This kind of borrowing, Miss Belmont, can, I believe, lead a woman to an unpleasant stay in the county jail."

"You will not have me sent to jail," she said with complete certainty. "It would be far too much of a scandal."

He raised an eyebrow and looked her up and down.

"I have never been afraid to cause a scandal, Miss Belmont. Surely you recall that."

In the dim yellow glow of the lantern he couldn't tell if she was blushing, but she did appear disconcerted.

"My aunt would never forgive you if you had me sent to jail," she suggested.

He thought about that for a moment.

"I don't know," he said. "Aunt Hen has always had a very forgiving nature. And she has forever had a soft spot in her heart for me."

"There would be no purpose in sending me to jail," Pru insisted. "Everyone in town would be angry at you. And at the very worst I would be free in ten days."

"Everyone in town is already angry at me," he pointed out. "And ten days would be enough to see that you are not able to put on a Harvest Moon Dance."

"You wouldn't!"

Gidry shrugged deliberately.

"Just by stopping me, you wouldn't stop the Ladies of the Rose and Garden Society."

"If you want to kill a snake, you cut off the head."

Her eyes widened, and her mouth dropped open in shock.

Intoxicated with the power of the moment, Gidry allowed her to puff and haw for several anxious, affronted moments.

"Of course, you could convince me not to mention it," he said

She looked up at him and swallowed bravely.

"How would I convince you?" she asked.

"You could try bribery," he said.

"Bribery?"

"You've already learned breaking and entering, contributing to the delinquency of a minor and robbery," he pointed out. "I think bribery is next on the list of criminals' behavior."

"I suppose you want me to give up the Harvest Moon Dance," she said.

"Would you?" he asked.

"Never!"

"Then I'll have to think of something that I want equally as much," he told her.

Deliberately he stepped closer. The scent of her was familiar, enticing. Roses. Yes, she'd always smelled like roses.

He stood inches from her now, staring down into her wary, upturned face.

"Kiss me," he said quietly.

"What?"

"Kiss me. A little bribe from your lips will suit me just fine."

Her expression was sweet confusion. She lowered her eyes hastily.

Gidry clasped her face in his hands. He could feel the heat in her cheeks as he raised her eyes to him once more.

"It's no great sacrifice, Pru," he told her. "It's not as if it's a thing you've never done before."

She was trembling.

"Kiss me, or I call the constable," he whispered.

The mention of law enforcement seemed to steel her determination. She raised up on tiptoes and quickly pecked a set of pursed lips against his own.

Gidry eased his hands around her waist and held her fast.

"Now, Pru, you could do better than that eight years ago," he said. "And I'm sure you've learned a trick or two since."

He pulled her into his arms, feeling the soft, full

length of her against his body. Bending his head to one side, he lowered his mouth upon hers. She opened for him as eagerly as she had eight years ago. He reveled in the taste of her. The indefinable spice that had lingered in his memory for eight long years. It was a taste of love. No woman, nowhere, at any time, had ever offered him that.

"Oh yes," he whispered against her lips before he deepened the kiss, using his tongue to tease and tempt her.

Her hands, which had lain dormant at her sides, were suddenly caressing his weary shoulders. Then featherlike fingers moved upward to bury themselves in his hair.

His hat fell off.

The unexpected calamity startled them both. Simultaneously they pulled back from the embrace and stared at each other.

Gidry's pulses were pounding like a racehorse's. His senses were heightened and his breathing rapid. He gazed down at her upturned face craving more, aching for more. Her lips were still parted and her eyes glazed with what he recognized as sexual desire. He could have her. Right here. Right now. He could press her back to this dusty floor and take his pleasure as he'd failed to do eight years before. She hadn't refused him then. She wouldn't refuse him now.

His body urged recklessness. His mind counseled caution. Reluctantly, he heeded the latter.

Gidry loosened her from his embrace. His hands lingered upon her waist. He was not ready to release her entirely.

"I've never been bribed before," he said quietly. "I found it to be a highly pleasurable experience."

Pru was embarrassed now, clearly embarrassed by her own unanticipated response.

"Let me go," she said, trying to pull away from him.

"Just a minute," he told her, lowering his hands until they rested high upon her hipbones. "I have something to tell you first."

She looked up into his eyes again startled.

"You may borrow my Japanese lanterns for your Harvest Moon Dance," he told her. "And in the future, Miss Belmont, if there is anything that you want from me"—he pulled her tight against the front of his trousers, certain that she could not mistake his meaning or the evidence of his arousal—"anything, you only have to ask."

Chapter 13

IT WAS as if heaven itself were smiling proudly upon the Harvest Moon Dance. The morning dawned bright and cloudless, and a pleasant westerly breeze commenced in the early afternoon. By three o'clock every boll of cotton in Chavis County and its environs had been ginned and baled and the horrible noisy commotion that had been plaguing town residents for days ceased abruptly into blessed silence.

Pru was fidgety and short-tempered. She was certain that most people chalked it up to anxiety and nervousness about the outcome of her speech. She only wished it were that simple.

The grounds around the church were gaily decorated. A hundred Japanese lanterns were hung around the dance floor and above the makeshift stage glowing with celebratory light. Every man and woman who beheld their splendor became all curiosity as to how Prudence had managed to come up with them.

For her part, Pru wasn't talking. She didn't even like to think about the night at the cotton gin. She'd behaved too stupidly to be believed. Trying to steal the lanterns was unconscionable. Involving Milton was even worse. And to then throw herself at Gidry Chavis was almost too much of a shame to be borne.

You want me to kiss you?

Pru had been incredulous. It was a bribe she'd never expected. And if she had any sense at all, she would have called the constable herself.

Kiss me.

Somehow at the time the words had seemed soft and sweet and seductive. He had said it was no sacrifice, but it would have been better if she'd been tossed into a flaming abyss. The touch of his hands upon her face was enough to overcome all her resistance.

It's not as if it's a thing you've never done before, he'd whispered. But it had been a wholly new experience, nothing like her eight-year-old memories or even the fantasy of a lonely dark night.

Gidry's hands upon her waist had eased her close and set her trembling. She could not recall his words, it was not at all what he had said, but the way he uttered them as warm and slow-dripping as maple syrup. She wanted to taste that syrup, savor it with her lips and her tongue. And when she did, she found it hotter, sweeter, and infinitely more suited to her appetite than she had ever imagined.

The feel of his long body against the length of her own was a sensation totally new and shockingly pleasurable. His broad chest, muscled stomach, powerful thighs were pressed in such intimate contact that she was unmistakably aware of his growing arousal.

He whispered gentle praise against her lips and she would have given him all she had to give. She could not resist touching him, caressing him, exploring the strange geography of the man who held her so gently, as if he feared she would break, yet so firmly it seemed he would never let her go.

Anything. He had told her with such meaning. *You only have to ask.*

The words could have been her own. Pru had thought herself long past carrying her heart upon her sleeve, but a few moments alone in a private, ill-lit room and she'd been his for the taking.

"Mrs. Johnson is arriving with the food. Do you want to supervise the setting of the tables?" Alice asked.

"No," Pru replied too sharply.

She was startled at the interruption of her wayward thoughts. Deliberately she counted to ten and apologized to the young woman.

"Could you take care of it yourself, Alice?" she said. "As you can hear, I'm as cross as a bear and no fit company for anyone."

Ever sweet, Alice patted her on the shoulder consolingly.

"It's all going to be wonderful," she assured Pru. "And everyone in the county is going to show up."

Pru nodded. Already crowds were beginning to gather, and it was not yet even dark.

"Yes, I'm sure we will be able to make our case at last," Alice said.

Pru should be practicing her speech, but she was so distracted. She was thinking of Gidry Chavis again. And she had to stop. She had to forget. She had to . . . she had to convince herself that the kiss had never happened.

To make it all worse than awful, she had seen him on two occasions since obtaining the lanterns. Both times he had tipped his hat at her politely and smiled.

Pru couldn't imagine what that could mean. Could

the man be laughing at her? It was certainly possible. Her behavior that night, however, had been no laughing matter. It was far too easy to love him. And it was a weakness she could not allow herself.

From the corner of her eye she saw Sharpy. He was helping Reverend Hathaway to move the church's piano onto the stage. Fay Tatum was to play the music, accompanied by Myra Beauchamp on the violin. Hathaway was not the most muscular of gentleman and Sharpy only a child. It began to seem unlikely that they would be capable of pushing the heavy instrument up the steep ramp they'd nailed to the end of the porch platform. Fortunately a couple of burly onlookers decided to lend a hand and momentarily the piano was in place.

Sharpy thanked them as if their help were a personal favor to him. The little boy had not had so much as a question about what had happened in the gin or how she had managed to return home, escorted by Gidry Chavis and with the Japanese lanterns wrapped neatly in folded newspaper.

If anything, the little fellow seemed almost guilty. As if it were *he* who had thoughtlessly involved *her*. The dear young boy would have never actually done such a thing had she not been so eager to aid him in the larcenous scheme.

In truth Pru was grateful not to have to explain herself to young Sharpy, or anyone for that matter. She didn't know what had happened in those dark, silent moments inside the gin. Her resistance had broken down. He had been there before her in the flesh, and she had been unable to resist him. She felt drawn to him in a way that was both tentatively tender and prodigiously powerful. It was not like the worship she'd felt for him as a young girl. It was complete, full-grown, and all-encompassing.

She had no idea how he must have felt. Pru would never have thought to describe Gidry Chavis as inscrutable, but she certainly didn't understand him. He had held her passionately in his arms. He had pressed her intimately against him. Then he had let her go.

Gidry had treated her much differently than he had eight years ago. But she had felt no sense of it being in the past. It was as if they were only unfinished. As if their parting were only a temporary lull in a storm that was brewing with great inevitability.

Pru recognized the direction of her thoughts and checked them firmly once more. There was no way that she was going to begin mooning over Gidry Chavis again. It was one thing to have been a lovesick young girl. It was quite another for a grown woman to make an utter fool of herself in front of a whole town.

Her only interaction with the man, if any, would be as president of the Ladies' Rose and Garden Society and, so far, it did not appear that he would be much involved with that organization at all.

Which was better for all concerned, Pru assured herself. She made a last walk-through of the area. It was as lovely as her ladies could make it. There were blooming flowers in every possible location and flowing ribbons twisting in the breeze. Boughs of vivid sumac had been arched over the entryway. And brightly colored vines twined the poles from which the lanterns were strung.

The women of Chavistown knew how to make things beautiful. And upon this occasion they had not hesitated to do so. Most were at the dance early. Each had her job to do. The refreshments had to be displayed. The last-minute details checked and re-checked. The dress rehearsal of the much-practiced tableau accomplished.

Alice was positively frantic because pretty little Callie Fenton had come down with chicken pox and wouldn't be able to do her part in the event. The group had frantically searched for a similar-sized child that could wear her costume. They had settled upon Sassy Redfern. Her mother was not in the club, being slightly less than respectable. But her daughter was sweet enough and very eager to participate.

To Pru's mind it had all worked out perfectly well, but the unexpected snag had completely rattled Alice, who was still not certain that it would all come off as it should.

It was not yet full dark, but the huge harvest moon was starting to rise. And people began to arrive. Farmers with families came in carts and wagons. Several lone gentleman rode in on horseback. More than one weary farmhand arrived on a mule. Stanley Honnebuzz showed up in his carriage, Judge Ramey at his side. But most people—the people of Chavistown—came walking, dressed in their finest, fittest party dress. They came to laugh and dance and celebrate the beautiful night and the success of the cotton.

Pru was dressed, modestly, in light and serviceable lawn shirtwaist and skirt. She did not anticipate an opportunity to dance. Younger ladies would have most of the attention. And married women would have the certainty of the first and final dances with their husbands. Spinsters were very clever if they developed an aversion to dancing. Prudence had.

She had come here tonight to save her garden and her community. And she could only hope that the people of Chavistown, eager to laugh and dance, had also come to listen to reason. That they came prepared to hear an opposing view on the subject of residential street lighting.

She felt for the pieces of folded paper and the small brown pamphlet that she had stashed in her pocket. Her speech was still there, and she was perfectly ready to make it. She took a cleansing breath as an antidote to nervousness.

Although public speaking was not as paralyzing for her as for many, the niggle of stage fright was common to all. However, she reminded herself, these were, at least in a very general sense, all friends of hers. There was no one in Chavistown that she had any cause to be nervous around. Except, of course, Gidry Chavis, and he certainly would not be here tonight.

Gidry Chavis sang to himself as he stood in front of his mirror making a knot in his tie.

He admired his appearance. With the ginning finally complete, he'd been able to make it to the tailor's shop and was sporting a pair of well-cut black cassimere trousers, a frothy white pleated shirt, and a blue pin-check cotton coat. The look was jaunty, urbane and particularly attractive on a tall man with dark hair. Gidry Chavis wanted to look his best tonight. Even with a most critical eye, he thought that perhaps he did.

With a spring in his step, Gidry left his own room and headed for his father's. He was grinning as he walked in, and the old man looked up at him, his eyes questioning.

"Oh good, you're awake," Gidry said. "You've been sleeping so much lately, I've gotten downright lonely. That's silly enough, isn't it? I've been gone for eight years and home barely a month. And I've already gotten so accustomed to being here with you, that I miss you when you're napping."

Gidry laughed out loud and seated himself beside his father on the bed.

"But I can't sit with you tonight, Papa," he told him. "I have a pressing social engagement. I'm off to the Harvest Moon Dance."

Gidry straightened his collar and adjusted his tie. "Don't I look spiffy in my new duds?"

He didn't wait for an answer.

"I'm very particular about how I look," he explained. "It isn't every night that a man asks a woman to marry him."

The old man's eyes widened at his words.

"I know, it's probably a bit of a surprise," Gidry said. "Though I don't expect it's as much for you as it will be for most folks in this town. The way I've been talking about her night and day since I arrived back home, I'm pretty sure you suspected my feelings."

He sighed heavily.

"I guess a lot of fellows would say it's too early," Gidry admitted. "She and I have hardly talked together at all. And there was just that one kiss. But I'm thinking myself that it's about eight years too late."

Gidry glanced out the window, his thoughts bittersweet.

"She loved me then, Papa," he admitted. "She truly loved me and . . . well the truth is I wasn't man enough to be loved. Her devotion terrified me in a way that all my experience with other women never could. I didn't want a woman to love me that way. I didn't believe that I deserved it."

He shrugged, embarrassed.

"I was too young," he said. "Although not all men are too young at that age. I was way too young."

Gidry turned to look with honesty into his father's eyes.

"And I was your son," he said. "Not at all an easy thing to be."

His brow furrowing, Gidry took back the words.

"I don't mean that exactly the way it sounded," he assured his father. "I was lucky to be your son. I was lucky growing up with your love and your example. I want you to understand that I know my good fortune. Not many motherless boys are as cherished and nurtured as I was. I thank you for that. But being the son of Peer Chavis was a more of a fight than I was up for."

Gidry took a deep breath, trying for once to sort his jumble of feelings into some kind of explainable order.

"I have always . . . always admired you so much, Papa," he said. "You were the biggest, the strongest, the smartest, the most powerful man in Chavis County. In my mind, Chavis County was the whole world. As a boy I thought that you were infallible, invincible. And I knew myself to be all too human."

He shook his head ruefully.

"As I grew up and realized, as sons will, that we were both very human, well I suppose that I still suffered a great deal with the comparison. I just didn't think much of myself. I wanted to be like you, but I knew I wasn't up to the job."

He leaned forward and grasped his father's withered hand in his own.

"I'm still not the man you are, Papa," he said. "But I'm my own man now. I'm careful and thoughtful. I

work hard and try to live right. I can be kind and I
can defend what is my own."

His firm tone belied any doubt.

"And I want Prudence Belmont to be my own."

Gidry sighed.

"I know that you always wanted me to marry Pru,"
he said. "But I have to tell you honestly, Papa, that is
not why I'm doing it."

He gave his father a wry grin.

"I'd do most anything you'd ask of me," he said.
"However, I have always drawn the line at a lawfully
wedded wife."

He chuckled.

"Truth is, I think about the woman all the time,"
he admitted. "Everything that happens, I want to tell
her about it. She avoids me as if I had the plague, so
I manufacture reasons just to pass her on the street."

Gidry shook his head.

"I guess I've finally decided that I deserve to be
happy, Papa," he told his father. "I deserve my own
wife and my own children. I deserve to be loved. I
love her, Papa. And I deserve to get to be her husband."

A long companionable silence lingered between the
two men. Gidry felt the warmth of his father's gaze
and knew that the old man was happy for him and
proud as well.

"I'm not saying it's going to be easy," Gidry said.
"There is apparently someone else. I don't know the
man, but I think I have more to offer her. I don't mean
materially, although I think I can keep her in comfort.
The fact that I can offer marriage and children and . . .
and my heart. That's a lot, don't you think. I hope it
is enough."

Gidry rose to his feet.

"So no wild cowboy stories for you tonight," he said. "I've asked Aunt Hen to sit with you tonight. So I guess we can both spend the evening making eyes at a fine handsome woman."

Gidry leaned forward, tenderly swept the hair from his father's brow, and kissed him on the forehead.

"I love you, Papa," he said. "Wish me well."

His father could not answer, but his fingers tightened around Gidry's and Gidry knew what was in the old man's heart.

He left the room smiling and singing once more.

Trotting down the stairs in fine high spirits, he picked his new-stitched linen fedora from the rack and placed it upon his head at a rakish angle.

"Oh dear," he heard Aunt Hen say from the room behind him. "The young ladies had best be on their guard tonight."

He turned and grinned at the older woman.

"The young ladies as a whole are relatively safe," he assured her. "I have my eye, however, on one female in particular."

Aunt Hen raised an eyebrow and giggled delightedly.

"What a very fortunate young lady," she said.

Gidry bowed low, feigning fine manners.

"I do hope she agrees with you, ma'am," he said.

He left the house laughing, his spirits very high.

The dancing was well under way by the time he arrived at the church grounds. Just as Pru had predicted, virtually everyone in the county was in attendance. And certainly none of those people expected to see him. He smiled and nodded as he made his way through the crowd, refusing to take offense at often astounded expressions upon the faces of his male acquaintances or the most blatant snubs of their wives.

At the refreshment table, he wondered for a moment if they were going to refuse to serve him. After several skeptical looks and a good deal of whispered discussion behind his back, he was eventually handed a glass of lemonade and two shortbread cookies. It wasn't much considering the abundance of sweets weighing down the table, but at least they were not willing to have him starve.

He sipped his drink and ate his fare as he watched the dancers cavort upon the floor. Most of the dances were exuberant reels and jigs; occasionally, to the apparent delight of the violinist, waltzes were played. Gidry watched and imagined. He had danced with Pru many times in his youth, but never as a man had he swayed and turned with her in his arms. It was an event to anticipate with great pleasure. He wanted to dance with her until their shoes wore through, until dawn peeped over the horizon, until the end of time.

He caught sight of Sharpy Kilroy in the crowd and waved welcomingly to the boy. The young fellow stared back at him, unsure. Gidry motioned him over, but to his surprise the child ducked into the crowd and was gone.

Gidry was puzzled, but shook his head. In memory he saw the boy's frightened eyes when they'd collided upon the stairs in the gin. The fellow must still think Gidry was angry with him. He was not, of course. He knew exactly whose idea it was to steal the Japanese lanterns and where the plan originated.

His brow furrowed thoughtfully. Of course, Pru would never have known her way through the back alleys like that. And she certainly would not have been able to get into the gin without the child's help.

The boy did seem to be pretty conniving for one so young.

Gidry glanced up again to take notice of the lanterns. They did look very good. He could hardly be sorry she'd come to steal them. And he wasn't even sorry that her little dance was such a success. Stanley Honnebuzz was wrong. If these ladies wanted to have a say in the street lighting project, then at the very least they should get to be heard. No matter how nonsensical or foolish their concerns.

The dance ended, and Alice Ramey came on stage. She was a kind of quirky-looking young woman with far too much brown hair. Actually, she looked a good deal like her father, but it was more attractive on the judge than on his daughter.

"Ladies and gentlemen of Chavis County," she said formally. "The Chavistown Ladies' Rose and Garden Society presents for the edification and education of the participants of the Harvest Moon Dance, a tableau entitled *Three Women of America*."

The pianist began to play a rousing rendition of *"My country 'tis of thee"* while behind the stage three women assembled dressed in what looked from Gidry's distance to be Grecian robes.

"The first woman of America," Alice announced over the sound of the piano. "Lady Liberty, who stands ever watchful shining her light into the darkest corners of land to guard us against oppression, despotism, and tyranny."

Elmer Corsen's wife stepped onto the stage, her draped gown not quite able to disguise her rather large girth. She carried in her hand a makeshift torch of colored paper with yellow and orange ribbons strung up a wire frame to resemble a flame.

The pianist finished that verse and Alice began speaking again.

"The second woman of America is Blind Justice," she declared, as the next lady made her entrance on the stage. "Forever vigilant that truth and equality prevail, she weighs only the facts with no regard for wealth and privilege."

Blind Justice did indeed have a folded scarf across her eyes. Her steps were, therefore, a little tentative. She reached her side of the stage and then with whispered directions from Alice moved over a little farther. The scales she held before her clattered a bit with the effort.

Alice waited for the verse to finish once again.

"And lastly and in some way leastly we have the American woman of the next century."

The crowd ohhed and ahhed as cute little Sassy Redfern took her place at center stage. The pretty five-year-old was bright and shining as a new penny. Her pale blond hair was tied in a half dozen little pink ribbons and her sweet chubby cheeks just begged to be pinched.

Alice began again. "The woman of the next century will bring her family into a world of freedom and liberty. She will touch the progressive world, but keep in trust the tradition of values handed down for generations. She will face the future with courage and joy, hope and enthusiasm. She will be the embodiment of all that is great and good in America."

A second trio of young ladies also in draped Grecian-looking garb walked onto the stage and took their place next to the piano.

Their voices blended in perfect harmony as they sang so beautifully the last verse of the beloved anthem.

"Ladies and gentlemen, join us as we sing," Alice cajoled.

The tune began again at the beginning. All around him voices were raised in song. Gidry joined in, his pleasant baritone, a nice foil for the high tones of the ladies standing around him.

"My country 'tis of thee, sweet land of liberty
Of thee I sing.
Land where my fathers died.
Land of the Pilgrims' pride.
From every mountainside,
Let freedom ring."

It was at this moment that he saw Pru for the first time that evening. She was standing to the side of the stage. She was as white as a sheet, and she was staring right at him.

Chapter 14

PRUDENCE COULDN'T believe that he was there. It was impossible, totally impossible. But it was true. And he was wearing new clothes. He had been unfairly handsome in his cowboy garb, he was patently irresistible in a well-cut suit.

He was smiling at her. Smiling at her. Was that his plan? To so unnerve her that she would be unable to give her presentation? She had to get ahold of herself. Her gardens, her community were counting upon her.

The tableau had been a rousing success. As beautifully done as any Pru had seen in larger cultural centers. But now the women were filing off the stage, and it was going to be her turn to speak. For the first time she doubted herself, doubted her cause. Perhaps the lighting would have no ill effects. Maybe she should just leave the thinking to the men. Who was she to point out the dangers of progress unquestioned?

She steeled herself deliberately. She was Prudence Belmont, a citizen of this town, this county, this state, country, and planet. If she did not use the knowledge and understanding that God gave to her, then it would be just as well had he not given it to her at all.

"Ladies and gentlemen," Alice began her introduction, "as you know the Chavistown Ladies' Rose and Garden Society has sponsored this dance for a high and honorable purpose. To speak with you about a topic of great import to ourselves and to all the people of Chavis County. May I introduce to you our president, Miss Prudence Belmont."

Pru hardly heard the smattering of applause as she took her place upon the stage.

Her hands trembled as she reached into her pocket for the crumpled speech and the small pamphlet bound in brown paper. She opened the latter to the first place she had marked.

"I would like to read to you," she said, her voice not betraying a hint of her nervousness, "a passage, very pertinent to our current situation, from the treatise by Avis Atherton Lafoon entitled *Observations Upon Progress as a Threat to the Natural World.*"

Prudence cleared her throat and raised her voice.

"The unconsidered, unthinking march toward progress takes no stock in the natural world or the needs of it," she began. *"To design a machine that allows a man to complete a task in half the time as he is naturally capable is to tinker with the purpose of time. It is said that the machine has saved time. But one might rightly ask if time can indeed be stored for later use. When time is saved does man live longer or is eternity expanded? I say, resoundingly no. No, the man has merely completed his task before he should and now stands idle and his unoccupation likely to lead to dissonance, perhaps even moral ruin."*

Pru glanced up to see her audience. She noted with some concern that not all of them were able to follow her logic. Only a handful had the wit or education to comprehend Mr. Lafoon's philosophy.

Pru found her place at the next bookmark.

"When man attempts to improve upon the order of the universe, it is as if he boasts that he knows more than God. But he does not. He cannot. His meddling is as an unlearned child allowed to conduct the affairs of Church or State, strictly upon impulse and with acumen unsound. Perversely unraveling the laws of universe may result in unanticipated, detrimental outcomes. The reason of creation in the natural world is multitudinous and unfathomable. Man in his simple ignorance seeks to make enhancements upon it, only to unleash a plethora of incomprehensible consequences."

Prudence looked up once more to see the reaction of the townspeople. Some looked confused, some bored.

"I don't see where this has anything to do with electric street lighting." Stanley Honnebuzz voiced the question that many had on their minds. "Or with ridding ourselves of a nest of thieves."

Pru was momentarily taken aback by the interruption, but she recovered quickly enough to answer his question.

"The purpose of deterring is fine indeed," Pru answered him. "But turning night into day may be too big a price to pay for a solution."

"What do you mean?" the judge asked. "The Commercial Club has agreed to pay for the improvements."

"I don't speak of that price, Judge Ramey," she said. "That price hardly bears mention at all. The price I speak of is much greater."

Those around her seemed to be listening at last.

"Our plants, our gardens exist within the bounds of two lives, daylight and dark. If one of those ceases to exist, we can't know what the effects might be."

"Do you think it might do something to our crops?" Amos Wilburn asked, wariness creeping into his voice.

"Some say yes," Pru answered him. "It's been suggested in many publications that exposure to constant light might have effects heretofore unanticipated or unknown. No one can say if that is true, sir, but I do know that morning glories open their petals at dawn. And four-o'clocks in the fullness of the afternoon. If night is turned into day, how will those flowers know when to reveal and conceal?"

There were murmurs of question filtering through the crowd.

"We know from the work of both Priestley and Ingenhousz that plant growth only occurs in radiant light. When the sun goes down, growth ceases. Can a plant work night and day with no rest? We know that man cannot. It would kill him."

"Maybe the plants will just grow twice as big as they are now?"

"Some have suggested that," she agreed. "There has been talk of our flowers growing tall as trees. But is bigger always better? What do we have to give up to have them so large? We know from the hybridization of roses that when we attempt to create a new color, for example, the resulting plant may be less supple-limbed or more thorny than either of the families of its origin. Perhaps we will be giving up blossoms entirely in order to grow bushes taller than cottonwood trees."

"Surely you don't think so."

"I do not know what to think," Pru answered honestly. "I know that night was created for rest. And that if people do not rest, if they do not sleep, they become witless and often insane. The eventual outcome in plants not allowed to sleep is unknown."

"There might be no effect at all."

"I'm sure that is what the gentlemen of the Commercial Club believe," she said. "I know they are only trying to do what is right for this community. But we do not always know what is the right thing to do."

Pru could feel the crowd moving to her side of the argument. She could feel her words reaching them.

Stanley Honnebuzz made a dismissive sound and shook his head at her.

"Many of us have electric lamps in our houses now," he pointed out. "And we have seen nothing amiss. The gas lamps on the courthouse square have been lit every night for years. The trees and grass still grow there just fine."

Pru made no attempt to dispute his word, just to explain away his meaning.

"The gas lamps provide very little light, not nearly as much as is being proposed by the gentlemen of the Commercial Club. And the changes may not be immediate."

Stanley Honnebuzz spoke up disdainfully. "For heaven's sake, what is the loss of a few roses when we are trying to safeguard ourselves from criminals."

"My dear Mr. Honnebuzz," Pru replied testily, "athough I value my roses highly, I am not suggesting that only the flowers in our gardens would be affected. Imagine, if you can, cornstalks tall as your house, with not an ear to feed man or beast. And if the cattle don't have corn, from whence will come our milk and butter?"

"Are you prophesying doomsday?" the lawyer asked.

"I am not prophesying at all," she said. "I am voicing concern for a new intrusion into the natural world that none of us knows enough about even to speculate upon the outcome."

"I believe it was God, Miss Belmont, who said, 'Let there be light.' " Honnebuzz announced loudly.

Pru's eyes narrowed as she focused in on him directly as she replied, her voice rising in anger. "And if you read on from there, sir, he 'divided the light from the darkness and saw that it was good.' "

The lawyer looked ready to make another volley when suddenly Gidry Chavis stepped upon the stage.

He held up his hands to get attention, and every sound on the grounds ceased abruptly as people strained to hear.

"Miss Belmont, Mr. Honnebuzz, I don't think we should allow this wonderful discussion to dissolve into a shouting match."

Pru opened her mouth to dispute his characterization, but she wasn't given a chance.

"You have made a good point, Miss Belmont," he said. "You have made a very good point. I wish I had bothered to listen to it several weeks ago. I publicly apologize that I did not."

Pru stared at the man, stunned speechless.

"The Commercial Club," he continued, "has made some decisions concerning the residential street lighting project without fully understanding the implications that you have brought up. Mr. Sattlemore, the representative from Big Texas Electric, is not here tonight, but I shall wire him first thing Monday morning. We need to have another meeting to discuss this. And I would like to ask you, Miss Belmont, to be present to bring up these concerns at that time."

"I . . . I . . ."

Prudence couldn't think of a thing to say.

"Would you be willing to sit down with us and Mr.

Sattlemore and see what the man has to say?" he asked.

"Ah . . . yes," she managed to get out finally. "Yes, I would."

Gidry's mouth curled into a broad, handsome grin.

"Thank you, Miss Belmont," he said more quietly, as if his words were just for her. "Do you have something more to say? I don't believe you were allowed to finish your speech."

She glanced down at the crumpled paper in her hand.

"No, no, I don't have anything more to say," she told him.

"Good." He turned to scan the crowd. "Where are our musicians?" he asked. "I don't know about the rest of you, but on a night like this, I really want to dance."

The crowd erupted in laughter, and a few moments later, with the help of the musically inclined ladies, the dancing began once more.

Gidry held out his hand, and Pru glanced down at it questioningly.

"Would you care to dance, Miss Belmont?" he asked.

"What? Why no, Mr. Chavis, I never dance," she answered.

She expected him to walk away, but he did not.

"Please dance with me, Pru," he said.

She looked up into his eyes and knew that her heart was there on her sleeve once more.

There is something about dancing in the arms of the man that you have loved all your life that is uniquely disconcerting. Beneath the mesmerizing rays of the harvest moon and gaily glowing Japanese lanterns, Pru placed her hand in Gidry's own and with him stepped out upon the dance floor.

A smattering of applause broke out among those near, apparently believing that having the two share a dance was the same as having the differences between the Commercial Club and the Rose and Garden Society worked out and settled. Pru realized they were seeing the dance as symbolic, but she could not join them in their delight. To her the hand that clasped hers and the arm so casually around her waist were the touch of a lover. And Prudence Belmont had absolutely no business being in love.

He was staring down into her eyes, his own bright and warm. He seemed so happy, so content and at ease, she wondered if he were secretly laughing at her.

"Don't hold me so close," she whispered to him.

Gidry raised an eyebrow and gazed at her questioningly.

"I'm holding you at the same length that I would hold Mrs. Hathaway," he assured her, then added with a warm smile, "Don't worry, my sweetheart. I would never do anything to expose you to sly talk."

Her eyes widened.

It was undoubtedly true. There was nothing untoward in his embrace, except that he was the one doing the embracing.

"Then do not call me *sweetheart*," she said, her voice clipped and cold. He was laughing at her, she was almost certain.

"My apologies," he answered. "It was a slip of the tongue. I used to call you my sweetheart all the time. You never seemed to mind it."

"That was when I was your sweetheart," she told him. "Now I am only your neighbor."

"And the sweetest sweetheart of a neighbor a man could want," he said.

She looked at him askance.

He shrugged. "The words in my heart just come out of my mouth."

Pru's brow furrowed worriedly. He was playing some kind of joke, some kind of cruel joke, and she was the butt of it.

"What is it that you're up to?" she asked him.

"I am up to nothing," he assured her. "I came here to dance tonight. And to be perfectly honest, there is no one with whom I'd rather dance than you."

She was skeptical.

"I don't know why you have decided to be so co-operative," Pru said. "But in case you were not listening to my speech, I can assure you that I am very serious about ensuring that the community does not perpetrate some drastic disservice to nature."

"I did listen to your speech," he assured her. "You were eloquent and made a good deal of sense. That is why I suggested that you be with the Commercial Club when we talk to Mr. Sattlemore. I would not suggest that for any other reason. This has nothing to do with that."

"This?"

"This chance to hold you in my arms again," he said as warm and smoothly as a velvet glove.

"Please do not think that I am so easily impressed by your manners that I will forget what I am about," she said.

He grinned at her.

"That is something I would truly like to see again," he told her. "I would like to see you, Pru, with your heart in your eyes forgetting about everything in the world but me."

She huffed with disdain. "Would that give you some kind of perverse pleasure?" she asked.

"Pleasure, yes," he answered. "But nothing perverse about it. Look at me, Pru. My heart is in my eyes right now. I have forgotten about everything in the world but you, sweetheart. There is nothing in my world but you."

Pru was incredulous.

"Do you expect me to believe that?" she asked him. His expression seemed almost hurt.

"I suppose my opposition to giving you a platform to speak as well as my recent vilification all over town has turned you solidly against me."

"I can't imagine why it would not," she said, "although I am certain that it was not you alone who was opposed to hearing us out. I know the gentlemen of this community all too well."

"Yes, you're right," he agreed. "I took on the role of scapegoat, not thinking how solidly I would be tied to playing the part."

"So now you are trying to say that you were not opposed to the dance?"

"No, I was against it," he admitted. "I believed that you and the other ladies had nothing important to contribute to the discussion," he admitted. "I was wrong about that. Over the years, I've been wrong about a good many things."

"At least you admit that," she said.

"I was never wrong about you, Pru," he said. "I knew you would love me and you would tame me. I was never wrong about that."

"I have no idea what you are talking about, Mr. Chavis," she said with extreme formality, keeping her head high and refusing to look at him.

He continued to twirl her around the dance floor;

she begged in her heart for continued silence, but it was not to be.

"I believe I did say that this was not going to be easy," he reminded himself aloud.

"What is not going to be easy?" she asked.

"Winning you back," he answered.

"What!"

She said the word so loudly and stopped in the middle of the dance floor so abruptly that all those around them stared curiously.

"Keep dancing," Gidry cautioned with a whisper. "People will be thinking I've made you an indecent proposal."

She resumed moving gracefully with him.

"I don't know any romantic way to tell you what I need to say, Prudence," he began. "I was wrong, very wrong all those years ago. And I know now that my father was right. You would make a wonderful wife for me."

Pru stared at him, shaking her head. A part of her was incredulous, disbelieving. Another part was trembling with hope.

"Gid, this is some joke or hoax or . . ."

"A joke?" He shook his head. "I have never been so sincere in my life. I was young and foolish, and I deliberately threw away my chance at happiness with you. Well, I want it back, Pru. I want you back."

The song ended. Everyone around them applauded. Pru did as well, but it was as if her hands were numb and her ears muffled. All the real world seemed so very, very far away.

Gidry's arm slipped easily around her waist and he looked down into her eyes smiling warmly.

All of it, all of the past came crashing back on her in a wave of nausea. She could see herself as she once was, craving the merest crumbs of his attention, pathetic in her need for the least of his regard. She remembered with vivid clarity the hastily written note saying merely good-bye, as well as the public pity when his hasty departure was made known.

The band struck up a new tune, this one a lively polka. Gidry led her away from the noise and lights of the dance.

In the darkened shade of the cottonwood trees on the far side of the church, he took her hand into his own. He brought it up to his mouth and laid a gentle kiss at the pulse point on the inside of her wrist.

"I'm sure a more wily fellow than I would have dragged you into the shadows to vie for another sampling of your sweet lips," he said. "I want that as well, but first I want to say my piece. Shall I go down on one knee? Would that help? Miss Prudence, would you do me the great honor of being my wife, for better, worse, sickness and health, all of that?"

"Stop it!" she said. "Don't joke with me this way."

"I am not, I would not joke with you, Pru," he assured her. "I do want to marry you. I want to marry you as soon as it can be arranged. I want you to move into the house with Papa and me. I want to give the old man grandchildren, we still have time. Be my wife."

"You are eight years too late," she said.

"I know you must find it hard to forgive me for that," he said. "I find it hard to forgive myself."

He sighed heavily as he offered explanation.

"I ran away, Pru," he whispered to her softly. "I was young and scared, and I ran away. But not from you. It was never about you, about whether I thought you would make a fine wife for me or not. It was about me and my father, I suppose. Or maybe just about me. I was running wild. There wasn't enough liquor in the county to quench my thirst, nor enough loose women to . . . well to suit me. My father believed that the burden of wife and family would slow me down if not tame me completely."

He rubbed the back of her hand against his cheek. It was smooth, very recently shaved clean, but there was still the hint of rough stubble.

"I knew he was right," Gidry said. "And I did not want to be changed. I was having too much fun. I was too carefree."

Those dark, expressive eyes that had once lured her into love, now watched her with such honest intent, his sincerity could not be denied.

"Pru, I am different now," he assured her. "I've got all that wildness, all that restlessness, I've got it out of my system now."

She stood beside him, feeling his warmth, his care; as inside her everything turned cold, brutally cold.

"Let me be sure I understand you," she said firmly, pulling her hand away from his grasp. "You didn't want a wife and family then because you were young and free. But now that you've got all that out of your system, well fortunately I'm still here and you can pick up just right where you left off."

His brow furrowed in worry.

"Well, no that's not exactly what I mean," he assured her. "I know that our lives have changed. I know that . . . that your heart has been or may be now engaged elsewhere. But, Pru, I can offer you so much . . . I can offer you marriage. I . . ."

"Marriage to you? Apparently in your mind that is a great boon, I take it," she said sarcastically.

"No, I didn't say that," he insisted, obviously becoming irritated himself. "But it is better than the alternative."

"Oh, so you are one who believes that for a woman to marry, no matter how miserably, is better than living in spinsterhood?" she asked with great sarcasm.

"I'm not talking about spinsterhood," he said, raising his voice slightly at her challenging tone. "I'm talking about . . ." He lowered his voice secretively. "I'm talking about loving without marriage."

"A subject you know a good deal about apparently," she snapped.

His expression was somewhat worried. He obviously did not care for the direction of this discussion, but he continued his argument nonetheless.

"I do know about it, Pru," he said with great solemnity, his mind focusing on the memory of her signature on the back of a vulgar French postcard. "I figured it out the first day I got home. But I am not a guiltless fellow, I am far from being blameless enough to cast stones. I don't want to know any more than I already do. And I can assure you that under no circumstances will I ever offer one word of reproach. We will put it in the past and never look back again."

"Reproach?" She was astounded. "How on earth could you have cause to reproach me? Yes, you want to put it in the past. You want to put it all in the past and never look back," she said. "Well I, Mr. Chavis, live with the past every day of my life. You come back in here and say, oh excuse me, I made a mistake eight years ago but now we can be married, no harm done. Well, there was plenty of harm done. There was harm done to me, there was harm done to your father, there was harm done to this community. And there was harm done to an innocent who has no idea who or why it has happened."

"What are you talking about?"

"I'm talking about Mabel," she answered sharply.

"Who?"

"Mabel Merriman," she said.

Gidry's brow furrowed in question.

"She died last year, you know," Pru continued.

"Who?"

"Mabel . . . Mabel Kilroy, you knew her as Mabel Merriman."

Gidry continued to look at her blankly.

"Mabel Merriman," she said, emphatically and a bit louder than necessary, "the woman you ran away with."

His eyes lighted with recognition.

"Was her name Mabel?" he asked. "Seems like it was Minnie or Mattie. Something a little more doll-like than Mabel."

"It was Mabel," Pru declared, horrified.

"Perhaps so."

"Certainly so!" Pru was red-faced furious. "You ruin a woman's life, and you can't even remember her name?"

Gidry's expression was incredulous.

"I didn't *ruin her life*," he answered calmly. "The day I met her she already knew more about life than most women ever learn."

"You *did* ruin her life," Pru said. "You ruined my life, you ruined your father's life, and now you're ruining . . . you are despicable!"

"I don't know what you are talking about."

"You don't know," she said, sneering. "I always gave that to your credit. The fact that you didn't know was in your favor. But now I see it all quite clearly. You didn't know because you didn't care to find out.

You just wanted to do what you're doing now. Put it in the past and never look back."

"What are you talking about?"

"I'm talking about why I would not, not if you were the last man on earth and I was commanded by the heavens, why I would never, ever consent to be your wife. And why I pity the woman who will be."

"Pru, for heaven's sake you are overwrought."

"And I have good reason to be so. You are . . ."

She did not have an opportunity to finish her sentence. Albert Fenton came around the corner of the church and spotted them.

"I've found him," Fenton called out to someone in the distance.

"Gidry, come quick," he said to the man beside her.

Chapter 15

HENRIETTA PAULING sat at the bedside of Peer Chavis. With all the windows of the house open on the warm night, the soft strains of music from her niece's Harvest Moon Dance carried into the room. The familiar melody captured her fancy and she began to sing it softly.

"Just a song at twilight, when the lights are low,
And the flick' ring shadows softly come and go.
Tho' the heart be weary, sad the day and long.
Still to us at twilight, comes love's old song.
Comes love's old sweet song."

She turned to smile at the old man in the bed. He was wide-awake tonight and watching her. The glow from the lamp showed him perfectly. He was still as handsome to her as he had ever been. His thick black hair was now mostly white. The prominence of his cheekbones and strength of his jaw were much evidenced in his gauntness, though somewhat disguised by the atrophied muscles on the left side of his face. His once-strong physique was now withered and fragile. And his powerful booming voice was now stilled indefinitely.

But she had never loved him for his handsome face, his fine-hewn body, or his impressive speech. She had loved him for the man that he was. And he was still that man as he lay among the tumbled bedclothes in the warm summer evening.

"I wish we were at that dance," she told him. "Prudence has had her mind completely full of it for a week. They've decorated the church grounds fit for a wedding and lit the place with enough Japanese lanterns to be seen on the horizon in San Antone."

She chuckled lightly.

"My little Prudence has not turned out to be any shy, wilting flower," Henrietta pointed out with pride. "When a fellow is foolish enough to tell her that she can't do something, then he best just get out of the way."

She raised a teasing eyebrow in accusation.

"I know what you're thinking," she told him. "You're thinking that she is a good deal like me. Well, you are right to some degree. She's sure got my dangerous streak. But I think she's got her mother's capacity for forgiveness. I sure hope that she does anyway."

She sighed thoughtfully, wishing, hoping the very best for her niece. She resolved not to dwell upon it. Pru and Gidry must sort through their lives as well as they could. Happiness not being an elusive quality to be found, but something integral to be lived.

"I do wish we were at that dance," she repeated. "I'd be done up in my very finest, sporting a brand-new hat, of course. And you in your cutaway coat. I always thought that cutaway coat made you look a fine figure of a man."

She laughed lightly.

"We would sure surprise them if we showed up at the dance," she said. "I'd make you lead me through every set. We were always the fittest partners on the floor. The two of us would dance till dawn in front of the whole town and then come back up here to this room together."

Henrietta widened her eyes feigning shock at her own words.

"That would brew up a scandal worth seeing," she said. "And you know how I hate a scandal."

The teasing tone belied the truth.

"It was a ruse, you know," she said. "Well, not completely a ruse, I suppose. It is absolutely true that if you got divorced, the entire town would have been scandalized. And marrying me afterward would not have helped poor Pru's chances for a happy marriage.

"That's why you pressed Gidry so to wed her," she said. "You should not have done it. I guess we all see that now. He was far too young and completely unready. It was very selfish of you. But I understand why you did it.

"Once they were safely married, you and I could marry as shockingly as we saw fit. It wouldn't touch them. They could have acted as outraged as everybody else and no harm would have been done.

"It was a good plan, Peer," she said. "But we both should have known better. In life, things are never quite what we plan.

"The truth is, Peer, and I imagine you always suspected this, Pru was an excuse, rather than a reason. I didn't allow you to free yourself from her and marry me, because . . . I wanted you to suffer."

She made her confession without any hint of apology.

"I wanted you to suffer as I had suffered," she said.

She leaned forward and adjusted his pillow, then gently caressed his brow.

"I was hurt to the core, wounded to my very being when you brought home your Alabama bride," she said. "I was crushed and disheartened at your inconstancy. And I was angry at the injustice of it all."

Henrietta's jaw tightened as she remembered.

"It all was so very unjust," she said. "You didn't love her, and she behaved unseemly. She had granted you the intimacies that, as a virtuous, innocent female, I would not."

Anger could be heard in Henrietta's tone for the first time.

"And what was her punishment for this wickedness?" she asked. "Did God cast her to demons? Was she publicly stoned? Forever ostracized from decent people? Oh, no, nothing like that."

Henrietta laughed without humor.

"For her lapse in morals she got your name. She got your child. Ultimately she got to live her chosen life among her friends and family upon your money."

She shook her head, incredulous.

"What did I get for my honor? My adherence to morality? What reward did I get?"

She answered her own question.

"I got loneliness."

Sounds of the distant music still drifted into the room as Henrietta swallowed her pain.

"It was all so wrong, so unfair," she said. "I had loved you since I was a girl, and I knew that you loved me in return. We would have been married if you had stayed, but you wanted to go. You didn't want to miss the war. It was to be a glorious adventure, and you wanted to go. I didn't try to hold you back. I loved you and wanted you to have whatever you wanted."

She shook her head, remembering

"What you also wanted was the transitory pleasure of a night of passion."

She turned to look at him once more, no longer feeling sadness or anger, only honesty.

"I wouldn't give that to you, but she did," Henrietta said. "You threw away everything that we were to each other, every dream we had shared together, every chance that we had for happiness, you threw it all away for a transitory pleasure. A few hours of unwedded bliss that ruined our lives. I couldn't forgive you for that, Peer. Truthfully, I didn't want to forgive you for that. I wanted you to suffer as I suffered."

She ran her hand along the length of his arm and down his long, narrow fingers.

"Foolish," she said finally. "I was so very, very foolish."

Henrietta looked up into his face.

"When I think of the time we wasted, Peer, the years we could have shared in this house, I am so angry. And at long last, I am more angry at myself than I am at you."

It was a hard-won confession, but having made it, she felt much better, much stronger.

"We were unable to be together not only because you betrayed me, but also because I was unwilling to forgive you.

"I forgive you now. I forgive you, and I beg your forgiveness," she said. "My lingering grief has kept us apart for thirty years. But it is all gone now. I cannot regret my life or yours and anything that has gone on before. Only my bitterness do I regret, and it is gone as if it had never been."

The lines on his forehead relaxed as if a burden had been lifted from him and Henrietta realized, perhaps for the first time how much her own sorrow had hurt him.

"I am here beside you now," she said, bravely acknowledging that it was only the present that truly mattered. "At last I am where I belong. It is far too late for wedded bliss, moonlight dancing, or even transitory pleasure. But I am here and, as always, I do love you."

He gripped her hand. It was strong and firm and full of hope.

She gazed into his eyes. They were bright with tears.

A guttural sound came from his throat. He was trying to speak. His words indecipherable.

"I know," she assured him. "Truly, I know."

She smoothed his cheek to comfort him.

"We have not had the lives that we had planned," she admitted. "We've not seen many of our childhood dreams come true. But we have had each other through it all. There was never a tear I shed that you didn't dry, not a worry that you didn't share, not a moment of joy that was not saved for the two of us alone. I have had in my life a man who truly loves me at my side. There are women all over the world who would envy me such good fortune."

Henrietta brushed his hair from his brow and leaned down to kiss him on the forehead. But instead, as she moved close, she lowered her mouth to his. She touched her lips to his own as she had not done in so very, very long a time. They were warm and soft, so familiar and beloved.

The tenderness of her kiss was as achingly wonderful as the tenderness of her heart.

His eyes shone up at her. Young again, strong again, loving each other as they always had. Their hands were clasped together as they had often been as youngsters, blushing and giggling as they chased together down narrow streets and through blooming fields of cotton. The strains of sweet music still drifted softly through the window. Two people truly one if thought and sentiment played any part. Love at last wholly complete. For one instant.

Then the expression in his eyes changed. He gasped roughly.

"Peer?"

Her question a cry.

His whole body went rigid. Pain ripped through him. Tearing at his side, his throat, his life.

"What is it? What is it?"

Henrietta knew what it was.

His expression was momentarily one of abject pain, followed by fear, then resignation. He looked at her. All his heart, his love, his life in his eyes.

"Please, no," she begged. "Please, no."

It was as if she could almost hear the apology that he could not speak.

His pupils widened hugely as if to take in the sight of her one last time, then narrowed quickly to pinpoints and glazed over. He was gone.

He still held her hand in his own.

"Don't leave me," she pleaded.

But he could make no response.

The black armband around Gidry's sleeve felt like a tourniquet upon his heart. The little graveyard just west of town was called Cemetery Hill because of the slight rise of elevation that allowed full appreciation of a cool summer breeze and frigid blast of winter wind. The former was in evidence this day. But in his broken heart Gidry felt the grip of the latter. The area was crowded with people. He should have expected as much, the house had been filled to overflowing.

Peer Chavis had been laid out in a fine cherrywood coffin in his own front parlor. The people of Chavis County had turned out to respectfully say their final good-byes to the town's leading citizen. Gidry had shaken hands, listened to well-meant consolation, and said "thank you for coming" a dozen, a hundred, maybe a thousand times.

He sat alone now on the long pine bench provided by the undertaker for the mourning of closest kin, understanding, perhaps for the first time, how his father must have felt coming home from the war to discover himself without family. His father was not without family now. All around him were Chavis gravestones as well as those bearing the names Gidry and Guidry, his grandmother's family. They were all here together.

He was upon the mourning bench alone.

A telegraph had been sent off to his mother yesterday, asking if the funeral should be delayed so that she might attend.

Her response had been prompt, brief, and to the point.

So sorry for your loss. Have no plans to return to Texas.

Gidry sat alone on the family bench, staring at the elaborately carved cherrywood coffin and the giant gash in the ground where it would be buried as he half listened to Reverend Hathaway's reading.

"A time to be born, and a time to die; a time to plant, and a time to pluck up that which is planted."

He had not believed it when they had come for him

at the dance. He was certain that a night so bright with hope could not end with such agonizing finality.

They were mistaken; he had been absolutely sure of that as he had raced home. His father might be asleep or he might be worse, but he was surely not dead. He had not thought it possible until he had seen Aunt Hen's face. Her complexion as bloodless as if she were deceased as well, Gidry knew that in fact it was irrevocably true.

"But though he cause grief, yet will he have compassion according to the multitude of his mercies. For he doth not afflict willingly nor grieve the children of men."

In the thirty-six hours since, he had held himself together by sheer force of will and the requisite numbness of the occasion. He had calmly ordered the disposition of the body with the undertaker. He discussed the details of the funeral service with the pastor. He had selected the songs to be played. And he had even personally requested that Judge Ramey give his father's eulogy.

"A hero to his country," the judge intoned. "A friend to those in need."

Gidry continued to stare at the coffin. It was draped in flowers, mostly roses. Undoubtedly Aunt Hen's roses. He would not have imagined that after the Harvest Moon Dance that there would have been any blooms left in town. But they were all here now, all decorating the cherrywood box that held the cold shell of a body that was once Gidry's father.

"The sorrows of death compassed me . . . I was brought low, and he helped me. Return unto thy rest, O my soul, for the Lord hath dealt bountifully with thee."

Finally it was over. The twelve sturdy men who had borne the cherrywood coffin from the hearse to the burial site began carefully to lower it down with ropes. At last it lay still at the bottom, covered with beautiful flowers.

"From dust to dust," Reverend Hathaway proclaimed as he scattered a handful of dirt atop it. He nodded for Gidry to do the same.

He picked up a handful of the waxy black dirt and cast it down onto the coffin. Gidry thought it would make him feel better. He'd thought it would make it feel finished. Neither happened. He remained numb. Numb on the surface, hollow inside. He was lonely and lost, bereft. And he needed something to do.

Deliberately he walked to the other side where the dirt was piled high. Gidry took up one of the shovels there. He began to fill the grave, one spadeful after another. If the community were startled or scandalized, Gidry did not notice. It was hot, hard work, it was also the last thing that he could ever do for his father. He took off his coat, handed it to Reverend Hathaway and began to utilize the shovel in earnest.

People passed by. Some throwing in a handful of dirt, others dropped in flowers. Gidry didn't speak to them, he continued his work.

Slowly, ever so slowly, the coffin was covered. Then the bright colors of the flowers disappeared from view. There were other men beside him before the job was done. The rest of the mourners had drifted away, but several stayed behind to help, Elmer Corsen, Albert Fenton, and a farmer that Gidry did not even know.

They piled the dirt high upon the grave site, knowing that it would sink and settle as it gave way to the nature of all things. Gidry's brow was drenched with sweat and his cheeks stained by tears. He didn't care if one was mistaken for the other.

Gidry tapped down the last spade of dirt with the

back of his shovel and stood silently before it as the men dispersed. He nodded as they patted him on the shoulder or expressed their sorrow.

He was thinking about his father. In his mind's eye he could see the old man as he once had been. Huge and vital, towering over his adoring son. He imagined his father laughing. It was not something he often did. Generally he was stern and gruff, a demeanor most suited to his position in the community. But Aunt Hen could tease him unmercifully and always wheedle a smile out of him, no matter the seriousness of the occasion.

In the far-distant past he recalled a picnic. It was just the three of them in a shady spot by the river. His father insisted that Aunt Hen must be invited to every picnic because her fried chicken was the best in town. On this particular picnic it happened to be Aunt Hen's birthday. A fact that was a surprise to Gidry, but apparently not to his father, who after consuming the famous fried chicken produced a small gift for her.

Gidry was excited when she unwrapped the paper and ribbon; he loved getting presents. Then he was keenly disappointed to see a cup. A little boy could only think, what kind of present is a cup? It had a rose painted on it, which seemed to please Aunt Hen, but it was still just a cup.

The sweet woman, apparently sensing his dismay began to make a joke of it.

"What on earth will I do with an empty cup?" she asked in feigned dismay.

"You can drink coffee," Gidry told her.

"Yes, I suppose I could do that," she said.

"Or tea," he said excitedly.

"Yes, I like tea as well."

Aunt Hen looked over at Peer. There was a teasing

sparkle in her eyes, and his father picked up on it.

"It's not a regular cup," Peer said. "It's one your Aunt Hen can use for a spittoon."

"A spittoon?"

"Yes, you know, for her chewing tobacco."

"Papa, Aunt Hen doesn't chew tobacco," Gidry told him.

"She doesn't?" His father's expression was all teasing puzzlement. "I must have got her confused with Mrs. Crenshaw."

The woman to which he referred did indeed chew tobacco. She was, to young Gidry's mind, at least a thousand years old and the dirtiest, smelliest old woman in Chavistown.

Aunt Hen giggled like a young girl.

"I am not Mrs. Crenshaw," she told them. "But what do you think, Gidry? Should I take up the tobacco habit?"

He didn't know how to answer.

"What's a habit, Papa?"

"It's something you like to do every day," Peer said.

Gidry nodded thoughtfully and turned to Aunt Hen. "Like gardening?" he asked.

She smiled.

"Well no, gardening is actually a hobby," she told him.

His father's voice was gruff, but his tone was teasing as he leaned forward to suggest to Gidry, "With your Aunt Hen, it *is* more like a habit."

She had feigned fury, and his father laughed. It was a broad, booming laugh that echoed off the river bluffs and filled the deserted clearing with its joy.

In his heart Gidry could almost hear it again, and it warmed him.

"Is there anything more I can do for you, Mr. Chavis?" the undertaker asked him.

He looked up, momentarily started. When the man had said, *Mr. Chavis*, Gidry had illogically thought that his father had arrived. But the only Mr. Chavis to be spoken to was himself.

"Nothing more, thank you, sir," he told the man.

Then he was alone.

He stood there. Wondering what to do. Wishing he knew what to do. Seemingly unable to think.

He heard a sound behind him and turned to spy young Sharpy watching him warily.

"Hello," he said quietly to the boy.

The little fellow nodded guardedly, then stepped closer to examine the hill of dirt that crowned the grave. He turned to Gidry, his childish face, solemn and sincere.

"I'm sorry about your papa dying, Mr. Chavis."

"Thank you."

"He was real nice to me, always," Sharpy said.

"That's nice."

"Are you going to get him a tupe-stone?" the little fellow asked. "I think the best graves are the ones with tupe-stones."

A ghost of a smile turned the corners of Gidry's mouth.

"Yes, I will certainly get him a tombstone," he assured the boy.

Sharpy nodded satisfied.

"Good," he said. "He got my mama one, so I wanted to make sure he had one of his own."

"He what?"

"He got my mama a tupe-stone," Sharpy said. "She didn't have one, just a two-by-four sticking out of the ground with her name wrote on it by the undertaker.

So I went to Mr. Chavis and say, my mama's gotta have a tupe-stone, and he got her one. Ya wanna see?''

Gidry nodded.

He followed Sharpy across the cemetery, noting with some surprise that the little boy seemed very much at home here, as if he spent a good deal of time upon the lonely hill. He pointed out graves to Gidry as he went. There was fussy old Miss Fern, who used to play for church, and Mr. Buster, Albert Fenton's father-in-law.

He even pointed out the grave of the Redfern twins, a pair of nine-year-olds who'd drowned in the river nearly fifty years earlier. One boy had gotten a cramp and the other had dived in to save him and drowned as well. They were identical twins, and when their lifeless bodies were found, even their own mother couldn't say for sure which was Ezra and which was Amos. So they'd been buried in one grave, lying together in one casket. It was the kind of local lore that was passed down to each generation. Gidry listened to Sharpy tell the tale with the same awe, enthusiasm, and embellishments with which he had once told it himself.

The boy stopped a little farther on. Gidry stood beside him looking down at the stones. The larger, more prestigious one said Thomas Franklin Kilroy and carried the epitaph, *Carried Home at Last.* Beside it was a very much smaller stone of plain gray granite. It read simply, *Mabel Merriman Kilroy 1862–1894.*

The name jogged in Gidry's memory. Pru had mentioned this very woman at the dance. He had not been able to recall her name at the time, but he remembered her quite well.

"I knew your mother," he told Sharpy.

"Really?" The little boy's eyes were alight with anticipation. "Is that why your papa bought her the tupe-stone, cause she was your friend?"

Gidry shook his head.

"No," he told him. "I'm sure my father did it because . . . because she didn't have one. He probably wasn't even aware that I knew your mother."

The little boy nodded, accepting.

"I remember how she used to laugh," Sharpy said. "She would laugh and laugh, no matter how bad things were."

Gidry's smile was bittersweet. Had he not been thinking similar thoughts of his father only moments ago? He understood the child's feelings as perhaps he could not have a week earlier. He comprehended fully the painful knowledge that the laugh would be heard no more.

"I remember your mama long before you were ever born," Gidry said suddenly. "She had a bright, spangly red dress, and she was so pretty, I could hardly keep my eyes off of her."

"For true?" Sharpy asked.

"For absolutely true," Gidry replied. "I thought she was the prettiest girl in Chavistown. I use to lie awake at night dreaming up things to say to her to catch her attention."

Sharpy looked up at him, eager to hear.

"And did she like you back?" he asked.

Gidry shook his head.

"Oh no," he replied. "She had no use for me at all. To her I was just a loutish, clumsy boy."

"I bet if she could see you now, she'd like you," Sharpy assured him.

Gidry leaned over and ruffled the boy's hair.

"And I'm sure she'd be as pretty as I always remembered her."

The little fellow smiled up at him, eased, Gidry hoped, by the words.

"It's getting close to dark, Sharpy," he said. "I guess we'd better head back toward town."

The youngster agreed, and they began walking together in that direction. Gidry realized that some of the numbness was receding. If he could feel the boy's pain, then eventually he would feel his own.

"Do you live in your father's old shack?" he asked the child. "Or with one of the families in town?"

"I got my own place," Sharpy answered quickly. "I'm really glad that you're not mad at me."

"Mad at you?"

"I started not to speak cause I thought you might be," Sharpy admitted. "But Miss Pru says that a man has to undress his can-dough-latches, no matter what."

Gidry disguised a chuckle behind a cough.

"Absolutely," he agreed. "Condolences must certainly be addressed. Why did you think I would be angry at you?"

Sharpy looked at him curiously, as if not sure if his mind was addled.

"Because you caught me stealing the Jack-a-knees lanterns," he said.

"I understood from Miss Pru that you two had borrowed them for the dance," Gidry said.

Sharpy rolled his eyes, but didn't immediately comment.

"I thought they looked very pretty that night," Gidry assured him. "I thought they looked very pretty indeed."

The two parted company in front of Gidry's door. As he watched the boy hurry on, he wondered once more where the little fellow lived.

"His own place?"

Gidry shook his head in disbelief at the idea.

The house was barren and empty. The scent of flowers still lingered in the front parlor. He didn't venture in there. He made his way to the kitchen. The table, counters, and shelves were full of food. Virtually everyone in the county had called while his father was laid out. Nearly all of them had brought a pie or ham or a mess of peas. Gidry surveyed the accumulation, thinking rightly that the amount of food available would feed a small army for more than a day.

He felt empty, very empty. But somehow nothing appealed to him. He made his way from room to room, finally finding his way upstairs to change out of his suit. Dressed once more in his cowboy duds he felt a little more relaxed.

Gidry stepped into his father's room. It was dark and empty, the shades all drawn. The bed had been stripped completely, the mattress tick gone. He tried to recapture the feeling of being here with his father. The few short weeks where they had, perhaps for the first time, met each other on an equal basis. The strange numbness pervaded him. He tried to recall the pleasure in his father's eyes as he regaled him with Wild West tales. But the only image that would come to his mind was the vacant, glassy eyes of death staring up at him.

Gidry shook off the emotion. The memory, however, remained.

He walked around for a long moment assessingly. It was traditional for a man to take the main bedroom of a house as his own when he inherited. Gidry couldn't imagine that. And looking around he could come up with no good reason for doing so. His own room was larger than this one and was nicely shaded by huge red oak that grew on the far side of the house. It was strange that his father had made this little corner his bedchamber. It was neither large nor had a good view.

Gidry walked over to the east window and drew up the shade. The only thing one could see really well from this room was Aunt Hen's garden. Of course, it was certainly pretty enough when in bloom, he decided.

It was then that he saw Pru. She stood at the back door, as usual, and her lantern was ablaze. Gidry's eyes narrowed at the sight. How many nights had he stood at this window watching that garden, waiting for Pru to leave the house to meet her lover.

"Damn!"

Gidry slammed his fist against the windowframe with tremendous force.

She was going to meet him now, again.

By God! He decided angrily. It was unconscionable. She was going to meet some worthless, lowlife adulterer. When it was he, Gidry Chavis, who needed to be held and soothed and comforted. It was he who should be finding solace in her arms. Because it was he that had gently and most ardently offered to make her his wife.

She refused him because of what had happened so very, very long ago. Well, she was not so blameless herself. And he would tell her so. He would tell them both!

Gidry Chavis tore down the stairs, his jaw set in determination.

Chapter 16

SHARPY WAS not in the milk shed this evening. Pru was disappointed. She'd hardly had more than a moment to spare for the little fellow in the last couple of days. Aunt Hen had taken the death of poor old Mr. Chavis very hard. But sad as she was, she was also determined to see that everything was done properly and to be of as much assistance to Gidry as possible. Pru didn't fault her aunt for her concerns or actions, but it did make it more difficult to keep up with the little boy whose care she'd taken upon herself.

They'd had only a moment to talk that morning. The little boy appeared very curious to compare the funeral for Mr. Chavis with the one held for his mother. He'd also shown a keen interest in Gidry and how he was taking the loss.

Seeing how sympathetic his young heart was, she'd urged him to formally offer words of comfort to him. The little fellow admitted to some trepidation at doing so. Apparently he thought the incident at the cotton gin would have soured his hero against him.

Pru hoped, for the boy's sake, that it had not.

It would be good for Gidry as well. He looked so lost and alone out on Cemetery Hill. She had thought to follow Aunt Hen's stoic example of graceful good breeding. When he picked up the shovel, however, and began to fill the grave himself, Pru's heart ached for him, and she'd been unable to hold back the tears.

She thought of the long years when he was away. Wasted. So very wasted. He'd returned to find his father forever altered. And now, after only a few short weeks, dead.

Pru hated that. She hated the pointlessness of it. She hated the pain it evoked. And she hated seeing Gidry so hurt. After all that had been said and done and left unable to be undone, she still loved him.

At that moment the door to the milk shed flew open and slammed back upon its hinges. He did not look hurt, or sorrowful. At that moment he looked at mad as the very devil.

"Where is he?" he barked after a hasty survey of the dimly lit room revealed Pru as being alone.

She was startled, puzzled, curious.

"He's not here yet," she said. "What do you want with him?"

"It's not what I want with him," Gidry said furiously. "It's what I don't want with him. I don't want *you* with him."

Pru was momentarily stunned. Had Gidry discovered the truth at last? Or was he admitting that he had known all along?

She raised her chin defiantly, ready for a fight.

"Whatever it is you have to say, Gidry Chavis," she challenged, "say it in plain English and say it now, or just get out of my sight."

Her words seemed to knock some of the fury out of him.

He stared at her for a moment, his brow furrowed and his expression pained. He sat wearily in the little chair next to the table and threw his head back as if to steel himself against the wounds that plagued him.

"I . . . I need you, Pru," he whispered at last. "I need your strength and your warmth. I need your love. Please, please just hold me."

His words, so unexpected, so sincere, so full of agony, melted the strength of her outrage like ice chips on brick pavement in July.

She dropped to her knees in front of his chair and wound her arms around his waist, pressing her face against his chest.

"I am so sorry, Gidry," she whispered. "I am so very sorry."

She didn't know if she was speaking about his father or about Sharpy, but whichever it was, she knew at that moment if it hurt Gidry Chavis, she was sorry about it.

He wrapped his strong, thick arms around her tightly as if he could not bear to let her go. He buried his face in the top of her hair. The way his body quaked and trembled, she knew that he was at last allowing himself the tears that he would show to no one else.

She held him, caressed him, ached for him. His heart was her own, and it was broken.

"All I wanted as a boy was to be like Peer Chavis," Gidry ground out hoarsely. "But I never even had time to really know the man. I never really even knew him."

Pru ran her hand lovingly along his cheek. "You knew him," she said with certainty. "In your heart you knew him better than your mind ever could."

"Oh Pru, my sweet Pru," he whispered. "You always know how to make it better."

Gidry, apparently not content with the barest distance between them leaned down to the floor where she knelt and lifted her in his arms to sit upon his lap. She could see his face now, clearly, his dark eyes redrimmed and bright with tears.

He clutched her to him, and she buried her face in the muscled curve of his throat. She ran her hands along the length of his strong back, coaxing and comforting.

She was still tight against him as his chin began to nuzzle at her throat. It was a sweet, loving gesture as she pulled back slightly, his lips were there, meeting hers.

It was not a kiss of teasing fire, like the one they'd shared in the gin, nor was it like the one she received upon her garden bench eight years ago. It was a light touch of flesh to flesh that spoke volumes of honesty and of love.

Their mouths parted, but their faces were intimately close.

"Comfort me, Pru," he whispered. "Give me comfort."

She turned her head slightly and opened her mouth more fully and kissed him again. This time there was passion, fire.

Pru had never explored a man's mouth with her own. She had never ventured into that realm of pleasure. She did so now with the highest of motivations, to comfort the man that she loved.

Gidry's need for her was almost mindless, desperate. It was as if he could not get enough of the taste of her mouth or the feel of her skin.

"Let me love you," he pleaded with her. "Let me . . . be inside you. I need you."

"All right." Her own voice sounded breathless to her. "Yes," she said with more certainty. "Yes, Gid, please, I want you inside me."

Pulling her snugly into his arms, he carried her to the small narrow bunk and laid her down upon it. His face was flushed, his breathing rapid.

Pru was trembling, now anxious, eager. She wanted to comfort him, she needed to comfort him, but she did not know how. Her only experience had been in his arms, and she had been innocent and passive. She wanted now to touch him, urge him, but she did not know how.

Gidry showed no evidence that he required any skills or found her lacking in any way. He made no attempt to so much as undo her collar button. He rucked up her skirts and pulled the drawstring on her drawers and drew them down over her stockings and shoes to push them on the floor.

Pru's eyes widened as he undid his trousers, but he didn't remove them or even take off his shirt. He lay down upon her on the cot. The weight of him was warm and welcome. He eased his thigh into the apex of her own, the sensation took her breath away. Gidry's mouth was on hers once more, kissing, coaxing.

"I need you," he whispered desperately against her throat. "Forgive me, Pru. I need you."

Then he was pressing his way inside her.

Pru steeled herself as best she could. Biting her lip against the discomfort and willing herself not to cry out or push him away. He needed her. He needed this. It was her gift of comfort, and she would not stint in giving it.

When he was finally buried deep inside her, there was a sense of rightness and a sense of being whole. It was not pleasure exactly, but it was no longer pain.

When she thought he was going to withdraw, she clutched at his shoulders, not quite ready to give him up yet. But she had been mistaken in his intentions. He began to move in and out inside her in an increasingly rapid pace.

He clasped her by the inside of her knees and raised her legs higher so that he could bury himself more solidly within her.

The tiny cot was rocking precariously, and the rhythmic weight of his body atop her own was having a strange effect upon her. It was almost as if she were becoming light-headed. Her heart beat rapidly. Her breathing increased. Her skin was suddenly alive and sensitive. And the feeling between her legs had gone from discomfort to not quite pleasurable to strangely urgent.

Faster and faster and faster until her vision was hazy.

Then Gidry stopped still, every muscle in his body taut with expectation.

"Pru!" he cried out her name.

She felt the hot flood of his seed inside her before he collapsed upon her, relaxed and spent.

She lay there beneath him feeling strangely bereft and slightly cheated. Of what she did not know. But there was no anger in her thought. And there was no regret. She loved him. He needed her this way. She had given herself to him as a gift.

He was so large and so wonderfully warm upon her. Is this what married women had that she did not?

A man to love and lie upon your body was not a totally unpleasant thing, she concluded.

Gidry's face was buried in the nape of her neck and his dark hair tickled her nose. It was nice, she decided. Holding him this way. It was really quite nice.

He startled awake; pushing up on his elbows, he looked down at her.

"I thought I was dreaming," he said.

"You weren't dreaming."

He lowered himself to her lips tenderly.

"Oh yes I was," he told her. "It was a dream come true."

She smiled up at him, warmed by his sweet words.

"I'm too heavy to lie on you like this," he said, easing off of her, and kneeling beside the cot.

"You're not too heavy," she assured him, trying discreetly to wiggle back into her underdrawers, which had been scandalously hanging from her right ankle.

Gidry assisted her in getting her drawers back in place, but when she would have pushed her skirts back down, he simply laid his arm across them, impeding her progress.

He shook his head. "I'm a heavy brute and lout, sweetheart, but I'm going to make it up to you."

She stared at him, puzzled at his meaning.

"I'm sure you don't need to make anything up to me," she said.

"I was completely selfish," he admitted. "I just . . . I just needed you so much. I apologize."

"You didn't seem selfish to me," she told him.

His eyes widened in disbelief.

"I didn't?"

"No," she assured him.

His expression was incredulous.

"Then I can only think that I must have saved you from a worse cad than myself."

She had no idea as to his meaning, and it was on the tip of her tongue to ask. His next words, however struck her mute.

"Let me help you get out of these clothes," he said.

Stunned, she abruptly sat up on the couch.

"Good idea," he said. "We'll begin at the beginning."

"I thought that we were finished," she said.

"You must not think very well of me, if you think I would leave you unsatisfied," Gidry said.

He kissed her again, his mouth sucking ever so gently at her own. Pru loved the sensation.

He undid the buttons on her shirtwaist and laid her back on the cot once more. He leaned over her and set his open mouth upon the taut flesh of her bosom covered only by a thin sheath of fine lawn chemise.

Pru gasped aloud at the wave of pure physical reaction that coursed through her. The pent-up desires that often troubled her sleep surged through her— hot, fiery, destructive, shattering the guarded reserve and inflaming the long-dormant passions of a fully mature woman.

"Oh my!"

She was shocked at her own reaction.

The unfamiliar contact set off surprising reactions at pulse points in unexpected locations on her body. She stiffened her legs together tightly and buried her fingers in his hair.

Gidry moaned low in the back of his throat as if tasting a delicious treat. The slight vibration the sound made against the sensitive flesh of her breast had her biting her lip. It was not uncomfortable as the mating had been, but in its own way it was an extremely disconcerting sensation.

His tongue and teeth worried her nipple.

Pru moaned, reveling in the feeling, yet horrified that such a sound escaped her own lips. But she could not seem to help herself. She threw her head back and arched her body, begging for his continued attention.

"Mmm, so you like that, sweetheart," he said languorously. "I'm so pleased that you like that."

Once his mouth was drawn away, the dampness of her thin chemise clung with diaphanous clarity to the turgid nubs. The contrast of her heated flesh chilling her in the night air was almost more thrilling than she could bear.

"Don't stop," she pleaded.

Gidry grinned down at her.

"Oh no, sweetheart," he said. "I promise I will not stop. Help me get you out of this chemise."

His words momentarily startled her. But she dutifully raised her arms as he pulled the chemise up over head and cast it aside.

Pru tried to cover herself with her arms, but Gidry determinedly held them to her sides. She watched his eyes as he looked at her. Without the added effects of corseting she was not nearly so well endowed as current fashion dictated a lady should be. And her bosoms had the strange nature of always seeming to tilt upward. Certainly that was some inexplicable bodily deformity.

"Oh my Pru, who ever imagined you were this beautiful."

His words were an awestruck whisper.

She had hardly a moment to savor the sweetness of his judgment before he lowered his mouth to each in turn, kissing and sucking until Pru was gasping for breath, unable to hold herself still.

"Oh my heavens!" she exclaimed as the pleasure of it became increasingly unfathomable.

Gidry was not in any way passive. His mouth was urgent and questing upon her. And his hands were never still, stroking her back, her shoulders, her arms.

"I'm going to make it so good for you," he promised hotly against her skin as he kissed his way down toward her navel. "I will make it good for you, I'll make it right with you, I'll see you never come to regret loving me, sweetheart. You'll never regret it again."

Pru hardly noted his words. Her whole body seemed to be almost twitching with need.

He ran a loving hand down the length of her leg, then back up to deftly draw the hem of her skirts around her waist.

He was looking at her down there now. The confidence of moments before was fading rapidly as she perceived him becoming the aggressor. She trembled nervously under his gaze. Her knee-length drawers were sufficient covering that she need not feel embarrassed, she assured herself. She was so grateful that she'd put them back on.

"Are you on your courses?" he asked.

"What?"

"Are you having your monthly? You have some blood here."

When he touched her intimately she nearly jumped out of her skin.

"No, no," she assured him, trying to pull away. "It is not my time of the mouth."

His expression was sorrowful.

"Then I must have hurt you," he said. "I am so sorry."

"It was nothing," she said.

His sad face slowly faded into a sly grin.

"Let me kiss it and make it better."

Gidry bent forward and placed a kiss so tenderly at the apex of her thighs. It was a sensation so unimaginable that she cried out.

"No!"

Gidry stopped immediately, looking thoroughly chastised.

"No?" he asked.

"No to that," she said. "Not . . . not no to the rest only . . . no don't kiss me there."

He relaxed slightly and nodded. Leaning back upon his heels and began discarding his shirt.

"All right," he said. "If you don't want me to kiss you there, I won't."

Pru sighed gratefully.

"Thank you."

"Can I touch you there?" he asked, as he allowed his hand to do just that.

Pru managed to keep a squeak from escaping her throat.

"Yes . . . ah yes, you may touch me there, but not too much," she told him. "For some reason I am . . . I am very sensitive there."

Gidry raised an eyebrow, chuckled and gave her a long look. "I do hope, ma'am, that *I* am the reason."

Gidry discarded his shirt on the floor and then sat down to take off his boots.

"Should I remove my shoes and stockings as well?" she asked him.

He did not answer immediately. When he was finally barefoot he reached over and ran his hand along the leather of her brown glove-grain button tops and whistled appreciatively.

"Definitely leave on the stockings," he said. "And the shoes would be all right with me, too."

Prudence gazed at him curiously, until he rose to his feet and began to shuck his trousers. Then she tried not to look in his direction at all. The exposure of skin in the light of the lantern inevitably drew her eyes.

"Scoot over, sweetheart," he told her. "It's not much of a bed, but it's all we've got."

Disconcerted, Pru eased over. It was strange to be mostly dressed but be so exposed. It was even stranger to be mostly dressed and lying next to a man who was naked.

He wrapped his arm around her and pulled her closer, firmly wedging his thigh between her legs.

"Does that feel better against your *sensitive place*?" he asked.

His grin suggested that he was making a joke, but Pru could not quite imagine what it might be.

"It's not truly uncomfortable," she admitted.

Gidry chuckled delightedly and kissed her, sweetly, tenderly. He trailed a line of tiny kisses along her cheek to her ear and down her neck. When he got to the base of her throat he made a deep bass growling sound and, to Pru's shock, nipped at her with his teeth.

"What are you doing?"

"Just a little love bite, sweetheart," he said, healing the minor injury with a gentle kiss. "Do you like bites, sweetheart?"

His whisper against her heated skin raised goose-flesh upon the curve of her shoulders and her naked bosom.

"I don't know if I like it," Pru answered. She was finding it increasingly difficult to catch her breath.

Gidry ran his hand down her back and grasped her bottom. Holding her firmly, he adjusted the thick-muscled thigh that was pressed so tightly to her body's apex. The more he moved against her, the more she wanted him to move against her.

"You do like that, don't you, sweetheart?" he asked.

Aching, straining against him, she was hardly capable of reply. The need to be close to him, very close to him, intimately close to him, overrode any other considerations.

With his hands at her waist and his thigh between hers, Gidry actually lifted her slightly and pushed her back until her buttocks were tightly flush against the wall. He continued to grind his thigh into her with pleasing effects. His hands moved back up to her breasts. Her nipples were stiff and raised as if to implore attention.

He gladly gave it, with his hands, his lips, his teeth, his tongue, the fine graze of beard along his jaw.

Pru was no longer capable of rational thought. She pressed his face more firmly to her bosom and desperately squirmed and wiggled against his thigh.

"Oh my. Oh my! OH MY!"

Gidry pulled away from her. She made a cry of objection and reached out for him. But he knew exactly what he was doing.

He grabbed her at the hips and turned her onto her back. He was already between her legs, and the change of position widened her before him. He grasped her booted ankles and raised her feet to his shoulders.

With his eyes upon her face, he kissed the glove-grain leather and rubbed his cheek against it. He kissed her again near the top of the boot. And then higher upon her black cotton stocking. The touch of his lips proceeded up the inside of her thigh with purposeful intent. A haze of lusty desire clouded Pru's vision and a mewling, begging sound issued from her throat.

Gidry was at the top of her hose now and nipped her again in the fine, pale flesh exposed above it. He buried his hands under her bottom and dragged down her fine lawn drawers, pulling with his hands from behind and with his teeth in front until her most private parts were exposed to his gaze.

His mouth was now poised above her thatch of damp brown curls. She was quaking, twitching, unable to hold herself completely still. He began to lower his head, then stopped abruptly and raised his eyes to hers.

"May I kiss your *sensitive place*, Miss Pru?" he asked politely.

"Yes!" she pleaded, and raised her hips to meet him.

The kiss was much like others he had given her, teeth and tongue and a lot of gentle sucking pressure. Its pleasurable effect, however, was much more intense.

Pru buried her hands in her hair, pulling at it like a wild woman as her head flailed side to side. She was incapable of coherent speech, but repeated his name a thousand times.

When he ended the kiss, she reached for him intent upon protest. He clasped her hand in his own and brought it to his erection.

"Put me inside you," he told her.

Eagerly, she obeyed his command.

This time there was no difficulty, no discomfort. He eased inside her like a hot knife in warm butter.

"This time you will know how selfish I was before," he promised.

Within a few short moments, she did.

Chapter 17

HENRIETTA PAULING awakened late—an unusual occurrence for her in her fifty years of life. But as she wandered into the kitchen to fix a cup of morning coffee, she was not disturbed by it. What did she have to get up for after all? Her niece? Prudence was a grown woman and could well take care of herself. Her garden? Roses might require tending, but flowers were pretty much on their own in this world. Her home? The little place was far more than what was necessary for two spinster women. And it had so many things, so many doilies and knickknacks and furniture. A person had no need of all those *things*.

Her niece was nowhere to be seen. Henrietta had peeked into her bedroom as she'd passed. It was neat as a pin, hardly looked slept in at all. The back door was as wide-open now as when Henrietta had gone up to bed last night. Clearly Prudence was long since up and gone.

That was just as well. Truly, she didn't wish to have to carry on a conversation with anyone this morning, not even her beloved niece.

Henrietta stoked the coals in the firebox and added

a small piece of wood before setting the water on the stove. Normally she would wash and dress while the coffee boiled. This morning, however, she simply sat down at the table and stared off into nothingness. A scrubbed face and fresh clothes seemed infinitely more trouble than they were worth.

There were chores she could be at, work that should be done. In her heart none of it mattered. Today, like yesterday and the day before, Peer Chavis was no longer in the world. And today, like tomorrow and a hundred years thereafter, Henrietta saw nothing on her horizon to look forward to.

In her mind's eye he was as vivid and real as he had ever been. She could recall the handsomeness of his youth. As well as the decline of the last few weeks. She had loved him all her life. Loving him was her life. How did a woman go on beyond that?

"One foot in front of the other," she admonished herself aloud.

But her heart was not in the words. Every step she made without him, every moment she lived, every breath she took was wrenching and painful. She no longer wanted to go on. The struggle to do so was hardly worth it.

Widows were pitiable. Everyone knew that. Even the Bible urged visiting them, along with the sick and injured. Henrietta was the widow who never was. In life she had been too proud to let her heart be known. In death she had been relegated to standing among the crowd. Holding back tears of grief and moans of agony by sheer force of will. Her secret forever safe. Her heart forever broken.

She had so much wanted just another moment alone with the body. A chance to say one last good-bye. To give one last kiss upon those cold, still lips.

But a *neighbor* could not request such a thing. It would have created a tremendous scandal.

Scandal. The word that scarred her life. If she had not been so afraid of looking the fool and facing the scandal, she would have been Peer's bride twenty years ago.

She wasn't afraid of scandal now. She wasn't afraid of anything. Except having to get up sunrise after sunrise after sunrise to a world where there was no point, no purpose, and no one to love.

Her life seemed to be behind her now. All of her mundane motivations, quiet daydreams, and unspoken hopes had been buried yesterday on Cemetery Hill. She could not get them back. And it hurt too much to try to move forward without them.

Henrietta glanced up at the coffeepot. It was just beginning to boil. She stared at it for a very long moment. Then she rose to her feet. She retrieved her favorite cup from the shelf. It was hand-painted with a bright pink Old Blush rose, a long-ago birthday gift from Peer.

She held it in her hand lovingly and ran her thumb over the delicate little painting. He had always been so attentive. For all those many years never a holiday or occasion was allowed to pass without the discreet arrival of some token of his affection to mark the day.

She had so often sat among the ladies and heard wife after wife complain that her husband could not be depended upon to recall birthdays or anniversaries, and she had held her tongue. Silently pleased, knowing how very cherished she was.

The sting of tears clouded her eyes, but she held her gaze steady. Peer Chavis was gone. In the past, in her most bitter and woebegone moments, she had thought herself alone. She had thought herself lonely.

Until now she had not known the meaning of the word.

Henrietta poured herself a cup of coffee and sat at the table once more. The sorrow and grief weighed upon her like a darkness she could not dispel. Deliberately, earnestly, she sought the light.

She remembered Peer. She recalled the sight of him young and strong in his uniform, full of heart and hope. She saw him despondent and determined as he picked of the pieces of his life after the war. He said good-bye to his family and his dreams as he forged ahead to make something fine and purposeful. She saw him as she had known him so often. Hardworking, casually generous, a proud father trying not to spoil a privileged child, and a bulwark of dependable strength for a whole community. And she saw him as only she had known him, tenderly romantic and, after the dissolution of his unfortunate marriage, enduringly faithful.

As tears stained her hollow cheeks she closed her eyes and tried for the hundredth time to pray.

"Dear God," she whispered, "why could you not give us more time together?"

God did not answer. He would not answer. The earth where she lived, where she loved was a place with sunshine, flowers, rainclouds, and weeds. It was not a place with answers.

She opened her eyes and brought the cup of coffee to her lips once more. She gazed at the hand-painted rose for a long moment and kissed it tenderly.

"God," she said, addressing the emptiness of the kitchen aloud. "I know that you have plans for our lives. And you know that I had plans for our lives. I know that I have to go along with *your* plans." She raised her chin mutinously. "But you must know that I don't have to like it."

She looked lovingly at the Old Blush rose on her cup once more.

"I don't have to like it, but I do have to go on."

Determinedly she got to her feet.

There were flowers to tend, chores to be done, friends to visit, a community that needed her. And there were two young people whom she loved dearly who might very likely make the same foolish mistake that she had made herself.

She went to the sink, washed her face, tidied her hair and set forth to make a new place for herself in the world that Peer Chavis had left behind.

At the back step she was startled to see a young boy waiting, elbows on knees his hair still tousled from sleep.

Sharpy Kilroy jumped to his feet, looking somewhat grimy and a good bit guilty.

"What do you want here?" Henrietta asked him.

"I'm not doing nothing, ma'am," the little boy said. "I'm just sitting here waiting."

"What on earth are you waiting for?"

He seemed hesitant to speak. "I ain't had no breakfast this morning, and I'm powerful hungry."

Henrietta was surprised at his words.

A bit uncertainly he glanced out at the old milk shed behind the house.

"Miss Pru, she usually feeds me," he said. "But . . . well I ain't seen her this morning. If you ain't got nothing for me, I can ask along the street until somebody does."

"Prudence usually feeds you?" Henrietta asked, puzzled.

The little boy nodded. "Yes'um. I . . . well I stay

around here most nights, and she usually feeds me supper and breakfast, but I ain't had neither. I ain't had nothing since yesterday morning."

"You stay around here?"

Sharpy nodded.

"Where on earth do you sleep?"

Once more the little boy glanced rather guiltily at the milk shed.

"Well, last night I slept on that bench in your garden," he said.

Henrietta stared at the youngster incredulously for a long moment.

"Well for mercy's sake," she said finally. "That is the most fool nonsense I've ever heard in my life. Get in here, boy, and I'll fry some bacon and stir up a mess of grits. Do you like biscuits?"

"Oh yes, ma'am," he assured her. "I love biscuits."

"I can make up a batch in just a shake," she said. "But you'll need to wash up. Go draw some water from the well. I'll need to see your hands and face clean. And don't forget to wash behind your ears."

"I never do, ma'am," he assured her.

Enthusiastically, he started out the door.

"You'll be needing a towel," she said, stopping him in his tracks.

She went to the linen drawer to get him one. When she turned back around he was standing by the table staring at her china coffee cup.

"Don't touch that!" she said rather sharply.

The little fellow appeared thoroughly chastised.

"I wasn't going to, ma'am," he assured her. "I just never seen anything so pretty as that. It looks almost like a real rose."

Henrietta picked up the cup and allowed him to examine it more closely.

"It's not a real rose," she told him. "It never was, and it never will be. But you are right, it's very beautiful. We can always admire it for what it is."

The little boy eyed her with questions. She smiled down at him and patted him on the head.

"Go wash up while I fix the biscuits," she said.

"Yes, ma'am," he answered eagerly.

"And you don't have to call me ma'am," she told him. "The young ones all call me Aunt Hen. I suppose that will do for you as well."

"Thanks ma—, thanks Aunt Hen," he said hurrying out the door.

Gidry awakened slowly, his position cramped and his muscles aching. It was a miracle that anyone could sleep in such a cramped space. But after the long night of such sweet passion who could not sleep.

Lying against his shoulder, snoring ever so daintily, was Prudence Belmont. He sighed with delighted pleasure. She was everything a man could want in a mate, Gidry decided. She was discreet and ladylike in public, thrilling in bed, and interesting in conversation. A man would be greedy to want more. Of course, he did. He wanted a long life together, several well-behaved children—there was still time—and a much better bed!

"Pru," he whispered, "it's morning, better wake up."

She gave a little moan of protest and snuggled more closely against him.

He didn't allow himself so much as one thought of dalliance. In a milk shed in broad daylight! They were both too old and wise for such behavior.

"Sweetheart," he said more firmly. "I want you to

get your rest, but it sure will be embarrassing if we have visitors."

She snuggled more determinedly and then as if suddenly realizing that things were not as they should be, her eyes opened and she stared up at him in wonder.

"Good morning," he said, smiling down at her. "Is this going to be my fate? A bride who's a lazy, slug-a-bed and can't get up until nearly noon?"

Her reaction was excessive. She rolled out of the bed in one moment and hastily began to drag on her clothing. In the light of day she seemed embarrassed about her nakedness, so Gidry did not tease her further. Their love was so new, so precious, it was natural to be a little overwhelmed at first.

Gidry began to dress as well. For the first time he actually took note of his surroundings. The place was neat and relatively clean, very much so for a deserted shed. It had a lived-in look about it. There were no clothes or toiletries, but the bed had fresh linens, the floor was swept, and a towel was hung to dry on a hook. There was such a myriad of things in storage. And it appeared to be somebody's hideaway. And Gidry didn't like the idea one bit. He had promised himself never to mention her lover nor reproach her on her behavior. But he could not stem his curiosity. What man had bedded her so frequently and yet taught her so little about lovemaking? Perhaps their affair was quite new. Still Gidry knew it had been going on since the night he arrived home. He had taught her more last night than she had learned in all those weeks with another man. And she was so wondrously tight.

He clamped down on that direction of his thoughts. They were trying to get out of here. Allowing himself the pleasure of reliving the night before would have him *too big for his britches*, literally, and this was not the time or place for that.

Besides, it didn't matter. He'd had enough experience to know that whether a woman was tight or not, had much more to do with her physical build than with her virtue. A narrow vagina was no more guarantee of inexperience than a large penis was the calling card of a great lover.

Gidry was fully clothed and Prudence was *hiding* in the far corner. With her back to him, she had one leg raised, her foot resting upon a crate as she pulled on her stockings. Gidry momentarily imagined himself lying on the floor beneath her. Ah ... what a pretty picture. After they were wed, he determined, after they were wed ... everything.

She turned back to face him, showing surprise to catch him watching her. Hastily she averted her eyes and found her shoes. She sat down in the chair next to the table and slipped them on. Without a buttonhook, the task of securing them to her feet was not an easy one. The tiny buttons were not so easily fitted into the small slits in the leather shoe. Gidry gladly knelt in front of her and pushed her hands away, eager to be of service.

"I'm supposed to meet with Judge Ramey today about my father's will," Gidry told her as he worked.

She made no comment.

"I don't know yet what matter of paperwork may be involved in the transfer of my father's property."

Pru maintained her silence as he finished the left shoe.

"I won't have to make a claim through the court," he continued. "The judge said that except for some small bequests, he specifically left everything to me."

Still she had nothing to say.

"My father made the will up several years ago," Gidry told her. "He said when I left that he was disinheriting me. So he must have forgiven me long before I came home."

He finished the right shoe and sat back on his heels to look up at her. She seemed unwilling to meet his eyes.

"He left Aunt Hen her house and a very generous income to maintain it," he said. "You and I, of course, would have always taken care of her. But he couldn't know that we would end up together at last."

Pru finally looked at him then. Her expression was unfathomable.

Gidry's brow furrowed.

"Did you not understand that?" he asked her. "Did I not make myself very plain? With the funeral just yesterday, it is probably the thing for us to wait. But not more than a month or six weeks. If we have a very small, simple wedding, I think it can be very soon. I don't believe it would show disrespect, and Papa would understand. More than understand, Papa is probably looking down on us and cheering."

He grinned mischievously.

"I hope he wasn't looking down on us last night," he teased. "He would have gotten more of an eyeful than is comfortable for me."

Gidry laughed and cocked his head to one side to look at her puzzled.

"Where is your sense of humor this morning?" he asked. "I hope you are not feeling that what we did was unseemly on the night my father was buried. I talked to him a lot about you. Believe me, he wanted us to be together from the very first."

"Gidry, stop it!"

Her first words were sharp and angry. She was upset. He wanted to take her in his arms and comfort her. As he reached out, she rose to her feet and stepped away from him. He stood as well.

"I am not sorry for what happened last night," she said firmly.

"Nor I," he agreed.

"You needed comfort and I was . . . I was very willing to give it," she said.

Gidry's brow furrowed. At first he had needed comfort, he had begged her for comfort. But that first, hurried, selfish coupling did not at all reflect their long night of passion together.

"Pru, I . . ."

She held up her hand, not allowing him to speak.

"I am not sorry for anything that happened between us, Gidry," she said. "I will, well, I will treasure it always. But there will be no repeat of it."

He was thoughtful for a moment and nodded slowly.

"All right," he agreed. "That is probably for the best. We wouldn't want our first child to come early and set tongues to wagging. I don't relish the idea of waiting, but I can take cold baths until after the wedding."

"There will be no wedding," she declared adamantly. "What happened last night happened. I am not sorry, but it is in the past now and best forgotten."

"What?"

"It is in the past and . . ."

"I heard what you said," he interrupted. "I just can't believe you are saying it."

"I told you the night of the Harvest Moon Dance that I would not marry you," she said. "I have not changed my mind."

"But surely . . ."

"Surely everyone remembers your treatment of me eight years ago as if it were yesterday," she said. "I have no intention of putting myself up for public discussion once again."

"Up for public discussion? What about marrying me would be up for public discussion?"

She raised her chin defiantly, fortifying her resolve.

"They would remember how I made a fool of myself over you. How I wore my heart on my sleeve," she said. "They would remember how you rejected me."

"But I'm not rejecting you now."

"Oh no," she agreed with heavy sarcasm. "What was it you said at the dance? Now that you've got all the youth and freedom out of your system, you are willing to settle down. Don't you think I know, don't you think everyone will know that what you mean is that you are willing to settle."

"I am not willing to settle," he insisted. "I am marrying the woman I love."

"No, I will not do it," Pru said firmly. "I have my pride, and I won't throw it away for you."

"I believe it was you who told me that pride is a meager emotion when compared to love."

"It may not be much," she agreed. "But it is all that you left me with, and it has kept me safe all these years. I won't relinquish it."

"It has kept you safe?" he asked incredulously. "It has not been enough to melt your heart, to teach you to love again."

"Is that what you are doing? Loving again?" she asked.

"I would think that after last night you would know that I love you," he told her furiously. "And as to what the rest of the world thinks, what should I care."

"Yes, that's the same old Gidry Chavis," she said snidely. "Suit yourself and let the rest of us sort out things like propriety, honor, reputation."

"Propriety! Honor! Reputation!" he bellowed. "How interesting that you should choose those words. I'm not fooled by this ridiculous argument you are making. You are not refusing me because of what happened eight years ago. You just don't want to give him up, do you?"

Gidry turned and furiously kicked the little cot, splintering it into a half dozen boards and a pile of bedclothes.

"You just want to keep your little secret rendezvous and your illicit lover and your . . ."

"Illicit lover?"

"Who is he?" Gidry questioned angrily. "I wasn't going to ask, I felt it wasn't my right, but now I demand to know."

"I don't know . . . why would you . . . how dare you *demand* anything of me!"

"By right of what we did here last night, I dare it!" he answered. "What if you are already with child? That can happen, you know. Good God! You could be carrying his child as easily as my own."

"I'm not carrying anyone's child," she snapped.

"Oh right, the blood, you just finished your courses," he said. "Thank God for that."

"Thank . . . get out of here!" Pru screamed at him.

"I'll leave in my own good time," he told her. "And I'll find out who it is. You think you can keep it a secret? In a town this small it is impossible to keep a secret this big. I'll figure it out. It's just a matter of time."

"I have no secret lover," she insisted. "You are being ridiculous."

Gidry was incensed at her denial.

"I've watched you walk out here to meet him every night since I've been home," he admitted. "And saw a note you wrote to him. In fact I remember it vividly. It was written on a postcard of a naked beauty in her boudoir. Guaranteed, I would think, to set a man's mind to rutting."

She gasped in shock and her eyes widened. The bright pink tint to her cheeks clear indications of embarrassment and guilt.

He was so furious, he wanted to break something else. He wanted to bring the building crashing down. He wanted to hack every board to bits. He grabbed a long, rounded stick with the intent of smashing it upon the table. He didn't do so when he realized that it was not simply a bat or wand. One end of it had some sort of padding and leather straps. Disgusted he threw it toward the other end of the room. Why in the devil would Aunt Hen have a wooden leg in her milk shed?

"Gimp Watkins," he said aloud.

"What?"

He retrieved it from the other side of the room and held it up in near disbelief.

"This is Gimp Watkins's wooden leg."

Prudence looked disgusted. "My heavens, what is it doing here?"

Gidry began wildly sorting through all the shelves and boxes.

"What are you doing?" Pru asked him. "What are you looking for?"

He began tossing items on the floor in front of her.

"A pearl inlaid hairbrush," he answered, retrieving it from a pile.

"Horse blankets.' They fell in a heap.

"And if I am not mistaken," he said, pulling down the photogram from where it hung on a rusty nail, "this will be Mrs. Hathaway's uncle Lucius, killed at Manassas, 1861."

"What on earth are you talking about?"

"You didn't know, I guess," he said.

"I didn't know what?"

"He is the one."

"He who? Is the one what?"

"Your lover, the man who brings these things here, he's the thief."

Chapter 18

PRU REALIZED it was the truth the minute Gidry made the accusation. Not having been burglarized herself and having her attention taken up with other things, Pru had not listened with great concentration during the crime-wave talk. But she did recall that valuables were often overlooked while strange and sometimes purely undesirable things were sneaked off.

And who in the world would be most likely to abscond with something no one else would even want. No one but her little friend Milton "Sharpy" Kilroy. She berated herself for not making the connection before. But then she never expected the thief to be anyone she knew.

"Who is he?" Gidry demanded.

Pru just stared at him, wondering what to answer. Where he had come up with the notion that she had a secret lover, she did not know. But if his belief could be used to protect the child, she would.

"I will never tell you," she answered.

"Then you'll have to tell the judge," he threatened. "He's using your property to store his loot, and you

303

knowingly allow that. It makes you an accomplice to burglary."

"This is your father's property," she pointed out. "At least until after the terms of his will are settled. Then it will be Aunt Hen's. I only live in the house."

Gidry visibly made an effort to control his anger and took long, deep breaths to calm himself.

"Pru," he said more quietly, "this is not about you and me. It's not about what happened between us last night or eight years ago."

He squatted down and placed his hand upon the pile of stolen goods in the middle of the floor.

"Crimes have been committed," he said. "People have been robbed of their possessions. Things that had real or sentimental value to them. Things that are irreplaceable. You are not the kind of person to be a party to that."

"You may return the items you've found," she told him.

"Return them? Do you think that will make everything all right?" he asked. "Do you think that once people have their things back they will sleep unconcerned? We have a criminal in our midst. He makes us feel threatened in our own homes. He violates our sense of privacy. He has used you, Pru, he has used you very underhandedly. You must tell me who he is."

Determinedly she shook her head.

"I will under no circumstances ever reveal his name," she said.

She turned without another word and walked out the door. Her thoughts were in a whirl. She had to protect Sharpy, the thieving little scamp, and she didn't know how she would do it.

"Prudence Belmont, you get back in here this minute!"

The loud bellow from behind her was so reminiscent of Old Mr. Chavis that she momentarily hesitated, accustomed to doing his bidding. But she need not obey Gidry. He was not her husband, her father, not even very much her elder.

He had been her lover last night. But in the clear light of morning nothing really had changed. She would never allow herself to be so much in his power again. And she would protect young Sharpy, Gidry's only son, she would protect him with her very life if necessary.

"What is all the shouting about?"

The question came from Aunt Hen, who was standing in the back doorway.

Pru was torn between the desire to share what she knew with a sympathetic heart and the need to keep the truth as closely guarded as possible. How much could Aunt Hen know without getting involved herself? Her aunt loved Gidry almost as much as she did Pru. And she hated scandal. How much would she do to protect him from one? And how much detriment to another could she allow?

"It's Gidry. He's . . . oh, never mind," she said.

Aunt Hen was not so easily dissuaded.

"Tell me what's going on with Gidry."

The gentleman in question was now coming out of the milk shed and heading in their direction. Prudence slipped past her aunt and into the kitchen. Her eyes widened in dismay.

"Milton! What are you doing here?"

The little boy looked up from his plate and answered with his mouth full.

"Eating biscuits."

"We've got to hide you," Pru said.

Aunt Hen looked at her as if Pru had lost her mind. But without further discussion the little boy grabbed up an extra biscuit in each hand and made ready for a quick getaway.

There was not time to run to the front door.

"Here," Pru said, opening the narrow pantry doors. The child squeezed inside, and she hastily closed them and turned just in time to see Gidry walk into the kitchen.

"I haven't finished talking to you, Miss Prudence," he bellowed.

"Gidry Chavis, for heaven's sake," Aunt Hen piped in. "What are you thinking, using that tone of voice in this house."

He cleared his throat thoughtfully and apologized to the older woman.

"I'm sorry, Aunt Hen," he said. "But your niece has information about the rash of burglaries that we've been having, and I insist that she tell me what she knows."

Aunt Hen's jaw dropped open in disbelief.

"Pru? What on earth could Pru know about the thievery?"

"The stolen goods are in your milk shed," he replied. "She knows who put them there, and she's not willing to say a word."

He was speaking to her aunt, but his eyes never left Pru's. It was as if he was staring right inside of her. As if he were looking to find her heart. Pru thought of the warmth in those eyes when he'd held her close last night. The tenderness with which they had beheld her. And the languor of lust that had shone there.

"Gidry," Aunt Hen said, breaking into the moment, "isn't it a mite early for you to be paying a call?"

Pru got the minor victory of seeing the man blush. He stammered an inconsequential answer, but her aunt was not so easily put off.

"You come bursting in here upon us," she said. "I'm just now dressed and still eating breakfast."

She pointed out Sharpy's plate on the table.

"And Prudence has not even had time to put her hair up this morning."

Pru's hands flew to the wild tangle of curls that still untidily graced her shoulders.

Her aunt continued. "I think, Gidry, that it quite an ungentlemanly hour for you to be paying a call."

"Aunt Hen, this business is very serious," he replied.

"I'm certain that it is," she agreed. "And it will be just as much so at, shall we say, two o'clock this afternoon. My niece and I will be receiving visitors at that time."

Gidry opened his mouth to protest, but apparently thought the better of it.

"I'll be back at two o'clock," he said.

The words sounded more like a warning than an announcement.

"We will be glad to receive you at that time," Aunt Hen told him formally.

He nodded with exaggerated politeness.

"And Gidry," she added, "I do believe that a shave would be in order before paying a call."

He ran a hand along the roughened stubble on his jaw and left without another word.

The two women waited, simply looking at each other for a long moment. Then Aunt Hen crossed the room and opened the pantry doors.

Sharpy was squatted chewing upon his biscuits, his young face as innocent as an angel's.

"Is he gone?" the little boy asked.

"Yes, Milton. He is gone for the present," Pru told him.

"Come out and finish your breakfast now," her aunt admonished.

The child did not need to be asked twice. He returned to his place and began eating again immediately.

Aunt Hen seated herself as well and motioned for Pru to take the other chair.

"We obviously have some things to talk over," the older woman said.

Pru signed with resignation and took her place at the table. She didn't know where to begin. She didn't know what she should say. She didn't know how much to tell.

"I take it," Aunt Hen began, helping her out, "that the stolen items in my milk shed have something to do with this young man sitting here."

She was looking at Sharpy. He hesitated, a spoonful of grits halfway to his mouth.

"I was just borrowing," he explained. "The folks wasn't using them, so I just borrowed them."

Pru nodded sympathetically. "See, Aunt Hen," she said. "He wasn't stealing at all."

Her aunt shook her head and gave Pru a long-suffering look before turning her attention to the child.

"How old are you now, boy? Six and a half? Seven?"

"He's almost eight," Pru answered for him.

Sharpy's mouth was full of food once more and he made no comment.

"He doesn't look that old," Aunt Hen insisted. "But no matter, you, young man, are plenty old enough to know the difference between right and wrong. Taking other people's things is wrong."

He nodded sorrowfully, but still offered his excuse.

"I didn't have nothing," he told her. "Other folks have so much."

"I'm sure that's true," Aunt Hen agreed. "But it is better to have nothing in this world than to take what does not belong to you. Promise me that you won't do it again."

Without hesitation Sharpy replied. "I promise not to steal nothing again," he said.

"All right, young man," she said. "I'm going to take your word on that. Prudence, you'll have to make up that little sewing room for the boy. We can't have him out in the milk shed anymore, with the place under scrutiny."

"Yes," Pru agreed.

"You should have brought him into the house from the first."

"I didn't want people to know that he was staying with us," Pru answered.

Aunt Hen looked her sternly and then at the little boy. There was firm expectation in her expression as well as a tenderness that bordered upon a smile.

"When you've finished your breakfast, fill up the woodbox and bring in a load of water for the reservoir," she said.

"Yes, Aunt Hen."

"Anything in this house that you want, simply ask for it," she continued. "I will not tolerate thievery of any kind."

He nodded.

"As long as you stay in my house, you'll have a clean place to sleep and plenty to eat. A young fellow shouldn't require much more."

The boy agreed readily, and, stuffing the last bite of biscuit down his already overfull mouth, he rushed outside to get to work. After a couple of weeks of helping Pru, he was familiar with the morning chores and eager to prove himself to Aunt Hen.

"What is it that you are not telling me?" her aunt asked as soon as the child was out of earshot.

"Nothing," Pru insisted a little too quickly. She did not sound at all convincing.

"That little fellow has been on his own for a year now, and nobody has even noticed," Aunt Hen said. "Why wasn't he taken in by somebody?" She shook her head and answered her own question. "I suppose because the poor fellow's mother was no better than she should be. You'd think at least the Hathaways would have been looking out for him."

"They might want to send him away," Pru said.

Aunt Hen nodded. "That might well be the right idea."

"No!" Pru's tone was adamant.

"Why not?" Aunt Hen asked her. "It might well be the best thing. A fine, clean orphanage where he'd get good care and a chance at an education."

"He shouldn't have to leave Chavistown," Pru said.

"A new place would be good," the older woman insisted. "In a city where no one knows his past, he'd have to be judged upon his own sins, not those of his parents."

"He belongs here," Pru said with certainty. "His . . . his heritage is here. His mother is buried here."

Her aunt's brow furrowed.

"Your mother is buried in Iowa," she said. "Would you wish to be there because of her grave?"

"No, it's not that," she assured her aunt. "It's . . . it's . . . Befuddle Kilroy was not Milton's father."

Now that the words were out, Pru felt better. She couldn't hold the secret to herself a moment longer.

"If you think I'm near keeling over in shock," Aunt Hen said, "I'm afraid you'll be disappointed. Mabel Merriman was a wild young girl. And set on that path, her troubles as a woman just got worse."

"Do you know who arranged her marriage to Befuddle?" Pru asked.

Aunt Hen shook her head.

"Peer Chavis."

"Really."

Her aunt did not seem unduly surprised or concerned.

"She apparently came to him seeking help, and he gave Befuddle money to wed her and set up housekeeping."

"It sounds like it was a pretty good idea," Aunt Hen said. "Mabel needed a name for her child, and poor Befuddle needed someone to take care of him."

"Well, I don't think Befuddle's family were as pleased about it as you seem to be," Pru said. "They never gave the child so much as a second look. When Befuddle died, they erected a fine tombstone. But when Mabel passed away only months later, they put up no marker at all."

Aunt Hen tutted with disapproval. "That Cloris, it's her doing, I'll avow. It's hard to imagine a human any more mean-spirited."

"Do you know who bought the tombstone on Mabel's grave?" Pru asked. "Peer Chavis bought it. Milton told me so himself."

"So?"

"So it makes perfect sense," Pru told her. "He's the one she ran to, he's the one who helped her, gave her money, arranged for her future, and he's the one who remembered her after she was gone."

Pru watched her aunt's expression change from puzzlement to abject displeasure.

"If you are trying to say that Peer Chavis is that little boy's father," she snapped, "then I've a good mind to go cut a peach-tree switch! It's is absolutely untrue and shame on you for speaking such ill of the dead."

"Oh I didn't mean Peer!" Pru corrected hastily. "I never . . . of course I never thought it could be Peer. He did what he did for Gidry."

"For Gidry?"

"Yes, of course. Gidry must be the father."

"Well, I think it's rather doubtful with Gidry having been gone for eight years," Aunt Hen told her.

"And Milton is eight years old," Pru said. "For heaven's sake, Aunt Hen, you must remember that they ran off together."

"I remember that they left town on the same train on the same night," she said. "Saying that they *ran off together* requires an interpretation that nobody in this town except Gidry has the certainty to make."

"You defend him always, even when he is obviously in the wrong," Pru said.

"Yes," she admitted. "I suppose I will always defend him, as I always will you. But I don't mind telling either of you when I think your brains are full of feathers, as yours is now."

"Aunt Hen, it is true. I am sure of it," Pru told her. "Look at the boy, he has Gidry's hair and eyes."

"The boy looks like his mother," Aunt Hen replied. "Mabel's mother had those dark looks of old French blood. You can't get away from it."

"Why would the old man have been so kind to her,

then?" she asked. "And kind to Milton as well. He put him to work in the cotton mill, just like he did Gidry. Why else would Peer Chavis do that?"

"Because beyond all his booming and blustering he was a kind and good man," Aunt Hen answered. "He had a weak spot for people who make mistakes. Lord knows, he made a few of his own."

"That may well be so, but it doesn't change the fact that the child could be Gidry's, and I believe he is Gidry's. He is a Chavis, and he deserves, at the very least, to be able to live his life in Chavistown."

"And what did Gidry say when you told him about his son?" Aunt Hen asked.

"Well of course I couldn't tell him," Pru insisted.

"And why not?"

"Because . . . because he obviously does not want to know," Pru replied. "He left her, just like he left me."

"You do the man an injustice, Prudence," Aunt Hen told her. "Yes, he did leave you, and perhaps he did leave her. But I will not believe that he would deny a child of his body. He is too much like his father to do such a thing."

Prudence shrugged. "Well, that remains to be seen."

"I don't think that's the reason you haven't told him," Aunt Hen said. "I don't think that is the reason at all."

"What other reason could there be?" Pru asked.

"A much more selfish, personal reason," Aunt Hen said. "A reason that makes me ashamed of you."

"Of me?"

"Yes," Aunt Hen answered. "I think you haven't told him because you know that if he is the father, he will claim the boy. And if he does, then you will have to give Sharpy up."

"What?"

"If the boy becomes officially Gidry's son, it will be obvious to anyone who sees your affection for the child that you love him because he is Gidry's."

"I care for Milton for himself," she insisted.

"Perhaps you do now, but that is not what brought him to your attention. You've never had any interest in children. But you saw in him a boy that might have been your own."

"That's not true!"

"I think there is enough truth in it to worry us both," Aunt Hen replied.

Pru didn't know what to say. For the first time she scrutinized her own motives, questioned her own actions.

"I can't see him sent away to an orphanage," she told Aunt Hen, her tone pleading. "Whether I'm right or wrong, you've got to help."

The old woman sighed.

"Yes," she agreed. "I suppose I must."

There was duty to one's community and loyalty to one's beloved. Occasionally those things were at cross-purposes. Gidry determined to serve them both, but hadn't managed to serve either particularly well.

He'd returned to his house to clean up and dress. He was still too mad at Pru even to see straight. She said that she was refusing him because of what he'd done all those years ago. Blaming him and yesterday for why they could not be together now. But the truth had come out, or at least part of it, he was certain. She was protecting her man. He turned out to be worst than a no-account, unfaithful, two-timing, adulterer. He was also a common thief, who by hiding his loot in Aunt Hen's milk shed had dragged the two most important women in Gidry's life into some criminal involvement. And Pru let him do it. That must mean she really loved him.

How did one fight against such a thing? he wondered. And the answer came to him. You choose a battle that is more important than personal feelings of the heart.

So before he went to call upon Pru and Aunt Hen that afternoon, he set up a meeting in his office with Arthur Sattlemore of Big Texas Electric. If the gentleman was surprised to see him the day after his father's funeral, he gave no indication. And as for the subject of discussion, Pru's speech at the Harvest Moon Dance had already managed to make the rounds of barrooms and barbershops all through Chavistown. Sattlemore was ready with his own explanations and arguments.

"We've encountered the objections of naturalists in nearly every town we have lighted," the man admitted.

Gidry's brow furrowed. "Why didn't you mention this to the Commercial Club?" he asked.

The salesmen shrugged and smiled. "I believe your Mr. Honnebuzz says it best: Why stir up controversy unnecessarily?"

Gidry was beginning to very much dislike that attitude.

"Because, it seems," he answered, "controversy often brings attention to facts that some people would wish kept unknown."

Sattlemore nodded in acquiescence.

"The fact, Mr. Chavis," he said, "is that we have no facts. Science has not determined any effects, helpful or harmful, related to artificial light."

"But that doesn't mean there aren't any," Gidry said.

"We don't know," the man admitted. "We've seen no effects in all the years of gas lamplight. But the use of electricity is still very new. We know that plants and animals, as well as humans, have within themselves electrical charges. Electricity is now being used in medicine for treatment of bodily ailments such as rheumatism and gouty complaints. In laboratories all over the world testing is being done. But the desire for electricity, the progress, security, and convenience that it offers has far outstripped any cautions from those who fear man's reach exceeds his grasp."

"So you are saying that we simply do not know what effects lighting our neighborhoods, even our homes, might have upon us."

"Nobody knows," Sattlemore told him. "But I can point out that numerous towns and cities all over the country have decided in favor of electric lighting and each month, each day, each year that goes by with no ill effects speaks for itself."

Gidry nodded slowly. "So we are actually testing this new science in our own towns on our own families and with our own consent."

Sattlemore chuckled.

"You needn't make it sound so ominous, Mr. Chavis," he said. "This modern innovation probably has no ill effects at all."

"Probably," Gidry repeated.

It was a word that held tremendous promise as well as consequences.

He called upon Pru at exactly two in afternoon. He knew exactly what he was going to say. He also knew that he was perfectly right in what he was doing. Still, his palms were sweating and his heart was pounding.

He'd never thought to lose Pru. He'd never thought that she couldn't be his if he just said the word. And his need to have her at his side had never been greater.

Determinedly he knocked on the door.

"Good afternoon, Gidry," Aunt Hen said. "It is so nice of you to call."

The formality was off-putting. Especially when the older woman escorted him into the tiny front parlor. He was accustomed to being treated as part of the family and to being entertained in the kitchen or the sewing room.

Aunt Hen seemed content to allow Pru to do the talking. Her message was calm and well rehearsed.

"We would like for you to take the items found in the milk shed and see that they are returned to their rightful owners," Pru told him.

"How would you suggest that I explain how I came to have them?" he asked her.

"Can you not simply say that you found them? Give them back and assume that all is well that ends well," she said.

"If we have a criminal among us, Miss Pru," Gidry answered, "I do not believe giving back the loot will be the end of it at all."

Pru appeared thoughtful for a long moment.

"I think you will have to trust me on this," she said. "There will be no more thievery."

"I am no longer sure," he replied, "that you are a woman that I can trust."

She appeared stung by his words. Gidry did not mean to hurt her, but he was determined upon his present course.

"I have come to discuss a compromise," he said.

"A compromise?" Her voice was hopeful. "Isn't

that what I have been offering to you? Return of goods and no further robberies as long as nothing else is said."

"That is not the type of compromise that I have in mind," Gidry told her.

"Then by all means," Pru said, "state your own thinking."

"The perpetrator of these crimes must be brought to justice," he said. "You obviously could be instrumental in helping to bring that about."

"I have no intention of helping you," she said.

"If you don't tell me, then you will certainly have to tell the judge," he said.

"I won't tell him either," Pru insisted.

"I believe that you will, Pru," Gidry said calmly. "I believe that you will be willing to tell me. You simply have to be sufficiently motivated to do so."

"I'm sure that nothing you can say will change my mind."

Gidry mentally braced himself. This was the big risk for him. The proposal that might alienate her from him forever.

"If you tell everything to me," he said evenly, "I will see that no electric lighting will ever be installed in the residential areas of Chavistown."

She gave a gasp of surprise.

"If you do not," he continued, "I will see a light pole raised on each and every corner of this town. From below the railroad tracks to Cemetery Hill it will be as bright as daylight from dusk till dawn."

"That is blackmail."

Gidry shrugged. "Blackmail, thievery . . ." He glanced over at Aunt Hen before continuing. "There are sins aplenty involved here, Miss Pru."

"One thing has nothing to do with the other."

"It certainly does," he insisted. "If we no longer have a criminal among us, then I would feel confident in letting the idea of allowing the street lighting project to drop."

"I told you to trust me, there will be no more stealing," she said. "That should be enough to make the project unnecessary."

Gidry was firm and sure.

"I don't care how well you think you know this man or how confident you are of your influence on him," he said. "You cannot speak for him. I cannot accept a promise from *you* for him."

Pru's expression was momentarily agitated, frustrated. Then she raised her chin in defiance.

"I can speak for the thief, Mr. Chavis," she said smoothly. "Because Mr. Chavis, I am the thief."

"What!"

The words came as shouted exclamations from both Gidry and Aunt Hen.

"Everything you find in that milk shed, I have stolen."

If the situation had not been so serious, Gidry would have burst out laughing.

"You caught me yourself," she said, "when I broke into the gin. You'll have to admit that in any court. I have broken into houses all over this town. I have taken things from people, and I have stored them in my aunt's milk shed, where you can find them now. I confess. I am guilty."

Gidry was shaking his head, and the words were on his lips to call her every kind of fool ever created.

"You will never get the people of Chavistown to believe such a thing," he said.

Pru raised a challenging eyebrow.

"You think you will have an easier time convincing

them that a dried-up old spinster who threw her cor-set across the amoire years ago is having an illicit af-fair with a thief in her milk shed."

"You are not a dried-up old spinster."

"In the eyes of this town, I certainly am," she said. "What do you think I have been doing in the last eight years since the scandal? I've been living a life of absolute chastity. None of the men who called upon me got so much as even a good-night kiss, and you are going to convince this town I am some wild Jez-ebel?"

Prudence shook her head, sure of herself.

"No one is going to believe such a thing of me. No one would imagine such a thing of me, except you. You, who judge all the faults of mankind by your own."

"Is that what you think? Maybe that's not it at all. Maybe it is because I know the passion that lurks be-neath the sour spinster facade."

Aunt Hen cleared her throat loudly.

"I believe that we are getting a bit far afield," she said. "Pru, don't be so ridiculous as to think anyone would believe you capable of being a common thief. Gidry, don't attempt to manipulate my niece by threats or coercion."

"But Aunt Hen!"

They both complained.

"A crime has been committed," she said. "It's time the authorities were called in to sort it out. Neither of you has the right of it. Hopefully, someone else will."

Chapter 19

THE HEARING was scheduled for the next morning at ten o'clock. Gidry had tried to keep it as quiet as possible. Unfortunately in a place as small as Chavistown, such a thing was impossible.

He had spoken privately with Judge Ramey, but Alice had listened at the door. She couldn't wait to tell Leda Peterson, who told her mother-in-law. She whispered it to Bertha Mae, who told it to every telephone patron in town. Henrietta was informed herself by a gossipy Mrs. Champion, as if it were possible to be personally involved and not be aware of what was going on.

But unlike Pru, Henrietta did not spend the morning rehearsing a set of lies she intended to present to the judge in order to be held responsible to burglary and face detention in the jail.

She dressed in a cool cotton day dress and filled her basket with the newest blooms of the garden. They were little more than buds, and normally she would have been loath to cut them. But this morning she did so without any sense of sadness.

She made her way up to Cemetery Hill. The sky

was a brilliant blue with only a few feathery clouds so high in the sky they might well have been throw rugs on the floor of heaven. A slight breeze in her hair eased the heat of the bright morning sunshine.

Henrietta walked with a smile upon her face and a lightness in her heart. She watched the butterflies flit from flower to flower and listened to the songbirds greeting the day. Her beloved Peer was dead. He was dead and all that he was to her heart was dead as well. But she was alive. Today she was perfectly, gloriously alive. It wasn't everything. But it was a lot. Today it was enough.

The cemetery was quiet and deserted. There was a feeling of peace, a feeling of permanence.

Henrietta stood at the foot of the hill of dirt that now embraced for all time the body of the man that she loved. She wanted him. She wanted him beside her. But today she would not, she could not, cry.

Henrietta knelt on the ground beside the grave and began arranging the flowers she'd brought in her basket upon the raised hill of black waxy soil.

"I wish you could have heard what my niece told me yesterday," she said. "She's thinking that poor Mabel Merriman's orphan is your grandson. It's wishful thinking if you want my opinion. He's a fine little boy, I know you'd be proud to claim him. But it's just not so."

Henrietta shook her head with wry disbelief.

"She thinks he's Gidry's child, and she's trying to keep him for herself," Henrietta said. "She's much too proud ever to just keep Gidry. Her wounded pride simply won't allow it.

"Those young ones we raised are something to watch," she said. "Two of the sharpest minds in this town, each bent on trying to outsmart and outmanipulate the other."

She tutted and shook her head.

"You would think that being in love as long as they have, they'd understand each other a good bit better than they do."

Henrietta sighed.

"I guess that's plenty true of all of us," she said.

The roses were spread out like a brightly colored fan along the top of the grave. Henrietta fussed with it for several more minutes, getting it exactly how she thought it would look best. Then she stood back and assured herself that everything was exactly where it should be and very well balanced. It was as near perfect as she could make it. And there was really no one to care how it looked except herself.

"You should have seen the folks at your funeral. Everybody was there to pay last respects. All the townsfolk in their best suits and nearly every farmer in the county showed up. It was a whole houseful of broken hearts. Poor old Ollie Larson, who never had a good thing to say about you when you were alive, was just sniveling and wiping his eyes until I could hardly keep my own self straight. They all miss you. Like a fine old shade tree blown over in a summer storm, they miss you. But the world goes on."

She turned her eyes to the sky. Overhead a flock of birds winged their way southward.

"I nearly gave up, you know," she said quietly. "I was just too broken to try to go on. I wanted to just give up."

The breeze whistled around her and she straightened a loose strand of hair back into its pins.

"I thought I loved you more than life," Henrietta continued. "But in truth, I believe that I love life very much. Enough to try to live it without you. I've raised Prudence the best I could, and she's a fine young woman. I couldn't be prouder of her. And I take some of the credit for Gidry as well. He's your very shadow, and he's his own man as well. They would miss me, I know. But I have more reason than that to stay."

She could hear the faint drone of a lazy bee buzzing almost languidly in the morning heat.

"Do you remember when I was a girl, and my sister and I went to Galveston with my father?" she asked. "We met an old fishing-boat captain that Daddy knew. He told me that in the middle of the ocean, on the clearest day of the year, you can only see three miles. Three miles. That's all. Total calm, perfect visibility you can only see three miles. The curve of the earth makes it impossible to see any farther. Three miles is not really very far."

Henrietta gave a long, heartfelt sigh as she stared at the ground before her.

"I've lived almost fifty years in this little town," she continued. "I walked every inch of it a thousand times and know the sight and scent of every season by heart. I've had my own little house and felt snug and safe and warm. I've grown some of the most beautiful roses that eyes that ever beheld. And I've loved one man for my whole life long."

She hesitated thoughtfully.

"Peer, I hate rowing this boat without you, but I just have to see what comes up on the horizon."

She paused to glance once more into the vivid blue sky, so calm and untroubled.

"Your soul may be in heaven," she continued, "but your spirit . . . your spirit is here in my heart." She folded her arms across her chest as if she were holding it inside.

"I will keep you there. And as long as I live, you live."

Henrietta rose to her feet. She brushed the dust from her skirt and then from her hands before she picked up her basket and turned to go.

Standing some distance away under the silvery yellow canopy of an autumn maple tree. Sharpy Kilroy stood watching her.

She'd had no idea that she was not alone in the cemetery. He had made no attempt to make his presence known. But he ran up to her now, bright-eyed and eager.

"Hello, Aunt Hen," he said tentatively, as if to test if he was still allowed to call her by that name.

"Good morning, Sharpy," she answered. "I didn't realize that you were here."

He nodded back in the direction from which she'd come.

"I saw you talking to old Mr. Chavis," Sharpy said. "I didn't want to end-er-up you."

Henrietta smiled at him.

"Thank you, that was very kind," she said.

The little boy blushed, pleased with her praise.

"I come and talk to my mom sometimes," he admitted. "I always tell her who I am, 'cause I've grown so big, she probably don't even recognize me anymore."

"Oh, I bet she would," Henrietta assured him.

"You think so?"

"Oh yes, any mother would know you," she said.

Sharpy grinned.

"So are you heading home now?" he asked.

"No, actually I'm heading for the courthouse," she

said. "I have to see Judge Ramey about the stolen goods in the milk shed."

"What are you going to tell him?" Sharpy asked.

"I'm not planning to tell him anything," Henrietta said. "Now my niece is planning to say that she was the one who stole those things."

Sharpy's eyes widened in disbelief.

"Why would she do that?"

"She is trying to keep you from getting in trouble," Henrietta told him. "So she is making up a big lie."

"No one would believe that about Miss Pru," Sharpy said with certainty.

"I couldn't agree with you more," Henrietta told him. "I personally make it a policy to tell the truth about things, difficult things, myself, in my own way. I always think that is better than just letting things come out as they always do. Somehow the truth eventually always comes out."

"You think I should go down to the courthouse and tell the judge the truth?" Sharpy asked.

"Yes, I think that would be the smartest and best thing to do," Henrietta told him. "You knew you shouldn't steal, and you did anyway. When you make mistakes like that, it's best just to take your punishment and get it over with."

The little boy was thoughtful for a long moment.

"Do you think they will send me to prison?" he asked.

Henrietta shrugged.

"I couldn't say. I'm not the judge," she told him. "But the thing to do is go down there, tell the truth, and throw yourself upon the mercy of the court."

Judge Ramey's chambers were on the second floor of the newly finished courthouse. Paneled in dark ma-

hogany wood, the accommodations were as sumptu-
ous and fine as any in Texas. The furniture was huge
in aspect and intricately carved, the judge insisting
that no expense be spared in providing the very best
for "the good people in Chavis County."

Since most of those good people would, with any
luck, never see the inside of the judge's chambers,
their appreciation remained unexpressed.

Prudence Belmont did not take note of her surroundings. She was as nervous and jittery as she had
ever been in her life. She didn't know what to hope
for.

If she were to be believed, there was a chance she
would be sent to jail. If, however, Gidry convinced
the judge that she were protecting a lover, once again
she would be the object of tremendous gossip and
pity. *Poor Prudence, love has ruined her twice in a lifetime.*

Either way a tremendous scandal was forthcoming,
and she had no idea how to prevent it. Except . . . except perhaps the truth. Did she really believe that
Gidry, knowing the child to be his own, would fail to
acknowledge him or send the boy away forever? Even
knowing him to be a man much flawed, Pru could
not really believe that he would deny his son.

She bit down upon her lip. She was worried that
Aunt Hen might be right about Pru's motivation for
keeping Sharpy's parentage a secret. It was true that
she had never shown much interest in children. And
if people realized that the boy was Gidry's son, she
would probably feel uncomfortable about showing
any interest in him.

But was that enough reason for her to allow whatever calamity that was shortly to befall them as the
result of this hearing? Pru was not certain that it was.

Gidry arrived, wearing his dress suit. He looked

urbane and quite handsome. Not at all her intimate cowboy lover. His glance found her immediately, although she was not difficult to locate among the cluster of businessmen. Their gazes locked for one brief moment before Pru lowered her eyes.

Why did *she* suddenly feel so guilty? She was the one who was trying to do the right thing. The right thing for Sharpy, so that he would not be sent away. The right thing for the town, so they would not thoughtlessly accept a modern convenience whose drawbacks were unresolved. And right for herself and Gidry.

That last one gave her pause. She had allowed herself to revel in a long night of passion with a man she had loved so long. Ostensibly it had been to offer him comfort, but he had given as much as he had taken. And he had assumed that marriage was part of the bargain. She had refused him because of gossip. She didn't want people to think that she had continued to love him. Now, people were going to think . . . heaven only knew what people were going to think.

Eight years ago, he had hurt her. He had embarrassed her. He had humiliated her. She had forgiven him, she assured herself, but she could never forget.

More and more people began to enter the room. There were no longer sufficient chairs and spectators now lined the walls and hovered around the doorway.

Gidry was speaking firmly with the judge, apparently concerned about the growing audience to the day's business. Finally the judge nodded and rose to his feet.

"Today's hearing will be closed to the public," he announced.

Noises of complaint rose immediately from the by-standers.

"This is a private matter at this time," Judge Ramey insisted. "We are merely asking questions. If it is determined that crimes have been committed, they will be tried in open court."

"We have a right to know if it's true that you've found the stolen goods," Ollie Larson proclaimed. "And we have a right to know who the thief is. Some of us had our own houses robbed."

"The court clerk will be taking notes," the judge stated. "Those who have actually been robbed, Reverend Hathaway, Tatum, Honnebuzz. You may stay. If the rest of you all will just move on out into the corridor."

Murmurs of disappointment grumbled through the crowd.

"Constable, you can stay, but stand by the door," Judge Ramey said. "We will be announcing the outcome of these hearings as soon as they are concluded."

As the mass of onlookers receded reluctantly into the hallway, Pru glanced nervously at those left in the room. Enough people certainly to ensure that nothing said in this room would remain private for very long.

"Now, Miss Prudence," Judge Ramey began. "For the record please state your name."

"Prudence Belmont," she said, her voice catching slightly with nervousness.

The judge smiled at her, apparently sympathetic to her disconcerted demeanor.

"This is not a formal court procedure of any kind," he assured her. "We are here upon a fact-gathering mission, and you are free to tell us what you know about the stolen property that has been found in your possession."

"It was not technically found in Miss Belmont's possession," Gidry clarified. "It was found in the milk shed behind her aunt's home."

"Yes," the judge agreed rather vaguely, unwilling to belabor the point. "Just tell us what you know, Prudence. The truth, that is all we want."

She had rehearsed her story a dozen times that morning. She would simply confess that she had taken up housebreaking as a hobby. In great detail, drawing upon her experience of sneaking into the gin, she would describe how she roamed the streets of Chavistown looking for doors left unlatched and windows open.

That is what she had planned to say. But she had spent most of the last decade trying to recover from the public embarrassment caused by Gidry Chavis. She knew that she would find it far more difficult to overcome publicly embarrassing herself.

"I . . . I . . ."

She just could not do it.

"I refuse to answer, so that I may not incriminate myself," she said.

There were murmurs of question all around her.

"Now, Miss Pru," the judge began.

"I know my rights," Prudence insisted. "I cannot be compelled to say anything that might implicate me in anything."

"No one is trying to implicate you in anything," the judge assured her. "You need not be afraid to tell us the truth."

The man's overly patient and increasingly patronizing manner grated upon her. She raised her chin defiantly and gave him a long, assessing glance, cold enough to keep ice in midsummer.

"I may not be a lawyer, sir, or a judge," Pru told him, "but I did complete a normal-school education, where I learned a good deal about the U.S. Constitution as well as the fifteen amendments to it. The one I'm referring to at this juncture is the fifth, I believe."

Gidry cleared his throat loudly.

Pru glanced over at him. His expression was extremely solemn, but in his eyes she detected something recognizable only as pride. Somehow he was proud of her. She was flirting with public humiliation, and he was proud of her.

Judge Ramey, however, seemed to be losing patience.

"Indeed, Miss Belmont," he said, "I, too, am familiar with the amendments. You cannot be forced to testify against yourself. But it has come to the attention of this court that you may be protecting someone. Whom are you trying to protect, Miss Pru?"

She had no idea how to answer that. Not for anything in the world would she point the finger at young Sharpy, but Gidry's conclusion, that she was protecting a man, would shortly be the conclusion of everyone. It was incalculably unfair. Pru had spent so many years restoring her reputation and avoiding romantic entanglements. Now all of that was to be undone in a few short moments. It was grossly unjust. But how could it be avoided?

Inexplicably her eyes were drawn to Gidry. His brow was furrowed in concern.

"Are you protecting a man?" Judge Ramey questioned.

Pru was close to tears of frustration. She didn't

want to be a laughingstock once more, but she couldn't imagine any other way.

"Miss Belmont, if you do not speak," the judge insisted, "I can hold you in contempt and put you in jail."

"She is not required to speak," Gidry said suddenly.

Every eye turned to stare at him.

Judge Ramey looked askance.

"Whyever not?" he asked.

Gidry's glance held her for a long moment before he replied. "A wife cannot be compelled to testify against her husband."

"Husband!"

The word was a gasp among the onlookers.

Pru's jaw dropped open in shock.

"Miss Belmont is a spinster," Judge Ramey stated flatly.

"I have reason to know that she is not," Gidry told him. "She . . . she has been secretly married for some time, and she believes that her husband is involved in this ongoing thievery."

"A secret marriage?"

Pru heard the words spoken incredulously by Reverend Hathaway behind her. What was Gidry doing? Why was he saying these things?

"How do you claim to know this?" Judge Ramey asked him.

Gidry was looking at her again as if trying to convey some message.

"I know this . . ." he said, "because I am the man she is trying to protect. Prudence Belmont has been for . . . for over eight years, Mrs. Gidry Chavis."

"What?"

The sound of Pru's horrified exclamation was lost

in the pandemonium that broke out all around her. Everybody was talking at once.

"Order! Order!" Judge Ramey bellowed.

"I am the thief, Judge," Gidry proclaimed. "I have been sneaking back into town for years to see my wife, and I, being often short of funds, I began a life of crime. Only when my father's health caused him to accept me back into my family was I able to stop stealing."

Pru stared across the room at him in disbelief, her heart near to breaking. Gidry, her wonderful Gidry, had struggled all his life with the inability to live up to the sterling example set by his father. Finally, at long last, he was accepted in this town, admired in this town, and he was throwing it all away. He was throwing it all away for her.

"He's lying," she said loudly. "He's lying about everything. We were never married. And he has never stolen anything. For heaven sake, he hasn't even been in town for years. I am the thief. I took all those things. He is trying to shield me from justice."

The roar of questions, speculation, backbiting, and gossip had risen to such a crescendo that the judge, having no gavel in his chambers, began pounding furiously upon the fancy desk top with a paperweight.

Pru and Gidry stared at each other as all around them the speculation swelled. Pru could not even cringe from that knowledge. She could only marvel at the man across the room who, after all that had and had not been between them, must in fact truly love her.

"Stop this instant, or I will clear the room immediately!" Judge Ramey was shouting.

His threats eventually began to take effect. The

crowd had just began to quiet when the door to the hallway burst open.

Judge Ramey rose to his feet.

"No one else is allowed in here."

Henrietta Pauling and Sharpy Kilroy stood on the threshold.

"I think you'd better hear what we have to say," Aunt Hen told him.

The little boy rushed forward, his eyes wide and his coattails flying.

"I confess, Judge, I did it," he said. "I'm here to throw myself in the murky-oven-quart."

"What?"

"I believe he wishes to throw himself upon the mercy of the court," Aunt Hen interpreted.

"Miss Pru didn't do nothing, it was me," Sharpy said.

Judge Ramey looked at the boy. He looked at Pru. He looked at Gidry. And he gave a long-suffering sigh.

"You can't all be guilty," he said. "Somebody here is lying."

"Judge, may we have a short recess," Gidry asked. "I think I need to talk to . . . to my wife."

The portly man leaned back in his chair and surveyed the entire room.

"Yes, Mr. Chavis," he said finally, "I do believe a short recess would be in order. Maybe you can all manage to get your stories straight."

Chapter 20

GIDRY, PRU, Aunt Hen, and Sharpy were relegated to a small anteroom on the far north side of the building. There was a large dormer window with a small balcony that overlooked the square and the town and the cotton fields in the distance.

In the hallway behind them, the incredulous chatter was nearly deafening. The gossips, the unkind and most-feared gossips of Chavistown, would never have a morning so fine as this one.

Gidry was as calm as he had ever been in his life.

"So it was you who has been staying in the milk shed," he said to the boy.

Sharpy nodded. "I took those things. Miss Pru wanted to take my punishment, but I can't let her," he said. "If somebody is going to jail, it's going to be me."

"No, we can't . . ." Pru began, her voice near pleading.

Gidry held up his hand.

"Why don't you sit here with Aunt Hen," he said to Sharpy. "I think I will talk to Miss Pru out on the balcony."

The two nodded, and Gidry took the arm of his supposed wife and let her into the warm sunshine of the morning. He shut the twelve-light doors behind them. Finally alone, Gidry felt unaccountably shy and incredibly foolish. How on earth could he have ever believed that she was seeing a lover? His sweet, honest, and faithful Pru, who cared so much for her reputation. How could he have ever thought something like that of her? He recalled with dismay the blood on her underdrawers. She had been an innocent virgin, of course, and he had taken her with the delicacy and finesse of a drunken sailor.

"Why on earth did you make up that story about us being married?" she asked him.

Gidry shrugged.

"I couldn't think of any other way to save you," he answered. "When you reminded us that you couldn't be forced to testify against yourself, it came to me that you also couldn't be compelled to testify against a husband. I've spent a good deal of time with my father these last weeks making up tall tales. If I was going to make up one about you having a husband, the man in question was certainly going to be me."

Pru's expression was marked with concern.

"Being accepted and respected by this community is so important to you," she said. "I couldn't believe that you would risk that."

"Any more than I could believe that you would swallow that hard-won pride that you have acquired," he said.

Gidry hadn't thought a great deal about what he was giving up. He had acted on instinct, as if throwing himself in front of a bullet. He had to save her from the damage that she was intent upon doing to herself. Sacrificing everything for her lover. Except now, of course, there was no lover.

"What about the postcard?" he asked aloud.

"What?"

"The French postcard. I found it in the gin," he said. "I thought you had written it to your lover."

Pru gasped in horror and covered her face in shame.

He pried her hands away from her face. He was unexpectedly rewarded when she stepped closer and hid her embarrassment in his neck and shoulder.

"I was looking for a piece of paper to write you a note," she told him in a whisper. "When I saw . . . when I saw what it was, I just got out of there immediately."

Gidry bit his lip to stifle a grin and took advantage of her nearness to wrap his arms around her waist.

"You shouldn't have such . . . such vulgar material in your office with young children like Milton around," she scolded him.

"I got that vulgar material from *Milton*," Gidry answered.

"What!"

Pru jerked back astounded.

Gidry nodded at her. "Not only is the little devil a thief, he's a smut peddler as well."

"He's just a little boy," Pru defended. "He's hardly had any upbringing at all. He can't be blamed for what he has done."

"He is guilty and must be punished," Gidry insisted. He could almost hear his father's voice in his own words. Deliberately he moderated his tone. "But he is very young, and the rest of us have good reason for shame in allowing him to get so far down the wrong road."

"It is more our fault than his own," she said.

Gidry shook his head. Clearly he could not agree.

"It is his own fault, and he's willing to own up to that, Pru. You have to let him do that."

"They . . . they might send him away," she said. "I just could not allow him to be sent away."

Gidry's brow furrowed in concern.

"There is a wonderful boy's home in Shockley," he said. "He'd get good care, a good education, and a thorough grounding in religion and morals."

"He mustn't be sent away," Pru insisted.

"Why not?"

She hesitated as if she was loath to speak.

"Is there something more about this that I don't know?" he asked.

She bit her lip, considering.

"Tell me, Pru," he encouraged. "If I am going to help the boy I'll have to know."

She stepped away from him, wringing her hands nervously, then turned to face him.

"Gidry," she said, softly almost comfortingly, "Milton Kilroy is your son."

He heard the words, but the meaning of them didn't quite register.

"What?" he asked.

"Milton is your son," she answered. "Your unlawful child, conceived with Mabel Merriman."

"What!"

"Befuddle Kilroy was not his father," Pru told him. "When Mabel returned to Chavistown, she was already carrying your child."

Gidry stared at her, incredulous, for a long moment. Slowly, very slowly, he began to shake his head, then a humorless chuckle escaped him.

"I don't see anything funny about this, Mr.

Chavis," Pru said, affronted at his reaction.

"Mabel Merriman has never carried a child of mine," Gidry told her with certainty.

"I know it is a shock and probably hard to believe that she wouldn't tell you but . . ."

"She didn't tell me because it simply isn't true," he assured her.

Pru's mouth thinned into a stubborn line.

"Gidry, I know that it is true," she said. "All the evidence points to it."

"What evidence?"

"Well, your father helped her financially when she came back to town," Pru said. "He actually set up the marriage with Befuddle so Milton would have a name. He bought her tombstone when she died, and he took a great interest in the boy always."

"And you think that proves that he is my child?"

"Of course it does," she said. "Look at him."

Pru gestured toward the glass door beyond which he could clearly see the child talking animatedly with Aunt Hen.

"He even looks like you," she said.

"He looks like a lot of people," Gidry answered. "And practically all of them are not his father. I fall into that group as well."

Pru's eyes were welling with tears of frustration.

"Don't deny him, Gidry," she pleaded. "For all that he has done, he is a very good little boy and . . . and I love him very much."

"Pru . . ." he began, but she was too emotional to let him speak.

"He has lived a life missing so very much," she told him. "He's been poor, alone, orphaned, unwanted, and reviled. He has done things wrong, but the conditions of his birth are not his fault, they are not his crime. He needs someone to care for him, to love him. I've been trying to do it. But a real father, a real father would mean so much to him, Gidry. Don't deny him that."

"Just listen to me, Prudence," Gidry began.

He was interrupted by a tap on the glass behind them. The constable had come into the anteroom. Gidry opened the door.

"Judge Ramey is ready to recommence the hearing," the man announced. "He says if you couldn't sort this out in twenty minutes, you never will be able to."

Gidry nodded and offered his arm to escort Pru.

"For your sake, Pru, because I love you, I will be everything that I can be to the boy," he promised. "And I will see that they don't send him away."

"Oh Gidry—"

"No more lies from you," he told her. "And this one time, let me handle it in my own way."

She didn't look too willing, but she did acquiesce.

Aunt Hen and Sharpy led the way as the growing throngs in the hallway parted to allow them to pass. The mood was reminiscent of a carnival. Folks might shake their heads and be anxious to condemn later, but right now they were enjoying the drama for all it was worth.

They reentered the judge's chambers, and Gidry immediately found a seat for Pru and stepped up to speak to Judge Ramey.

"I would like to question the boy," Gidry told him.

"Why should you question him?" the old man asked. "These are my chambers."

"Yes, Your Honor, I realize that, but I think I know just what to ask to get this whole thing cleared up in a hurry," Gidry said.

The judge lowered his voice, his tone disapproving. "No more games, Gidry," he said. "You are no more married to Prudence Belmont than I am."

His expression solemn, Gidry nodded. "We're all through protecting each other, Judge. Now we only want the truth," he said.

Finally Ramey nodded. He gestured toward young Sharpy to take the chair beside his desk.

"I'm going to allow Mr. Chavis to do the interrogation," he announced.

There was a buzz of commentary about that, but no one dared question Ramey's judgment.

Sharpy sat in the huge mahogany chair looking very young, rather defiant, and more than a little worried.

Gidry smiled at him, hoping to give the boy courage. He had always liked the brazen little fellow. And if Pru loved him, well who could question her choices in people to love.

"Sharpy," he began softly, "I am going to ask you some questions, and it is very important that you answer them absolutely truthfully."

The little boy nodded. "I'll swear on the Bible if you want me to," he volunteered.

"That won't be necessary here," Gidry said. "Just promise us that you'll answer all my questions with the truth."

"I will," he agreed, swallowing nervously. He scooted back to make himself more comfortable, giving onlookers an excellent view of his slightly scuffed new shoes.

"What is your name," Gidry asked as he began pacing the short distance between the judge's desk and the chair where the young boy was seated.

"That's easy," Sharpy answered, bouncing a little in the chair. "It's Milton Kilroy."

"Where do you live?" Gidry asked.

The little boy had to consider that one thoughtfully.

"Around," he answered finally.

"Don't you have a home?"

"Well, I had one with my mother in Befuddle Kilroy's shack," he said. "Then, after Mama died, I was there by myself, but the roof fell in one day, so I left."

Gidry allowed his gaze to drift slowly to the faces in the crowd around him.

"And where have you been staying most recently?" he asked finally.

"In the milk shed behind Aunt Hen's place," he said. "Miss Pru fixed it up nice for me. And she didn't charge me no rent nor nothing as long as I wash up and practice reading."

"She made you practice reading?"

He nodded enthusiastically. "Every night she'd bring out some supper and a lamp and after I ate, I'd read some for her. I read real good."

"I'm very glad to hear that," Gidry said. "I'm very glad indeed."

The little boy was so proud of himself he was beaming.

"I understand that mostly you don't go by your given name, Milton, but by a nickname," Gidry said.

"Yes, sir," he said. "Folks mostly call me Sharpy."

"And why do they call you that?" he asked.

" 'Cause I'm kind of a sharpster," he answered. "I mostly got an angle going all the time."

Gidry nodded encouragingly at the boy.

"Some of the folks here might not know what that means," he said, gesturing to the onlookers. "Can you explain what that means, Sharpy? Having an angle going."

"Well, it's . . . it's kind of like a job or something," the little boy said. "I try to figure out ways to get things."

"Like money?" Gidry asked.

The little boy shrugged. "Sometimes money," he agreed. "And sometimes other things. I trade, and I make bets on things."

Gidry nodded thoughtfully. "And do you win most of these bets?" he asked.

Sharpy looked momentarily sheepish. "Yes, sir. I usually bet on things that I already know I'll win. Like card tricks and the like."

"So you get along in the world as kind of a swindler," he said.

The little fellow hedged. "Some folks just aren't really a lot smart, and when I beat them on a game or something, I guess they'll get smarter."

"Hopefully so," Gidry agreed, clearing his throat to disguise the inappropriate chuckle that bubbled up from inside him.

"So you go along in this manner, and you manage to do pretty well on your own," he said.

Sharpy nodded. "Yes, sir, mostly I do."

"But you started stealing," Gidry said.

The child lowered his head slightly and nodded.

"When?" Gidry asked him.

"Last winter," the boy admitted quietly. "But I didn't really think of it as stealing, at the time I mean."

Gidry folded an arm across his chest and held his chin thoughtfully.

"What did you think of it as?" he asked.

"Kind of borrowing," Sharpy said a bit lamely.

"Borrowing?"

"Well, nobody was using it and..." His voice trailed off.

"When did you start this borrowing?" Gidry asked him. "What did you take first?"

"Some horse blankets," he answered, glancing a bit nervously in the direction of Mr. Tatum.

"Horse blankets," Gidry repeated. "You don't have a horse, do you?"

"No, sir," he answered.

"Then why did you break in to steal horse blankets?"

"I didn't," Sharpy said. "It . . . well, it was real cold that night." The boy seemed almost hesitant to explain himself. "It was after the roof had fallen in, and I'd just been sort of camping out wherever I could. But it was real cold that night, so I thought that it would be warm in the stable with all those horses. So I used a willow switch to unhook the latch, and I went inside. I wrapped up in some horse blankets and was about asleep when I heard someone coming. So I jumped up and left out of there the way I came. But I took the blankets with me."

Gidry listened thoughtfully.

"So stealing from the stables was not really premeditated," he said.

The boy looked momentarily confused.

"I don't know nothing about no pree-muddy-taters," he assured Gidry. "I was pretty hungry, but I didn't see no taters at all in there."

There was a little flurry of giggles at his words. Sharpy looked around, obviously wondering at the source of the joke.

"So you began stealing by accident," Gidry said.

"Yes, I guess you could say that."

"But it didn't continue to be by accident, did it?"

"No, sir, I figured out that I could pretty much get into anywhere I wanted and take whatever they had," he said. "Being little, nobody watches you much, and you can squeeze through places that would keep a grown somebody out."

"What kind of things did you take, Sharpy?" Gidry asked him.

"Just kind of things that I wanted," the child answered vaguely. "Pretty shiny things. My mama liked pretty, shiny things, so I'd take them to . . . to remember her."

Gidry nodded.

"I took a curly-cue from Mrs. Corsen cause I thought it'd make a real fine spinner on my fishing rod," he said. "And I got a minnow bucket from Mr. Crane because I knew I could trade it at the penny arcade."

"What about Gimp Watson's wooden leg?" Gidry asked.

"Oh, that." He looked a bit embarrassed. "I used that to scare the kids that live down by the railroad track. I told them that ghost story, have you heard it? Where the man comes back and says 'give me back my golden arm'!"

Sharpy voiced the words in a deep, throaty tone sure to frighten children.

"Yes," Gidry admitted. "I heard that story when I was about your age."

"Well, the way I told it to them it's Gimp Watson saying 'give me back my wooden leg'!"

Gidry could not keep the smile from his face. He remembered old Gimp and how much he loved children. He would have been tickled to live on in their fantasies, no matter how fantastic.

Sharpy began giving a verbal inventory of all the things he had taken and why. His explanations were sometimes poignant, but often comical. Victim after victim learned the reasoning behind their losses and one after another their outrage at being robbed seemed to disappear.

"So you never tried to sell any of the items you stole, you never attempted to make money on them," Gidry said.

"Well no," Sharpy answered. "Except for the postcards, you know the po-knock-rafee. I used to let the other boys see them, two looks for a nickel until I sold them all to you."

There was a startled gasp from several of those present. Reverend Hathaway made a noise as if he intended to interrupt.

"You stole the postcards as well?"

Gidry was surprised to hear it.

"Yes, sir, from Mr. Honnebuzz," Sharpy replied, gesturing to the lawyer, whose expression was horrified and whose cheeks were bright red with embarrassment. "I didn't figure he'd even miss them. He must have a million others. Just drawers and drawers full of naked ladies."

The completely dressed women present in the room were shocked speechless and glared with unspoken censure at the formerly eligible bachelor. Even Judge Ramey looked horrified. His daughter Alice had lately been keeping company with Honnebuzz.

Gidry decided to end his questioning there. End it when all attention was now focused upon a new scandal within the community.

"So you admit everything and wish to throw yourself upon the mercy of the court," Gidry said.

The little boy nodded. "Yes, sir," he answered bowing his head. "I'm ready to take a whopping or go to jail or whatever I'm going to get."

"That's for the judge to decide," Gidry told him more quietly.

Glancing back behind him, Gidry's gaze locked with Pru's. She loved this little boy, and if she loved him, Gidry definitely could as well. But he couldn't allow her to believe the lie that she did.

"One more question, Sharpy," Gidry said. "And remember you've promised to tell the truth. When were you born?"

"My birthday is November eighteenth," he answered.

"Do you know the year?"

"1888," he answered.

"So you will be just seven on your next birthday," Gidry said.

Sharpy agreed.

"Sometimes in the past you've lied about how old you are, haven't you?"

The boy shrugged. "Just little fibs, Mr. Chavis," he said. "Little fibs don't hurt nobody."

"Little fibs are a lot like borrowing things that don't belong to you," Gidry said to him softly. "Sometimes they can hurt others very much."

Gidry stared into space thoughtfully, trying to recall events from the past. After a long moment he smiled.

"I remember 1888," he declared pleasantly, as if he and the child were having a simple conversation. "I remember the year you were born. I'd helped take a herd of cattle up to Montana the autumn before. We got a late start and were delayed on the trail several days. We finally made it to our destination just in time to get snowed in by the worst winter they'd seen in years." He turned his gaze away from Sharpy and looked directly at Pru. "I didn't even get back to the Pecos until May Day," he said with certainty.

"Someday, I'm going be a cowboy like you," young Sharpy declared adamantly. "Or I'm going to work in a cotton gin."

Gidry smiled at the boy and turned to Judge Ramey.

"That is all the questions I have," Gidry told him. "I think that it is clear that the child is guilty of these crimes. But I do not believe that he is beyond our redemption. I would like to add my voice to the plea for mercy from the court and—"

"I'd like to do more than ask for mercy."

The words came from Aunt Hen, who had unaccountably risen to her feet.

Judge Ramey looked over at her questioningly.

"You have something to add here, Miss Pauling?" he asked.

"Yes, Judge, I do," she said. "This boy has been living in my milk shed for some time. The stolen property was found there, so I feel that I have more than a passing interest in this case."

"I'm willing to hear what you have to say," Ramey agreed.

"This boy is the shame of this town," she declared, glaring accusingly at the people gathered in the room. "He was left alone to fend for himself, and no one, not one of us, gave so much as a thought for his welfare."

Silence filled the room.

"Well, I suppose not all of us were completely blind," she admitted. "Peer Chavis gave the little boy a job. And my niece gave him a place to stay. What he needed, of course, was a home and a proper upbringing. School by day, church on Sundays, three meals, a clean bed, and a person who cared enough about him to see that he learned the rules of society and disciplined him when he didn't obey them."

She looked around once more, her eyes on all, condemning each one in turn.

"This whole town should be throwing ourselves at the mercy of this court," she said. "For our neglect of this little boy makes us all to blame. Not as much as this child, of course, but we all had a part in what has happened here."

No one disputed that truth.

"I am just as much at fault as the rest of you," she said. "Wrapped up in myself and concerns of my own, I hardly noticed this child existed. But I'm noticing now."

She gave the boy an encouraging smile.

"I know that it has occurred to many in this room that the easiest thing we could do is just send young Sharpy here away from us," she said. "There are places, schools and institutions where children with no guidance and no family can be sent. They are raised by well-meaning people to find their way in the world the best that they can. It would be really easy for us here in Chavistown to find a nice place, send young Sharpy there, and wash our hands of him completely. We could do that with very clear consciences. He would probably turn out fine. But I doubt that we would learn anything in the process."

The judge's eyes widened in respect.

"This child is ours. He is a part of all of us," she said. "His mother was kin of the Gidrys or Guidrys. His heritage here is as old as any we have in this town. The first French families to settle here were Chavis, Guidry, Ramey, and Corsen. I know the Kilroy clan doesn't claim him," she said, looking pointedly at Cloris, "but I think that the rest of Chavistown must. Sharpy belongs here. And we owe it to him to find him a place among us."

A long thoughtful silence filled the judge's chambers.

"I've moved the boy into my sewing room, Judge," Aunt Hen said. "I've never had children of my own and am past such a thing these days. But I raised my Pru through her toughest years, and I take some credit for young Mr. Chavis being the fine fellow he is. I'm willing to love the boy and care for him. But there are plenty of things the rest of you can offer here."

Reverend Hathaway spoke up first. "Certainly the child is in need of moral instruction," he said. "It is my duty to take on that aspect of his upbringing."

There were nods of approval.

"I doubt if the boy has ever been on the back of a horse," Elmer Corsen said. "I could certainly see that he learns to ride."

"More important that than," Oscar Tatum added, "he'll need to know how to handle a team and care for harness. My son and I can see that he learns that."

"He will certainly have to go to school," Albert Fenton said solemnly. "I can't afford to pay the whole tuition for another child, but I can get his slate and books from the store."

"I suppose I could pay his tuition," Judge Ramey said.

"I wonder if he would like to play the piano?" Mrs. Tatum asked.

Chapter 21

PRUDENCE WAS working in her garden. The heat was draining, but the work was good for her soul. Keeping her hands busy was always a good idea when her mind and thoughts were chaotic.

She hadn't spoken to Gidry since they'd left the courthouse yesterday afternoon. He had squeezed her hand very intimately and looked into her eyes.

"I want to speak with you alone very soon," he'd whispered.

She had not known how to answer. She had pulled her hand away and walked on. Pru did not want anyone to see them together. Nothing had changed. Nothing had changed at all.

Except for Sharpy, of course. For him everything had changed. It had all been settled. He would live with Aunt Hen. He would go to school. He would personally return all that he had stolen and apologize individually to each person that he had wronged. Everyone in town would be involved in trying to raise him up in the way he should go. He would not be sent away. He would grow up in the town he was born in. And Pru would get to see him every day.

He was not Gidry's son. Strangely she'd felt disappointed by that. She loved them both, and she'd wanted somehow to connect the two. She wanted to be able to bestow her attention freely on the boy and for him somehow to be connected with the man. She loved Sharpy for Sharpy and Gidry . . . she had always loved Gidry.

His very shocking allegation that she had been his wife all this time was thankfully discounted by the gossips. They undoubtedly had sufficient opportunity to bring up the memories of her public jilting once again. And undoubtedly marveled at how easily the two of them seemed to have overcome their differences. But this time at least, she was not the main target of speculation. Stanley Honnebuzz and his hoards of pornographic photographs were center stage in the gossip circus.

Alice Ramey had broken off with him immediately upon hearing the story. And housewives all over town were insisting that any business or personal relationships between Honnebuzz and their husbands be terminated immediately.

It was rumored that he was thinking to move his law practice to Killeen. Good riddance, most folks were willing to say.

Pru could almost feel sorry for the man. He was not at all pleasant or personable. Perhaps the only woman he could have would be one on a picture postcard. She had never really liked him much, but she certainly could understand his loneliness.

She heard voices and glanced back toward the house. Aunt Hen was directing Sharpy to his morning chores. The two had formed a fast bond. Her aunt seemed to understand little boys a good deal better than Pru herself. Aunt Hen made it clear to the child that obedience was the minimum requirement for respect. Sharpy accepted her despotism with good grace and appeared eager to please her.

They were a good match. Her aunt had taken Mr. Chavis's death rather hard, Pru thought. And now that she was no longer having to nurse and care for the old man, she would have more time to devote to her garden and to herself. A small, eager, enthusiastic little boy would surely brighten her day.

"So what are you up to this morning?" Aunt Hen asked as she came up beside her.

"I'm just mulching a bit," Pru answered. "I thought I'd take some cuttings of these old moss roses."

Aunt Hen leaned down and examined the bush, nodding with approval.

"Looks like a good time," she said. "Where are you going to plant them?"

"Oh, I don't know," Pru answered. "Maybe I'll put them up at the cemetery on the grave of old Mr. Chavis. Do you think Gidry would appreciate that?"

"No, not there," Aunt Hen said. "I'm already planning to put Yellow Rose of Texas on his place. You know what they say about it. Plant it today, and it will outlive your grandchildren."

"I hate to be the one to point this out, Aunt Hen," Pru said, teasing, "but if you are hoping to have grandchildren, you'll need to get very busy."

"I've been busy enough," she answered. "What about planting those old moss on the grave of Sharpy's mother?"

"That's a good idea," Pru agreed.

"And you could get him to help you," Aunt Hen said. "You do the cuttings, and once they're ready to plant he could put them on poor Mabel's ground himself. It would teach him a lot about plants and allow him some sweet memories of his mother as well.''

Pru smiled at her.

''You are always so right,'' she said. ''You always know exactly what to do. Do you think I will be that smart when I get to be your age?''

Aunt Hen waved away her praise. ''The way you get smart,'' she explained, ''is by learning from your mistakes. I've learned so much because I've made so many.''

Pru chuckled, disbelieving. ''What kind of mistakes have you ever made, Aunt Hen?''

The older woman ignored her question.

''Have you been over to talk to Gidry?'' she asked.

''Why no,'' Pru answered, immediately defensive. ''What on earth would I have to speak to Gidry about?''

Her aunt looked disapproving.

''Well, at the very least you owe the man an apology for thinking the worst of him,'' she said.

Pru demurred. She couldn't argue with that.

''And I would think that after the man compromised himself on your behalf, you would at least offer to make it right,'' she continued.

''To make it right?''

Pru didn't comprehend her meaning.

''Yes, I think that you should go over there and ask the fellow to marry you,'' Aunt Hen said.

Pru felt a painful, hollow pit in her stomach.

''Don't be ridiculous,'' she said.

''I'm not,'' Aunt Hen told her. ''Gidry Chavis loves you. It took him a long time to realize it, but it's true. Any fool can tell it just by looking at him.''

Pru shook her head.

''It doesn't matter,'' she said. ''It's too little, too late.''

"Is it?" Aunt Hen asked. "I've never known love to be measured or timed."

"Well, it is," Pru insisted.

Aunt Hen seated herself in the dirt next to Pru. The expression in her eyes was one of caring and concern.

"I know that he hurt you," she said more softly. "Do you forget that I was here? I saw how broken you were, first by his faithlessness and then wounded when you were set upon by town gossips like wolves. I saw it all, Prudence, and I was helpless to do anything but offer sympathy."

"I appreciated having you at my side," Pru assured her. "I don't know how I could have ever faced the world if you had not been there holding my hand and forcing me to stiffen my spine."

"You are my niece," Aunt Hen said. "Your mother was dearer to my heart than you can ever know. And you were her sweetest gift to me. Had you been my own daughter, I could not have loved you more."

Pru managed a wan smile and kissed the old woman's cheek.

"You have given me the only home I've ever had," she said. "In my own way I was as alone in the world as little Milton, and you filled my emptiness with all things right and good. If I haven't thanked you for that in the past, I do now."

"Seeing you grow into a fine woman is thanks enough for anyone," Aunt Hen said. "You are intelligent, devoted, hardworking. I'm pleased to see those traits in you. You remind me a lot of myself, and that makes me proud."

She reached over and cupped Pru's chin in her palm and turned her face toward her.

"It also makes me sad, because I see you making

the same kind of foolish errors in judgment that I made myself."

"I don't know what you mean."

"You're letting the opinion of the people of this town have far too much weight in your own thinking," Aunt Hen said. "People talk. They always have, and they always will. If you let what they say, or the fear of what they might say, have too much influence in your life, then you end up with no life at all."

"I don't believe that," Pru told her.

"It's true, I'm living proof of it."

"You? When have you ever let gossip bother you?" Pru asked, genuinely surprised.

Aunt Hen hesitated a long time as if unwilling to answer.

"A long time ago I did," she said finally. "A long time ago I chose to do what I thought other people expected of me."

Aunt Hen glanced off in the distance as if recalling long-ago memories.

"I was in love once," she told Pru simply. "I loved a man, and he loved me. But because of things that were in no way my own fault, it was not considered an acceptable match. If I had married him, it would have been a grand scandal. It wasn't that I was so afraid of scandal for myself. At first I couldn't do it because I didn't want to bring a bad name upon my sister and ruin her chances of finding a good husband. And then my parents were old, and I was afraid it would be too much of a shock to them. Then after they died, there was you, and with all you had to contend with in a new place I didn't want you embroiled in anything unsavory. So I never married him. I always loved him, and I never married him. I did what I thought people expected of me, instead of what I wanted. I regret that. When you get to be my age, Pru, I don't want you looking over at that house next door and having those regrets."

"Oh, Aunt Hen," she said. "I never knew you loved somebody. It's not too late. I'm grown and I can take care of Sharpy myself. Why don't you go to him and spend your golden years together. It's not too late."

Aunt Hen raised an eyebrow and looked at her niece sternly.

"Pru, if you think it's not too late for me," she said, "then how can you suggest that it *is* too late for you?"

She had no answer for that.

"You and Gidry are flowers that bloom at the end of summer. It's taken you both a bit longer to find your way in this world. But you have a full, long life ahead of you, and you can be together. You can share it. I don't want to see you throw that away."

Pru's spine stiffened along with her determination.

"It needs to be thrown away," she said firmly. "It was all ruined eight years ago. There is nothing left worth saving."

"Pru, he loves you. You love him. What is ruined about that?"

"You just don't understand how it was, Aunt Hen," she said. "It was perfect. It was all so very, very perfect."

She shook her head thinking painfully of the past.

"He was charming, handsome, the best catch in town. I was the plain, little girl-next-door, poor and orphaned. But he loved me. And I loved him."

Pru laughed lightly, but there was no humor in it.

"I remember hearing other girls talk about *how to catch a boy*. If you really liked him, you should pretend that you don't. You should always try to be where he is, but then ignore his presence. You should only smile at other boys. That will drive him crazy and make him determined to get you to smile at him."

She rolled her eyes at her aunt and mimicked the high-pitched whine of schoolgirls.

"I heard them talk this way, Aunt Hen, and I secretly laughed at them. I told Gidry about it, and he laughed as well. We were not like that at all," she said. "I told Gidry every day that I was in love with him. I told him and you and anybody else that would listen."

Pru closed her eyes as if the memory of it was more than she could bear to look at.

"We were going to get married in this garden," she told her aunt. "That's what we decided. No stuffy church for us; we would marry outside in the open air with everyone in town watching. We would move into the house next door and we were going to have nine children. *Nine*. He wanted to be able to field his own baseball team. We laughed and talked and planned it all so well. It was perfect, totally perfect. And he ruined it."

Pru stabbed the spade she held into the ground with lethal force.

"He desired another woman and he ruined it. It can never be that way again."

"No," Aunt Hen agreed quietly. "But it probably wouldn't have been that way in the first place."

Pru looked up at her surprised.

"Only perfect people have perfect lives, Prudence," her aunt told her. "Like the rest of us humans on this earth, you and Gidry are flawed. The fairy tale you keep dreaming about is just that, a fairy tale. Nobody's life is free of pain and grief and sorrow. You should be grateful that what you've seen is all that you've had. Quit concentrating on what is lost and see what is there."

She reached out to grasp the bush of moss roses that was near her and held one pale pink bud up for Pru's inspection.

"This is beautiful," Aunt Hen said. "It is absolutely beautiful, isn't it. It's worth cherishing."

"Of course it is," Pru agreed.

"But look here along its stem, what are these, Pru?" Aunt Hen asked. "They prick me and draw blood. What are they?"

"For heaven's sake, Aunt Hen, those are only the thorns," Pru said.

"Yes, they are thorns," the older woman agreed. "There are thorns growing on your roses, Pru!"

Her words feigned surprise, which turned dramatically to sarcasm.

"Oh you poor, poor dear. There are thorns growing on your roses," she said. "Thorns on your roses. And that has made you cry."

Aunt Hen shook her head sympathetically. "They are not at all perfect, they are cursed with those thorns."

Her tone became serious.

"Or perhaps not," she said. "Perhaps they are only thornbushes. Normal, healthy, natural thornbushes, whose purpose on earth is to grown thorns but which, by some special favor of God, have been given the opportunity to produce a beautiful flower."

Aunt Hen fished her rose knife out of her pocket and cut the flower from the bush, thorny long stem and all, and handed it to her niece.

"Pru, I love you and I want the best for you," she said. "And learning the truth about this sooner, rather than later, is all for the best."

She cupped her niece's chin in one hand and looked into her eyes.

"Maybe the perfect love you thought you dreamed about, you'd thought you had, maybe it has truly turned out to be a thornbush. But won't you give it a chance and see if perhaps it can bloom in this garden and brighten the life of all of us?"

Aunt Hen walked away.

Pru sat there holding the beautiful rose in her hands, admiring the lovely blossom and considering the cruel thorns.

The harvest moon had waned to gibbous but still provided a modicum of light as Pru surreptitiously made her way to the loose tin sheet at the back of the cotton gin. Gratefully, it had not yet been secured, and she made her way inside into total darkness.

Once inside, being fully prepared for what she would find, she retrieved a match from her pocket and lit the lantern she carried. On her own, and with only a few wrong turns, she wound her way through the hulk of machinery to the small set of stairs that led to the office.

Her step was light as she hurried up them and through the doorway. As she expected, the place was deserted. With ginning complete, no one would have cause to venture this way until next summer. Certainly not in the middle of the night.

She set her light upon the desk and opened the drawer. There was relief in her sigh and she laid them out in front of her and within the dim yellow circle of the lantern glow selected the one she found most pleasing.

Not an hour later, Gidry Chavis was standing shirtless in front of his washstand readying himself for a night of sleep. The loud clamor of the front-door knocker was startling, unexpected, and urgently persistent.

Worried, he hurried downstairs.

"Coming!" he called out as he ran.

The sound abruptly ceased. He continued hastily.

He opened the door to find the porch deserted. There was no one in sight. Puzzled, he stepped outside and looked around. There was no one. Not a soul.

He shrugged and shook his head. It was a child's prank, and he briefly wondered if young Sharpy was the culprit.

He reached for the door, only to notice that a piece of paper had been wedged in the handle. Gidry picked it up and saw that it was actually a postcard. He stepped back inside and walked into the parlor, where he lit a lamp.

There in his hands was a photograph of a short, buxom female lying naked upon a chaise, a diaphanous drape between her thighs and a rose between her teeth.

He quickly turned it over to read the words penned upon the other side.

My only lover,

You will find me tonight in our secret place dressed in just the manner as the lady pictured here. I am ready to fulfill your every desire, if you will agree to grant my dearest wish, to love, honor, and obey you as long as we both shall live.

Yours soon to be,
the notorious Mrs. C.

Gidry's stunned expression slowly blossomed into a full-fledged grin. He turned the postcard back to the picture and with a sigh of pure pleasure, he planted a kiss upon the bared bosom of the anonymous female.

Then, with postcard in hand, whistling a bawdy tune, he walked through his house and out the back door. Not bothering to collect his hat or coat, or even a shirt, he made his way to that oh-so-secret rendezvous of lovers. What man needed pornography, he thought to himself, when he had a milk shed next door?

Epilogue

May 12, 1899

THE WHOLE of Chavistown was on hand for the illumination. A dais sporting yards of red, white, and blue bunting was erected at the foot of the 150-foot tower in the middle of Main Avenue right in the front of the home of the city's first family. It was nearing dusk, and the street was blocked off to make room for the crowd who vied for a good spot close to the stage beneath the great tower. Refreshment tables stretched across the front lawn of the Chavis home. The ladies were serving punch and root beer along with their fresh-baked cookies and slices of pie. Warm taffy was being pulled by ethusiastic children who ran wild, as children will, not aware that this auspicious occasion in the town's history would live in memory all of their lives.

The entire Chavis family was not all present for the festivities. Mr. Henry Pauling Chavis, only two days old and already known by the nickname SugarPaul, was not yet fit company for crowds. Therefore, both he and his mother, Prudence, had chosen not to attend.

The young man's sister, however, tagged along after her papa as quickly as her chubby little legs would carry her. Her thumb was tucked firmly into her rosebud mouth and her thick black curls bounced upon her head with every step. The little girl was completely undeterred by her father's sometimes booming voice and occasional stern demeanor. Bright and pretty, Peerlene Chavis was, so gossips said, the luckiest little girl in Texas.

Upon the advice of his wife, Gidry Chavis had invested his own money quite heavily to create a brand-new industry in Chavistown. Chavis Cottonseed was already producing as much cottonseed oil and oil products as their nearest competitors, and the plant would not be fully operational for another year.

The Chavis family, always affluent, was quickly becoming wealthy. That was at least part of the purpose of today's presentation. To share personal good fortune with an entire community.

On his way to the stage, Chavis stopped beside a strapping boy who, if arms and legs were any indication, was destined to be a very tall young man. Surrounded by fellows his own age, clearly he was the leader of any group were he was present.

"Can you watch this little dumpling, while I take care of business," Gidry asked, indicating the wide-eyed two-year-old behind him.

"Sure I can," the youngster replied easily. "Come here, darling, you want me to teach you a card trick?"

The boy squatted and opened his arms. The little girl rushed into them eagerly, hugging the boy's neck with a ferocity that had those around him chuckling.

"Thanks, Sharpy," Chavis said.

"It's no trouble," the boy told him. "You know how she likes to follow me around."

"Aunt Hen is here, but I didn't want to ask her. I worry that she's going to get more than her share of nursery duty now that we have two of these sticky little people to contend with."

"Sticky? Did you say sticky?" Sharpy feigned surprise. "Well, let's get this girl some of that taffy they're making across the street. We'll make her so sticky I won't need to carry her, I'll just attach her to my shirt."

Gidry laughed and waved them on as he marched up the dais and took his place in front of the podium.

"Good evening, folks," he called out to those gathered.

He had the relaxed and certain demeanor of a man who knew his place in the world. And understood that those gathered around him, friend or foe, newcomer or longtime resident, realized that he was simply trying to do what he thought best for his community.

The crowd quieted and began to gather more closely around the makeshift stage.

"I suspect it's time to get this started," Gidry said. "If we wait much longer, we won't be able to see what we're doing." He hesitated momentarily, then gave a boyish grin. "I guess this is the last night that will happen."

The crowd laughed along with him.

"You all expect me to give a speech, tonight" he said. "I pretty much leave the speech making to Judge Ramey. But my wife has written a couple of pages here of things she wants me to say. And since she's probably listening from that second-floor window over there, I guess I'd better read them."

There were knowing chuckles from the crowd. Gidry glanced toward the window as if to assure himself that she was there for him. Then he unfolded the paper he carried and began to read.

"We are here tonight to dedicate the first of seven planned towers to be erected throughout our city for the purpose of providing modern illumination to neighborhoods and businesses."

He paused to take a long breath.

"Each tower, equipped with six carbon arc lighting units, generates light equal to two thousand candlepower and was specifically designed to mimic natural moonlight."

Gidry paused to glance upward at the huge wrought-iron tower erected behind him, the likes of which had never been seen in this part of Texas.

"Once these artificial moons are illuminated they should provide sufficient light on the darkest night to read the time on an ordinary pocket watch within a circle three thousand feet in diameter."

There was murmur of disbelief among the crowd.

"Moonlight towers have been extensively tested through much of the United States, including our state capital, Austin City. The conclusion of these scientists and engineers is that the only effect of the lighting upon local vegetation is that it makes it look prettier at night."

Gidry glanced up hopefully at the crowd.

"The moonlight towers project is a gift from Chavis Cottonseed to the city and the people of Chavistown provided at a cost of $26,000."

Astonished whistles were heard among the crowd at the enormity of the price.

Gidry folded his paper and stuffed it in his coat pocket.

"I would now like to ask Mr. Albert Fenton of the Commercial Club and Mrs. Bertha Mae Corsen, president of the Ladies' Rose and Garden Society, to please come forward."

The two were standing at the bottom of the steps and quickly took their places near the huge switch that greatly resembled a railroad brake. It had been designed especially for the occasion.

"Mr. Fenton, Mrs. Corsen," Gidry said. "Please light up our town."

They grasped the handle in unison and a moment later the area was bathed in the soft silver glow of artificial moonlight.

At first there was wondrous amazement among the onlookers. It was not like turning night into day at all. It was turning night into . . . into night you could see. Astonishment was followed by cheers and shouts, whistles and applause.

Upon the dais, Fenton, Mrs. Corsen, and Gidry Chavis were lauding the innovation as well. Chavis turned toward his house and waved. Certainly his wife could see him as clearly as day.

As the noise died down, Gidry returned to the podium.

"Now that we can see what we doing," he said. "Let's celebrate!"

More cheering ensued as the local Chavistown Band, resplendent in their new blue-and-gold uniforms, took to the stage.

Within minutes the music had begun and beneath the bright light of an artificial moon the local citizens paired up and began to dance. Old Plug Whitstone had Eula on his arm. Conrad and Ethel Peterson soon joined them. Elmer Corsen stepped out with his mother. And Amos Wilburn escorted Mrs. Butts, who, according to the record keeping of the gossips, had attended Sunday service with him four times in the last two months.

Henrietta Pauling watched from the sidelines, genuinely enjoying the crisp rhythm of the tune and the swirling dancers in the middle of the street. Since Prudence couldn't be here, she'd insisted her aunt have a new dress for the occasion. Henrietta felt positively fashionable in the dark Copenhagen silk. She wore an Amazone rose at the throat, the first bloom of the season.

On the edge of the crowd she spied her young charge. Sharpy was ignoring the hopeful, adoring glances leveled in his direction by the younger of the young ladies, those pigtailed misses not yet allowed to pin their hair up. He seemed content to entertain little Peerlene, who was busy getting taffy all over herself.

A gentleman stepped up beside her.

"Good evening, Henrietta," he said.

She smiled at him and nodded.

"Good evening to you, Judge. It's a wonderful night for a party."

He nodded agreement.

"We missed you at the wedding," he said.

"Peerlene was very croupy, and I didn't want Prudence to have to stay at home," she said. "Alice was always so dear to her."

Judge Ramey smiled, understanding.

"I heard it was a beautiful ceremony," Henrietta told him.

He shrugged. "I don't know a thing about ceremonies, but I do know my little Alice looked pretty as a picture that day."

"All brides are beautiful, that's what they say."

He grunted, but he looked proud.

"Are they still on their trip?" she asked.

"Ought to be back next week," he replied. "I've never been to Europe myself. But Alice tells me it is absolutely the only place to go for a honeymoon."

"Well, it was certainly a fateful day when you hired Mr. Chester," Henrietta said.

"And I have you and that Sharpy to thank for it," Judge Ramey answered. "When you told me what a head that boy has for botany, well, I just had to find him a worthy tutor."

"The man has been a godsend," she admitted. "The boy had become so bored at school I began to worry that we'd have trouble with him again."

"It is still going to be difficult to keep him occupied," the judge agreed. "Chester tells me he's nearly as bright in math as science and that he could pass the high-school examinations today."

Henrietta smiled proudly. "Yes, our Sharpy is quite an achievement for this town."

The tune ended, and the two of them joined the dancers in offering applause. When the music commenced once more it was a slow, sweet waltz. One that Henrietta recognized immediately.

"The renovations are almost done on the house," Judge Ramey continued, making conversation. "I swear, it's a misery living amid all that sawdust. Carpenters and painters making themselves at home every hour of the day."

Henrietta said nothing.

"It's going to be as fine and modern a place as any in Chavistown," he went on. "Alice wanted every convenience, and she has surely got it. Electric lights in every room, and the wires are actually hidden within the walls. Isn't that something?"

"Yes, I'd say it certainly is," Henrietta replied politely.

She was listening to the music. Listening and remembering.

"When they get back, I'm thinking to move out. I loved that old house, but I think a newly married couple ought to have the privacy of living on their own," the judge said.

"I'm sure they will miss you."

Henrietta was examining her feelings. Attempting to locate an ache in her heart. To her amazement, there no longer seemed to be one.

"Actually, I'm more than ready," Judge Ramey told her. "I've been wanting to sort of get on with my own life for a while now. But I just had to see that girl settled. I owed that to her mother."

"Yes, I suppose so."

There was no pain, no sadness. Henrietta could only recall sweetness to memory, only the sweetness.

"I'm thinking about getting a smaller place," Judge Ramey continued. "A man by himself really doesn't need anything all that big."

"No I would imagine not," she said, distracted.

She couldn't quite believe it, but somewhere, sometime, somehow her heart had healed.

"Of course, if I were to marry again, I suppose a new wife would want some say in what kind of house she's to live in."

"Probably so," Henrietta agreed absently.

The judge was silent beside her so long, she eventually noticed it and turned to him. He was looking all around.

"This lighting is really pretty, isn't it?" he said. "I don't think I expected that."

Henrietta agreed. It was in fact very pretty indeed.

Slowly the judge's expression softened as if recalling something sweet and pleasant. "Do you remember . . . no you wouldn't. It was such a long time ago."

"What?" she asked him.

"That fall when we had the pumpkins made into jack-o'-lanterns all over town," he said. "Do you remember that?"

Henrietta smiled. "Yes, yes, I remember it very well."

The old judge chuckled and shook his head. "It was so pretty and so *romantic*. That's when I fell in love for the very first time."

"Me too," she answered quietly.

The judge grinned broadly at her, but when he spoke his tone was soft and respectful.

"Miss Henrietta," he asked, "would you care to dance?"

She stared at him for a long moment. He had kind eyes, she decided. She had never noticed it before, but he had very kind eyes.

"Yes Judge Ramey, I would like that very much."

"Call me Nathaniel," he said.

"All right, Nathaniel."

He led her out among the dancers and took her into his arms. He was a tall, rather portly man, and being in his embrace gave her the unfamiliar but somehow pleasant sensation of being small and delicate, feminine and sheltered. They moved together so well and so naturally, it was hard to believe they had never waltzed before.

"You are a wonderful dancer," she told him, unable to keep the surprise out of her voice.

"Not usually," he replied. "But you're so graceful, ma'am, what fellow could help but be in perfect step."

Upon the brightly lit street, on a fine spring night,

amid friends and family, they laughed together and swirled to the music as the band played.

> *Just a song at twilight, when the lights are low,*
> *And the flick' ring shadows softly come and go.*
> *Tho' the heart be weary, sad the day and long.*
> *Still to us at twilight, comes love's old song.*
> *Comes love's old sweet song.*

THE WORLD OF
AVON ROMANCE SUPERLEADERS

Cross-promotion and rebate offer in the
back of every book!

MEET THE MEN OF AVON ROMANCE . . .
They're fascinating, they're sexy—they're irresistible!
They're the kind of men you definitely want to bring
home—but not to meet the family. And they live in
such romantic places, from Regency England to the
Wild West. These men are guaranteed to provide you
with hours of reading pleasure. So introduce yourself
to these unforgettable heroes, and meet a different
man every month.

AND THE WRITERS WHO CREATE THEM
At Avon we bring you books by the brightest stars of
romantic fiction. Christina Dodd, Catherine Anderson
and Pamela Morsi. Kathleen Eagle, Lisa Kleypas and
Barbara Freethy. These are the bestselling writers who
create books you'll never forget—each and every
story is a "keeper." Following is a sneak preview of
their newest books . . .

Enter the world of New York Times *best-selling author* **Catherine Anderson**. *This award-winning writer creates a place where dreams really do come true and love always triumphs. In April, Catherine creates her most memorable characters of all in* **Forever After**.

County Sheriff Heath Masters has a hard enough time managing small-town crime, and he doesn't need any complications—especially ones in the very attractive form of his new neighbor, Meredith Kenyon, and her adorable daughter, Sammy. But when Heath's giant of a dog causes trouble for Merry, he finds himself in trouble, too . . . of the romantic kind.

FOREVER AFTER
by Catherine Anderson

HEATH VAULTED over the tumble-down fence that divided his neighbor's patchy lawn from the adjoining cow pasture, then poured on speed to circle the house. He skidded to a halt about fifteen feet shy of a dilapidated woodshed. A child, dressed in pink pants and a smudged white T-shirt, stood splayed against the outbuilding. Her eyes were so wide with fright they resembled china-blue supper plates.

Fangs bared and frothing at the jowls, Goliath

lunged back and forth between the child and a young woman Heath guessed to be her mother.

"Stay back!" he ordered.

At the sound of his voice the woman turned around, her pinched face so pale that her dark brown eyes looked almost as large as her daughter's. "Oh, thank God! Help us! Do something, please, before he hurts us!"

Heath jerked has gaze back to his dog. If ever there had been an animal he would trust with a child, Goliath was it. Yet now the rottweiler seemed to have gone berserk.

Heath snapped his fingers. "Goliath, heel!"

At the command, the rottweiler whirled toward Heath, his usually friendly brown eyes glinting a demonic red. For an awful instant Heath was afraid the dog might not obey him.

What in the hell was wrong with him? Heath's gaze shot to the terrified child.

"Goliath, *heel*!" He slapped his thigh for emphasis.

The rottweiler finally acquiesced with another frenzied bark followed by a pathetic whine, massive head lowered, legs stiff, his movements reluctant and abject. The second the dog got within reach, Heath grabbed his collar.

"Sammy!"

The woman bolted forward to gather her child into her arms with a strangled cry. Then she whirled to confront Heath, her pale, delicately molded face twisting with anger, her body quaking.

"You get that *vicious*, out-of-control dog *off* my property!"

The blaze in her eyes told Heath she was infused by the rush of adrenaline that often followed a bad scare.

"Ma'am, I'm really sorry about—"

"I don't want to hear it! Just get that monster out of here!"

Damn. Talk about starting off on the wrong foot with someone. And wasn't that a shame? Heath would have happily fixed this gal's plumbing late at night—or anything else that went haywire in the ramshackle old house she was renting.

Fragile build. Pixieish features. Creamy skin. Large caramel brown eyes. A full, vulnerable mouth the delicate pink of barely ripened strawberries. Her hair fell in a thick, silken tangle around her shoulders, the sable tendrils curling over her white shirt like glistening ribbons of chocolate on vanilla ice cream.

Definitely not what he'd been picturing. Old Zeke usually rented this place to losers—people content to work the welfare system rather than seek gainful employment. Even in baggy jeans and a man's shirt this lady had "class" written all over her.

Nationally best-selling author **Pamela Morsi** *is known for the trademark wit and down-home humor that enliven her enchanting, memorable romances that have garnered rave reviews from critics and won national awards. This May experience the charm of Pamela Morsi in* Sealed With a Kiss.

When Gidry Chavis jilted Pru Belmont and left Chavistown, the nearly wed bride was devastated, the townsfolk scandalized . . . and Chavis was strongly discouraged from showing his face again. But now he's back, a bit older, a whole lot wiser . . . and rarin' to patch things up with Pru.

SEALED WITH A KISS
by Pamela Morsi

THE COWBOY allowed his gaze to roam among the customers. There was a table full of poker players intent upon their game. One tired, sort of half-pretty woman looked up hopefully and pulled her feet out of the chair next to her. He didn't even bother to meet her glance. A couple of rowdy farmhands seemed to be starting early on a weekend drunken spree. A few other men drinking quietly. No one that he recognized for certain.

At the near end of the bar a dandied-up gentleman in a plaid coat and summer derby sat alone, his traveling bag at his feet.

The cowboy almost smiled. If there was anyone more certain not to be a local, it was a drummer in a plaid coat. Without any appearance of haste or purposeful intent, he casually took the seat right next to the traveling bag.

"Afternoon."

The little man looked up eagerly.

"Good afternoon to you, sir," he answered and in true salesman fashion, offered his hand across the bar. "Arthur D. Sattlemore, Big Texas Electric Company."

The cowboy's only answer was an indecipherable grunt as he signaled the barkeep to bring him a beer.

"Hot weather we've been having."

The cowboy nodded. "A miserable summer," he agreed. "Good for cotton."

"You are a farmer, sir?" Clearly the drummer was surprised.

"No," the cowboy answered. "But when you're in Chavistown, it's hard to talk about anything here without mentioning cotton."

The drummer chuckled and nodded understanding. He leaned closer. "You have the right of it there, sir," he admitted. "I was asked to come present my company to the Commercial Club. I've been here a week and haven't been able to get a word in edgewise. The whole town is talking cotton and what will happen without old man Chavis."

The cowboy blanched. "He's dead?"

The drummer shook his head. "Not as of this morning, but without him to run the gin and the cooperative, the farmers are worried that their cotton will sit in wagonloads by the side of the road."

"Ginning time has just begun," the cowboy said. "Surely the old man will be up and around before it's over."

The drummer shook his head. "Not the way they're telling it. Seems the old man is bad off. Weak as a kitten they say, and the quacks warn that if he gets out of bed, he won't live to see winter."

"Doctors have been wrong before," the cowboy said.

The drummer nodded. "The whole town hopes you're right. The old man ain't got no one to take over for him. The gin's closed down and the cotton's just waiting."

The cowboy nodded.

"They had a meeting early in the week and voted to send for young Chavis, the old man's son."

"Is that so?"

"Young Chavis created some bit of scandal in this

town eight years ago," the drummer explained. "Nobody's seen so much as his shadow since."

The cowboy listened quietly, intently.

"So they sent for their son and they're hoping that he'll come and save their biscuits," the little man said. "But for myself, I just wouldn't trust him."

"No?"

The traveling man tutted and shook his head. "They say he was all but married to a local gal and just left her high and dry."

"Is that what they say?"

The drummer nodded. "And I ask you, what kind of man blessed with plenty of money, an influential name, a fine place in the community and an innocent young sweetheart who expects to marry him, runs off with some round-heeled, painted-up saloon gal?"

The cowboy slowly picked up his beer and drank it down in one long swallow. He banged the glass on the bar with enough force to catch the attention of every man in the room.

"What kind of man, indeed," he said to the drummer.

*Best-selling author **Kathleen Eagle's** marriage to a Lakota Sioux has given her inspiration to write uniquely compelling love stories featuring Native American characters. She's won numerous awards, but her most gratifying reward was a note from a reader saying, "You kept me up all night reading." This June, stay up all night with **The Night Remembers.***

Jesse Brown Wolf is a man living in the shadows who comes to the rescue of kids like Tommy T, a

*street-smart boy, and Angela, a fragile newcomer to
the big city. Jesse rescues Angela from a brutal robbery and helps nurse her back to health. In return,
Angela helps Jesse heal his wounded soul.*

THE NIGHT REMEMBERS
by Kathleen Eagle

H E HADN'T been this close to anyone in a long time,
and his visceral quaking was merely the proof.
He sat on a straw cushion and leaned back against
the woven willow backrest and drank what was left
of the tea. He didn't need any of this. Not the kid, not
the woman, not the intrusion into his life.

A peppering of loose pebbles echoed in the air
shaft, warning him that something was stirring overhead. He climbed to the entrance and waited until the
boy announced himself.

''I had a hard time gettin' the old grandpa to come
to the door,'' Tommy T reported as he handed the
canvas bag down blindly, as though he made regular
deliveries to a hole in the ground. ''Some of this is
just, like, bandages and food, right?''

''Right.''

The boy went on. ''I said I was just a runner and
didn't know nothin' about what was in the message,
and nobody asked no questions, nothin' about you.
You know what? I know that old guy from school.''

''A lot of people know him. He practices traditional
medicine.''

"Cool." Then, diverting to a little skepticism, "So what I brought is just roots and herbs and stuff."

"It's medicine."

"She might be worried about her dog," the boy said, hovering in the worlds above. "If she says anything, tell her I'm on the case."

"You don't know where she lives."

"I'll know by morning. I'll check in later, man." The voice was withdrawing. "Not when it's daytime, though. I won't hang around when it's light out."

On the note of promise, the boy left.

The night was nearly over. The air smelled like daybreak, laden with dew, and the river sounded more cheerful as it rushed toward morning. Normally, he would ascend to greet the break of day. The one good thing about the pain was the relief he felt when it lifted. Relief and weariness. He returned to the deepest chamber of his refuge, where his guest lay in his bed, her fragile face bathed in soft candlelight.

He made an infusion from the mixture of herbs the old man had prepared and applied it to the tattered angel's broken skin. He made a paste from ground roots and applied it to her swollen bumps and bruises, singing softly as he did so. The angel moaned, as though she would add her keening to his lullaby, but another tea soon tranquilized her fitful sleep.

Finally he doused the light, lay down beside her, closed his eyes, and drifted on the dewy-sweet morning air.

STRANGER IN MY ARMS
by Lisa Kleypas

HE WAS so much thinner, his body lean, almost raw-boned, his heavy muscles thrown into stark prominence. His skin was so much darker, a rich bronze hue that was far too exotic and striking for an Englishman. But it *was* Hunter . . . older, toughened, as sinewy and alert as a panther.

"I didn't believe . . ." Lara started to say, but the words died away. It was too much of an effort to speak.

383

She backed away from him and somehow made her way to the cabinet where she kept a few dishes and a small teapot. She took refuge in an everyday ritual, fumbling for a parcel of tea leaves, pulling the little porcelain pot from its place on the shelf. "I—I'll make some tea. We can talk about . . . everything . . ."

But her hands were shaking too badly, and the cups and saucers clattered together as she reached for them. He came to her in an instant, his feet swift and startlingly light on the floor. Hunter had always had a heavy footstep—but the thought was driven away as he took her cold hands in his huge warm ones. She felt his touch all through her body, in small, penetrating ripples of sensation.

A pair of teasing dark eyes stared into hers. "You're not going to faint, are you?"

Her face was frozen, making it impossible to smile, to produce any expression. She looked at him dumbly, her limbs stiff with fright and her knees locked and trembling.

The flicker of amusement vanished from his gaze, and he spoke softly. "It's all right, Lara." He pushed her to a nearby chair and sank to his haunches, their faces only inches from each other.

"H-Hunter?" Lara whispered in bewilderment. *Was* he her husband? He bore an impossibly close resemblance, but there were subtle differences that struck sparks of doubt within her.

He reached inside his worn black broadcloth coat and extracted a small object. Holding it his palm, he showed it to her. Eyes wide, Lara regarded the small, flat enameled box. He pressed the tiny catch on the side and revealed a miniature portrait of her, the one she had given him before his departure to India three years earlier.

"I've stared at this every day for months," he murmured. "Even when I didn't remember you in the days right after the shipwreck, I knew somehow that you belonged to me." He closed the box in his hand and tucked it back into his coat pocket.

Lara lifted her incredulous gaze to his. She felt as if she were in a dream. "You've changed," she managed to say.

Hunter smiled slightly. "So have you. You're more beautiful than ever."

Barbara Freethy's poignant, tender love stories have garnered her many new fans. Her first Avon romance, **Daniel's Gift,** *was called "exhilarating" by Affaire de Coeur and Romantic Times said it was ". . . sure to tug on the heartstrings." This August, don't miss Barbara's best yet,* **One True Love.**

Nick Maddux believed he'd never see his ex-wife, Lisa, again. Then he knocked on the door to his sister's house and Lisa answered—looking as beautiful, as vulnerable as ever. Nick soon discovered that, despite the tragedy that lay between them, his love for Lisa was as tender—and as passionate—as ever.

ONE TRUE LOVE
by Barbara Freethy

NICK MADDUX was surrounded by pregnant women. Every time he turned around, he bumped into someone's stomach. Muttering yet another apology, he backed into the corner of his eight-by-twelve-foot booth at the San Diego Baby and Parenting Fair and took a deep breath. He was hot, tired and proud.

His handcrafted baby furniture was the hit of the show. In some cases, it would be a challenge to have his furniture arrive before the stork, but Nick thrived on challenges, and Robin Wood Designs was finally on its way to becoming the profitable business he had envisioned.

Nick couldn't believe how far he'd come, how much he'd changed.

Eight years ago, he'd been twenty-five years old, working toward getting his contractor's license and trying to provide for a wife and a child on the way. He'd kept at it long after they'd gone, hammering out his anger and frustration on helpless nails and boards.

Two years had gone by before he ran out of work, out of booze and out of money. Finally, stone-cold sober, he'd realized his life was a mess.

That's when he'd met Walter Mackey, a master craftsman well into his seventies but still finding joy in carving wood. Walter made rocking chairs in his garage and sold them at craft fairs. Nick had bought one of those chairs for his mother's birthday. She'd told Nick he'd given her something that would last forever.

It was then Nick realized he could make something that would last forever. His life didn't have to be a series of arrivals and departures.

Nick had decided to focus on baby furniture, because something for one's child always brought out the checkbook faster than something for oneself. Besides that mercenary reason, Nick had become obsessed with building furniture for babies that would nurture them, keep them safe, protect them.

He knew where the obsession came from, just not how to stop it. Maybe Robin would be proud of all that he'd accomplished in her name.

Nick felt himself drawn into the past. In his mind he saw Lisa with her round stomach, her glowing smile, her blue eyes lit up for the world to see. She'd been so happy then, so proud of herself. When she'd become pregnant, they both thought they'd won the lottery.

He closed his eyes for a moment as the pain threatened to overwhelm him, and he saw her again.

"I can't believe I'm having a baby," Lisa said. She took his hand and placed it on her abdomen. "Feel that? She's kicking me."

Nick's gut tightened at the fluttering kick against his fingers. It was the most incredible feeling. He couldn't begin to express the depth of his love for this unborn child, but he could show Lisa. In the middle of the baby store, he kissed her on the lips, uncaring of the salespeople or the other customers. "I love you," he whispered against her mouth.

She looked into his eyes. "I love you, too. More than anything. I'm so happy, it scares me. What if something goes wrong?"

"Nothing will go wrong."

"Oh, Nick, things always go wrong around me. Remember our first date—we hit a parked car."

He smiled. "That wasn't your fault. I'm the one who wasn't paying attention."

"I'm the one who distracted you," she said with a worried look in her eyes.

"Okay, it was your fault."

"Nick!"

"I'm teasing. Don't be afraid of being happy. It's not fatal, you know. This is just the beginning for us."

It had been the beginning of the end.

Award-winning author **Christina Dodd** *is known for captivating characters and sizzling sensuality. She is the author of twelve best-selling romances, including* **A Well Pleasured Lady** *and* **A Well Favored Gentleman.** *Watch for her latest this September,* **That Scandalous Evening.**

Years earlier, Jane Higgenbothem had caused a scandal when she'd sculpted Lord Ransom Quincey of Blackburn in the classical manner. Apparently everything was accurate save one very important part of Lord Blackburn's body. Jane retired to the country in disgrace, but now she has come back to London to face her adversary.

THAT SCANDALOUS EVENING
by Christina Dodd

London, 1809

"CAN YOU see the newest belle?" Fitz demanded.

"No."

"You're not even looking!"

"There's nothing worth seeing." Ransom had better things to do than watch out for a silly girl.

"Not true. You'll find a diamond worth having, if you'd just take a look. A diamond, Ransom! Let us through. There you go lads, you can't keep her for yourselves." The constriction eased as the men turned and Fitz slipped through the crowd. Ransom followed close on Fitz's heels, protecting his friend's back and wondering why.

"Your servant, ma'am!" Fitz snapped to attention, then bowed, leaving Ransom a clear view of, not the diamond, but the profile of a dab of a lady. Her gown of rich green glacé silk was *au courant*, and nicely chosen to bring out the spark of emerald in her fine eyes. A lacy shawl covered her slight bosom, and she held her gloved hands clasped at her waist like a singer waiting for a cue that never came. A mop cap covered her unfashionable coil of heavy dark hair and her prim mouth must have never greeted a man invitingly.

Ransom began to turn away.

Then she smiled at the blonde with an exultant

bosom beside her. It was a smile filled with pride and quiet pleasure. It lit the plain features and made them glow—and he'd seen that glow before. He jerked to a stop.

He stared. It couldn't be her. She had to be a figment of his wary, suspicious mind.

He blinked and looked again.

Damn, it *was* her.

Miss Jane Higgenbothem had returned.

Nationally Bestselling Author

Pamela Morsi

"Her stories are gently humorous, wise and wonderful."
Susan Elizabeth Phillips

SEALED WITH A KISS　　79638-4/$5.99 US/$7.99 Can

Having forsaken her girlish dreams of romance years ago
after being abandoned by the man she loved, Prudence
Belmont is startled to learn the reckless cad has returned
and moved in next door.

NO ORDINARY PRINCESS　78643-5/$5.99 US/$7.99 Can

Brash Princess "Cessy" Calhoun firmly believes in love at
first sight. But she has never fallen—until a sophisticated
gentleman named Gerald sweeps her off her feet.

THE LOVE CHARM　　　78641-9/$5.99 US/$7.99 Can

"Pamela Morsi writes about love and life with laughter,
tenderness, and most of all, joy." *Romantic Times*

How to get your special rebate on seven Avon romances

Avon Books would like to offer you a rebate on any or all of the following seven paperback romance titles:

A WELL FAVORED GENTLEMAN by Christina Dodd;

FOREVER AFTER by Catherine Anderson;

SEALED WITH A KISS by Pamela Morsi;

THE NIGHT REMEMBERS by Kathleen Eagle;

STRANGER IN MY ARMS by Lisa Kleypas;

ONE TRUE LOVE by Barbara Freethy; and

THAT SCANDALOUS EVENING by Christina Dodd.

We will send you a rebate of $1.00 per book, or $10.00 for all seven titles, when you purchase them by December 31, 1998. To claim your rebate, simply mail your proof(s) of purchase (cash register receipt(s)) with the coupon below, completely filled out, to Avon Books, Dept. ROM, Box 767, Rte. 2, Dresden, TN 38225.

Yes, I have purchased

    _____**A WELL FAVORED GENTLEMAN**;

    _____**FOREVER AFTER**;

    _____**SEALED WITH A KISS**;

    _____**THE NIGHT REMEMBERS**;

    _____**STRANGER IN MY ARMS**;

    _____**ONE TRUE LOVE**;

    _____**THAT SCANDALOUS EVENING**, or

    _____**ALL SEVEN TITLES**.

My total rebate (at $1.00 per title OR $10.00 if all seven are purchased) is $ _____
Please send it to:

Name_____

Address_____

City_____ State_____ Zip_____

Offer expires December 31, 1998. Void where prohibited by law.